The Lies He Told Me

To
Barb + Karisse!

SYLVIE GRAYSON

Sylvie Grayson

The Lies He Told Me is a work of fiction. Names, characters, places and incidents are products of the author's imagination or are used fictitiously. Any resemblance to actual events or locales or persons, living or dead, is entirely coincidental.

For information write to:

GREAT WESTERN PUBLISHING 220 Bay Street,

Victoria, British Columbia, Canada V9A 3K5

ISBN: 978-0-9938288-4-3

Great Western Publishing is a registered trademark of Sylvie Grayson.

Cover art by Steven Novak novakillustration@gmail.com

DEDICATION

I am blessed with wonderful support that has enabled me to write. To my husband, who gives me time to work when I need it but is always ready to listen, read and lend a hand with difficult passages. To my children who had faith in me and helped with their support and practical suggestions, the choosing of titles and cover art.

To my critique group: Anna Markland, author of *Hearts and Crowns*, Reggi Allder, author of *Money, Power and Poison* and Jacquie Biggar, author of *Tidal Falls,* who all supported me to polish the words for publication, my many thanks.

Any errors or omissions are mine alone.

Sylvie Grayson

www.sylviegrayson.com

other books by Sylvie Grayson

Suspended Animation

Legal Obstruction

I just finished reading your book, what a great story. I loved it and can't wait for your next book.

Interesting characters, family conflicts and divided loyalties make this a book that kept me up half the night... - Amazon reader

The Lies He Told Me

CHAPTER ONE

Well, he's gone. I don't know where he went, but he isn't coming back today. I know at least that much.

Tears welled in her eyes, and Chloe Bowman fiercely blinked them away. *I'm not going to cry, I'm just not. It hasn't helped.*

At first she'd been too numb to cry. The tears wouldn't come because she couldn't believe her husband had simply disappeared. But as the weeks went by, the tears started and wouldn't stop. She felt more bereft than ever.

She looked over at her young son. Davey had fallen asleep on the patio behind her, lying beside Plutie on his bed. The dog saw her glance their way and gave his skinny white tail a thump but didn't move. *He's committed to Davey. That's a nice thing in a dog friend.*

She should pick her son up but she didn't have the energy. *He might get fleas.* Still she didn't move. Her gaze rested on his face and the half-moon crescents of his dark blond lashes. Not as fair as Jeff. But his thick blond hair showed strong red highlights in the sun. His chubby hands were half curled in sleep.

She thought she saw Jeff sometimes, driving past her in a pickup truck or walking down the street. She'd catch a glimpse of a tall redheaded man and some tilt of the head, some angle of his jaw would start her heart leaping in her chest with sudden recognition before she got a clearer view. Then she'd have to stop to catch her breath, allow her heart to slow. It might be the height, the breadth of shoulder, that certain shade of brown in his leather jacket.

It wasn't that she was still looking for him. And yet, somewhere beneath conscious thought, her mind and body yearned toward him. It was exhausting.

She looked out over the yard. The lawn looked like a golf green, smooth and perfect. That had been strange. She'd tried to cancel the lawn installation because she'd run out of money. But they said no, the bill was paid when the order was placed. An underground sprinkler system was part of the contract.

She shrugged. The installers had done a great job, it looked wonderful. Same thing when she went to pay the property taxes, they'd already been paid. It was puzzling. Jeff was obviously better at taking care of detail than she'd given him credit for.

She still had some tradesmen coming. With a new house there were always a lot of final touches to take care of. The fireplace mantels went in last week. Again, it had been booked and prepaid. They looked good. She was getting used to this.

Bees buzzed around the flowers in her patio flowerpots, lightly touching each bloom. Tomato plants gave off a strong herbal scent in the heat. It was so quiet she could hear the dragonflies as they patrolled the yard like small aircraft across the expanse.

Dog Two prowled the shade over by the workshop, moving methodically along nose to the ground or watching the drive with expectancy in his pose. Overhead, red tailed hawks circled. There were three today. They must have their baby with them, training it to hunt. Even the hawks had a partner to help raise their baby. *She wouldn't cry, she just wouldn't.*

Chloe looked down at the pad of paper on her lap, tapping the pen against her thigh. *Now what?* She had promised herself she'd make a decision today. Any decision. It'd been months with no word, no clue of where her husband had gone. Things were falling down around her ears. With no cash flow the mortgage payments were mounting and people called her daily to sort something out. She had to make a decision.

She'd been waiting for Jeff to come back, walk in the door and take up the reins of their life. He'd have some outlandish explanation for why he'd been gone, something unreasonable that would make her angry as hell but so relieved that he was home. They'd have a huge fight and then begin their lives again, together.

But it never happened. No matter how she longed for him, how often she prayed, how fiercely she ignored her circumstances, it didn't happen. She had to take up the reins herself.

There were two vehicles at the house. Jeff's Mercedes had disappeared with him. But his pickup truck and her convertible were still here. The convertible was in her name so she could sell it. The truck wasn't.

She'd loved that little car when he bought it for her. "No," she said, slightly aghast, "we can't afford that, at least not right now when we're building a house and buying a commercial building."

But Jeff just chuckled and handed her the keys. "Try it," he said. "You'll change your mind. It rides like a dream." They laughed and jumped into the car, Chloe taking the driver's seat. It did ride like a dream, so much power she could pass any other car on the road. Never mind that it had no back seat to speak of, or trunk space for groceries or luggage. That was Jeff, so generous, so impractical. Tears welled, but she impatiently brushed them away.

Just then her house phone rang and Dog Two stopped pacing to gaze at her expectantly. Chloe snatched it up from the wicker table in front of her, heart thumping. But she saw from the call display that it was her mother. Not who she hoped. Not Jeff.

~~~

Ross Cullen shifted on the seat of his truck and cranked his neck sideways to snap the stiffness out of it. Surveillance duty was hard. He was staff sergeant now and had become detective a year ago. He didn't have to do a lot of the grunt work anymore. But he'd wanted this case. He'd already had Jeff Sanderson in his sights.

A middle aged divorced woman had laid a complaint months ago that she'd been swindled. Ross was convinced Sanderson had been involved. Although she couldn't pinpoint exactly what had happened, she was out thirty thousand dollars. She thought she was buying an investment. The gentleman she was dealing with, who called himself Tom Dickson, was selling a share of ownership in an apartment building. The deal sounded exciting.

Tom introduced her to the building manager, a guy named Monty. Yet when the dust settled Tom Dickson and Monty were both gone along with her money and the building was owned by someone else, someone she'd never heard of.

Sanderson was an easy guy to profile, six foot three, broad shoulders and lean, erect bearing, with bright red hair and blue eyes. He was handsome, most women thought so and this woman was no exception. She'd given a very thorough description.

Ms. Brandon didn't want to go public. Her ex-husband had given her the money as part settlement of their divorce. She was afraid he wouldn't carry out the rest of the agreement without a fight if he found out she'd lost the first lot of money on a scam.

But Sanderson had already been a person of interest. Ross had his staff following a money trail and it seemed to lead straight to him.

When a few months later the Missing Persons Notice crossed his desk, it all seemed too convenient. After the
~~~

husband disappeared, the house got finished, the lawn went in. The property taxes were paid. He'd checked. How did Chloe Bowman have the money to do all that if the husband had taken off leaving her high and dry? He didn't buy it.

Today was his day off and he didn't have to be here. But now and then he came over and parked, keeping an eye on the yard. Dan might be right, he had too much time on his hands. Dan Parker was the Constable who'd drawn surveillance duty on the wife right after she laid her Missing Persons information. He had lots to say about her. He certainly couldn't fall asleep with this kind of duty, he reported.

Ross had thought Dan was joking, but from where he sat Ms. Bowman was wearing a tight camisole and not much else. Well, maybe a pair of shorts if he looked hard and squinted his eyes. Good God, didn't she have neighbours? He panned the area with his binoculars. No one could look into her yard, she had a lot of privacy. And she took advantage of it.

She looked darned good too, at least from this distance. She had a chest that he'd already heard about from Parker. If he was Jeff Sanderson, he wouldn't just take off. What if she got tired of waiting? That idea would keep him up at night if he were the husband.

The house was situated in a grove of evergreens with a big yard to the south. There was a smaller building, a workshop across the lawn. Even that was far enough away so that it didn't impinge on her privacy and the windows of the apartment above were on the other side of the building, affording the Sanderson yard and grounds a lot of seclusion.

If he hadn't found this old logging road on the hill and tucked his truck in behind a few fir trees, he wouldn't be looking into her yard either. The acreage, partly treed, had been farmed once but the field now looked like pasture with two sheep inside the fence.

There was also the dog. He'd spotted the serious looking beast as he walked down the road the other day. It kept its eyes locked on him the whole time he sauntered past, growled low when he paused at the side of the fence. That was a trained animal, part German Shepherd. He'd have serious concerns about entering the yard without an invitation.

He'd seen the tapes of Chloe Bowman's first interview at the station. After she filed the report about her missing husband, she'd been asked to come in and answer some questions. Her brother John Bowman came with her and sat in the interview room as she was questioned.

At one point John objected to the tone the officer was taking. Was his sister under suspicion because her husband had taken off? At that point Chloe burst into tears and the officer told John that he didn't need to be there. It was Chloe Bowman they were interested in talking to.

Bowman stated, while leaning over the table into the officer's face, that when he left, Chloe left. The constable continued his line of questioning. But the confrontation sparked some police interest into the brother and his possible connection to Sanderson. After some fairly extensive and unfruitful sifting of information, they found nothing to connect him other than the sibling relationship.

But Chloe herself had been impressive. She was obviously shaken. She'd looked tenuous but dogged as she recounted everything she claimed she knew about her husband's last days in Victoria. Her husband was gone, his laptop, his cell phone, his dog and car were gone. She answered the same questions over and over as they were put to her different ways, until she sagged back in her chair in exhaustion.

"Well," she said. "I've had enough. If there's anything else you want to ask that might help find my husband, then please ask now. Otherwise I'm going home."

She stood, looking down at the officer who sat with his finger midway down the page and a surprised look on his face. "You may have more to say but I'm through. Now you've had my cooperation and I want yours. Find my husband. Quit dragging your feet, quit pretending he ran off and find him!"

She turned her back and headed toward the exit, followed closely by her brother. The officer at the door looked past her to see what his instructions were, then opened the door and escorted them out. It was Ross's opinion that Chloe Bowman and her brother John were cut from the same cloth. Chloe was just younger and hid her steel under her feminine nature. But she was just as tough in her own way and just as determined.

And beautiful. He'd been fascinated by her dark glossy curls and fair skin, the large liquid eyes. He'd watched the recording more than once and it irked him to know that it was as much to look at her as to analyze the information.

He watched from his truck as Ms Bowman called across the yard to her little white dog and leaned down to ruffle his ears. Ross slowly panned the binoculars over her form, feeling his temperature rise. Maybe this kind of surveillance wasn't healthy. He might get a fever just watching her.

~~~

Brent called by the house next morning and Dog Two barked and lunged at the yard gate. Chloe gave him a command and he stopped barking, the hair on his neck still standing straight up.

"I don't think he likes me," her brother said.

Chloe shook her head and gave him a hug. "It's not you, it's everyone. Since Jeff left and Dog One is gone, Two is especially defensive. I find it's some comfort to know he's out here."

Brent chuckled. "Who calls their dogs Dog One and Dog Two, anyway? No wonder he's defensive." He joined them for a late breakfast. Davey sat on his knee throughout the meal, refusing to use his booster seat.

"It's okay, Chloe. I miss the little guy, I should come around more often."
~~~

Chloe frowned at him. "Yes, you should. And where's your wife this morning?"

He grinned. "She's still in bed." Diana was a school teacher and Chloe knew how she loved to sleep in.

"Brent, I need to pick your brain. This commercial building that Jeff has –well that I have now. I can't access the bank account, I don't have signing authority and the lawyer Art Rowbotham says he'll act on Jeff's behalf, I don't need to worry about it. He gave me a verbal pat on the head. It's infuriating.

"But I need to pay bills, make sure the rent deposits are made by the tenants and handle the business. I'm going to have to get in there somehow. And the mortgage company called the other day. I'm afraid to call them back."

"How do they call you, Chloe? Do they have your home phone number?"

"I bought a cell phone and had it programmed with Jeff's old number. It wasn't being used." She swallowed hard at what that could mean. "All his business calls and contacts have to come through that number, so I need to receive those calls."

He reached to squeeze her fingers. "Good plan, Chloe. You're a clever girl." He looked at her quizzically. "Still no word from the police?"

Her face went pale. "No. Nothing. I'm sure they aren't even looking. It makes me crazy."

Brent took her hand again, this time hanging on. "They interviewed John and me, and our wives. They've talked to everyone involved with Jeff's construction crews. His foreman Fraser Hodge said they got the third degree. He said being paid in cash made it difficult to answer the questions. Did you know that? That Jeff paid his crews in cash?"

Chloe stared at him, then shook her head impatiently. "I find that hard to believe, where would he get the money? Besides, he'd need records, wouldn't he? Why would Fraser lie about that?"

He shrugged. "I don't have a clue. But the police talked to all John's guys. Everyone who knew him has been questioned. They're taking it very seriously. It's just hard to wait, with no word, right?"

"Mummy, don't cry, you promised." Davey patted her arm.

"I know, sweetheart. I promised." She wiped her cheeks with the palms of her hands. "That's the last time today!" She gave him a watery smile.

"At any rate," Brent continued, rubbing her shoulder, "I think you need to be firm with Rowbotham. There was no will, but you're Jeff's wife. It's logical that you take over, at least while he's gone. So go back and tell him how it's going to be. I always quote Dad when talking about lawyers. They're job is to take instructions, not give them. You tell them what you need and their job is to get it done for you.

"Now, why don't you come over for dinner? Diana asked me to invite you. You need to get out of the house. Just for an evening, Chloe. You have your cell phone, if anything happens people can reach you. Come on, you'd enjoy it."

"I know, Brent. Thanks, really. But since the break-in it makes me nervous to leave. It was awful coming back home and finding we'd been burgled."

It had happened right after Jeff left. Chloe couldn't believe the timing. And the police had been awful. The thieves had entered the house through a broken window into the garage. The window wasn't visible from the road and Dog Two was in the fenced yard around the other side of the house.

The entire place had been ransacked. Not that they had much to ransack. They'd only been living in the house a couple of months. Some of the rooms were still empty.

But her bedroom had been rummaged, every drawer dumped onto the floor, all the closet shelves swept clear. The freezer had been emptied onto the hardwood floor in the back hall.

When the police arrived, they looked everything over carefully. The officer thought they must have been looking for something specific but Chloe didn't know what. Money, wasn't that the prime motive for these crimes? And she didn't have any money. She wasn't able to identify anything that had been taken.

Meanwhile they sat her down and did an interview. The questions got tougher and more personal, more insistent. She got up and left the room to get her purse but the interrogating officer followed her. So she took her purse back into the dining room where they'd been sitting at the table, pulled out her cell phone and made her call right in front of him.

Her older brother John answered on the first ring. She told him what had happened. "So," Chloe continued into the phone, "I need you to come if you can. They don't stop with the questions and I answer over and over again. I need some support."

Her brother had arrived fifteen minutes later, although she knew full well it took her twenty five minutes to get to town. She barely had time to make a sandwich for Davey and sit him up to the kitchen table, with the officer following her from room to room. John simply asked the officer to leave. He didn't fool around with whether he'd finished his questions or had anything more to ask. The officer left.

Then he looked through the house. "What happened to your alarm system?"

She shook her head. "I don't know. I always put it on but I just don't remember. The police kept asking about that. They checked the wiring and say it's okay. I have a call in to the alarm company."

John nodded. "Well, better change your password and the master code. That's the first step. If this person knew the password, that should stop this from happening again."

She stared at him.

"What, Chloe?" he demanded. "That's what the police are thinking. That's why they were hounding you. Someone got into your house and tossed it and the alarm didn't go off. Either you're in on the break-in or this other person knew the code. And it doesn't look like you were in on the break in, there won't be an insurance claim. So they must be thinking the second scenario, the person knew the code."

"Just Jeff," she whispered. "Jeff knew the password. Do you think this means...."

"No, I don't." John shook his head. He gripped her shoulders and looked sternly into her eyes. "I haven't a clue what the police know, but I don't think Jeff did this. If he was here, he'd come and see you. He loves you. I may not have been in favour of his style of business but he's not sneaking around hiding. Don't go thinking that, Chloe. It'll drive you crazy. If Jeff isn't here, it's because he can't be here."

CHAPTER TWO

Chloe alternated between fear and rage, total numbness and intense pain, frantic activity and paralysis. While she was in one of her active phases, she got an ad onto the web and sold her convertible. Surprisingly, she got her asking price but didn't think twice, just went straight to the bank and deposited the rather substantial payment. Some breathing room at last.

Her meeting with Rowbotham, Jeff's lawyer, didn't go quite as well. He was adamant that he retain control of the company. "After all, Mrs. Sanderson," he said in a condescending tone, "You're not a business woman and Jeff would find it incumbent on me to keep things on an even keel."

Chloe gritted her teeth. She'd told him more than once that her name remained Bowman. However, she had a different purpose today and would ignore the irritant for the moment.

"That isn't satisfactory, Art." She smiled to herself as he frowned at her use of his first name. Two could play at this game. "There are numerous business decisions that need to be made. There isn't time or the need to consult you. It's entirely too costly to have a legal firm run my company." She was quoting what Brent had said to her the other day, it sounded pretty good to her ears.

"These aren't things a lawyer needs to be involved in. And I do have business experience. Jeff and I shared most decisions so I'm very aware of what needs to be done." That last was a bit of a stretch but everything else she'd said was totally valid.

"I need your help. I need signing authority for the company and the bank. I can look after the rest once that's in place. I want to go before a judge in Chambers to get an order. Will you help me?" She smiled winningly and held his gaze.

His face was flushed. "I can certainly take it under advisement," he said through tight lips. "I'll have an answer for you next week."

Her smile disappeared. "Don't take too long. I'll have to consult other legal advice if this drags. Please let me know Monday."

She stood. "Thank you, Art. I know Jeff would be grateful for all the help you've given me." He shook her hand with a short grip and let it go. She felt his gaze follow as she left the office.

Stepping onto the sidewalk, Chloe let out a pent up breath. She'd sounded pretty good in there. She may have exaggerated, given that she and Jeff didn't share most decisions, considering she often didn't even know decisions were being made. But Rowbotham didn't know that. When the nerves eased a bit, she felt good. After months of indecision and disappointment, it felt right to start moving forward.

She'd call John, see if his lawyer was any good. Maybe she needed better legal counsel. She needed something to happen.

~~~

Next morning, she faced a full day. "Come on Davey. We've got people coming to stay and we need stuff."
~~~

Amanda was the daughter of her mother's friend, and Vivienne had talked her into this arrangement. The girl was eighteen, very shy and coming to Victoria to start university. Vivienne had offered Chloe's house for room and board. At first Chloe had been furious. She had enough to deal with, Jeff had just disappeared. The police weren't helpful, acted as if she was mixed up in it. She was convinced they never looked for him, never conducted a proper search. Everyone else was pelting her with questions and requests, and in the middle of all the mess Vivienne phoned with a boarder.

Well, now it didn't seem so bad. She could use the money.

"What kind of stuff?" Davey was slowly eating his cereal, one flake at a time.

Chloe looked hopefully into his bowl to see how much was left. "We need beds and blankets and stuff. Probably towels too."

"What kind of people?" He popped one more flake into his mouth.

She gave him a look. "You know what kind of people. School people. First Amanda is coming, and then hopefully a few more students."

"When are they coming?"

"Come on Davey, no more questions. Let's get your shoes."

Throwing his breakfast bowl into the sink, she hustled him toward the door. "Where should we go first?"

They found a decent bed frame and headboard at the thrift store plus a comforter that looked brand new. She bought a mattress from a mattress shop to be delivered later and dropped the comforter at the cleaners. Then they went to a couple of home discount places for sheets, blankets and another comforter. They also needed pillows.

Well, not today. She had enough pillows for Amanda and Davey had had enough shopping for one day. When they got home, they lugged most of the things upstairs and made the bed in Amanda's room. She put the new sheets on it and added pillows. Not bad.

Chloe dragged a bedside table in from the room across the hall and added the lamp. It needed a chair, probably some kind of desk and it would be very comfortable. She'd have to head back to the thrift store or try the internet.

~~~

The boarder arrived that evening. She'd taken the bus from Salmon Arm in the interior of British Columbia at seven in the morning. Chloe went down to meet her at the bus stop near the house. Amanda was a little thing, mousy and terrified. Chloe wondered if her family knew that the woman she was going to live with had lost her husband. Well, hadn't lost him, just couldn't find him. Gone. Vanished. Kaput.

She couldn't think like this for too long. She had a hideous feeling that she'd either burst into tears or start laughing and be unable to stop.

She walked over when the door of the bus opened and waited for the driver to get Amanda's things from the luggage compartment below. "Hi Amanda, I'm Chloe. You'll be living with me for the semester." She held out her hand and Amanda took it in a surprisingly firm grip for such a little thing.

Chloe smiled. "Let me help. The truck is right over here. My son Davey is in the back seat, so we can't leave him for long." Amanda grabbed her duffel bag and laptop satchel. Chloe took the other two heavy bags and they headed over to her vehicle.

"You drive a truck," said Amanda in admiration. "That's great. I always thought I'd get one when I get a vehicle. They're so handy, you can do just about anything with a truck."

Chloe examined it with new eyes as they threw the bags into the bed of the pickup. She supposed that was true. She'd made the best decision about the vehicles. She pointed Amanda to the passenger door and walked around the cab to
~~~

climb in. The girl chatted to Davey as they drove. Then she turned to Chloe. “I knew you had a little boy. Is he ever cute. Is he like your husband?”

She nodded. “A bit. My husband is a red head. But Davey is more blond.” She held out a fistful of her dark hair. “And he didn’t get my curls either. Maybe he was lucky.”

She showed Amanda her room upstairs and toured the bathroom. Chloe explained she’d be sharing the bathroom with others once everyone arrived. There wasn’t anyone else lined up to board but she wanted to lay the groundwork. It looked like that would be a good move in the short term.

She pointed out the half-sized fridge, microwave and coffee maker on the second floor, explained that she’d make dinner but breakfast and lunch were Amanda’s concern.

Chloe’s other problem was what to say about Jeff. She didn’t know quite how to phrase it. *Oh, by the way, my husband left.* That sounded like they’d divorced. *Oh, by the way, my husband ran off.* That didn’t sound any better.

He disappeared? That sounded creepy. It was creepy, and she didn’t want to scare her boarder. She had to come up with some story that was truthful and left it open for Jeff to come home, and at the same time wasn’t so terrifying that Amanda’s parents took her somewhere else for her own protection.

At dinner the girl was very patient with Davey as he told her a story about his dog Plutie. This plan might work. She hadn’t realized how lonely and quiet it was with just her and Davey eating together, mostly in silence as she sank in mental gyrations of where Jeff was and what might have happened to him.

~~~

Chloe bundled Davey into the truck. She had a meeting with the realtor at the building that afternoon.

It didn’t go as well as she’d hoped, however. She bluffed her way as far as signing the listing agreement and showed him around the last empty space for lease. A large
~~~

area, it had a number of offices down one side. But the realtor wasn't hopeful about finding a tenant. He talked about overstock, a glut on the market, grade B space as this clearly was.

She looked around with a critical eye. Grade B space, was it? Yes, she could see that. She pulled Davey down from the wire fence enclosure that surrounded a former stock room and turned back to the realtor.

"At the same time, it's solid concrete construction. The services are all here, gas heat, electric air conditioning, internet and phone lines. There are four bathrooms. There's a huge staff room and the boardroom sized table and chairs are still there. And it's reasonably priced. I'll bet there aren't many spaces on the market at this rate."

He started nodding encouragingly. "Yes, yes, I see your point. I may have someone I can bring through next week to look at it."

When he drove off, she locked up and headed over to John's little office on the same side of town. Her brother brought out an extra chair for her and got glasses of water for them in the heat. Davey played with the small figurines his uncle kept in the box in the corner.

John listened with interest about the realtor, nodding in agreement of her points in favour of the building. Then he frowned as she rehashed her visit with the lawyer, Rowbotham. He reached for his phone. "Is Bill available? It's John Bowman calling. Just a quick question." He waited on the line.

Finally Chloe heard a voice at the other end and John nodded. "Bill, I have my sister here in the office with me. She has a complicated question and she needs help to find an answer. Can she come over to see you for a few minutes?"

There was a pause. "No, it's more like a second opinion. But complex, she needs to explain it herself. Yeah, I know. You're always busy." He listened. "Yes, now would be great. She can be there in ten minutes. Her name is Chloe Bowman. And don't charge her an arm and a leg!"

He laughed at something the lawyer said. "Get out. I pay through the nose and we both know it. Good, good. She needs your help, man. Thanks."

John hung up and smiled at her. "There you go, get yourself another opinion. Tell him everything, even stuff you don't tell me." He held up his hand at her outraged look. "I mean it, Chloe. Legal advice is only as good as the information you give your lawyer. Davey can stay with me. I've got paper work to do for an hour or so, and there's stuff in the fridge for us to munch on. Here's his address."

A few minutes later Chloe found herself in Bill Hodson's reception area and ushered almost immediately into his office. She introduced herself and he showed her to a chair. "Nice to meet you, Chloe. I knew John had a sister, but I've only met Brent. I did your father's estate. That's how I know your family. So, what seems to be the issue?"

Chloe spelled it out for him. He didn't say much, but his gaze sharpened as she talked and he reached into the mess on his desk to find a legal pad and started to take notes. He nodded when she mentioned Art Rowbotham, but kept on listening. Finally she fell silent.

He looked at his notes for a minute. "Any children?"

"One. Davey, he's four."

"How long have you been married?"

"Five years."

He nodded. "What kind of family does Jeff have?"

"Just his parents. His folks didn't come to the wedding, but I've spoken to them on the phone. They live in Florida but Jeff grew up in different places across Canada. He came here for University. Since Jeff disappeared, I've spoken to his parents a couple of times. They said they didn't know where he was. Otherwise I don't know much about them."

She twisted her hands in her lap. "I have a diploma in business administration. I also worked for my father. He talked about the company all the time at home and especially once John started working with him. He was a thoughtful man and a good business man, I couldn't have learned from a better teacher."

Bill Hodson gave her a sympathetic look. "I knew your father quite well, Chloe. He was a very good man."

She gazed at him through suddenly teary eyes. "And I have my brothers to rely on. I know what needs to be done and I'm quite capable of doing it. I can't afford Rowbotham to handle it, it'd be a ridiculous waste of money. If I'm very careful I'll be able to hang onto my home and the building. And if not, I don't want it to be because Rowbotham got in the way."

"Well," he looked at his watch. "Here's what I recommend. See Rowbotham on Monday. Tell him you've sought a second opinion. Let him have a chance because he has all the documents and agreements, the company seal. It's faster and less expensive than switching. But his action has to be speedy, by that I mean it should be done inside two weeks. If he's so booked up he can't do it, there has to be someone in his office who can."

Bill waggled his brows at her. "If he doesn't want to go to court and ask for authority on your behalf then you need to get different counsel. Because there's no will, something has to be put in place to protect the assets until that can be sorted out or Jeff shows up. That doesn't mean you can't make a living off it. It's a fairly easy thing to get a Court Order like this that lets you administer the property."

He stood and held out his hand. "Nice to meet you, Chloe. John's a good man too and he can be a real resource for you. Let me read the document Rowbotham comes up with if you like. That way we can make sure you're asking for enough authority. No point in going to court twice."

Chloe headed back in the truck to pick up Davey, feeling more confident. She cursed Jeff for leaving this mess. If he had to disappear, why couldn't he have made better arrangements? Why didn't he include her in the business so she'd know what was going on?

Tears formed and she pulled over to the side of the street. She couldn't bear to think about what it meant, that he hadn't made those arrangements. She sobbed, her hands trembling on the steering wheel.

Well, she'd cry later. She had to pick Davey up and get home to make dinner for her new boarder.

~~~

Ross took the phone call in his office Monday morning. The carcass of a dog had been found in a ditch on the mainland, south of Vancouver in Ladner. The collar had registration numbers on the tag that had been traced back to Victoria. The city clerk had recognized the name of the dog's owner and knew he was missing. The collar had been found five weeks ago.

He groaned inwardly at the delay and took down the details. Then he summoned Constable Dan Parker to follow up when the collar arrived from the City office.

"Where are we on this case?" he quizzed Parker. "Where are we on the fraud allegations from Marion Brandon about Tom Dickson? Can we not find *anyone* who knows something about that?

"How about the car that Sanderson was driving, what's new on that front? Damned little, that's what." He banged his fist on the desk top in front of him. "Why are we getting nowhere? It's been months."

Marion Brandon must have given up hope that the police would ever find her money or the men who took it. Ms. Bowman however seemed to carry on just fine without her husband. He'd been out to watch her house again. Even if he didn't learn anything from a police perspective, it was pretty interesting if he just got a glimpse of her.

His chest felt tight when he thought about her on the interview tapes. Watching her in the yard just added to his fascination. That wasn't the best way to feel about an investigation and he heard an alarm sound in his head. He'd better get his mind back on business.

~~~

Jayde Farrell stirred drying leaves in the basket on the table, her fingers disappearing into the dark green curled foliage. Chloe's neighbour, was a widow and had been a Godsend since she'd moved in. She'd talked her into growing dahlias in the spring.

Now she was harvesting her herb garden. "You see, lavender is hard to grow here because it gets too cold in the winter and it's damp. That doesn't mean you can't grow it, it just means that some of them might not make it. Maybe you'll find special spots in your yard that are more protected, and it will survive there.

"That's what I've done. See, just here by the back door seems to be dry enough, and out by the side of the shed. It gets a lot of sun and stays warmer during the winter, probably because the building retains the heat. Makes sense, doesn't it? But lavender looks so lovely in the garden that I mostly leave it there and just dry the leaves. I add a few of the flowers in the potpourri to give the lovely lilac colour of the bloom."

Chloe sniffed another basket and Jayde said, "That's sage. Isn't it great? It's such a pungent scent. Pleases me no end. Then this one's rosemary. Do you know, I've always liked rosemary the best. It has a robust perfume and it's good for moths.

"Now, the rosemary has more moisture in it than you might think. When you strip the branches down to remove the needles, they seem pretty dry. But not so. If you pile them into a basket and stir them the next day, you'll find that the centre is really damp. Surprises you, doesn't it?

"And these are rose geranium leaves. They're quite a lovely low bush and the flowers aren't huge but they look good along the border of the garden. And the leaves smell wonderful. They have oil in them. When you pick them your fingers get covered in it. They take the longest to dry, you have to stir and turn them for days."

Chloe's fingers twirled in the dry leaves. "But how do you have time to do all this and sew up little bags for it, too? You're amazing, Jayde, you really are."

"Pshaw. It's nothing. What else have I got to do? Besides, who says I sew pretty little bags? I might if I were making gifts. But for the rest, to put in my sweater drawers and the linen closet, I just do this."

She pulled a bolt of light cotton cloth from the sideboard and lay it out on the table. "See, I cut squares. Then when I've mixed all the leaves together, I just fill them up and tie the top. Easy. Here, this basket is ready to make up."

Chloe grabbed the basket and leaned over it, mixing the leaves together. "Oh my Lord, that smells heavenly. You could patent this and make a killing"

Jayde beamed. "Pile it up on this square of cloth and we'll tie the top shut."

They made three or four and Jayde insisted she take them home for her closets. "You'll love it when you pull a fresh sheet out and it smells like herbs. As a matter of fact, if you like the rose geranium, you should take some plants home for your garden. It grows really easy, then you can use the leaves. I'll dig you some up in another month or two, it's too hot and dry right now. I have lots, look at them out there. I don't have room for it all."

Chloe chuckled. When Jayde gave her something it was always because she absolutely didn't need it and simply couldn't use it. She was the most generous person she'd ever met. She gave her a hug.

"Hey, what was that for? They're just plants, heck, a dime a dozen."

CHAPTER THREE

"There you are," the locksmith called from the door to the workshop across Chloe's yard. "I just took that first lock out and replaced the second one. It operates okay." He worked the lock with one of the keys. "I'll send the bill, or you can settle it up now if you like."

"I'll pay you now, save sending me an invoice." She went to get her purse as Dog Two kept a wary eye on the man. As he rolled up the driveway in his service van, Chloe took her new key and approached the building. What could possibly be in there that required two big locks on that door? She was almost afraid to look.

Stepping inside, she turned on the light. At first glance it looked exactly like it always had. Yards of Jeff's construction scaffolding leaned against one wall. There were tools neatly placed on the shelves across the back. Her husband was amazingly neat for someone so impulsive. There was a lot of stuff in here, it would take a week to go through it all. At least now she had the chance to conduct a search whereas before she couldn't even get in.

She was turning to go when the sparkle of broken glass on the floor caught her eye. Glancing up, she realized there was no glass in the back window. Someone had broken it and removed all the jagged edges from across the bottom. She walked closer and found muddy boot prints on the floor.

She looked around fearfully. What had been taken? She'd probably never know, this was construction equipment and she wasn't aware of what else Jeff kept in here.

She'd been broken into again and still didn't know who was doing it or what they were after. Maybe it happened at the same time as the house burglary. She felt a shiver move over her, the hair on her arms stirring. This was so creepy, she was afraid it would drive her crazy. She pondered whether to call the police, shuddering as she thought of how they'd treated her last time.

Her phone rang and she pulled it out of her pocket. It was a response to her ad for boarding students. She already had one person coming out tonight so she encouraged this one to come at the same time. Then, scrounging around for a piece of plywood, she took it outside with a hammer and nails. She found a ladder and hefted the plywood up to rest it on the lower edge of the window. It was slightly too big for the space, but would do for now. She hammered the nails into place.

That evening, in the middle of talking to two young men who wanted to see what she had available for boarding, a police car came slowly down the drive. Chloe lost her train of thought and finally asked Amanda to finish showing the students around.

She was already waiting at the front door when the vehicle stopped and one of the officers climbed out of the cruiser. He approached the step. "Ms Bowman?"

She nodded, her hands gripping the edge of the door.

"Can we come inside?" He gestured behind her.

She paused, then shook her head and stepped out onto the porch, closing the door behind her. "I have two young people looking at the rooms upstairs to see if they want to board with me, I don't want to spook them." She stalled, watching his hand which held a piece of paper.

She glanced back up. "Have you found something? Is there any news?"

The police officer motioned her down the steps and along the driveway a few paces. "I'm Constable Parker, Ms. Bowman, and we do have some information." He paused, "Your husband's vehicle has been located, a black Mercedes."

Chloe nodded emphatically. "Yes. Yes, that's what he drove. And his car went missing at the same time he did. You've found the car? Well, that could be..."

He held up his hand. "The car was burned out. It was gutted by fire. There's nothing to find inside it."

She just stood there, looking at him. Her hand slowly rose and covered her mouth but no sound escaped.

"There was no body in the car," he added. "You can be assured of that."

She nodded, her fingers glued to her face, her eyes wide.

The officer finally looked away. "The car was found in Washington State. We've requested the tapes of nearby border crossings to see if we can pinpoint when it went through the border and perhaps who was driving. Did your husband do business in the States, do you know?"

Chloe was still wide-eyed. She shook her head slowly, then lowered her hand. "He didn't go to the States as far as I know. His parents live in Florida, but you know that. It's not like he'd take off to drive down and see them, without telling... without telling anyone."

She floundered. She felt the officer's piercing gaze on her face but didn't care. "This isn't any progress, is it? We're no closer to finding him than we were before." She turned her head and gazed sightlessly at the woods across her drive. "He may never come back," she whispered. "He might never be found. I may never know."

The officer said something but she didn't hear. He touched her arm to get her attention. "Ms. Bowman, this is some information. It gives us a little more to go on than we had before. We haven't stopped the investigation, we're still searching for your husband."

She nodded but didn't answer. There was nothing to say.

~~~

Chloe had four boarders plus Davey and herself living under her roof, when for months there'd been just the two of them. She was never much of a cook, being given to whipping up a salad and a bowl of soup, or a sandwich. Now she felt compelled to produce a real dinner.

She put roast chicken on her list. Then, macaroni and cheese. Finally, curry. She could do a decent curry. That and a pot of rice and dinner was served.

Jayde had some advice. Her house was a ten minute walk down the road where she lived alone, her husband long dead. She'd subdivided her property a few years ago and sold half of it to Jeff. "My son will never live out here and farm it," she'd said. "He's a city guy, and no harm in that, is there? But it's not for him.

"And my daughter has been in town for a long time now." Jayde's daughter lived on the street, a drug addict who was often to be found in doorways or soup kitchens. It was the sorrow of her life. "So why not sell some of it off and have the money? I won't have to worry about my finances, I can do what I need to and live here as long as I want."

She had been a rock when Jeff went missing. Chloe's mother at first brushed it off, saying men will be men and he'll be home soon, sorry for being a bad boy. Vivienne had made the remark that if Chloe would only make a bit of an effort, put on some makeup, she wouldn't have any trouble keeping her man at home. "I don't mean to blame you that he's left, darling," she said, "but really, you could make more of yourself. You used to when you were at university."

Chloe had been devastated by these comments, but Jayde put it all into perspective. "Chloe, use some common sense. You're a beautiful young woman and your husband loves you. Did he show any signs of not loving you? No, he
~~~

didn't, so don't go there. Come now, something has happened and we don't know what. Jeff usually worked all hours, you've told me that. He'd leave before you woke in the morning, right? And sometimes he didn't get home until after you were asleep. But there were reasons for that, weren't there?

"You were finishing up your house, he was running a construction crew and he'd just bought that building downtown. So of course he was busy. Now, he could have asked for your help on some of that, but he didn't. He was bullheaded, so sue him."

Jayde had always been able to make her laugh, even through her tears. She was such a morale booster. What would Chloe have done without her down-to-earth approach?

Now she bustled around to put tea on the table and a glass of juice for Davey. He wouldn't stay long at the table though. There was a new litter of kittens and Jayde had kept one. He was both curious and fascinated by it.

"So, Chloe, you're putting dinner on the table for six. You know, it isn't that much more work than for two, except you have to plan ahead a bit, that's all, make sure you have enough volume. Let's see." She poured the tea and pondered the problem.

"One thing my crew always liked was squash soup. Have you ever made it? It's no trouble at all and full of flavour. You can make it up in advance and have two or three meals out of it. You cut the squash up and roast it in the oven with a few apples and onions. Adds all kinds of flavour. And I have tons of squash, I got twenty-nine off of one vine this year, imagine that! I've never seen the like. Just went crazy.

"Then you make some grilled cheese sandwiches to go with it, especially for the guys. But it doesn't have to be roast beef and mashed potatoes every second night, does it? No, just simple stuff, and it'll be twice as good as what those others get in the dorms, won't it?"

Jayde nattered on. Davey slid out of his chair and headed into the living room. They could see mother cat curled up sleeping on a cushion on the sofa, the kitten lying peacefully at her side.

"Don't hurt her, Davey. Be very gentle."

"Don't worry so. He's a good boy, he won't hurt her. The mother cat will scratch him, more like. She's a fierce one, that one."

Chloe turned to the older woman, and lowered her voice. "I have to tell you something. About Jeff. They found his car."

Jayde's eyes grew round. "They found his car. Where?"

She shook her head. "I'm not sure. In Washington State somewhere, close to the border."

Jayde didn't say anything, but motioned for her to go on.

"There was nothing in it. Someone torched it and burned everything. Except his phone, they found what was left of his phone but it was burned, no information to be gotten from that."

"So, was he inside the car?"

Chloe mutely shook her head.

"Well," she puffed out. "That's good then. He wasn't inside it. What does it mean, I wonder?"

Chloe shuddered. "I have no idea. I don't know what to think any more. At first I thought he'd gotten busy and lost his phone. Then I thought he'd been kidnapped and I'd get a ransom note and have to sign over the house to have him released. But at least we'd be together again, you know?"

Her friend nodded in sympathy.

"Now I have no idea what to think. Does someone run off and go to this much trouble to disappear? Does someone else kidnap him and burn his car? It doesn't make any sense. I don't know what to tell Davey. I don't know what to tell these boarders who've just moved into my house."

Jayde shook her head, "Don't tell them anything. They'll just assume you're living separately or that he works in another country, and who cares? It doesn't matter what they think, does it? Except the police, it could matter there. Just make sure you're always honest with them. Then you'll be fine. And by fine, I don't mean everything will be the way it used to be. I can't tell about that. But you'll manage. Come here."

The older woman threw her arms around her as she wept on the comfortable and comforting shoulder of a friend. Finally she pulled away to find a hanky and mop her face.

"Oh, Jayde, you're crying too."

"Never mind. Tears never hurt anyone, did they? I'll just get my recipe box and you can copy that recipe for squash soup. Now, you don't want to make it too hot. It has curry in it and it can make the eyes water. But it's tasty and filling, you'll love it. I'll give you three or four squash to get started and that will be a blessing to get rid of them. Really, I have way too many to use."

~~~

Chloe had an appointment with Rowbotham on Monday and waited anxiously in the reception area of the law firm. Finally he seated her in his office and closed the door. Sinking into his chair, he unbuttoned his jacket. "Well, Mrs. Sanderson, I have here a document that I feel will be sufficient to address Chambers on the issue of your husband's company. We have a court date set for next week, Tuesday morning. I think this will deal with the issues in a way that allows you to handle your business affairs and retain control for when Jeff returns."

Chloe smiled brilliantly, a feeling of relief washing over her. "Excellent. I'll take a copy and read it over tonight."

He frowned. "You can just look it over now if you wish. I assure you, it deals fairly and equitably with the situation in question."

"Good, then there won't be a problem. But I'll take a copy. I want to read it, Art, make sure all the bases are covered."
~~~

His frown grew darker. “My instructions don’t come from you, Mrs. Sanderson, I work on behalf of your husband.”

“Well, that’s where we have a problem. My husband isn’t here telling you to get the Court Order. So I’m your client now. If you don’t think so, then we’re at cross purposes. I don’t want to waste your time or any more of my own.” She felt her muscles tighten as she glared at him.

Rowbotham rose from his chair and paced around the cramped room. “This is a difficult question, I hadn’t thought of it in those terms. Give me a minute. Jeff’s my client. However Jeff isn’t here and you’re asking for control of his company. In the short term, there’s no way I can agree to that. But we aren’t dealing with the short term any longer. And a company needs action on its behalf to look after its interests.”

He stared out the window. “I have to say I still think I’m doing the right thing. Very well, come out and I’ll have Bertha print you off a copy of the Application and we can go from there.”

Chloe took the document to her car and read it. Not sure, because of the legal language, that she understood entirely how it addressed the issues, she drove over to Bill Hodson’s office. He wasn’t in, so she left a copy and headed home.

Poor Jayde was looking after Davey more than she should have to and there was a daycare operated out of the church just down the road from the house. Maybe they had room for him part time.

Three boarders home tonight. Jose was out and it was the first night of macaroni and cheese. She added coleslaw to the menu for nutrition. A few cookies for dessert. Not her best effort.

Dinner was fun. Beth and Amanda got along really well, and the one man home tonight was Dennis which cheered the girls.

He had come in from up island, his father was a logger in the forestry industry and he looked like he'd done some logging of his own. He was a big boy, only twenty but husky and well muscled. He had the kind of face that girls swooned over, a heavy sensual mouth and large dark eyes.

Both of them were already half in love with him.

CHAPTER FOUR

Chloe was dreaming. It was a relaxed dream, she was having fun, but then it changed and grew darker. It seemed to move and roll. She didn't recognize the feeling and slowly rose to semi-wakefulness where she thought the bed was moving and shifting. A roaring sound came from somewhere far off.

She sat up with a start, now fully awake, confused and alarmed by the unfamiliar feeling. Then she leaped from the bed, tangling her legs in the blankets and nearly falling. The noise grew louder, coming gradually closer, seeming to come straight into the house and hovering there. She flicked on the light, ran to grab her robe and tore across the hall to Davey. Just as she grabbed him up in her arms, covers and all, the roaring increased in volume and the house shook beneath her feet.

She darted down the hall to the front door, Davey screaming in her arms. She shrieked up the stairs to the boarders. "Get out! Get out of the house!"

Unlocking the door, she yanked it open and raced onto the front step in her bare feet as the roaring seemed to increase in volume. She stood motionless, trying to get her bearings and catch her breath. Her bewildered gaze swept the night as the noise filled the house behind her. Then it started to subside, moving off past the field into the distance.

Her arms were tense around her son as she poised uncertainly on the porch step. Then the roaring started up again to her left, like a train headed straight for them. It was ferocious, growing louder and stronger as it approached. The house shook and jerked, the timbers groaning and snapping. She could hear things banging and hitting the floor behind her, the crash of glass shattering.

Racing into the gravel driveway on her tender feet, she held Davey against her chest as Plutie howled around her ankles in the din. The trees whipped in the air above her head. Dog Two could be heard in the yard giving a mournful howl. A tree cracked like a gunshot beyond the fence and she ran across the gravel onto the lawn, as far away from the trees and buildings as she could.

Dimly she heard the others running out behind her. What had her attention now was a new sound from the side of the house, like rocks falling and crashing onto the ground. Then all the lights in the house went out.

Dog Two cowered at her side, whimpering in the back of his throat. Davey was grizzling, patting Chloe on the shoulder to make himself feel better. She rubbed his back as she peered through the gloom, watching Amanda and Beth come down the walkway onto the lawn.

"Oh, you're okay," she breathed. "Where's Dennis?"

"Oh, my God!" Beth was hysterical. "That was just awful! I swear, I thought I was dead!" She shivered and rubbed her arms. "Amanda, that was just awful!" She cried. The girls hugged each other.

"Dennis ... is just…just...." Beth couldn't get the words out.

"He's coming," Amanda interjected. "He just stopped to see if Jose came home." The shocked group stared at each other in the moonlight. The noise had receded down the valley and it was dead quiet. The street lamps all around them were out, no light showed in the few houses they could make out through the trees.

"Well," Chloe gasped and suddenly sat down on the damp grass. "I don't know what to do. My legs are like rubber." Dog Two uncharacteristically sat right beside her with Plutie lined up leaning against him. She tightened her grasp on Davey and wrapped her other arm around the dogs.

"I thought the house was falling," Amanda said. "It was shaking so badly."

"I know. I thought I was having a nightmare," Beth confided. "I was dreaming but it turned real." She shuddered.

The silence became eerie. Dennis appeared around the side of the building alone. Jose had not returned, and after a while they ventured cautiously back inside to find a light. None of the flashlights they found had batteries that worked. The best they could come up with was candles.

The house was totally silent. The usual hum was gone and Chloe realized how noisy their existence was with all the electrical gadgets around them. They did a quick tour ending upstairs, each carrying a candle, but found little damage.

Chloe finally went back downstairs to put Davey to bed, making sure there was no broken glass in his room. As she tucked him in, he cried again and clung to her neck. Plutie whimpered at her feet. "Come on, Plutie," she whispered. "Come up here and make Davey feel better." She patted the little boy's back.

"Mummy, what happened?" he sobbed wetly against her neck.

"It was an earthquake, Davey, but it's over now. So we can go back to bed till morning. Then we'll see what our yard looks like." *And our house.* "It's okay, baby. It's all over now. It's all finished."

Plutie came over and leaned against the bed so Davey could reach him and stood there meekly as the child's fingers scrubbed in his fur. She smoothed her son's forehead until he dozed and the dog subsided on the floor with a sigh. Then she went back down the hall to the front door, pulling shoes and a coat out of the closet.

"Chloe?"

"Oh, Dennis. I can't go back to bed until I make sure Jayde is alright. She's by herself at her place."

Dennis found a flashlight in his car that worked and walked with her down the trail to Jayde's. There was a dim glow in the front window so Chloe knocked softly on the door. Jayde's face appeared through the glass and Chloe waved to her. She and Dennis stepped inside. "I just had to see if you were okay. Did you suffer any damage?"

Jayde took her arm, waving Dennis in behind her. "Well, I just don't know. I can't see much and my flashlight is out of batteries. But it didn't sound like it, if you know what I mean. It sounded fierce, something terrible, but I didn't hear the sound of any part of the house collapsing."

"We're a fine pair, aren't we?" said Chloe. "We had an awful time finding a flashlight that worked, we're using candles."

"What does your place look like? Everyone okay?"

"Well, part of the chimney fell down, that's all I've been able to see so far."

Dennis took his flashlight and looked around the outside of the house while the women talked in the kitchen by candlelight. When he came back, he shook his head. "I don't see anything. I guess we'll just have to wait till daylight."

"I've had the radio on," Jayde said, "I haven't heard anything but chaos from the local station, part of their building came down." She locked the door behind them as they left.

They trudged back along the trail. "We better see what we can find out. I have to call my family, make sure everyone is okay."

"And your husband, will he be involved in this?" Dennis didn't look at her as he asked, keeping his eyes on the path in front of him where the flashlight beam illuminated the hard packed dirt and gravel track. She could almost hear him holding his breath.

"I don't think so, Dennis. I doubt he's in Victoria tonight."

As she stepped back into the house, the smell of vinegar and something sweet hit her. She took the flashlight into the kitchen to see a river of liquid seeping out from beneath the pantry door. There were piles of tins and shattered glass on the floor. Pickle jars, juice jars, jars of sauce lay broken in an uneven layer, their contents spilled. Grabbing some towels, she mopped up what she could, then put everything into a plastic bag and set it outside on the deck. She'd clean and sweep in the morning.

In her room, she phoned Vivienne first and got her on the second ring, but they were barely able to say a few words before the call was cut off. At least Chloe knew she was alive and well. She tried calling her brothers, but got a busy signal. The system must be overloaded. Then she sent a text message. One went through to John, but the one to Brent hung there and refused to budge. She prayed that her family was fine, it didn't matter about the buildings.

~~~

When she woke, she heard Davey moving around in his bed and talking to Plutie. Sighing, she stretched leisurely then froze, remembering the events of the night before. The house was silent as a tomb. This was going to be interesting. The smell of vinegar still hung in the air.

The news was devastating. Buildings had fallen, roads collapsed, the Pointe Ellice Bridge in the centre of town was partially dismantled and unusable. Many were dead, even more were injured or homeless, but the numbers were unknown.

Her chimney had indeed broken off at the roofline. It had hit the deck and taken out the railing and glass wall. Chloe looked at it in dismay. This would mean no fire in the fireplace and it was getting cold. And with no power, there would be no heat.
~~~

There were a few cracked windows. She wondered whether to put duct tape on them to keep the glass from falling out. She'd ask John. The wall in the dining room had a huge crack down the drywall. It didn't look pretty but wasn't anything that would harm them.

The first thing she discovered was the water had been shut off. She immediately put signs on the toilets warning everyone not to flush. They needed every bit of water they could conserve. By the time the boarders were up, the news was coming in. iPods and communications gadgets abounded and it was clear the city of Victoria was a disaster area.

Roads were closed due to damaged overpasses or subsiding roadbeds. There were tall buildings collapsed into themselves, shorter structures leaning drastically. Several had simply sunk into the ground losing a storey or two in the process.

Chloe wondered about her own building in town, but knew she wouldn't be able to find out today. The police had issued warnings to stay home. There was enough chaos without people coming to rubberneck. Only those that absolutely had to be at work should attempt it.

Grocery stores, gas stations, hardware stores and pharmacies were asked to stay open if possible. Everyone in emergency services was to report in. Chloe went across the yard to check the workshop. The door was a bit stiff and she had to put her shoulder to it to get it open, but everything seemed fine. She should have spent the time to do a thorough search in here once she got the locks sorted out, instead of getting pulled away by other things.

Her gaze fell on a laptop bag in the corner behind the tool shelves and she started forward, a sudden hiccup in her stomach. She recognized that bag, it belonged to Jeff. Stooping, she pulled it out, brushing off a light layer of dust and a few cobwebs. Had it been there all the time? Flipping back the flap, she looked down at an empty cavity. Jeff didn't go anywhere without that laptop, so it had probably gone with him. But why was the bag here, hidden behind the shelves? She quickly rifled through the pockets but only found a few papers. Hoisting it onto her shoulder, she headed back to the house, legs trembling.

She shoved the laptop bag under her bed and went back to the kitchen. Food first. She made a big pot of porridge, setting milk and brown sugar on the table. The gas stove worked fine, although she had to use matches to light it, but thank God it wasn't electric or they'd be trying to cook on the barbeque. She and Davey ate and she pointed the others to the stove as they came down the stairs. She was drawing water from the hot water tank, and warned everyone not to turn on a tap or flush.

Meanwhile she phoned her tenants at the building. The grocery store didn't answer for the longest time, but finally she was able to get through. They were so busy they couldn't answer questions, just confirmed that the premises were fine save for a broken window and business was brisk. This was such welcome news she was momentarily unable to speak. If only she could escape damage this easily.

After many tries she got through to StreetSmart, her non-profit tenant, only to reach an answering service. No one was in the office. That didn't tell her a whole lot more, other than that the damage to the building seemed to be minimal at the Grover's Grocery end of the structure. She didn't even know where the insurance papers were. She slapped a pad of paper onto the counter, found a pen and started a list.

The food in the freezer was worrisome as it could be days before she'd be able to shop for more, and perhaps weeks before the power would be restored. She remembered the installation of a generator in the garage, something Jeff had been quite proud of, and went to take a look. Not that she knew how to work it, but the monster machine was still residing in the back corner.

The diagram on the wall above told her it would service the freezer, the fridge, some plugs and lights in the kitchen. She talked to Dennis and he agreed to start it up that night. When the generator was going, they could charge everything, and use their laptops if they wanted to bring them into the kitchen.

Then she put Davey down for his nap, went into her bedroom and closed the door. She rummaged through Jeff's laptop bag, finding his usual paraphernalia, a few invoices and a bank statement stuffed into a side pocket.

She read every piece of paper. The bank statement was from April, the month before he disappeared. The information was now six months old. But it gave her something to go on. There were two automatic withdrawals that month, those must be the payments for the first and second mortgages. Pretty hefty payments.

There were two deposits made by bank transfer, so those must be rent payments from the tenants. They were also fairly hefty. Thankfully they added up to a larger figure than the withdrawals, but she'd have to keep in mind those deposits included amounts dedicated to building expenses and property taxes. It wasn't all to pay the mortgage. Then there were deposits of cash about twice a week. Those must be from Jeff's construction jobs. The bottom line looked pretty good.

She relaxed, then tensed again. Six months was a long time, and she didn't know what had happened in the interim. But she could bet that any cash deposits had stopped.

She sat on the bed, a sense of absolute loss overwhelming her. Why did Jeff do it this way? Why not let her in on the running of the business and the construction work? She knew about business, she could have done the mundane, making bank deposits, checking the statements, balancing the check book or paying bills. When she asked Jeff about it, she never got a real answer. He'd ask her a question in return, change the topic or remember a phone call he had to make.

Yet she was doing most of the business now, wasn't she? Or would be as soon as she got Rowbotham off his ass. She snickered at the silly analogy, then leaned her head back as tears leaked out of the corners of her eyes and into the hair at her temples.

When was she going to stop crying? Jayde had said the first six months were pure hell, no way around it. Then a kind of small healing took place, and she'd find she could go a while without thinking about the loss, then a bit longer. It was slow progress but it was progress.

Well, if that were true, and it probably was because her neighbour seemed to know these things, then she had a little way to go before she got a grip on her emotions. That seemed an eternity. It was already one eternity since Jeff left, but it looked like an even longer road ahead of her without him, on her own. With Davey.

~~~

Dennis started the generator that night. He found gas in a couple of jerry cans and poured it into the tank. Then he pulled the line until it fired. Everyone cheered as it stuttered, then settled down to a steady roar.

They rushed back into the kitchen to turn on lights. Laptops appeared and everyone checked email or searched for information. The wireless service was working but it gave spotty coverage. Chloe plugged in her own laptop to charge the batteries. There were extension cords all over the kitchen.

Jose returned home that night, having taken the bus partway from town and walked the last three miles. It was chaos, he reported. The buses were running in an abbreviated run making use of the roads that were clear. He had a printed sheet from the bus driver showing the routes that were being serviced at the moment. The university was closed.

Police were everywhere, fire trucks and ambulances littered the landscape. Trees were down, houses had collapsed, and whole buildings were damaged or destroyed. Jose had been at the university dorms overnight with friends and there were buildings damaged there. He figured they wouldn't be back in class for a while.

Water was off all over the city. They had promised it would be back on tomorrow in some sections of town,
~~~

perhaps for only a few hours. They were trying to glean information on water mains, pipes, and the damage done to the dam at the Sooke Reservoir. If the dam was seriously impaired it was possible water would be a partial service for months. Information slowly trickled in.

Chloe opened her laptop to search for information on the earthquake and found a joint website set up by the city of Victoria and the province. She lugged her printer into the kitchen, plugged it in, and started to print.

Amanda came over to look. "Good idea," she said. "When you're finished, can I print information from the University?" After a bit Chloe sent Dennis to turn off the generator.

Immediately candles were lit and the students started a card game at the kitchen table. Davey wanted to play so they began a game of Go Fish, until Chloe pulled him away to get ready for bed. Then the game changed and the boys were all about poker. Amanda didn't have a clue, but they would teach her and Beth was willing. Dennis brought down a six-pack of beer from upstairs.

"Don't catch your hair on fire from leaning too near the candles," Chloe warned. "Remember, we don't have any water to put it out." Everyone thought that was hysterically funny and even she was laughing as she herded her son down the hall to bed.

Next morning, the boarders put a forty five gallon drum in the bed of her pickup truck and took off, Dennis driving. They were going to find a lake, any lake that could be reached by vehicle. The bucket brigade would bring back water to flush the toilets.

Chloe went down the road with Davey in the wagon to check on Jayde. In the daylight, she saw the cracks in her porch steps and places where the concrete had pulled away from the front of the house.

Jayde herself was doing fine, although her phone was dead. Chloe pulled hers out of her pocket and offered it up. "You'll have to be quick because it's running low on charge."

Her neighbour called her son and left a message that she was fine and wanted to hear from him. She gave him Chloe's number.

Leaving there, Chloe carried on to the church hall. Davey climbed out of the wagon and took her hand to go inside. There was one woman in the daycare and two children playing with blocks in the corner. Davey stood for a minute watching the play, then let go of his mother's hand. He walked slowly over and crouched down, putting his fingers on one of the blocks. No one said anything, so he sat down and played.

The supervisor smiled. "Hello, I'm Sonya."

Chloe shook her hand and introduced herself. "I've been wondering about daycare for Davey. He's four and I've gotten so busy… But then we had the quake and things have changed."

Sonja laughed, then sobered quickly. "They certainly have. Thank God the loss of life has been minimal, but it's terrible, isn't it? This building is apparently unharmed, although no one is allowed in the church itself until it's been thoroughly checked out.

"And most of the children who come to daycare aren't coming at the moment as you can see, people are staying home. We usually have about eighteen children, with three of us running the programme. But we have room for Davey. He looks like a nice young man. Where do you live?"

Chloe pointed back down the road, "Not far. And I really only need him here one or two days a week to start."

Sonja took her over to a table in the corner to work on forms.

~~~

Ross Cullen pawed through the files on his desk. There were too many open cases, too much work backed up. He wanted to get a handle on things, because they needed to solve the Jeff Sanderson file. Something wasn't right about it and he wanted to find out what that was. Ms. Bowman was a fascinating suspect.
~~~

"Dan," he called across the room. "What about Sanderson's background? What have we got on that?"

Dan shuffled through his file and brought some papers across to show him. "Not a heck of a lot. His parents are in Florida, retired. They were Canadian citizens, but now have dual citizenship. Father worked for oil companies, they travelled quite a bit during their married life. One child, Jeff.

"They didn't hear from Jeff a lot once he left home, hadn't met his wife. They knew about the grandchild but have never laid eyes on him. To tell the truth, the cop who interviewed them said they didn't seem all that interested in the fact that their son is missing. They have an active social life, read that as an active drinking life. They did say to keep them posted on finding him."

Ross raised his eyebrows. "Nice."

"Then we have a couple of Sanderson's buddies from university. We have, uh…" Dan searched through the papers, came up with one near the bottom. "We have Buddy Slots who knew him at university. Saw him in a bar around Christmas last year. They had a drink together. He hadn't known he was married, so they obviously didn't see each other often. He was surprised Sanderson was in construction, thought he was more the information technology type. When he knew him at school he was always talking computer programmes and games. He mentioned Sanderson was a bit of a drinker, you'd find him in bars a lot. Conducted his meetings in bars, that kind of thing."

"So a drinker. A womanizer?"

"Well, he didn't say that, nor did this other guy. A fellow named Uhjal Singh, also from university. Singh works in construction, his father owns a heavy equipment operation. He remembers Jeff dropped out of university, Singh finished. But they'd meet up once in a while around town.

"Jeff talked to him recently about a project where he needed a road built and parking lot paved, but it didn't come together. That was last year sometime. He said he could probably dig out the bid they put in on the job if we really needed it. He thought Sanderson was always looking for the fast track, the shortcut. He wasn't surprised when he quit, university was too slow for him. There were no quick results to be had there."

Ross nodded. "Maybe you should get that quote from Singh, it might be the same building where the fraud was involved. Could be something there."

"Right. Also, both these guys remembered another fellow who was a good friend of Jeff, one said his name was Ron, the other said Ray, but they seemed to be talking about the same guy. This was another nerd type, played computer games. They spent a lot of time talking theoretical business deals, spending time in the cafeteria instead of studying. They both quit university about the same time."

"Try to find more on that. Check with admissions up there, see if they have any records that are useful from that long ago, must be, what? Eight or ten years ago. I know the earthquake has created a huge upheaval, but try to fit it in, maybe take Cheryl with you. She's good at that kind of stuff and she's trying to make us hire her full time."

Dan laughed. Cheryl was Dan's current girlfriend. She'd come on the job in the office part time the year before and after a lot of effort finally caught Dan's attention. "That's a good idea, I might take her along for the ride."

Ross snorted at his sly grin and waved him away.

~~~

Chloe set off for town the following day as early as possible with a road map in her hand. She desperately needed that court order. The mortgage company had called again. Chloe needed signing authority to deal with them.

She'd relied on the earthquake to explain why it would likely take a few weeks, and promised to get back to them as soon as she had some positive news. In the meantime, she reported she'd lost all her mortgage files in the quake and needed copies of the documents. She gave them her email address and John's fax, and threw up a prayer of
~~~

thanks. Somehow she'd weaseled out of that one. And as a bonus she'd get a complete file. Now for step two.

The trip to town was horrendous. There were backups and delays, there were detours. She drove slowly in a long line of cars past the buildings at Houston Way, a pile of rubble beside the highway interchange. A large part of her route was one-way traffic, with police and flaggers controlling the flow of vehicles. It took forever to make progress.

Finally she arrived downtown, or what was left of it and parked on the street. There were no meter readers, so she just found a space, left her truck and walked. As she went, she gazed around. What she saw was astounding. The downtown looked in remarkably good shape on one block and a total wreck on the next. A skyscraper would appear untouched, standing beside a low rise building that had caved in.

One huge exception was the facade of the massive Anglican cathedral. The whole thing had collapsed. Quadra Street was impassable, mortar and stone rubble piled eight or ten feet high. She could look straight into the body of the building from blocks away, where the pews were lined up facing the altar. Remarkably, the back half of the structure looked in perfect shape. Even the embroidered altar cloth was still spread on the altar, pinned down by candle sticks, one end lifting in the light breeze. There was a peculiar gritty smell, as if the dust from cutting the stone still hung in the air.

Her first stop was Rowbotham's office. She had to walk a circuitous route to reach it. The building was damaged at the far side. It looked like someone had placed a giant foot on the roof and stood, squashing one end. Inside were rows of shelving waving unevenly down the wall with stacks of books scattered everywhere. Files lay open and spilled, file boxes ripped. The offices were empty and businesses closed, but at the other end companies were operating as usual and Rowbotham's law office was open. She waited fifty minutes before Art Rowbotham came out to see her.

"I know you must be overloaded," she said. "But I insist that we move ahead on the court order. I can't wait any longer. I have the document with me. If we go across the road we'll see when we can get into Chambers."

Rowbotham gave a supercilious smile. "It's not that easy, Mrs. Sanderson. And right now I have some pretty important files to take care of."

"This file is pretty important, at least to me." Chloe stood up. "Are you saying you won't come to court and make this application, Art? I need an answer."

Rowbotham's face turned a dull red. "I'm saying, Mrs. Sanderson," he gritted out with stiff-necked emphasis, "that today I am unable to help you. I don't know at this point when I can make the court appearance. Hopefully soon, but not now."

Chloe nodded, looked around the reception area. Two other people were sitting on chairs waiting for an appointment, and the receptionist was working at her desk between calls. They were all staring at her. She smiled and turned back to him. "Art, you have been less than helpful from the very beginning." She walked out the door.

CHAPTER FIVE

Walking straight across the street, Chloe turned the corner to the court house on the next block. An imposing double staircase came off the second floor and led down to the sidewalk. After some muddling around inside the building, she found her way into a chambers courtroom. She waited for the case before the Judge to finish, then spoke to the court clerk.

The judge listened as the clerk explained something to him. Then he looked at her with interest and motioned her forward. After some consultation with his clerk over the rest of the day's schedule, he offered to hear her application that afternoon around four o'clock. "Everything must be in writing," he remarked. "And the application should be supported by whatever evidence you have."

Chloe left on the run. Her first stop was John's office. His secretary helped produce a copy of all the documents for the judge. Chloe attached the missing persons report, a paper for John to sign backing up her statement of facts and placed a quick phone call to him to come back into the office to sign it. She made out a new chronological list of events that she thought would be helpful, then put it all in order.

A quick trip to get a sandwich and wolf it down, and she was back at the court house, walking up and down the hallway and looking hopefully about for her brother.

She had to begin without him. Going up to the bar on wobbly legs, she sat where the clerk pointed. "You're to address the judge as 'Your Honour'," she said, "And you stand when you address him." There was no one else in the courtroom.

Finally the judge appeared, robes flapping and ascended to his high seat behind the bench. He looked over his spectacles and nodded at Chloe before grabbing the file the clerk handed up and pulling it toward him. The clerk announced *The Application of Chloe Bowman in the Matter of the Disappearance of her Husband Jeff Sanderson*. Not sure what to do, Chloe stood.

"Sit down," the Judge said. "Let me read this document."

As he read, the door at the back opened and John came quietly into the courtroom. Chloe waved her brother forward and handed him two copies of his statement to sign. The judge watched with interest as he read over the paper, signed both copies and handed them back to her. She tiptoed up and handed one copy to the clerk who passed it on to the judge. He took it, scrutinizing John for a moment before briefly reading it. Then he settled back in his chair. "Okay. Ms. Bowman, please give me a brief outline of why you're here."

Chloe gave as succinct a summary as she could, then sat down. The judge looked at her for a minute. "Why exactly are you representing yourself?"

Chloe paused with her mouth open. "Uh." She stood again and stammered for a minute. "I had legal counsel, Your Honour. The lawyer who acted for my husband in his company matters. At first he wouldn't take any steps. But after four months, and there was no word from Jeff....." Chloe could feel her eyes tearing up, so she glanced down and focussed on the papers in front of her. "I went back to see him again because something had to be done."

She was now able to raise her gaze. "That was two months ago. The earthquake made it even more important that someone take control of the company. I can't do repairs or deal with the insurance. The document he gave me doesn't allow me to handle the bank or financial matters. It doesn't make me a signing authority. It doesn't allow me to take any profits."

The judge nodded. "And you want all those things."

"Yes, Your Honour. I need all those things."

"I see." He looked at her for another moment. "And how long since you last saw your husband, Ms Bowman?"

Chloe thought for a moment. "Six months and twenty-seven days, Your Honour."

The judge pondered that. "What kind of income do you require?"

Chloe stalled. "I'm not sure, but if there's profit I'm going to need it. My husband had just built a new house for us before he..... before he left. And the mortgage payments are pretty steep. I've taken in four boarders, but that only goes so far. Then there's the commercial building, I'm uncertain what the expenses are going to be."

The judge regarded her for a moment longer. Then he looked down at the clerk and said, "Alright. I'm issuing an Order from this Court that provides the following.

"Ms Bowman shall have full signing authority over the company," here he consulted the documents, "Sanderson Holdings Ltd.

"Ms. Bowman shall have full signing authority over the bank accounts, accounts, and any other assets, liabilities or commitments of Sanderson Holdings Ltd.

"Ms. Bowman shall have authority to make decisions…" The judge continued talking for a few more moments, then added, "This Order shall stand until such time as Jeff Sanderson shall appear in person to make application to alter this Order, or such other interested parties who can show standing come forward for the same. It is open to Ms Bowman to appear in this Court to make application to change the Order if she sees fit."

He added for the record, "Clerk, we'll keep this open and add anything that needs adding that we've missed. But give her the Order now."

The Judge paused. "There are other issues you'll need to deal with, of course, such as transferring the corporate shares into your name, but this is a start." He hammered his gavel and stood.

"Order in the Court," said the clerk and everyone stood. The judge nodded and walked out.

She stood for a minute in shock, then turned to John and whispered, "John! Did you hear that? I've got it. I can do something now."

John slanted a look at the clerk and Chloe closed her mouth. She gathered her papers together and tucked them under her arm.

The clerk stood. "You can pick up the Court Order tomorrow after ten o'clock at the court house office on the first floor. That Order can be copied and used to change things over into your name. Good luck, Ms. Bowman."

She nodded, tears gathering in her eyes, then sat down unsteadily as the clerk left through the back door of the courtroom behind the judge. Her palms were wet with sweat and her legs shaky, but she'd done it. She had the court order.

~~~

From there, Chloe took John to look at the building. As they drove past the Pointe Ellice Bridge, she saw a part of the foot bridge twisted out of shape and one lane of the car bridge hanging in mid-air over the inlet. "Were there any cars on the bridge, John? When the earthquake hit, I mean."

John shook his head. "Nope, none. Just lucky I guess."

They crossed the Gorge to find the building looking solid. At first glance they found a few cracked windows. But as John poked around he saw some cracking in exterior walls
~~~

on the single floor structure. "You'd better let us take another look, Chloe. I'll have Ralph come over with a couple of the guys sometime this week and do a closer examination. And I'll ask Brent to come as well. Might as well get the official version with an engineer's stamp on it." He grinned. John was proud of his 'little' brother.

"This is a solid building. I've seen the drawings and I know it has a lot of earthquake upgrades. It looks like your non-profit is still closed down, and they don't even have any cracked glass."

They looked through the glass doors but there was no movement inside. Chloe took her keys and opened up the vacant space that ran down the side of the building. John looked around inside and pronounced it in good shape, no crumbling plaster or concrete.

She considered the abandoned detritus from the last tenant. There was some furniture here she might be able to use at the house. She was short of night tables for Dennis and Jose, which made it difficult for them to read in bed without a place to put the lamp.

A couple of these desks would work as well. She might bring the boarders in on the weekend. They could take some things back home in the pickup.

As he was putting her back into her truck, John suggested a quick fix to her fireplace chimney that would get her back in business for heat. He'd gather the materials and try to get out later in the week. His days were getting longer with all the deconstruction and reconstruction work that was being prepared in the city.

"Good going today, Chloe," he added. "You spoke well for yourself. Turns out you didn't need that lawyer after all, eh? I'd change law firms. I know he's worked for Jeff for years, but he simply isn't on your side. Think about it, anyway."

He gave her a hug and closed the cab door. "Drive very carefully." He gave a tap on the side of the truck as she pulled away.

~~~

On her way home Chloe stopped at the farmers market at the edge of town. In the back of her truck were four dozen eggs, sacks of potatoes, carrots, onions and some other vegetables.

Now she sat in a line-up of vehicles waiting for gas. Her tank was low and she'd decided to stop while there was still enough left to wait it out in the line. It didn't look that bad when she first pulled in but it had been fifteen minutes and she wasn't that much closer to the gas pumps.

Amanda answered the phone at the house and said she'd be happy to go down to Jayde's place with the wagon and bring Davey home. It was nearly eight o'clock and he'd be getting tired, Jayde too for that matter.

It was closer to nine when Chloe finally pulled down the drive. To her delight, there were lights on in the house. The garage door opened with the remote the way it was always meant to and she drove inside. She left all the vegetables in the bed of the truck, picked up the eggs and her bundle of papers. Dumping everything on the kitchen table, she stared gloomily at a sink full of dishes.

There were voices coming from upstairs. Amanda was working on some project at the coffee table on the landing and Davey was playing Lego on the floor. Jose was propped up on one elbow beside him. She could hear the shower going in the bathroom.

"So this," Jose was saying, "is the pirate ship. That's why this guy has a patch over one eye, because he's a pirate. See, these other guys are soldiers. I like the soldiers."

"I like the pirates!" said Davey. "They have the best clothes."

"Really?" said Jose, looking sceptically at the tiny figure in his hand. "They look ragged, maybe they can't afford new ones."

"Maybe," said Davey doubtfully. "Mum!" he yelled, spotting Chloe. He leaped to his feet, Lego pieces scattering, and launched himself at her.
~~~

Jose sat up and smiled. "Hi, Chloe. We were just getting our Lego worked out here."

"Were you? Thank you so much, you guys. I simply couldn't get back in time to pick him up and I don't know what I would have done without you."

Amanda waved her away. "It was no trouble. Jayde says hi, and thanks for loaning your son for a while."

Chloe laughed. "She's cute. Loaning my son. I just had a killer of a day today and I had no way around it. How long has the power been on?"

"It came on about six o'clock, the internet site says we'll have more or less steady power from now on, steady as in coming on at the same time. I printed it out for you." Jose found a sheet and handed it to her. "Dennis is down the road still. They came door to door asking for help digging out a house, someone was trapped."

"Oh Lord, how awful. What happened?"

"We got the guy out, injured but basically all right. The house shifted and sank, and when it shifted the stairs sheared off so there was no way out of the basement. They were just finishing up when I left, so he should be back soon."

"Good for you for going, Jose."

He grinned at her but sobered quickly. "Everyone's just doing what they can, right?"

"That's for sure," she said. "Okay. So I guess that means showers tonight to take advantage of the lights and the hot water. I'll load the dishwasher and get it going while I can. See you all in the morning. By the way, if anyone has emergency laundry, you can drop it in the laundry room. If there's water and power during the day, I'll put on a load or two."

Chloe put Davey to bed, made sure everything was charging, put a load of her son's laundry into the washer, turned off all the lights downstairs and threw herself into bed.

~~~
~~~

John came out Saturday morning with one of his men. Chloe had just gotten up when the doorbell rang. She quickly slid a warm sweatshirt over her head as she went down the hall to the front door. "John, long time no see."

He laughed and gave her a hug. "Well, at least you weren't still in bed. I thought you were a sluggard when it came to getting up."

"Not after you have children, you aren't," she replied acerbically. "If you're still in bed at six o'clock after your child turns two then he just isn't doing his job."

She waved them in and Ralph headed straight over to the fireplace. Ralph had been John's foreman for years and his father's before him. He was so knowledgeable, John always said, "If Ralph doesn't know how to do it, it can't be done." He'd said it once in front of him and Chloe had been delighted to see the slightly grizzled older man blush.

He installed some plywood behind the glass fireplace doors then went outside and climbed up onto the roof. She heard scraping and banging inside the chimney and the sound of rocks falling. The men set a metal chimney extension in place, cementing it in to seal it for smoke. They patched and mortared some of the fallen stones around it for support.

When they were finished, Ralph opened up the fireplace doors and took the fallen chimney stones out. The two men pulled chairs up to the kitchen table and Chloe plunked mugs of coffee in front of them.

"I've got a package of paper for you, Chloe. It's in the truck. Don't let me forget, it's from your mortgage company."

"Oh, thank God. It finally came."

"Yeah, it's all there. Now," he paused to take a sip of coffee, "We've got a big job starting and one more following, I guess we'll be working on both at the same time. Ralph here is up to his eyeballs trying to hire guys. Everyone is committed, working twelve hour days. There's so much work it'll last into the next decade."

Ralph nodded.

"I have an idea for the empty space at your building. The Construction Association needs more office space to deal with all the new contractors flooding into town. I suggested your place. It's about fifteen hundred feet, right? And with the four offices and open area for another four or five people, they're interested. Do you want to show them around? Because I already told them about you, so..."

"You told them what? The poor widow?" Her face flushed.

"Come on, Chloe. Of course not. Just that you're my sister and they know me. The connection's a good one, why not use it? Plus they have certainly heard about Jeff. This city is too small to keep something like that from coming into the conversation." He frowned sternly at her, leaning forward aggressively in his chair.

"Okay. I'm sorry." She sighed. "Give me the contact information and I'll call them this morning. It would be good to have income from part of that space."

Her brother settled back in his chair. "Good. Now I have another idea. We have crews coming. Ralph's been hiring out of town, out of province in a lot of cases, right?"

Ralph nodded again and drained his coffee.

"And they need a place to stay. There isn't a thing available in the way of bed and breakfast, motels, rooms to rent. There are people who have no housing who are taking most of those places. So what about a hostel arrangement in the rest of your space? Ralph here suggested it actually."

Chloe turned her smile on Ralph, who nodded awkwardly and stared into the bottom of his mug.

"There are three bathrooms with showers," John continued, "You have a huge lunchroom with a fridge and a microwave oven, sink and all. And then the big open space. My idea was this, build temporary partitions to provide a cubby for each man. We could install a washer and dryer, and we'd have someone sleep in to supervise, 'cause with a room full of guys…" He slanted a glance at his foreman who looked glum. "You could have trouble. Anyway, if it was done properly it would give you a good income and solve a problem for us. What do you think?"

Chloe nodded. "Would you pay by the bed, or would you rent the whole space?"

John stared at her for a minute. "I haven't thought it through yet."

"What about zoning? I'm not zoned for housing."

"No problem. We just don't apply for zoning. We'd never get it, or it would take too long to be of any use. The need would be over before the city made the decision."

"Yeah, you're right. But you'd build the partitions? Who supplies the beds, the mattresses, the sheets and blankets, etc.?"

John looked at Ralph. "See this? Her brother is doing her a favour and she's talking nitty gritty dollars and cents, how much am I going to put in."

She laughed. "This is no favour. I see all kinds of problems. I can just imagine what it will be like with thirty guys in there, a few with too many drinks under their belts. However, for you, I guess I could... "

Ralph snickered. "You two deserve each other."

CHAPTER SIX

Sunday Chloe loaded everyone into the truck and headed for the building. Whatever they could use in the way of furniture, they'd bring back. "These are mostly big office desks," she explained. "It's more likely the side tables and other things that will be useful."

It turned into a kind of hunting expedition. They trooped through the space, looking in each office and all the back rooms, shouting when they found something that looked interesting.

It was fun and had a flea market feel to it. John had already started clearing the space and laying out the design of the temporary structures that would house his workers. The furniture had been shifted to the side, and wood framing laid out on the floor.

She walked through, surprised at how many men could be housed here. She wondered at the size of each cubby, but if the guys were working for two or three weeks before they went home on leave, it would drive them crazy to be in a really tight space. As always, John was doing a good job of thinking it through before he started.

There were some wheeled office chairs that were chosen along with a side table, bookcases and a corner table.

They dragged it all to the entrance and left it there while they explored further. They found boxes of paper and envelopes and hauled it out to go with the rest. Finally Dennis stumbled across a small desk that would fit in his room and got Jose to help him move it.

Chloe took a long folding table to use as a work bench. Davey spent his time picking up any small object and carrying it around. He came up with boxes of tacks and paper clips. There were binders and report covers, file folders and clipboards.

They eventually carried everything out to the truck. Dennis and Jose loaded the desk in first and as they lifted it, the lower drawer opened. "Oh my God," Jose murmured. "Would you look at that?"

"Look at what?" said Chloe. She turned around at the sudden silence and found herself looking into the open desk drawer at Jeff's laptop.

"Chloe, is this yours?" Jose was looking at her curiously.

"No," she said clearly. "That's my husband's." More silence. She glanced up to catch the looks being exchanged between them.

Dennis cleared his throat, leaned over and picked it up. "Well, I'd say it's still in good shape." He handed it to her over the side of the truck. She caught it with both hands and set it down on the nearest chair. There it was, sitting in plain view more or less. She opened the lid and pressed the power button but nothing happened.

"It's probably low on battery after all this time," said Dennis.

"I have the charger," said Chloe. "I found the laptop bag in the workshop at home."

"So is it your husband's?" he asked. The others looked at him because they dared not look at Chloe.

She nodded.

"How long has he been gone?"

She stared at him, but she didn't really see him. "Seven months," she said. She looked down again at the blank screen of the laptop then shut the lid and picked it up. "Well, let's get everything loaded." The mood was more sombre as they headed home, everything piled and tied down in the bed of the truck.

By the time they arrived, chatter had resumed. Furniture made its way to various parts of the house. Chloe wrestled the folding trestle table into the garage with Dennis's help.

"It's okay, you know," he said. "You can talk about him and it would be okay. We all know he's gone, we just don't know why. A lot of people separate, we can understand that."

Chloe nodded. "I guess that's true, Dennis. But you see, I don't know why any more than you do. He just disappeared. There isn't any information."

Dennis was silent for once.

That night when the generator was running, Chloe had the laptop charging along with all the other equipment on the kitchen plugs. While it charged, she lifted the lid. She looked around uncomfortably but everyone was busy with their own devices. Booting it up, she immediately met a password demand.

She hit her forehead with her fist. Amanda looked at her questioningly. Smiling vaguely, she looked back at the screen. What would Jeff have used? She tried all their names, middle names, last names, parent's names. She tried numbers that meant something to them, combinations of numbers and names. Finally it was the dogs that got her in. The password was DogOneDogTwo.

Well, that had taken her forty minutes. She checked her watch. The generator would have to be turned off soon. Their power service had been fairly stable, but on the days that it didn't come on, she still needed the generator to keep everything going. She quickly opened up the email account. Immediately emails downloaded from months ago.

There were very few. She organized them by sender and deleted the spam right away. There weren't many left, and they all dated from the day Jeff left, up to a few weeks later. Obviously word had gotten around that he wasn't available to answer messages.

She scanned through them. Two from the bank, each confirming a transfer from the general account into a term deposit in the amount of fifty thousand dollars. Okay, that was a lot of money and she didn't know anything about a term deposit. The police must know the details of this bank account, yet they had never asked her about it.

She gave up in exhaustion and asked Dennis to shut the generator down as everyone packed up. Chloe quickly scanned the rest of the emails. There was one from someone named Bam, wanting to know when the concrete was needed. The last message was from a person named Rainman, confirming a meeting for the day after Jeff disappeared. She sighed. *I guess Jeff didn't make that meeting.* She powered the laptop down and closed the lid. She'd have another look when she wasn't so tired.

~~~

Rainman walked into the bank dressed in a way that allowed him to blend with the crowd and not be noticed by the casual observer. He'd made a study of it, what was most common, most ordinary, least likely to attract attention. He wore coloured contact lenses, the same ones each time he came into this bank, had done for months.

He produced his corporate bank card and asked for cash, nine thousand eight hundred dollars. The teller gave him a hesitant look and said she'd have to call her supervisor. "No problem, you people say that every time," he replied with a disarming grin. His crooked front tooth flashed for a moment. "I'll wait right here."

The teller nervously made a phone call and asked him to step to the side while she took the next customer. Finally the teller motioned him to the till and introduced a bank official who smiled at Rain.
~~~

"Hello, Mr. Humphreys, thanks for being patient. You know it will take a few minutes to open the safe. You can have a chair over there if you like, Annette will call you when it's ready. Annette, the prohibition on cash is when a customer is *depositing* over ten thousand dollars with us, not when they are *withdrawing* it. Just have Mr. Humphreys sign the form please, and then proceed."

Rain signed, waited patiently on the chair and finally came back to the wicket to pick up his packet of money. He smiled and thanked Annette before tucking it into his briefcase and strolling back out the door.

Walking around the corner, he pulled a handkerchief out of his pocket. Mopping the sweat on his forehead, he examined the makeup smearing the fabric and shrugged his shoulders. He did what he had to do.

His beater of a car, a Kharman Ghia, was sitting on a side street near the bank. It looked old and rough but was in very good mechanical condition. He replaced his vehicle every year, bought with a phoney driver's licence for ID when he went to register it and get insurance. But this one had been purchased early, just after Jeff left. He wasn't taking any chances. Best to cut all ties and erase the connections.

He made four more stops identical to the first one at four different banks. This was something he did every week, sometimes varying it by a day or two, but hitting each account for a cash withdrawal. The banks didn't always like it, but he would patiently explain that it was his money and he could withdraw in cash if he wanted. They always gave in.

By the time he was finished, it was late afternoon. Cindy would be up by now. Time to get moving on the next job for the day. When he got home, he walked into a silent house. Still in bed, he guessed. He carried on down the hall to her bedroom. "Come on, Cindy, you've slept long enough. Time to get up." He shook her arm.

Cindy rolled over and covered her eyes with the back of her hand. Rain noticed there were even scabs on her arms now. That crystal was dreadful stuff, it did strange things to people. He'd never tried it and never would. But Cindy couldn't resist it now, she was hooked.

"Come on." He shook her again, then went to the kitchen and put the kettle on.

He rifled through the mail while he waited for the water to boil. Nothing of interest, it was all for the former tenant of the house. His own mail went to a post box. Rain had been in this house for six months, he'd moved right after Jeff had gone.

A lot of things changed when Jeff left.

He'd tried to alter his routines. He made an even bigger effort to leave fewer traces of himself. He had no credit cards now, paid them off and cut them up. He had a driver's licence and one credit card in the name of Bob Humphreys. He knew he'd need credit for something, just not in his own name.

He wandered into the bathroom to take a leak and examined himself in the mirror as he washed up at the sink. Time for another hair job. He'd have to stop at a different pharmacy, pick up a box of dark brown colour. He tongued his crooked tooth, it didn't even budge. Damn, that worked fine and changed his appearance dramatically. It had been Jeff's idea, such a clever man. Just not clever enough apparently.

The kettle boiled and he made a cup of instant coffee, adding a lot of cream and sugar and took it in to Cindy who'd pulled the covers back over her head. He pulled them down again. "Come on, Cindy. No more lollygagging. Here's your coffee."

She lifted her arm and sat up. He was always a little horrified these days when he saw her naked face in daylight. She hadn't looked like this when he first met her. She'd been quite a beauty. She was using different drugs then, but nothing too debilitating, and she'd been gorgeous. Now she looked old, and the scabs on her face were disfiguring. He left her to get dressed but went back to hurry her along because they had an appointment.

She finally appeared in the hallway, a short red skirt and nylons barely covering her private parts. She wore a cream coloured V-necked sweater tight enough to read her nipples through. "Let's go," he said, "you're looking fine."

She wobbled down the steps to the car in her spike heels and fell into the passenger seat. Rain fired it up and backed out of the drive. "Now, Cindy. You know this guy is getting harder to deal with. He's starting to ask for a bigger cut and we can't give it to him. This is your job. Your part of the bargain is to make sure he pays us our share. You have a job to do. Don't let me down."

They pulled into a tool rental site. He parked the car against the back fence, facing out and produced a sheet of paper. "Here you go. Here's the tally for this month. This number is what's been deposited into his account."

He pointed at a figure that he'd circled on the page. "This number is his cut, and the one at the bottom is our payment. I've highlighted it for you, so it's clear what you're collecting. Don't let me down," he said again.

Cindy nodded and heaved the car door open. He watched her sway across the parking lot and pull the front door of the shop open just as a customer stepped out. The man stopped to stare after her as she walked into the office on her black heels. She was the only person in there now. Rain watched as the owner came out to lock the door. Then he took Cindy into his private office at the back.

This man was Cindy's contact. She'd had eight or ten of them originally, but one by one they'd disappeared. One went bankrupt, one backed out, one sold his business and others just fell by the wayside. But this fellow had been getting more and more demanding. Rain figured this was their last call here.

Finally the office door opened and she emerged carrying a manila envelope under her elbow. She unlocked the door, walked back to the car and fell into the seat, slapping the envelope down on the dash. "There you go, big boy," she said. She wiped her mouth and pushed her hair back behind her ears. "Piece of cake."

~~~

Rain picked up the envelope and weighed it in his hand. "You were gone a long time," he remarked. He watched the owner come out of his office, adjusting his trousers. He locked the front door and went around the shop to turn off lights.

Rain opened the envelope and counted. It was all there.

"He paid up, don't worry. He didn't want to, he tried to whine his way out of it. But then I showed him why it was to his benefit to pay in full, so he did." She smiled triumphantly at him.

He grinned back. "Good girl. One more stop now, off to the house."

When he pulled up in front of a derelict house at the end of a worn gravel drive, he realized this was one more piece of shit that weighed him down. He and Jeff Sanderson had lived in this house for three years when they first started out. There were enough rooms, counting the two damp ones in the basement, for seven guys. That left a living room and kitchen for common use. They had dragged in a bunch of men to help pay the rent, and essentially lived for free most of the time they were here. Jeff moved out shortly after he met Chloe, just before they married. Rain stayed on for another year, pulling in more guys as needed to fill the place.

But by then he and Jeff were making good money. He didn't need to live in a rat hole any more. He moved into a nice rental house, clean, dry and freshly painted. It had a decent driveway and garage, three large bedrooms. But he didn't let the rundown house go, just kept it, finding a few older guys to run the place and bring in the younger ones who paid the rent on a transient basis.

The landlord didn't care. He got paid monthly, on time, in full. He didn't give a shit what happened to the
~~~

house. He never got a call to fix something or paint it, and that's just the way he liked it.

Rain walked up the stairs and opened the door, stepping into the front hall. There was some kind of ruckus going on, a new guy who was trying to throw his weight around. "What's up, Buster? Have you got my stuff?"

The young man whirled around to nail him with a glare. "Who the fuck are you?"

Rain gave him an assessing look, then turned back to Buster.

"This is Troy," Buster said hurriedly, just as Troy grabbed Rain's arm and jerked him forward.

"I said, who are you, fuck face?"

"Well, Troy." Out of the corner of his eye, Rain watched Cindy move out of his way as he leaned past her toward the door jamb. Her face went blank as he grabbed the two by four that leaned there and whipped around, nailing Troy across the ribs. The young man grunted and doubled over. Rain hit him again from the other side, then casually leaned the lumber back against the jamb.

"Now, Buster, what have you got for me?"

Buster pulled a wad of bills out of his pocket and handed it to Rain. He counted it carefully, pulled out a few twenties, folded the rest of it and put it in his pocket. "You're a few bucks short, I'll leave it to you to collect as part of your commission."

The older man nodded.

He walked over and took a seat on the dingy cushions of the couch and looked at Troy. The young man was standing straight now with great effort and glaring at him from a flushed face. "How old are you, Troy?"

"None of your business."

"Come on, now. We don't have to be enemies. Let's just treat each other with respect. Come and sit here." He indicated a chair across from him as he watched Cindy wobble across the living room and into the kitchen in her spike heels, following one of the other men. She'd found her supplier.

Troy glowered at him, his dark blond hair bristling and blue eyes blazing.

"Come on. Sit down. What have you got in the way of identification?"

Buster motioned Troy to the chair, and he grudgingly moved over to it and sat down heavily. "Who wants to know?"

"Well, I do. I'm the one who's asking, aren't I? Pull out your wallet and let's see."

"What do you want to know for?"

"I just want to see if you have a driver's licence."

"Sure, of course I do."

"Well, let's see it." Rain held out his hand.

Troy finally reached back and extracted a wallet from his pocket. He pulled out his license and handed it to Rain who examined it carefully. An Alberta license, that wouldn't be too bad. No one here would be looking for one from Alberta. He noted Troy was a year younger than he was, same height but heavier build. That worked. His eyes were as blue as Rain's. It'd be nice not to wear contact lenses for a while. He could bleach his hair to Troy's colour, no problem. He was getting good at it. It all looked workable.

He glanced up. "What else have you got there?"

Troy raised his brows and pulled out a social insurance card.

He took it and looked for more. "Got a birth certificate?"

Tory shook his head.

"Okay, this'll work. Tell you what. I'll give you a hundred bucks to borrow your ID for two days. How about that?"

He looked doubtful.

Buster said, "He's good for it, Troy, and you know you're short of money."

"Two hundred. Cash."

"Done." Rain shook his hand and took the cards.

Troy handed over a student card, but Rain declined. "I won't need that. The driver's license and social insurance number are enough." Tugging some bills out of his pocket, he counted out two hundred dollars. "There you go. I'll be back day after tomorrow."

He walked into the kitchen at the back but the girl was gone. "Buster, give this to Cindy when you see her." He handed over a fifty. No point in giving her any extra. She'd just get more blasted than she probably already was. "Tell her I'll be in touch."

He went out to his car and backed down the rutted drive. Yes, it was time to give this place up. He'd been attached to it too long, and too many ties led back to him. He'd offer Buster the option of taking over the rental, and if he didn't want it, he'd quit the place. It wasn't in his name anyway, it was in Jeff's. But still, best to lose the connection.

Rain took the old Island Highway out of town toward Westshore. He continued on through Colwood onto the Sooke Road, then turned just before East Sooke, heading down a narrow feeder road that soon changed from paved to gravel.

Finally he steered off into the long grassy driveway of a house nestled back in the trees. He put the car in park and sat staring at the building. There was a light on in the kitchen. He turned off the motor and climbed slowly out of the car. Stooping slightly to avoid banging his head, he stepped up under the low roof of the porch and gave a couple of sharp raps on the door. He waited, finally hammered again. A few minutes later he heard what he expected to hear, the rustle of long grass in the yard behind him.

"Who's bangin' on my door?"

Rainier turned at the sound of the gravel voice. "Jimmy, you old geezer. It's Bob Humphreys. Why don't you invite me in? I've got some work for you." He pulled the two pieces of ID out of his pocket.

CHAPTER SEVEN

"Your turn, Davey. Hit the ball." It was a beautiful day, the sky a sunny blue without a cloud. But it wasn't as warm as it had been. Chloe felt a warning in the air that it wasn't fall any longer and she and Davey both wore heavy jackets.

Her dahlias were still blooming like mad, huge spiky flowers of every colour and hue. Some of them were so big she hadn't been able to stake them up properly, so she just cut them as they came and dotted vases all over the house.

She had leaf lettuce and chard in the garden, her salads had all been home grown and wild tasting in the last month, and she was very proud. Her son liked to follow her around the garden, picking different leaves to eat. She had to keep a close check on what he was picking. She wasn't sure how edible the daisy fronds or other decorative plants were.

Davey lined up his croquet mallet and walloped the ball through the wicket to the other side of the lawn. "Oh, too bad. You have to come back here to this side. But the good news is you shot it through the wicket so you get another shot."

"Okay." Davey looked determined as he clumped over to hit the ball again. They played what Chloe called 'abbreviated croquet'. She told him there were different rules for smaller people, with only three wickets set out in an 'S' shape with the posts hammered in at each end.

Chloe took her turn, missed the wicket and leaned on the handle of her mallet as she waited for Davey to take another shot. She turned her face to the slight breeze coming across from the field below. It smelled like winter. The grass down there had turned golden brown. Jayde's two sheep were still inside the fence, but she had mentioned that soon they'd be moved over to her pasture. There they could go in and out of the barn when the weather turned bad.

Chloe liked that her neighbour put her sheep in their field for the summer. It kept the thistles and other pest plants down and stopped the brush from taking over. Plus it looked like she was part of the farming community.

What would she ever do with the field if left on her own? She wasn't a farmer but it was nice to look out and see the animals grazing. Jayde sheared them in the spring and Chloe had seen the fleece. It was spectacular, impenetrable, muddy looking wool. Someone in the community liked to card and spin it. Many a pair of heavy winter slippers had been knit from that stuff, Jadye assured her, not to mention sweaters and mittens.

"Look, Davey." She pointed into the trees beyond the yard. There was a flock of forty or fifty tiny birds, swarming like bees from the giant red cedar tree to the Douglas fir and back. "Those little birds are getting ready for winter. They practice flying together in flocks like that so they can go south where it's warmer."

As she spoke a crow appeared in the sky. When the birds settled on the branches of the cedar like tiny knobs lining each bough, the crow fluttered in and landed among them. Alarmed, the birds scattered like confetti to land in a line on the next branch. But the crow followed. The tiny birds rose in a cloud and landed on the lowest branch, lined up like soldiers.

"Maybe the Crow thinks he's one of them," said Chloe. "Maybe he doesn't know he's a crow, and thinks he's a tiny bird."

Davey looked at her in puzzlement and went back to make his shot. His ball went two feet in the dense grass. He hit it again and it flew across the lawn, landing in the dahlias on the other side.

She couldn't let go of that thought. Maybe the crow thought he was a little bird. And it was apparent to the little birds that he wasn't, but it didn't seem to be apparent to the crow. She thought about Jeff. Was Jeff the crow? She was a little bird, her family and friends were all little birds.

Maybe it just hadn't been apparent to Chloe that he wasn't like them. She'd fallen in love overnight and never looked closer. Jeff was so engaging, so endearing, she was always happy spending time with him. She didn't want to be without him, which was one reason why she'd cut her university career short, achieving a business diploma rather than going on to complete a degree. She wanted to be with Jeff. She was married within months of meeting him, and pregnant with Davey inside a year.

Her brothers, especially John, seemed well aware of the fact that Jeff was different. He had been silently critical of the business activities, questioning everything, asking how Jeff ran a big business with two small crews of men and a couple of little jobs on the go. He wanted to know where the money came from to buy the land and build the workshop and then the house, because in his opinion Jeff couldn't finance that kind of purchasing power from the few jobs he was working on.

Chloe had taken it all in stride. John was protective of her, and in her mind was just doing more of the big brother role. But now she looked at it from a different perspective. Jeff didn't let her see the books, he said he left it with the accountant. He didn't include her in the business, he used Fraser Hodges for everything. He said it would muddy the waters if too many people got involved. He always maintained he could run the business in his sleep, control the jobs out of the back of his truck.

Maybe she should talk to John again, try to see things through his eyes. In reality she wasn't anxious to hear what he might have to say. Was there something there that she hadn't seen while Jeff was here?

She put her hand against her heart. She'd almost thought, *while Jeff was alive.* It scared her to think in those terms. She couldn't go there. Not yet.

~~~

She spent the rest of the morning making phone calls. After she fed Davey lunch, she hauled her bike out of the garage and tucked him into the trailer, putting saddlebags on the back. They were short of meat and bread. The wait at the gas station had been harrowing, even at eight o'clock at night. She vowed not to use her truck unless she absolutely had to.

"Come on, Davey. We're going on an adventure."

She called Dog Two and they set out along Wilkinson Trail. The trail ran past the back of their property all the way from Interurban Road to town. It had once been a railway line that left the city, ending at Tod Inlet. The right of way had been converted to a pedestrian and bicycle trail years ago.

Several deer stepped out ahead of them, then stepped just as quickly back into the trees. They were males, mostly two pronged, although she did see one with three. She always wondered what happened to the older males, she never saw a four or five year old buck. Dog Two didn't chase them but stuck to her side, trotting obediently next to the trailer.

They were more than halfway to the grocery store when Chloe was forced to come to a halt. There had been a landslide down the nearby slope and right across the trail into the slough water on the other side. She stopped in dismay. A crew of men worked, digging with a backhoe and hauling the dirt away in trucks. One of them approached and Dog Two growled deep in his throat. Chloe stayed him with her hand.

"Don't worry, Ma'am. You can get through. We've made a path to make sure bikes and pedestrians can pass,
~~~

because a lot of people are using the trails for transportation. Just come this way."

He showed her where to steer onto a temporary boardwalk that had been erected. "We'll be finished here in a few days, but we'll always make sure you can get through. Heading to the store, are you?" He waved at Davey and ushered them around the obstacle.

Chloe peddled hard and finally parked her bike a few feet from all the others at the side entrance of the grocery store. She tossed her helmet into the trailer, ordered Two to stay with the bike and took Davey inside.

She was tense. Everything had a hitch to it, nothing was straight forward, not even a bike ride to the store. The interruption in their ride was just the latest example. The morning had been fraught with problems. The bank wasn't happy with the wording of the court order and said they wanted one that named the bank specifically. She had been ready to scream.

She made an appointment to see Art Rowbotham but he didn't have any free time until late next week. The earthquake had thrown everything into chaos. No one was doing routine business anymore.

Probably not even this store. She put Davey in the seat of a grocery cart and walked down the aisles looking at half empty shelves. At the meat counter, they had a choice of chicken or pork. There was no decent beef, so she crossed that off her list. She bought three chickens. A chicken would probably only do one meal with so many in the house. Then she looked at the pork and bought a huge roast. Perhaps a pot of curry big enough for two meals, then what was left of the pork could be roasted or barbecued. She got a sack of rice, sugar, toothpaste and dish soap, and looked for bread.

Davey hauled a small bag of sweet cherry tomatoes out of her purse, taken from her plants on the patio at home. He'd fallen in love with them. He ate a few and had tomato all over his face and down the front of his shirt. She stopped and pulled a wet cloth out of her bag.

She cleaned him up and examined the tomatoes that were left in the bag. "I'd better take that big one, Davey or it'll be all over the place."

He offered her the bag and she carefully selected the large tomato. When she placed it in her mouth and bit down, a stream of juice shot out and hit him square in the forehead. Davey's mouth rounded in an 'O' of surprise and then he burst out laughing.

Chloe joined him and soon the two of them were in stitches. Chloe hung onto the handle of the cart and leaned over, laughing into her other hand to try to keep the juice from running out of her mouth. Finally she managed to get control. "I'm sorry, Davey," she giggled. "I didn't mean to get you with that."

"It's okay, Mummy." He helped himself to another tomato, the matter forgotten.

She took her cloth and cleaned his face again. He grinned at her, mashed tomato showing between his little front teeth.

"Well, we'd better see what else we can manage to carry with us." It took twenty-five minutes to get through the checkout with their purchases. The store owner was running the till and her husband was working on the floor, she told Chloe. It was a choice between closing the store or staying open and being slow. "Our staff couldn't get here and we're on our own today."

"Well," said Chloe, "I, for one, am glad you stayed open. We're out of a lot of things and this is a big help."

When they finally got outside dusk was closing in. Two waited patiently beside the bike. Chloe hurried to get Davey into the trailer and put on her helmet, then placed as many things as she could in the saddlebags and put the rest in with her son. Then she peddled, with Two trotting beside her. She could hear Davey talking to her from the trailer. "I can't stop for you, Davey," she called. "We need to get home, it's going to be dark soon."

As they approached the landslide, she saw that the workmen had left for the day. But the slide was worse. Piles of dirt covered the boardwalk and there was no place to get the bike past the obstruction. This wasn't good. She'd have to go back more than a mile to a crossroad that would take her out onto the main road and thus around the slide. She didn't even have lights on the bike.

Just then Two growled, his ruff standing on end. Chloe felt the hair on her arms rise in sympathy. Glancing behind, she saw two men on the Trail. They approached cautiously, fanning out to come at her from both sides. Her breath caught in her throat and she struggled frantically to turn the unwieldy bicycle and trailer in the narrow space.

The men came faster, Two barked and Chloe shouted at them, "Get back. You stay back! Get away from me!"

She shrieked, tugging on the bike and dragging it sideways in an effort to turn it around. Davey screamed.

The first man reached her and grabbed her arm. Two launched himself, hitting the man in the chest and knocking him to the ground. Chloe could hear shouting and growling but dared not turn to look. The second man was trying to tear the pack off her back and rip the saddlebags from the bike.

She yelled and struggled with him, falling to the ground. Leaping back up, she tackled him from the back but he threw up one arm and sent her flying to land in the dirt. Davey was crying and Chloe crawled desperately toward the bicycle and her son. Two growled, holding the first man pinned to the ground, when Chloe heard another voice join the din.

"Stop right there! You fucker! You stupid bastard! Stop there!" A figure rushed past her, slamming into her attacker at full tilt. He lifted him by the throat, tossing him to the side. The man landed in the slough. Chloe heard the breaking of branches and splashing water. She tried to get to her feet as this man turned and reached for her. Dog Two promptly dropped the first attacker and turned to rush at a new threat.

He stalled and held up his hands, palms out. "Hold it. Hold on. I'm just trying to help." He backed up a couple of steps. Two stood his ground, growling. Blood, something dark smeared his muzzle.

"I'm just trying to help. I heard you yelling."

Chloe slowly got to her feet, leaned on the trailer and reached in to touch Davey and try to comfort him. She didn't take her eyes off him. "Who are you?"

"I'm Ross, Ross Cullen. I was biking along here and heard the ruckus." He gestured as Chloe looked over, but the second man was gone.

Ross shrugged. "He's going to be sore in the morning. I think your dog had him by the arm. That's quite a defender you have there." Two growled low in his throat but backed up a couple of feet.

He glanced at Chloe. "Are you okay?

"I don't know," said Chloe. "I'm not sure." She knelt down in front of the trailer and patted Davey awkwardly. "It's okay baby, it's okay. We're safe now." She kept her eyes on Ross.

"What happened to the trail? When I came along here earlier it was open, they had a walkway built to get around the slide."

"I know," said Chloe faintly. "I think...." She stood and swayed on her feet.

"Whoa," said Ross, "Wait a minute." He took a step toward her as she started to fall. He made a grab and caught her before she went down. Dog Two growled again but didn't move. Chloe felt his arms holding her up, and she leaned into him. His chest was solid, she laid her head against a thick shoulder and sobbed. It was too much, simply too much. Davey sat in the trailer and grizzled miserably to himself as his mother sobbed harder and harder on this man's shoulder. She leaned, his arms tightened.

~~~

Chloe slowly realized she was being held in strong arms against a stranger's chest. The arms were firm around
~~~

her, one hand rubbed up and down her back. Her sobbing had slowed, she pulled back and wiped her face with her hand. "Well." She stepped away and glanced up at him. "Ross. Sorry about that."

He nodded and gave a little smile. "My pleasure, ma'am." Then, "You can't stay here. It'll be dark soon. We'd best get going. Where do you live?"

Chloe felt like her head was stuffed inside a bag of cotton. She wasn't making good decisions. Could she trust this man? Did she want him to know where she lived? He'd saved them from the robbers. He could be in league with the robbers. He came along at just the right moment. He could be stalking her. She must be paranoid.

She gulped back another sob, bent her head and wiped her face with the hem of her shirt. She tried to pull her backpack onto her shoulders but one strap was broken, so with shaking hands she stuffed it in the trailer with Davey.

Ross lifted her bike around and made sure the trailer hitch was properly attached. Davey had fallen silent, an occasional hiccup emitting from the trailer.

He picked up his own bike. "You don't have a light, do you? Well, I have one, so maybe it's best if I go in front, that will give us a light at the front and your reflectors will work for the back. Are you ready to go? Which way now?"

Just as they reached the cross track that would take them up to the main road, two other bikers came along. Ross told them the slide was worse and they'd have to travel on the road. Then he suggested they could travel together, as one of their bikes didn't have a headlamp.

So in the end Chloe found herself in a cavalcade of bicycles travelling along the road. It made her feel safer, both from the attackers and from this stranger who'd taken control of her journey. They finally reached her house, and it couldn't have been too soon. She felt like she was on her last legs. Anything else, any tiny incident and she'd simply lie down on the ground.

Stumbling off the bike, she wobbled over to dig Davey out of the groceries. He wailed as soon as she picked him up. Ross put his arm around them both and helped them toward the doorway of her home.

He got them seated in a chair in the kitchen, then stood there for a minute contemplating the sorry scene they made. Finally he disappeared into the family room and came back with a throw that he laid across her shoulders and tucked around Davey as he wept in her arms.

She didn't see him for a few minutes, and when he reappeared his arms were full of groceries. She just put her head down on Davey's, but she could hear him unpacking the saddlebags and placing everything on the counter. She heard the click of her fire lighter and the hiss of gas.

She finally lifted her head to see him placing the kettle on the burner and opening a couple of cupboard doors until he found her stash of tea. She sat there watching him read the labels and then pick out the green tea. Not a bad choice. He put a bag into a large cup and sniffed the black tea before taking a second bag for himself. Then he pulled out the hot chocolate and a third cup. She closed her eyes and snuggled Davey who had fallen silent on her shoulder. Eventually the kettle boiled.

She opened her eyes again to see a cup of tea set on the table in front of her. Davey's came next, the chocolate cooled by a big slug of milk. He drank quick sips from his own tea, standing at the counter. "Well, that's it then."

He looked around the kitchen, then back at Chloe. "Are you okay now? Sorry about what happened back there. I guess if the workers hadn't left it in such a mess….."

She sighed and lifted her arms away to let Davey sit up. "Here, Ross made you some hot chocolate. Drink a little." The little boy swivelled around on her lap and slurped at the rim of his cup.

"It wasn't a mess when we first got there," she said. "They'd moved the dirt so we could get by on the boardwalk. And they said they'd leave it open, they'd make sure it was passable for all the people who were taking the trail. Maybe those men dumped the dirt back onto the walk so they could stop people and rob them."

Ross rubbed his jaw. "That's more or less what I thought," he admitted. "Seemed too convenient that they were right there waiting where the trail was blocked. I've called it in to the police. They should come out and have a look. And those guys may be camping out there. They probably aren't too far away from that spot. Well," he stood with his hands on his hips, surveying the scene. "I'll go, then."

"Thank you, Ross. This is very nice." She waved at the tea in front of her. "Stay and finish your drink."

Ross eyed her for a minute then sat down at the table with his cup.

"Do you live near here?" Better to get a little information about this guy, a stranger they just met who was now sitting at her table.

"Nope, just riding out to see a friend. I stopped at the grocery store, he asked me to get him some bread but they were out. That trail's probably a good way for you to get back and forth to the store."

"I go there sometimes, but maybe not anymore." She thought about it. "I guess it might be safe enough in the daytime."

Ross nodded. "Yes, but even then don't go by yourself. Maybe ride when there are other people on the trail. Or go with a group. I'll bet there'll be more than a few places that become less safe in the short term. I come out here occasionally. I could ride with you if you need company."

Chloe raised her eyebrows and looked at him in speculation. "Well okay, if you like." She pushed a piece of paper toward him and he pulled a pen out of his shirt pocket.

He looked suddenly uncomfortable. "A friend of my mother's lives out here and I offered to drop by and see how he is. If I'm here anyway…" He wrote a number on the paper. "There you go, give me a call and I'll be glad to ride along."

She picked up her tea cup and took a sip, placing it back on the table with a sharp sigh, feeling as if her arm was too weak to support it. She was suddenly overcome by the events of the day.

Davey looked at her, concern pinching his face. "What's the matter, Mummy?" He looked at her hand pressed over her heart. "Are your boobies in the way?"

Ross choked on his tea.

"Davey."

"Well, sometimes they're in the way."

She gave him an exasperated look, then turned her head to find Ross eyeing her chest. When he raised his gaze it was to receive her glare.

He flushed. "They don't seem to be in the way now," he observed.

"Nope, they're not," said Davey and drank his chocolate.

Ross held her gaze, a slight smile on his face as if daring her to explain that conversation. She chose to ignore it.

"Have a good night, then." He rose from the table. "Just remember, don't go along there alone. I can come out the same day every week, so if you call we can arrange a ride."

Chloe saw him to the door and closed it behind him. She stood with her back leaning weakly against the panel. What was happening to them?

On the surface it was pretty straight forward, those men had attacked them and Ross had just happened to be on the trail following behind. Lucky for them. Thank God.

But when she put this incident together with the disappearance of Jeff, the break-in of the house and then the workshop, it took on a much larger and more sinister significance. She was frightened down to her core. Her knees felt weak, her breath came in ragged bursts. Something was underway that she couldn't predict and could barely protect her child from.

She pulled her mind back from that brink. No electricity again tonight but at least the water was running. The boarders would be home soon and no dinner in sight either. Maybe it was a good day for wieners and beans. She was unable to contemplate anything more complicated.

When she tucked Davey under the covers that evening, he cried and she lay down beside him on his little bed, Plutie's nose poking over the blankets on the far side of the mattress. "It's okay, Davey, it's okay baby."

Gathering him into her arms, she rested her head beside his on the pillow. She and Davey both reached across to touch Plutie's fur, scrubbing their fingers into its softness. She needed the comfort as much as he did.

CHAPTER EIGHT

Ross put his helmet on his head, switched on his headlamp and swung onto the bike. *What the hell am I doing*? He rode down the trail to the next crossroad and turned off his lights. Coasting in the dark, he arrived at the old logging road where his truck was still parked amongst the trees. Hoisting his bike into the back of the truck bed, he slammed the camper door down and climbed into the cab. *Am I nuts?* His old boss and training partner would tell him he was. Just broke all the rules about surveillance.

Not that he shouldn't have followed her. That part made sense. He'd seen her get the bike out with the trailer attached and the thought struck him that it would be the simplest thing in the world for her to ride her bike along the trail to where her husband was hidden and have a conjugal visit. If that was the case, it was no wonder they hadn't found hide nor hair of Sanderson. His wife was communicating in the most elemental way possible. No cell phones, no email, no letters, just ride a bicycle over to his hideout. That part of his actions at least made sense.

So he'd followed her past the landslide, ending up to his surprise at a grocery store. He'd shopped for a few things, putting himself through the cash ahead so he'd be back outside waiting when she emerged to retrace her steps.

But not before the episode with the tomatoes. That had been the most incredible thing, Chloe bent over holding her mouth, and she and the little boy howling with laughter about a squirting tomato. He noticed other shoppers grinning at them, taken in by the sheer silliness of it.

It had touched him in some way. It had tickled him, that was it. He couldn't remember the last time he'd been *tickled* by something. There wasn't much in police work to affect him that way.

He stared through the windshield at the dim light of her living room that he barely caught through the trees. He'd better be careful, he didn't need to be tickled or affected any other way by a suspect under surveillance.

And he'd been affected. If he was honest with himself, he'd have to admit that. He'd waited outside the grocery store, watching the dog watch him, till he saw them come out. She dumped everything into the trailer, talking a mile a minute to the boy, then took off down the trail.

He'd followed, riding far enough behind that she wouldn't notice him. She didn't travel very fast, with the load she was pulling. He'd been thinking that this mission had been a waste of time. To get back to his truck, he was going to have to go in the same direction anyway, so he would keep going till they got to her house.

And then he heard her scream.

The sound had jolted him into action, the action he was trained for, the protection he was paid to provide. But at the core was another emotion altogether, a sense of panic and ferocity. Thinking about it now, it shocked him. That wasn't the action of a police officer. A cop should deliver an instant reaction of purpose and informed response, aided by but not controlled by the shots of adrenaline that were flooding through his system. Not the hot madness that had gripped him as he raced ahead to see Ms Bowman and her child being attacked by two thugs waylaying them in the middle of the trail. The adrenaline was madness in his veins.

He couldn't remember what happened to the first attacker. He just removed him, that's all. And the second one ran while he was dealing with the dog and Chloe.

A police officer should have left that scene with one, if not two, suspects under arrest. Instead he stood there with a 'person of interest' crying in his arms. And he hadn't minded a bit. He could still feel her, hear her low sobs. Still knew her warmth against his chest and the shape of her. Lord, he was in trouble. He moved his head sharply, stretching the tight muscles in his neck.

The little boy had been undone by the events. He cried in his mum's arms, patting her and touching her. All he could think of was to make tea. He snorted. What he wanted to do was pick them both up and sit them on his knee, just wrap his arms around them. They'd looked so alone, so forlorn in that chair. They were essentially unprotected and his gut instinct was to protect, especially Ms. Bowman.

He shook his head. He'd better get that out of his system. They didn't know what had happened in this Sanderson scenario, but it wasn't apparent by any stretch that she was uninvolved.

On the other hand, were her boobies in the way? Not to his way of thinking. He put his head back and laughed aloud. What had that been about? Something. Little Davey was satisfied they weren't in the way this time. Well, they hadn't been in the way when she was in his arms crying against his chest. They'd felt more than alright pressed against him.

The feel of her was imprinted on his brain. He looked at his hands, flexed his fingers. He'd touched her and there was no turning back. She felt like he'd imagined she would when he watched her interview. He wanted her.

~~~

Davey wet his bed that night. Chloe patiently changed the bedding, put the plastic sheet back under the bottom bed
~~~

clothes so the mattress was protected. She didn't even mention it as she stripped him of his wet pyjamas and sponged him off in the bathtub, chatting to him about other things.

She knew what was going on. The same thing had happened after Jeff disappeared. He had just begun to sleep through the night on a regular basis with a dry bed. But the shock of losing his father had set him back. Davey started crying in the night. She would comfort him and put him back to sleep. But then he'd wet the bed. Slowly she weaned him of the habit.

Vivienne had suggested putting diapers back on him, until he got over the upset. But Jayde had said, "Just let it go. Pretend it doesn't happen. Smile and chat to him while you fix him up, and don't get him upset about it. He's already upset."

That plan had worked, and within a week, he had started to sleep through the night without crying, and a few days after that the bed wetting stopped.

~~~

Ross gritted his teeth in frustration. "We're not getting anywhere here, Dan. I need something, anything. What about the tapes at the border crossings that might tell us who drove the car across the border? Nothing there either, huh? Still waiting. Well, keep looking."

He threw his head back and thought about last night. He hadn't slept well, knowing he'd crossed the line with Chloe Bowman. He now had a way to get in there, but the house had been very thoroughly searched after the break-in. They'd milked that opportunity. If there was something to be found, they should have already found it.

He thought about Davey's comment. It made him snicker every time he thought of it, which was often. It also made him hot. His face went red.

It was such an offhand statement made by a little person who thought he understood what was going on. And
~~~

it roused much different thoughts in Ross. He determinedly put his head down and went back to work.

~~~

It took Chloe a while to recover from the attack. She'd called the police as Ross had suggested. The clerk said she needed to lay a complaint, so she went through that process. The officer who came out to the house told her the same thing Ross had, things might be different in the short term while the city was disrupted with the after-effects of the earthquake. It would be better to travel in groups, and in daylight hours.

But he took down all the particulars and promised to do a follow-up along the trail. She had to be satisfied with that. In her limited experience with the police, she wouldn't get any feedback and would never know if they cleared out campers along there or found nothing at all.

She was left feeling significantly weakened. The loss of her husband had begun a chain of events that each grazed her, grated some of her strength away and left her less than she had been. The break-in at her house had been such an immediate and personal assault that it left her reeling so soon after Jeffrey left. The small incidences with the police after the disappearance continued to whittle her personal self, until she was unsure of her footing and felt distinctly off balance.

But now there had been a direct physical assault on her, with Davey at risk. She kept thinking that she must have made a misstep somewhere, made a mistake in judgement, that she should be the target of each new insult to her person. She felt seriously wounded.

The following week she managed to get the bank account changed over with herself as signing authority. It was a big step. The reason she got that accomplished was Art Rowbotham suddenly became her most cooperative ally. He took a copy of the court order and put it in his file. Then he promptly cancelled the fifty shares of Sanderson Holdings Ltd that had been issued in Jeff's name and issued the same fifty in hers.
~~~

It was as simple as that. Those shares in the company allowed her to go to the bank and change signing authority. She ordered a new set of cheques and deposit books and asked the teller to print out the list of transactions for the previous months and balances for all accounts. She was informed that the bank statements had been mailed to a post box.

A post office box? Just one more thing to turn the court order loose on. She was afraid of what she might find, especially given that it hadn't been emptied in a long time.

She had another call from her tenant, StreetSmart. They wanted a meeting with Jeff. She told them Jeff was no longer the building manager, but she'd be happy to talk to them. They set a time for the following week.

When she tucked Davey into bed that night after another hasty supper, she crawled up onto her bed with the bank information. As she combed carefully through the documents, she saw that the chequing account was looking fairly healthy. Even more amazing, the term deposit stood at three hundred and forty thousand dollars.

She sagged back against her pillows. How was that possible? When she thought of Jeff's almost frantic activity to come up with the down payment on the building, she couldn't imagine the account blossoming this way.

She checked again. There was no information about when the money went in, but there was definitely a huge sum in there. Huge to her at any rate. But what was it for? And who had a claim on it? It was frightening to contemplate because she knew the money wasn't hers to use.

The next day she presented herself, Davey in tow and court order in hand, to open the post office box. They couldn't do that at the branch, but recommended she go to the head office downtown. She managed to get there just before the office closed and ran through the post office bureaucracy. Not much inside, a few envelopes and some flyers. She tossed the flyers. The bank statements were there, although this was old news. She already had back copies for the last year. But here she had the checks. She'd see if they told her anything new.

She forwarded the company mail to her home address and popped the rest of the envelopes into her case, wondering why Jeff had left the mail here instead of getting it sent to the house. Just one more question she'd probably never have an answer for. The thought gave her a pang in her chest but she didn't cry.

That night she woke from a dark dream, her heart thudding heavily in her chest and the sweat standing out on her forehead. She couldn't remember the dream other than that it was like being in a maze while needing desperately to get to the other side. She flopped back on the damp sheets, waiting for her breath to return. Even her bed wasn't a refuge, she was in it alone and lonely, obsessing with everything that had gone wrong.

What was going right? Maybe that was a better way to look at events. Because what was going wrong seemed a very long list.

Davey liked daycare. He was always in a good mood when she went to get him, usually dirty but cheerful. It was good that he got dirty, it meant they played outside or painted, some activity that he got right into. Maybe he'd been a little lonely here. That was one thing that was going right.

She'd gotten the bank to change the names on the bank account. Lots of things were possible now. That was number two.

The company had been changed over into her name, the shares transferred. And the lawyer, Art Rowbotham was cooperating. That was a big number three.

She smiled to herself in the dark. She was becoming a list maker. She was becoming her father. Davey Bowman had always told her to write it down and she wouldn't forget to look after it. He bristled with lists. They were in his truck, in his pockets, in the folder that he carried. He'd sit down after dinner and write himself a new list for the next day based on the old partially completed lists from the week before. Maybe it wasn't such a bad thing. It was a way to organize life when she had so many details on her plate and so much of it was out of her control.

She got up to check on Davey. In the dim glow of the nightlight in the hall, she could see his fair hair halfway down the mattress, the covers rucked around him. Plutie lifted his fuzzy white head from the mat beside the bed and thumped his tail. She shuffled inside the door, patted the dog's head and straightened the blankets. Walking softly around the house, she checked the locks on all the doors and went back to bed.

When she woke in the morning it was with the sense that she'd overlooked something. Some small thing was stuck in the back of her mind that she should be paying attention to. Well, she'd just have to wait. She'd always found that if she left a hidden thought alone, it would eventually come to her.

Today was for sorting out the space at the building. John met her there to decide a preliminary layout for the boarding space and a management plan. His first group of workers would arrive shortly.

Her meeting with StreetSmart deflated any feeling of accomplishment she might have had. They stated flatly that they couldn't pay the rent and wanted her to let them out of the lease. She didn't know what to say in reply, but knew a lease was a lease. She was bound by it as much as they were. At the same time, she didn't want a tenant going broke. Her mortgage wouldn't get paid.

"I need to see your books," she said firmly.

The Executive Director looked taken aback. "Why would you ask that? It's confidential information. I'm shocked you'd suggest it." He pushed back his chair and rose to pace his office.

She watched him, wondering if this was theatrics or if he was genuinely upset. "I'm shocked you'd suggest you won't honour your legal obligations under the lease."

His face went red and he sat back in his chair. “What about confidentiality? We have donors....”

“My lips are sealed,” she said. “I’ll sign an agreement to that effect. Show me your books and I’ll see what I can do.”

Suddenly much more conciliatory, he held out his hand to shake hers. “I’ll have a financial package to pick up in the next few days.”

“Just send it to my accountant.” She pulled his card out of her purse and wrote her name on the back. “He’ll give me an opinion so I can decide what can be done. Make sure it’s a complete picture.”

The Executive Director was much more effusive as she left, thanking her for taking the time to come in and listen to him.

Once she was back in her car, she called the accountant to let him know the StreetSmart accounts would be coming within a few days, and to get further information from their office if he needed it. One thing he should be particularly attentive to was where their core funding came from, and how much their people were being paid, especially the executive. She needed to get an idea of their ability to pay rent.

That night, Jose took her aside and apologetically told her he was quitting university. His folks needed him in the family business and school didn’t suit him very well. He’d paid her till the end of the month, but wouldn’t be coming back.

Chloe gave him a big hug. School wasn’t for everyone, but she was sorry to see him go. And sorry to lose the income. The money in the term deposit wasn’t hers, and she was sure a bomb would drop sooner or later as to its purpose. Back to the internet for a new boarder.

CHAPTER NINE

Earthquake numbers rolled in. There were more than a thousand people confirmed dead, and another eight or nine hundred still missing. The number of injured rose daily, now standing at over seven thousand. People had been flown out to hospitals elsewhere on the island and across the Province.

Some of the medical workers who had flooded into Victoria after the quake were still in the city, even after long weeks of work. They were mopping up and caring for people who had nowhere to go. Everyone was affected. People had suffered a fundamental emotional insecurity. Chloe wasn't the only one dealing with major upheaval on every level.

Thanksgiving dinner for the family was at John's house this year. Chloe mentioned to Diana, Brent's wife, that she was bringing a poison control kit to test the food and they'd shared a laugh. But she was surprised that Rosemary was willing to host.

Vivienne was already there when she arrived, looking lovely, tanned and toned. "Mum," said Chloe, giving her a hug. "You're looking great. Don't tell me the gym is open already after the damage they suffered during the quake."

Most of the family used the same gym, Chloe had brought Jeff in as a new convert shortly before they were married. She herself had gone twice a week for years. Even John went, busy as he was. Their father had started them all there and it was one thing that had carried on as a tradition.

Vivienne shook her artfully streaked blond hair over her shoulders and smiled. "Yes, dear, and you should go, too. You can't afford to let yourself go, especially now that Jeff isn't around anymore. You'll be looking for a new man soon and…"

Vivienne faltered under Chloe's dark glare. When Brent stepped in and steered the conversation around to other things, she gave him a grateful look. They sat down to a roast beef that Rosemary had had delivered from the caterers. But she'd made some salads to go with it, and baked potatoes.

At the dinner table, it was Rosemary who mentioned Jeff again. "Chloe, it can't be possible for someone to simply disappear," she said.

"Apparently it is," Chloe muttered.

"Rosemary," warned John, giving her a hard look.

"No, but I mean there must be some trace. For instance, the car being found in Washington State. Surely there's information about how it got there."

"You'd think so," she countered. "But the police don't seem to be able to put it together. I'm not sure how hard they're trying."

"Well, they certainly grilled us," said Rosemary. She speared a small piece of beef on her fork. "They were here for an hour or more, weren't they, John?"

John frowned but just nodded.

Chloe looked at him questioningly. He shrugged. "They were in my office for half a day, Chloe. Then they called in all my crews and talked to them one by one over the next while. I thought the questioning was thorough."

Rosemary looked at him. "You didn't tell me that, John. What a waste of your time. You must have been furious."

"No, I wasn't furious. And I didn't think it was a waste of my time. If anything we had to say might lead them to find Jeff, it was worth it."

Rosemary pressed her lips together, but went back to the topic. "Well, I think someone must want to get lost to be gone this long without any clue as to where they went."

John shoved his plate aside. "Rosemary, I've asked you not to do this. It hurts Chloe and it hurts me. Please stop."

His wife got a stubborn look. "Really, John. You don't have to react like a child. I'm just saying what everyone else is thinking."

"Well, you don't speak for me," said Brent. "That's not what I'm thinking by any stretch." His mouth was hard as he glared at his older brother.

Chloe interrupted, putting her hand up just as Diana opened her mouth to speak. "Look, we don't need everyone taking sides on this. Jeff has disappeared. Contrary to what Rosemary might think, we didn't have a huge fight, we didn't fall out of love, and we didn't decide to separate. He's gone. And yes, people do disappear. One shining example is Jimmy Hoffa. Do I think Jeff is buried under the concrete of his latest project?"

She choked up, but went on in an emotional voice, "No, I don't, Rosemary. So you can speculate all you like, your opinion isn't relevant. You don't seem to pepper your speculations with any weight, so I'm going to ignore your comments. Thanks for having us over for dinner."

She snatched Davey out of his seat, yanking him up into her arms.

John stood, tipping his chair backward onto the floor in his haste. "Chloe, don't leave like this. Please don't. Rosemary just says things…" He threw his hands out helplessly.

Rosemary interjected, "Oh, Chloe, don't go. I'm sorry, I really am. I don't know what I was thinking, to say that." She looked at John sideways, embarrassment evident on her face.

Chloe stalled with Davey half in, half out of his chair. When he reached for a piece of apple in his salad, she manoeuvred him back into his seat. Taking a deep breath, she held it while she willed her temper to cool as she slid into her chair.

Her gaze connected with Diana and they both raised their eyebrows. Hard to know with Rosemary. She looked around at the faces at the table, all family, all dear to her in some way.

"Is that how everyone feels? That Jeff dumped me, dumped us?" She peered through her tears to a chorus of 'no' from the others at the table.

"Don't be silly, Chloe," Brent interjected. "He loved you, wouldn't leave you for a minute. Protected you from everything. We may not all have loved him as much as you did, but we know that isn't what happened. Rosemary knows that, she also knows how to push your buttons. She's just jealous." He shot another look at John.

Rosemary's mouth opened and then clamped shut as John wrapped his hand around her arm in what looked like a death grip.

"Chloe, you know in your heart that isn't what happened." Vivienne's voice was soft but it silenced the rest of the comments. "The problem is, if we accept that he didn't leave you of his own accord, which none of us believes, not even Rosemary, the alternative is something we don't want to think about. Isn't it?" There was silence in the room.

John twitched in his chair. "Well, at some point, we have to face the reality that he's gone. We may never know. That's very hard. But we probably have to understand that he either can't return, or he's dead."

There was silence around the table.

"I'm not saying that's true. I'm sorry, I don't mean to sound so blunt."

But Chloe nodded. "I already know that, John. Everyone, we've all thought of that. It's been months. Not a sign from him, not a word. Those are the only conclusions to draw. I'm getting there, trying to anyway."

"I'm sorry, Chloe," Rosemary looked down at the table. "Sometimes these things just pop out of my mouth."

She gave her a hard look. "Yes, they do. You should maybe try a little harder to control your mouth."

Rosemary looked up at Vivienne as she continued, avoiding Chloe's eyes. "I have some news. That is, John and I do. We're expecting, we're having a baby next summer. I'm scared stiff." She burst into tears. There was stunned silence at her announcement.

"Well, I guess congratulations are in order," she said into the void. "I'm happy for you both." She gazed at her sister-in-law with an unsettling mixture of pity and dismay, when her mother's cool hand slipped into hers. Vivienne just looked at her. She breathed deeply and squeezed back. John was seated in his chair again with an embarrassed and pleading look on his face that was totally foreign for him.

"Well, big brother," said Brent. "I'm surprised. I mean, you've been married for what? Six years? I decided that you just didn't know how it was done."

John tried to cuff him from across the table with his long arm but Brent jerked out of reach and they all laughed.

She and Davey stayed for dessert.

John discussed the hostel and the crew of workers who'd arrive any day. Diana suggested they talk to the boarding schools. One of them hadn't opened this fall, people were withdrawing their children from a school in a dangerous earthquake zone.

"But it's always been an earthquake area," said Vivienne.

"Yes, but now it's harder to ignore that fact."

~~~
~~~

Chloe found a local restaurant to take the contract for all three meals for the men at the hostel. Ralph lined up one of Jeff's old construction workers to live in the building and supervise the space.

Mike LaTorre, a man in his late sixties, had been a nice presence on the jobsite when Chloe stopped by her husband's projects. She'd never warmed to the foreman, Fraser Hodges, and had always been uncomfortable and ill at ease around him. It was partly the way he looked at her, at any woman. But also she suspected he was not a nice man, nor an honest one.

Mike and his wife Maria were the survivors of a condo building that had collapsed into the street and they currently had a single room in a local boarding house that they'd been staying in since the quake. They were pleased to live onsite at the hostel and earn an income as well. Mike would keep order with the men, and the two of them would handle the laundry, cleaning and meals.

"John, I can't quite imagine how it's going to work. I keep thinking there'll be more to this than we've thought." Chloe frowned.

John grinned. "Don't borrow trouble. The main problem's going to be keeping order among the men, especially the younger guys. I've been telling Ralph to find some older workers to add to the mix, because we're going to need cooler heads when things get rowdy.

She made a face at him. "I hope they don't just tear the place apart."

"Well, what can they do to it? It's just a shell of a concrete building with some partitions."

She nodded. After all, it would be John's problem to sort, not hers.

The Construction Association had taken possession of the office space and Chloe was thrilled to have another lease signed. The rent would start flowing at the beginning of the month. She was afraid to touch the money in the term deposits, having no idea where it came from or what it was for. She'd gone over the bank statements and couldn't make any sense of them. She called Jeff's accountant, who told her he only worked with whatever documents were presented at the end of the year. He gave her the accounts from the previous year, but had nothing else to tell her.

Once the office rent started, it looked like she'd be making a profit. So with boarders and new tenants, her finances would start to balance. It took a great weight off her shoulders.

Just to take a little shine off the day, the administrator at StreetSmart called to complain that their premises weren't what had been promised in the agreement. "How is it not what you were promised?" Chloe asked.

"We're just not happy here, it's not the right fit."

"I see." She stared at the phone. How bizarre could it get? "I'll call you back. I just have to check something."

She promptly called the realtor who handled the lease and the fellow just laughed. "Don't let them jerk your chain. They knew exactly what they were getting. No one, and I mean no one, is going to buy that. Those agreements were gone over with a fine tooth comb by lawyers from both sides before they were signed. There's no getting out of that lease.

He promised to dig out the leasing agreement and make copies for her file.

Chloe called the administrator back. "I'm sorry you aren't happy. It was my understanding you didn't have any damage from the earthquake. Is there damage that I haven't heard about?"

The administrator's voice turned sullen. "Not earthquake damage. But it's not comfortable."

"Perhaps you should take it up with your boss, then. Is Martin Barrymore there? I'd like to speak to him." Chloe doodled on a pad as she waited. When she was finally put through to his office, she got voice mail. She left him a message, she was still waiting for the financial statements he'd promised.

~~~
~~~

Chloe woke that night in the pitch black. There was no moon, the only sound the breathing of the house. The power must be on. She glanced toward her bedroom door and saw the dim glow of Davey's nightlight reflected along the floor.

What had woken her? She lay there for a minute, listening for Davey but there was no sound from his room. She ran over the day in her mind, the busyness of it, dropping Davey at daycare and charging into the city.

The days she went downtown were always packed. She was hard pressed to get home in time to pick him up. Traffic was still terrible. So many sections of road were impassable and the arteries that did work were jammed with vehicles. The city had made a new regulation that deliveries had to be made after business hours because the streets and highways had become almost impassable.

She'd spent ninety minutes in Rowbotham's office. Even with him on her side, as John put it, she couldn't seem to get much done. But something was niggling at her in the dark of night.

She rolled over to go back to sleep, and just as she sank toward oblivion, she thought of the email on Jeff's laptop, the one from Rainman setting up a meeting with Jeff for the day after he disappeared. Except it wasn't for the day after, it was for the day he left.

Chloe sat up with a jerk. Staring in the darkness, she tried to concentrate. Yes, she was sure. Soundlessly she rose from the bed and searched around for her slippers. She walked softly down the hall. There was light cascading down the stairs. Someone up there was studying. In the office she turned on the desk lamp. Jeff's laptop sat humming where she'd left it, and she quickly started it up. When the email flipped up, she stared hard at the letters in front of her. They spelled out the same message that was engraved on her brain, the meeting was to have occurred the morning Jeff disappeared.

She felt the breath leave her lungs as she sank back in the chair. Did this mean anything, given how long ago it had happened? Did Rainman meet with Jeff and then Jeff left afterward, or did Jeff never turn up for the meeting? And who was Rainman? It was a generic and untraceable email address. For her. Maybe the police could trace it.

She stared at the screen until her vision blurred. She flipped back and forth between the 'sent' and 'delete' files. She checked the trash. Nothing. Jeff had obviously not believed in keeping records. There was nothing in the email file except new emails that showed up after he'd disappeared.

But there were other ways to look for information, other places that old emails might be stored on the hard drive. On the other hand, Jeff had been very accomplished with computers. If he didn't want his information found it might not be found by anyone.

By early morning, Chloe was on the phone asking for the officer in charge of the Jeff Sanderson missing persons case. She spoke to Constable Dan Parker. "I've found my husband's laptop," she said. "It had a password on it but I was able to figure it out, and I've read his email. There isn't much, he deleted it as it came in, so there are only messages since the night before he disappeared." That was a whole other issue. Why was there no history in his email account? But she kept that thought to herself. She knew the police would think of it without her help.

There was silence on the phone. "Where did you find it, Mrs. Bowman?"

"It was in the commercial building we own. One of the desks we brought home had the laptop in the drawer."

"So what do the emails tell you?"

She took a deep breath. "Well, most were junk. But one was about a bid for concrete and the second one was about a meeting for the day Jeff disappeared. I wondered if that might shed some light on things. There isn't any history in the email file. I don't know how to do it, but perhaps someone in your office knows how to find deleted emails. It could lead us to something that we don't know."

"I think we'd like to get the laptop, and have another look through the building. How about later this morning?"

"That would be fine," she said. "The laptop is here at the house. As for the building, it's changed quite a bit. We've done a lot of work there. Most of the desks and things have been taken away or used in the office space."

She spent the rest of the morning searching the laptop for anything useful. She was looking for business information, something to help wrap up Jeff's final construction projects and the running of the building. Given what the accountant had said about a lack of records, she'd be grateful for anything at all.

She found a curious spreadsheet, a list of companies with dollar amounts and dates beside each name. The one that caught her eye was the Personal Fitness Gym, where she and her family worked out. There was a note beside it, 'April, 12 months, double membership'. The property taxes were listed, the lawn and sprinkler installation. She ran her eye down the sheet. *Was this a list of prepaid expenses?* The dollar figure beside the property taxes matched the amount that had been paid on the house.

She called the gym and asked for Randy. He was pleased to hear from her. Vivienne had been in and John was still attending most weeks. When was she coming back? He knew she'd had a hard time lately, and expressed his sympathy about Jeff.

"Hard to know what to say, isn't it?" Good old Randy was always straight from the shoulder. "I can't say sorry he's passed, but I can say sorry for your loss. Because however it happened, he's still gone. This must be absolutely terrible to handle, Chloe. How's your little boy doing? But really, working out at the gym would help. It is always one of the best ways to handle stress."

"I know. I was wondering about the fee, Randy. Jeff told me he'd paid our membership, but I don't remember what he said about when it would expire."

"Hold on, let me look." There was the click of keys, and then he was back. "Jeff paid for a year, starting May. But it hasn't been used, so it would begin again when you come back, which you should do soon. It'd be good for you. Let me give you a new trainer, her name is Mikki and she's really enthusiastic. She'll take it easy on you till you get back into it. And daycare is still available, so Davey will be well looked after while you're working up a sweat."

His voice dropped over the phone. "To tell the truth, business has been terrible. People have more important or just more immediate things to keep them busy, such as where are they going to live? I'm having trouble paying my lease here, with the drop in membership. I hope it picks up soon."

Chloe promised to start her workouts again and hung up. She looked down the list on the screen in front of her. There were lots of services named. Did Jeff prepay all their expenses, then call in the services as he needed them? How would he have that much cash to pay in advance for things? There was a big deposit at their favourite Japanese sushi restaurant. When she was in town next, she'd try out her theory, take John to lunch and charge it against the balance. She didn't hesitate, quickly printed out a couple of copies of the list. Then she hit delete.

~~~

Ross read the report Parker had given him. It showed the year Jeff Sanderson quit university and the names of all males who quit the same year. There were two hundred and thirty nine names on the list. "Any Raymond or Ronald?"

Parker nodded. "Four named Raymond, two Ronalds. Then three who have Ronald for a last name. A few with Ronald or Raymond for a second name. We've called them all, no one fits. They don't know Jeff Sanderson, they don't know anything about computers, they live across the other side of the country. One Ronald Thompson lives here, he
~~~

knew Sanderson he thinks, had a vague recollection when he read in the paper about him missing. But Slots and Singh both say no, that's not him.

"Now, Slots says his name is Ran or Ren. Can't remember. Singh came up with the info on the Sanderson construction quote. It was for the building that he bought, the one Ms. Bowman is managing. I guess he got someone else to do the work, because there's new paving there but Singh didn't do it."

Ross nodded, looking down the list. "His friend could have quit the year before and just hung around at university. There were a few guys who did that when I was there. Or maybe he never actually went to university at all, just spent time there." He shoved the list back across his desk. "Border tapes, where are we?"

"They're on their way, emailed to Central. I should have them this morning. The work on the car has come in. There was nothing, the fire took care of pretty well everything. No DNA, no trace of anything, other than accelerant."

"What kind of accelerant?"

"Straight gasoline, probably right out of the gas tank. They likely siphoned it out and threw the siphon tube in before they lit it."

"And the dog collar?"

"Yep, it was Sanderson's. I'm going out to see Ms. Bowman this morning to pick up Sanderson's laptop, so I'll find out what I can about the dog. There were apparently some bones at the site."

"A laptop?" His tone became sharp. "This is the husband's laptop? Why hasn't she handed it over before now? Where has it been and why didn't we find it?"

"She says she just found it. It was in the drawer of an old desk at the building in some unused space."

"And she just found it. So she's been going through the desks in the building suddenly?"

Parker raised his brows at the sarcasm. "I believe her. She has boarders living with her, and you know yourself there isn't much furniture in the house. They'd just moved in. Some of the rooms were empty when we searched it after the break-in. She said they went to the building to see if any of the office furniture would be useful for the boarders and they brought back some stuff. The laptop was in the desk drawer."

Ross grunted and waved him away. He was going back out there tomorrow and he'd try to get another look inside the house. Who knows what he'd see? But he knew what he was looking for and he grew warm at the thought. Chloe Bowman was a beautiful woman and he couldn't wait to see her again.

~~~

Chloe was just lifting Davey into the bike trailer as Ross wheeled into the yard. He'd seen her get the bike out while he was still in his truck. He lifted the visor on his helmet and took in her sunny smile.

"Hi, Woss," Davey yelled.

"Hi there, Davey." He turned to Chloe. "Are you just heading out?"

She nodded.

"Have you got someone to go with you? I've got time, I just left my friend down the road." He pointed vaguely north, hoping she didn't want specifics on his 'friend'.

"Well, okay. That would be nice. I'll get some money." She darted back into the house.

"Are you coming with us, Woss?"

"Looks like it. Do you like riding down the Trail?"

"Yeah. But Mummy can't talk to me when I tell her stuff, 'cause she can't hear me."

"You weren't going down that trail by yourself, were you?" he said as she locked the door and came down the step.

"Not you, too," she groaned, tucking a handful of keys in her pocket. "My brother drummed that into my head three times this week already. Brent was pretty upset about the last time. He made me promise."
~~~

"That's good. Well, at least someone's looking out for you."

She flushed. "Of course, you're right. Thank you again for helping us. It could have been so much worse."

He held her gaze. "I'm just glad I was there."

"Well." She glanced away. "Here we go, then."

Chloe led the way and Ross pedalled along behind. He found himself watching her butt as she rode. It was a fascinating sight, and it embarrassed him to find his eyes drawn back there again and again. He should be riding out front because things were way too attractive back here. He tried to focus on his chat with Davey, who wanted to comment on everything he saw.

He asked what kind of shoes Ross had, and where did he get his bike. He talked about Two who trotted alongside them, and why Plutie was left at home. "Plutie is a rescue dog," he said. "He had to be rescued so we got to keep him. But Two comes with us on the trail because he's a work dog."

Ross had to smile. The little guy was pretty engaging. He enjoyed answering his questions and asking some of his own. He was surprisingly observant.

By the time they'd returned to the house the boy was hungry and Chloe invited Ross in for lunch. She served some pretty tasty curry leftovers and then put Davey down for his nap. When she returned to the kitchen, he was studying the schedule on the bulletin board.

"This is quite a list. You look pretty organized."

She gave a lady-like snort. "Pure illusion."

He smiled, watching her face light up with her teasing. She was very lovely. Maybe that's why he'd been so convinced she was an accomplice with her husband in his disappearance. He thought that meant she was shallow or that she'd use her beauty to her advantage to deceive the police. What kind of prejudice was that? It didn't mean he wasn't attracted to her, because he was.

He turned back toward the door. "Well, it looks like you're managing." He paused. "The police found some nests along the trail. They rousted out a couple of guys, said they'll keep a watch on it. So that should be some comfort."

"How do you know that?"

He hesitated for a second too long and hoped she didn't pick up on it. "I talked to a buddy of mine, Dan Parker. I asked him to look into it."

"What do you do, Ross, what's your job?"

He grinned. "I work in security. It pays the bills. We're pretty busy right now."

"Yes, I can imagine."

"Well, I'll be going. Give me a call if you want to do the trail again. I could let you know when I'm coming out here. Would that work?" Would she let him go with her again? He hoped so.

She laughed. "Maybe," she said, then seemed to relent and reached for a pen. He felt some tension ease in his gut. Good. He could come back because she was asking him back. That made it easier. His eyes roved over her face and along her cleavage as she bent to write her number. If he could solve this case, maybe there was something here for him. He felt a jolt in his gut. What was he thinking? That way lay trouble.

~~~

When he left, Chloe thoughtfully moved around the kitchen, gathering the lunch dishes and stacking them in the dishwasher. Ross intrigued her. He was a good looking man in a very physical way. He was tall, not as tall as Jeff, but close to six feet. He was thick with muscle, where Jeff had been lean and wiry. Yet he was lithe and light on his feet. His dark hair was wavy but cut short and his eyes, just as dark, were large and intense.

When he was looking at Davey, talking to him, he was just as focussed as when he was talking to her. Davey responded to that. He liked the attention and answered very solemnly when Ross asked him a question. She'd heard them talking as they rode along the trail, smiling to herself at Ross's questions. Did Davey like his dog, and why was he called
~~~

Plutie? She couldn't hear Davey's replies but she could hear his little voice rising and falling as he spoke.

If she weren't a married woman, she'd be very interested in Ross. He made her feel things she hadn't felt in a long time. Her body was waking up. She closed her mind to that thought and tidied the kitchen. Jeff was still out there waiting to be found.

CHAPTER TEN

Ross's supervisor pulled him in for a review of the case the next day. "Get me up to speed, Cullen. I want to know where we're at on Sanderson."

He went over the details of the case but didn't have much progress to report. Finding the dog was a small detail that tied in with the car going across the American border. Parker had found the tapes for the border crossing pretty insignificant, but they did show the car going through and the name of the driver on record was Sanderson. He wasn't able to tell who had actually been driving the vehicle, the quality of the recording was poor and the window too dark to give a useful picture.

However the Canadian border patrol found records showing Sanderson returning to Canada two days later by bus. Ross found that odd, but it seemed to direct their search back into Canada. Perhaps it was a red herring.

They'd sent Sanderson's laptop to the lab and were awaiting results. The focus was on any deleted items on the hard drive that might tell them what Sanderson had been up to in the last two weeks before his disappearance.

Inspector Marsh listened, his gaze intent. Ross had found him to be the quickest mind he'd ever worked for. His attention was absolute. No matter how long he talked and how much information he covered, Marsh stayed with him. Ross finished his report, and Marsh weighed what he'd been given.

Finally he shifted in his chair. "Just a few comments, then. First, that's pretty poor that we didn't find the laptop months ago. Did no one look through the building?"

Ross nodded. "Yes sir, we did, but we didn't conduct a thorough search. We were looking for Sanderson himself, his body. The stuff in there was old and covered in dust. No sign of someone in there setting up an office."

"What about these friends of his from university? Any chance they're lying, that they've kept in touch? I mean, where would it be easier to hide a body than in some gravel pit or road bed?"

Ross nodded again. "I know, but we've checked them out. Nothing there to think they aren't telling the truth. We can't find any current link between either one of them and Sanderson. We're still looking for another buddy of his that both remembered. Parker's gone through the university files but nothing so far. However we got an email off the laptop from someone arranging a meeting with Sanderson for the morning he disappeared. Parker's following up with his friends. It may be the guy they told us about. See if we can get an ID or a last name."

"You've checked his bank accounts and credit cards, I take it?"

"Yes, and that's where things don't add up. Too much cash. He paid all his credit card bills with cash, but the credit cards were seldom used, usually by his wife. His business account had constant cash deposits. He had a small construction crew. His foreman, Fraser Hodges, is a regular construction type, a bit rough but probably competent. He doesn't seem to have done much work for Sanderson, there's little trace of a paycheque. Yet he still managed to support his wife and drive a big truck. So maybe he was getting cash as well. He says not. But we plan to talk to him again."

"Okay." Marsh stared at his hands. "One other thing." He pinned Ross to the chair with his pointed gaze. "I gather you've met Ms.... uh..... Ms. Bowman, is it? And that you've been out to her house. Is that true?"

Ross felt the heat rising in his face. "Yes sir. I have met her. I was following her a couple of weeks ago on my bike. On my time off I've sometimes put the house under surveillance. It didn't seem logical that Sanderson would just disappear. Yet he leaves a trail of cash behind him wherever he goes.

"So I was watching the house, and I saw Ms. Bowman put the little boy in a bike trailer and ride down Wilkinson Trail. I thought that was the perfect way to communicate with her husband. No cell phones, no email, no text messages, nothing that can be traced. Just ride a bike down the trail, so she's not even on the road where she might be followed by a surveillance vehicle. It clicked as a very clever way to communicate, and Sanderson is nothing if not clever. So I jumped on my bicycle and followed her."

Inspector nodded and motioned him to continue.

"We ended up at the grocery store. I waited, and she came back out. There's nothing more suspicious than groceries."

Marsh laughed. "True."

"But I had to follow her to get to my truck, so I was hanging back when they were attacked by two guys who jumped out to rob her near the landslide. Lucky I was there, sir. She had a good dog with her, he knocked one fellow down and pinned him. But the other one was throwing her about and trying to steal her purse and the food. I don't know how it would have turned out, the little boy was screaming and so was she by the time I got there. I called it in once I got them off the trail. Then I followed them home to their house."

Marsh was silent. Finally, "Do you still think she's a person of interest in this matter?"

Ross shook his head and shifted uncomfortably. She was definitely a person of interest, just not how Marsh meant. "I don't think so. She cooperates, calls us if something happens. Her house was burgled a week or two after the husband disappeared. That can't be coincidence. She seemed really shaken up by it, according to Parker."

"Cullen," Marsh said. "There's an old saying, and it goes like this. *No plan survives contact with the enemy.* You know what I mean. You form a strategy for investigation, the best you can given the circumstances. But once you engage the fight, the plan is essentially out the window. In this case, it might mean the investigation goes off the tracks. Even if Ms. Bowman isn't the suspect, she isn't part of this investigation. And your plan will not survive intact when you have dealings with her. Just keep that in mind." He waved him out and went back to the files on his desk.

Red faced, Ross headed down the hall to his office.

Dan Parker stopped him. "I had an interesting call this morning from Mrs. Bowman."

Ross flushed a darker shade of red.

"She asked me if I knew Ross Cullen, so I had to admit I did. She said, and I quote, 'he said you were a buddy of his, and that the police had found a couple of guys by the trail and moved them out. Is that true?' So I had to admit it was." Dan paused, clearly enjoying Ross's discomfort.

"It's all true," he protested. "I told her so she wouldn't worry about the men along there. The trail runs past the bottom of her property."

Dan nodded exaggeratedly. "Right. Of course. Then she said, 'can you vouch for Ross Cullen, is he a good man, reliable'." Parker threw up his hands. "What could I possibly say to that?"

He gave him a vicious jab in the shoulder. "You'd better have said he's one great guy, because if you didn't, you're in deep shit!"

Parker doubled over with laughter.

"Aw, get back to work!"

~~~

Chloe cleared the sewing things away and set a pot of tea on the table. "Jayde, you're a miracle worker. Those overalls for Davey are great. I can manage through the winter now with the addition of a sweater or two, even if I can't get anything else for him. How are you finding it with your boarders?" Jayde had taken in a small family whose house had shifted off its foundation. They had two little girls and both parents worked.

"Well, I don't see them that much. Of course, it's pretty busy there in the evenings, with the two little ones. The mum drops them at the daycare because she leaves later for work and he picks them up because he's off work first. They sure are cute. They cried quite a bit when they first came. I think they're settling in more now, but it's shocking for little ones to lose their home, isn't it? I like them. And they do a lot of the cooking. Now and then I'll do it. Works out okay."

"And how is Will, do you see much of him?"

"Yep, every week. He's like clockwork, that boy. Doesn't stay long, but he always checks on me. He'll phone sometimes in between visits. I wish that man would find himself a wife. That's what he needs, alright. Can you imagine, coming up on forty years old and no wife? And no chance of one either, if I don't miss my guess. He's a loner. Doesn't like to socialize. Prefers his own company and his little band of cronies. Doesn't know how to talk to women, that's his problem. Too shy at school, and just got used to being alone."

"And Jannine, how is she?"

Jayde's smile faded. "Not sure at all. I couldn't find her when I went downtown the last few weeks. No one has seen her. The people at The Open Door say she hasn't been in for a meal. I'm that worried." A tear leaked from her eye and she wiped it impatiently away.

"I don't sleep so well when I don't know how she is, do you see? It just unsettles me. Well, that's as may be. Those
~~~

trousers look darned good, don't they Davey?" She finished her tea and stood up. "I'll be off then. Thanks for the visit."

Chloe laughed. "The visit? It was a work bee and you're so generous to share your time and skill with us." She leaned in and gave her a strong hug. "Don't worry, Jayde. I'm sure Jannine is okay. She's done this before and she'll just show up one day, you'll see. God bless you."

~~~

Rainman wiped his feet and inserted his key in the lock. As the door opened, he looked casually back over his shoulder. It was habit. In a sweeping glance he noted all the vehicles within sight and anyone walking on the street. He did it every time he went through the door and stored the information away for future reference. If the same vehicle appeared more than once on the street, he'd find out who owned it and if they were resident in the neighbourhood. If he saw someone strolling down the sidewalk, he'd have a look again in five minutes and then ten, to ensure their presence was innocent. He felt his constant alertness and attention to his surroundings was the only reason he was still an anonymous person, even though Jeff had been removed.

He stepped inside and closed the door behind him, hanging his coat on the hook positioned just inside the closet. Cindy's shoes were there, so she was home. But she was becoming a liability, and the time was fast approaching when he'd have to take steps with regard to her.

"Bob?" Cindy's head poked around the corner of the hall. "Are you home already?"

He smiled. "Surprised?"

"No, it's just later than I thought. I've got dinner almost ready."

His eyebrows rose in surprise but he kept any comment to himself as he walked into the kitchen. It looked like a hurricane had struck while he was out. Dishes were piled to overflowing in the sink, all the burners were covered with pots, some steaming, some cold. "What did you make?"

"Just some pasta. See?"
~~~

He stepped closer and saw a tomato sauce bubbling gently on the back burner. "Mmm. Smells good."

Her answering smile was so sunny, Rain felt he'd stepped back two years. That's what it had been like before the crystal meth hit, the deluge of drug that had demolished her.

"What are you staring at?" she said.

"Sorry, just hungry. When is it ready?"

"In about ten minutes, as soon as the pasta is cooked and drained."

He nodded. "I'll just wash up." He picked up his laptop case and walked into the bedroom. Laying it on the bed, he opened the back pocket and took out the bundles of cash. He carefully stored them in the small safe he kept in his top dresser drawer.

Cindy knew the safe was there but didn't know how to open it. He wondered daily when she'd simply steal the safe itself and take off, hoping to find someone who could help her jack it open. He wasn't too worried about it, it was only one day's take, but it did constantly raise the issue of how long to keep her around. The money was only stored there until she was out of the house, when he moved it to its next hiding place.

"Dinner's ready!" she sang from the kitchen, and he heard a pot lid hit the floor. He washed up and took his sweater off.

When he reached the kitchen, she had two plates balanced in one hand with a salad bowl in the other, heading precariously for the table. "Here, let me help." He relieved her of the plates and set them on the table, dragging chairs into place. "This is nice. What got you going on dinner? We haven't had any cooking here in a while," he teased.

"That's what I thought," she pouted. "It's been too long." She flipped her napkin onto her lap. "Would you like some salad?"

He helped himself and took a bite. "This is really good, Cindy. You're quite a cook. I'd forgotten."

She fluttered her lashes at him. He stalled again. It was like Cindy before the meth tide. Was she really sober for once? He watched her steady hand winding the spaghetti on her fork. Maybe this was a new leaf she was turning over.

After dinner, he offered to wash dishes and she laughed. "I couldn't let you do that all by yourself. I made quite a mess in there. Come on, we'll both do it." By the time the stove was wiped down and the table cleared they were laughing together like old times. Rain was pleasantly confused. He'd been half in love with her when they first got together. He'd even considered he might marry her in time. But the drugs had changed everything about her, so that dream was a long way down the road from here.

"Do you want some dessert?"

"What have you got?"

She reached for the top button on her blouse. "Something you'd really like."

He stared at her for a minute, then placed his hand over hers to stop her fingers, "Sweetie, later. I just got home and want to relax." He hadn't slept with her in more than six months. He didn't know what she did when she went out to get high or who she did it with, and he didn't want to be the one to find out what diseases she'd picked up.

She pouted prettily. "Well, I don't want to wait. We haven't done it in a long time."

"I know, and that's why we should take it slow. Let's just sit down for a while, watch a little TV and cuddle."

Her pout turned to a frown. "Bob, you bastard. I cook a nice dinner and look what you do? I'm out of money, my allowance isn't enough and you know it. Can't you lend me a little against my draw next weekend? Come on, Bob." She whined, dragging on his arm and tugging him toward the bedroom. "You've got lots in that safe of yours. I deserve some, why don't you ever share with me?"

Rain dropped his head, staring at the toes of his socks as she pulled on his hand. What a fool. Just for a moment there, he felt like his life could be good again, at least for a little while. He glanced at her angry face and let himself be pulled along. "Just this once, Cindy. Just this once I'll give you some extra. Don't ask me again."

She smiled brightly and skipped beside him down the hall.

~~~

Ross did the routine search of information lists: fugitives, arrests, wanted, warrants, suspects. He was scanning down the screen when one item caught his eye and he highlighted it. As the full information unfolded, he read it with rising excitement. This could be Sanderson's partner in the apartment building scam.

A suspect had been arrested in Edmonton on fraud charges. He'd been selling an interest in an apartment building to an older single woman. He introduced her to his building manager and she was encouraged to deposit a cheque with him for fifty thousand dollars. He tried to cash the cheque. She'd become suspicious and issued a *stop payment* order on it, the bank wouldn't take it.

But in trying to cash the cheque, the suspect had to deal first with the head teller and then with a manager. There was a lot of security film footage by that time, and he was identified when his photo went out in the newspaper as a man of interest to the police.

The story was very close to the one he'd heard from Marion Brandon of the incident in Victoria. He clicked on the picture and watched it open. This guy looked a lot like the description of Tom Dickson, the scam artist that might have been working with Sanderson. He printed it out and notified Parker to get Marion Brandon in to look at the photo. Then he called the Edmonton detachment and had a long chat with the detective on the case.

Meanwhile, the dog bones from the Ladner Trunk road site had arrived. The tag on the collar led directly to Sanderson, but they were anxious to see what could be found from the dog skeleton. Forensics had it but it was not a high priority. Ross made a note to follow up with them later, just a
~~~

push to see if they couldn't get a preliminary opinion on the type or breed of dog and how it had died. Parker had taken information on Dog Two out at Mrs. Bowman's, and they'd do a comparison, given the two dogs came from the same litter.

He glanced at the phone. It was too soon to call Chloe. But his hand itched to dial her number. He'd been thinking about her, couldn't get her out of his mind. Riding his bicycle behind her had been dumb. Dumb, dumb, dumb. Just the memory of her pedalling along, his temperature rose at the thought. He should have known better, should have ridden on ahead. But no, he saw her climb onto that bicycle seat, imagined her mounting something else. He huffed out a breath and glared out the door of his cubicle.

"What?" Parker looked in inquisitively.

Ross shook his head. "Nothing."

He waved Dan away and looked back at the phone. That little guy, Davey was as bright as they came. He knew they'd been in danger when Ross found them that first day, and now he worried. Were they still in danger? Were the bad men still along there? Had they been caught? He wondered if Ross would come with them every time so they'd be safe. Once he'd been reassured about that, he seemed to relax.

He told Ross about the deer they saw and how he knew how old they were by how many forks they had on their head. He held his little fingers up against his forehead to demonstrate his point. He rattled on about other topics, and Ross could see his mind was like a little sponge soaking up everything. He was cute with his surprisingly insightful comments.

And one of the comments was about Rainman. Then Ross asked him if he knew Rainman, because he remembered that Chloe maintained she didn't. Davey said, "No, but Daddy did."

"Daddy knew him?" Ross asked.

"Daddy said Rainman was really mad at him." Davey looked seriously back at him.

"Rainman was mad at your Daddy?"

"Yep," he replied.

Ross wondered what kind of connection this was with Rainman, Jeff and possibly Chloe. No cop took the word of a four year old. But Davey had brought the topic up himself, Ross wasn't prompting him. And he was a very observant child.

But the picture that stayed in his mind was of Chloe riding the bicycle, Chloe bending over to put Davey into his trailer seat and showing him a shadow of cleavage from those magnificent breasts, Chloe laughing up in his face when she teased him.

He moved uncomfortably in his chair. He was getting too warm. Thumping his fist on the desk, he rose to start organizing his staff for interviews of a group of eight year old hockey players. There had been a complaint from one of the parents regarding their coach that had to be ruled out or brought forward for processing.

~~~

Chloe hung up the phone with a smile on her face. Ross was coming out tomorrow morning to ride the trail with her. Her heart lifted. She thought it was cute that he took this chore so seriously, but she was also flattered. He obviously didn't need to come out here every week to see this friend of his mother's. She suspected he was doing it so he could supervise their ride to the grocery store. He must be in the right business. Jeff used to do that too, when he wasn't off night and day on business.

She felt a pang in her heart and paused for a second to catch her breath and wait for the film of tears to subside. Funny, she hadn't thought about him all day, but there it was, that hitch in her heartbeat, that flutter of loss in her stomach.

But if she were honest, when she thought of their safety and Jeff, she realized he hadn't been there for them in the last several years. He'd been distracted and irritable. He was obviously under a lot of pressure, with the house, the building, his construction jobs.
~~~

She breathed deeply, gripping the back of a chair and letting the loss wash over her. It was okay, they were okay. She had Davey's birthday coming up and wanted to plan a party for him. She'd concentrate on that. A party involved fun, and they all needed some.

There would be a family event, of course. He was the only grandchild and they made much of him. Vivienne had already phoned to book it at her condo. He was pretty excited.

But she wanted a children's party. Maybe she could do it at the daycare. It'd be short. She'd provide cupcakes and drinks, a couple of games. She started to get enthused. Her son was going to be five.

He'd been waiting a long time for this event. His fingers were already practiced in showing his age, with the four digits up and the thumb tucked in. Soon he could use his whole hand.

When Davey heard the doorbell next morning, he ran to arrive at the threshold just as Chloe opened the door. "Woss! Are you going to ride wiff us?" She watched the big man smile at her, eyes half closed in a lazy grin, and squat down to talk to her son. How kind. Although kind wasn't quite what she thought about when he appeared at her door. Exciting, sexy. Goodness! She put a hand to her cheek and grabbed her jacket.

The ride to the grocery store was uneventful. They stopped on the way at the small cafe that had opened up again. These were supposed to be the best sandwiches on the island, so they should at least sample them, Ross had argued.

Davey was all for it. He couldn't even get his mouth around the sandwich it was so thick, but he opened his half up on his plate and picked away at the cheese, chicken, pickle, tomato and sprouts that tumbled out. Chloe had the other half, but she noticed Ross polished off a sandwich with dispatch, then watched as she helped Davey struggle with his. She dragged the little boy off to the washroom before they carried on to the store.

There were more chickens for sale, which was good. She had found a dozen ways to cook chicken, her latest being rice with a chicken and vegetable stir fry that had received rave reviews. She had four boarders again, a man named Don Murphy had joined them just last week.

He was older than the others, probably older than Chloe, working full time at a high-tech company on the peninsula and finishing his Master's degree in Computer Engineering at the university at the same time. What he wanted was everything done for him, so he could just work. Chloe hadn't offered a three meal a day service. She had too much on her plate to do that, and she secretly didn't think anyone was so busy they couldn't find themselves some food. So she left him on his own for the extra meals, and he took his laundry to the cleaners because he couldn't be bothered to do it himself.

She bought ground beef and found the bakery section actually had some stock left. She got hamburger buns and bread to freeze. By the time she'd stocked up on the items on her list, Ross had discovered the freezer section at the back of the store.

"Did you know they have things like hamburger patties already made, chicken stock ready for soup, stuff like that? That would be easier when you're feeding so many people, instead of making hamburgers yourself."

Chloe frowned at the packaged food. "I think the meat isn't as good a quality when it's in pre-made patties. And I can make soup stock from the chicken bones. Jayde showed me all of that."

Ross looked startled. "Jayde? Who's Jayde?"

Chloe graced him with a brilliant smile. "She's my neighbour. She's the nicest woman in the world. She helped me make Davey's overalls, because I couldn't find pants his size in town."

Ross backed up a step. "Huh. That's neat. Okay, anything else?"

He stayed for a cup of coffee when they got back. Chloe walked him to the door as he gathered his windbreaker and helmet.

"You won't go along there without me, will you?" His look was so serious, she had to smile.

"No, I promise." It was cute that he was so concerned about them.

His glance fell to her mouth and her smile faltered under the heat. When he leaned in closer and placed his hand at her waist, her breath caught in her throat. He pressed his mouth over hers, his lips wide and firm, the kiss tender. He lingered and she put her palm against his chest to hold him back, then just to touch him as his heart thundered under her hand.

He lifted his head, nodded and walked out the door, the colour high in his cheeks. Chloe stood in shock, lips still tingling. Yet it was just a kiss. A wonderful kiss that she suddenly missed with a sharp pang in her breast.

Flustered, Chloe looked at Davey playing on the floor with his trucks, making little engine noises as Plutie watched curiously. He seemed to really take to Ross. He talked to him a lot, and today he'd insisted on sitting on Ross's knee while he had his hot chocolate.

Should she be worried? He was getting attached to him, straddling Ross's leg as if he was tired, his head leaning against his chest as they talked. He rolled his head from side to side, then put his little hands carefully over the heavy arm that held him in place, rubbing his palms up and down on the springy dark hair.

Ross didn't seem to mind but Davey didn't want to get down from his lap, right up until he said he had to go. Maybe he was missing his dad. He never mentioned him, and Jeff's name never came up when she was talking to Davey. She should make more of an effort.

"Davey, do you want to see some pictures of Daddy?"

"No," he said, and resumed his engine noises as the truck prowled slowly across Plutie's paw.

CHAPTER ELEVEN

Monday, Rainman made his rounds. Each bank took their time collecting the cash, today it was eighty-five hundred dollars. It was getting close to the end of the year and he knew he couldn't carry these accounts over to the New Year. The year-end accounting was always waiting to trip him up.

His practice was to stop deposits the first week of December and empty the accounts over the next two weeks. Then he closed them. The year-end statements would arrive sometime in February at the post office box, and then he gave up the post box. If he gave it up earlier and the mail was returned to the bank, it waved a red flag. Always better to take delivery of mail. Business shut down for a few weeks over Christmas.

He'd open new bank accounts as soon as he could in January, usually five were enough. It was too much work to handle more than that. Next would be a new post box at a different postal station. This time he'd be Troy Smith. His new pieces of identification looked darned good. He almost believed they were real. Because the eye colour was blue he wouldn't need contacts. Business would be back up and running.

He'd given notice on his house for the end of December and planned to have his things moved out before then. He hadn't chosen a new place yet but he always went for a house, it offered privacy. He didn't risk meeting the same person in the hall every day wondering why he didn't have a job, or fending off someone who wanted to know why he was moving twenty computers into his condo. People needed space, they got too nosy in condo buildings.

But he had cut off the tool rental guy, a deteriorating situation if ever he saw one. And because he didn't use him any longer, he didn't need Cindy's services.

She didn't know his real name, called him Bob like everyone else. But she could describe him, she knew what he drove and where he lived. When he moved out of this house, he was leaving her behind. He'd already moved her into the old house. Buster had agreed to take over the rental of the place, so at least she'd have a place to live for a while. Rain paid her rent for six months and left her to fight it out on her own.

His supplier found him a new vehicle, an old pickup with camper top. It looked good. The body was solid, but more importantly it ran like a charm. Rain would use it to move his things at the end of the year. Till then it sat hidden in the garage, registered in the name of Troy Smith. Everything was under control.

~~~

Chloe left Rowbotham's office and walked down the sidewalk to where her truck was parked. It was sleeting, and the road was slippery. She could still look up the street and see directly into the cathedral. Very little work had been done, other than to clear the road so traffic could get by. Supporting beams had been installed to keep the roof stable, but the wall was still missing. She had heard people were camping inside but hopefully not in this weather. It was very cold.
~~~

She'd finally fired her lawyer. Now that it was done, she wondered what had taken her so long. It was like a weight off her back.

Her truck started easily. John had gotten his mechanic to tune it up and put good winter tires on it. What a big brother he was, always looking after her. Although if she'd been on the ball, she could have done it herself. There was a mechanic and tire shop on that list of prepaid services she carried in her purse.

Turning the vehicle around, she headed across town to Bill Hodson's office. Time to take a step she should have taken a long time ago and take her file to John's lawyer. As she progressed down Government Street she saw a mass of people moving toward her. She pulled over to the curb. Past her marched an orderly file of people, mostly men, waving placards and heading for the Parliament Buildings at the foot of Government.

The signs talked about housing, demands for government assistance for repairs so people could move back into their homes. Chloe had heard about this march and was astonished at how many people were in the street. She wondered if the Legislature would respond, because winter was here and something had to be done. She made a mental note to see if she could have another person move in, even temporarily. Everyone had to do what they could.

At Hodson's office, Bill's assistant agreed to send a request to Rowbotham for the company records and file. "We'll send you a copy of everything in the file when it arrives, and I can make a note. Everything that comes in or goes out can be copied to you. After a while you may decide you don't need that, but it isn't a problem to provide it for you, Ms. Bowman."

Chloe conceded the point and realized just being called Ms. Bowman instead of Mrs. Sanderson was already worth the cost involved in switching lawyers.

She'd spent the morning searching for receipts for expenses at the building. She contacted the gas company and ordered back bills using the earthquake as her excuse. She already had a property tax invoice. But the power company gave her static and reluctantly agreed to bring the files out of their archives for a fee. What kind of archives were they talking about? It was less than a year since they bought the building. How deep could those archives be? Wasn't that all electronic anyway?

She was cranky and tried to keep her sarcastic comments mental rather than audible. She needed all the cooperation she could garner. She was aware the city was a mess in terms of paperwork. There were gaps in everyone's receipt chain

There were other issues however that weren't reflected in the bank statements. There was new paving in the back parking lot. There'd been line painting done, a building sign installed. She found the name of the sign company but they had no records. Their office had gone up in flames from the quake.

As she drove home, she couldn't help thinking about the people marching toward the Legislative Buildings. Would there be civil unrest? She was suddenly glad she lived so far out of town. There weren't crowds of people marching anywhere near her house.

The sleet was heavier north of town, almost snow. The road was slippery and she hoped Dennis was driving carefully in his little old car. It needed new tires. She'd convince him to invest in them, even if she had to finance it herself out of her tire fund. At least it would be used.

She had grilled cheese sandwiches and hamburger tomato soup on the menu for dinner tonight. She wondered what her new boarder, Don Murphy, would have to say about that. He had a way of making comments that really annoyed her. Seriously, if he wanted gourmet dinners he would have to find them somewhere else. She did have dessert though. She'd made scones this morning, and thawed some strawberries. All they needed was a little whipping cream, which was resting at the bottom of her bag.

~~~

Ross took the early flight to Edmonton, landing just before eight thirty in the morning. He was in the RCMP detachment office by nine thirty and had an interview booked with Tom Dickson at eleven. That gave him time to catch up with the arresting officer and get the background on their case. Back home, divorcee Marion Brandon had already confirmed from Dickson's picture that he was the man who had tried to sell her an apartment building. Ross was anxious to see what he had to say.

When he met the arrested man in the interview room, he found a mild mannered slightly suave individual who spoke well, seemed composed and anxious to please. The interviewing officer introduced himself and then Ross Cullen as an officer from the Victoria detachment. Dickson looked mildly interested and squared his chair around to politely face both men. They went through preliminary questions and he admitted to having lived in Victoria years ago, but not recently. Nothing seemed to throw him off stride.

Ross explained he had Marion Brandon, a divorcee, who claimed to have been bilked of thirty thousand dollars. She had positively identified Dickson from his mug shot as the man who played the major role in the scam. His identification was not in question. The only issues now were who had been working with him, and where was that second man.

At that point, the accused asked for a smoke break. Cullen watched him standing out in the compound staring off into space, a cigarette forgotten in his hand. When he returned, he said he had nothing else to say until his lawyer arrived. The lawyer was sent for, but word came back he couldn't get there until the following morning.

Ross had dinner with the arresting officer and they compared notes on the scams. The accomplice in the Edmonton case had already given his story to the police and mentioned that Dickson was angry with how he carried out his part of the job. He kept saying that Jeff was the best he'd
~~~

seen, not quite in such polite words, and too bad he wasn't available for this job. The fact that he had named Jeff got Ross excited but he tried to keep it in perspective. There were lots of men named Jeff.

Next morning, Tom Dickson consulted with his lawyer in a lengthy meeting. At the end of it, the lawyer asked to sit down with the police officers and laid his proposal on the table. Tom would cough up his accomplice if this second fraud charge could be tried with the first, two counts instead of one and the sentence would be concurrent. In other words, no extra time for the second charge.

Ross tried to play hardball but knew there wasn't much of a case and he needed the information on offer. He called Inspector Marsh in Victoria, who called the Attorney General's office and received approval for the deal. Emails and faxes were exchanged and by late afternoon Ross sat down with the accused to hear the full version of what had happened.

Dickson said he and Jeff Sanderson had cooked the deal up between them. Dickson had done a few scams before, nothing major. But Sanderson had all kinds of ideas and was not averse to carrying them out.

Was he violent?

No, he didn't think so. Had never seen any sign of that.

What other scams had they talked about?

Sanderson was partial to computers and ways to suck money out of people that way. But he wasn't comfortable with that. He wanted direct contact, something he could control. It was Sanderson who found the marks.

Marks? So how many times had they done this in Victoria?

Just the once, but they had tried with two other women before this one bit on the bait. Mostly the women didn't have enough to invest and they were firm that they weren't going to do this for peanuts. It had to be enough money to make it worthwhile. Sanderson posed as the apartment manager. He had a contact in the building, someone living in one of the units. They explained to the mark that they couldn't take her through on a tour until she was committed.

But they could show her one suite and arrange a complete tour once her money was paid in and they had a firm deal. Sanderson was a handsome man and the ladies loved him. They trusted him. Dickson grinned at the memory. He was a smooth talker, and it kept them from asking too many questions. Sanderson talked them in circles.

Who was the man in the suite who let it be shown?

Dickson didn't remember, didn't know his name. On the other hand he thought it might have been a woman.

Where was Sanderson now?

Dickson didn't know, lost track of him when he changed location to Edmonton.

Who else was involved?

He looked puzzled, then whispered to his lawyer again. After a hurried consultation, he turned back to the interrogating officers. No one else was involved but Sanderson had a partner that he worked with on other projects. His name was Rainman. He never met the man, just knew of him from Sanderson.

What about this time, how was he going to launder the money?

Well, this time he had the money coming in smaller amounts over four months. He was cashing the cheques at a bank where he'd opened an account and withdrawing over a longer period. Not nearly as efficient, but he didn't have a Sanderson here working with him.

On the flight home, Ross sat in his seat and stared out at the sea of cloud beneath him. This case still didn't make any sense. Sanderson and someone named Rainman had a scam going where they laundered money. For someone else? Why did it take two of them to launder it? What was Rainman's role? Did Tom Dickson tell them everything he knew? When Ross thought back over the interview, he felt like he'd gotten the main information from him.

Ross waved away the drinks being offered by the stewardess as he shifted uncomfortably in his seat. He thought of Dickson's description of Sanderson - tall and handsome, the ladies liked him, trusted him, a smooth talker.

On a gut level, he knew he was in competition for Chloe with Sanderson or his memory. And he didn't know how he stacked up. He suspected not very well and he wasn't sure who would come out the winner in such a competition.

On the other hand, he thought grimly, he was here and Sanderson wasn't. At least for now. That must count for something. But it was a strange feeling to think he was competing with a man who might be dead. Now he wished he'd had that drink the stewardess had offered.

CHAPTER TWELVE

Vivienne hosted the family at her condo for Christmas dinner. She always cooked a turkey with all the trimmings - stuffing, gravy, mashed potatoes, candied yams, Brussels sprouts. It was one of the few big meals she made and it was always delicious.

Chloe had given up eating sprouts when she was about fourteen and had only gone back to eating them again a few years ago. She actually liked them now.

The family didn't exchange gifts any more, although they all brought something for Mum. She loved perfume, gift certificates, chocolate. Chloe got her a massage and manicure. John gave her the same perfume he always bought her. And Brent surprised her with tickets to the symphony.

Rosemary looked well, her pregnancy just starting to show. She didn't talk about it much for once, just took her time getting up out of her comfy chair to sit at the dining room table.

Davey was tired. They had spent Christmas Eve at Vivienne's so she could watch him open his stocking in the morning. He got cranky during dinner and had to sit on Uncle Brent's knee. After a lot of conversation and banter, everyone headed home. Chloe strapped him into his seat in the back of the truck and he fell asleep halfway there, which she knew would be a problem.

As she pulled up to her house, she saw the inside hall light was on. The rest of the house was dark. She parked in the garage and closed the door, collected all the bags and hauled them into the house. Then she went back for her son. He wailed when she lifted him out of his car seat, and clung to her neck like a limpet.

She tugged his arms out of the sleeves of his jacket and it landed on the floor in the hall. Off came his clothes and on went the pyjamas, through flailing legs and weak cries. When she tucked him under the covers and rubbed his back, he was asleep almost at once.

It was quiet in the house. And dismal. Wandering into the living room, she flicked the switch. The Christmas tree lit up like a candle. It was made up of pretty little winking lights, tinsel reflecting them back. *Merry Christmas, Chloe.*

Loneliness rose like a tide in her chest, held back by the lump in her throat. Christmas was for sharing and here she was alone. Well, not entirely alone, she had her son.

Was she really a widow at twenty-seven? It didn't seem real. And yet, her mother was more alone. All by herself in her condo. She didn't have to feel too sorry for herself. The boarders would all be back in a bit. She wandered into the kitchen and put the leftovers into the fridge that Vivienne had packed up for her.

The doorbell rang. Startled, she banged the fridge door shut with her elbow and peered around the stairs to the front door. There was someone standing on the front step. *Well, of course there is, stupid.* That's why the doorbell went.

But she hadn't heard Dog Two bark so she was unnerved. She cautiously peered through the peephole. Ross! She unlocked the door and pulled it open. "Hello, stranger."

Ross laughed. "Hello yourself." He had a bulky bag tucked under one arm.

"Come in."

Ross stepped inside and looked around. "The tree looks great. Did Davey like it?"

"Let me take your coat," she said. "Yes, he loved it. He helped put the decorations on the lower branches, so you can see a distinct line between where he decorated and where I did."

Ross shrugged out of his jacket and hung it on the newel post at the foot of the stairs. "It's okay there. Here, this is for you and Davey. Maybe put Davey's under the tree."

Chloe peered into the bag, and pulled out two packages. The larger one was for her son. She looked at him questioningly.

"It's just a bike helmet, and there's a light on the front so he can see where he's going, even though he'll never be riding at night. It's just for fun." His face went red.

Chloe laughed. "Perfect. He loves gadgets." She walked over and placed the present on the cloth apron under the tree. The second one was smaller with her name on it. 'For Chloe' it said in bold handwriting, 'Merry Christmas from Ross.'

She sat on the sofa and removed the ribbon. A little box inside contained a shiny charm bracelet with three charms, a bicycle, a pickup truck and a little dog, all in silver.

Chloe laughed, and blushed. "That's nice, Ross. Thank you." He watched her, so serious. She tried to put it on and he moved forward to fasten the clasp. His hands were warm and steady on her skin. Like the man, she thought.

"Would you like a drink?" she said, slightly flustered. "I'd love one, myself."

"Sure. What do you have?"

He settled for a cold beer. Chloe pulled out tarts from the cupboard and some fruitcake that Jayde had given her. She poured a weak gin and tonic for herself and led the way back to the living room. She turned on music, some Christmas carols.

Ross settled on the sofa beside her in front of the Christmas tree and lifted his glass. "Merry Christmas," he said.

"Yes," Chloe said softly. "Merry Christmas. Did you celebrate with your family?"

"No. I was on duty today, just got off. So I thought I'd see if you were home and safe."

She huffed. "And safe. You'd think... well, never mind." She took a deep breath and let it out slowly. "We had a nice Christmas. We had dinner with my mother, my brothers and their wives. Davey and I stayed at Mum's last night so he could open his stocking at her place. She loves that kind of stuff. When he woke up, he was giddy with excitement. Once he had his stocking, I don't think he cared what was under the tree."

She smiled and he leaned over and kissed her softly on the lips. The next kiss was more insistent and he pressed her back against the sofa. Ross reached to set his beer on the coffee table and carefully placed his hand on her waist. He bent toward her, his head bowed over hers, his mouth strong and firm.

At first Chloe sat frozen, too shocked to move. His hand massaged her waist and his other arm slid along the back of the sofa and around her shoulders.

"Chloe, kiss me."

She turned her face up to him and wrapped her hand around his shoulder. "Ross," she said. "I don't know…"

"It's okay. It's okay," he murmured and kissed her again.

She opened her mouth and was lost to the sensations he roused. He pressed her back against the cushions and she pulled at him, tugging him down on top of her. Her arms wound round his neck, one hand pushed into the thick black hair. It felt soft under her fingers, dense, a wave falling forward over his forehead. He flattened her breasts against his chest with his tight grip. His muscles flexed against her.

"Chloe, oh my God," he said, his face buried in her throat, one hand moving up to touch the side of her breast.

A flush of heat suffused her body. "Ross, wait."

He stopped, his mouth resting open against her throat. Then he lifted his head to stare into her eyes. "I just want to kiss you," he whispered hoarsely.

Her fingertips skimmed over his strong cheekbones and down his jaw. He shuddered at the contact.

"I've waited for this, Lord how I've waited."

"Why have you been waiting?" she whispered.

He laughed low. "I'm not sure. You didn't give me too much encouragement."

"Well, a woman doesn't have to show all her cards at once," she teased, her cheeks hot under his scrutiny.

"No, but a few would do for a start." His mouth was back on hers with slow sweet kisses, then meandered down her throat to the V of her sweater. He nuzzled her, inhaling her scent. She shivered.

He put his hot mouth over her nipple and she felt it right through her clothes. She jumped in reaction and started to pant, her body alive with sensation.

His lips moved back up, raining kisses on her neck and ear, then across her cheek. "You're so lovely. I've thought all along how beautiful you are." He placed his lips over hers and just breathed out into her mouth. Then he kissed her again. When his hand slid under her sweater and cupped her, she moaned into his mouth. She was like a woman starved. She *was* a woman starved.

Ross bent his head, lifted her sweater and her bra came away. Oh, he was good. His hot mouth covered her nipple and he suckled slow, gentle, insistent. She strained upwards, his hand under her back helping to lift her. He moved to the other breast, she moaned in his ear.

"Just a minute." She grasped for sanity.

Ross pulled back with visible effort and she sat up, tugging her sweater down. His hand stayed on her waist, just beneath the swell of her breast, rubbing her gently. She leaned against the solid wall of his chest, panting softly. His heart thundered under her ear, his fingers threading through her hair and cupping her against him.

"Maybe it's too soon," he said. "I just wanted to kiss you, that's all." He put his finger beneath her chin to judge her expression. "But your kisses are something else. I kind of forgot myself." He grinned. "Chloe, you make me forget myself."

Her eyes were fixed on his mouth, her pupils dilated. "You're good at it, that's why," she said.

"Really?" His lips quirked. "You liked it?"

She nodded.

He leaned forward again, watching her face, finally laying his mouth over hers. As he pressed his kiss home, she caught fire again. She tugged his shirt up his back, clawing to get at his skin. "Let me," he panted and struggled with the buttons.

She ripped at the shirt and pulled it off his shoulders. Those beautiful shoulders. He was heavily muscled, with smooth brown skin. A mat of jet black hair covered the centre of his chest and curled down his flat belly. His hands were on her and his mouth ground her down onto the sofa.

"Oh, Chloe, Chloe, you make me crazy." He tugged her sweater over her head, and sat for a moment gazing down at her. "Your breasts are magnificent. I can't think of another word." He reverently lowered his mouth as his hands glided over her skin to cup her.

"Oh baby." He buried his face against her, then moved his head to lave her nipple.

Chloe clung to him and held on as her body lit up with passion.

"Ross, I need you."

"Oh, God! I'll gladly beg for both of us." He seemed to gather himself, then rose. Shrugging the shirt back onto his shoulders, he grabbed her up in his arms. "Which way? Show me," he panted.

Chloe pointed at the front door and he leaned forward so she could lock it. Then he carried her down the hall to her bedroom, following her directions. He stopped at her door. She opened it for them as her heart beat hard under her breast, and he stepped inside.

~~~

It was dim but the outline of the bed showed against one wall. He lowered his arm and let her slide down his body till her feet reached the floor. Holding her tight against his heat, he searched her face in the gloom. Then he kissed her again, slow mesmerizing kisses till she was out of breath.

"I'm clean, Chloe, I'm healthy," he panted. "And I don't womanize. My last girlfriend was quite a while ago, if you're wondering. I'm pretty anxious here, it's been a while for me."

"Me, too. You know how long it's been for me." Emotion welled in her throat, desperation seizing her. She needed him, needed this.

He leaned around her and whipped the bedcover off, sending it sailing to the floor at the foot of the bed. Then he started work on the button of her slacks.

"Let me do that." She wrestled his hands away and tugged the button undone.

He had his shirt off in a flash, shucked his pants and socks in one motion. He didn't give her time to take him in, just stepped forward and used his hard body to press her back onto the bed, his arms breaking her fall. He wrestled the blanket out of the way and rolled her onto her back. "Chloe, tell me now. If you've changed your mind, tell me now, for God's sake."

She heard the desperation in his low voice.

For answer she tugged his head down and kissed him. Immediately she was lost, they were both lost. He scrambled back off the bed and felt around in the pocket of his trousers, coming up with a condom. Putting it under the pillow, he leaned on his elbows looking down at her, breathing hard. He
~~~

shuffled lower on the bed and placed his mouth on her thigh. His hands stroked up her legs and he pushed her knees apart.

His mouth trailed along her inner thigh, then between her legs. She gasped as he opened his mouth on her and licked the delicate tissue. His hands adjusted her and he pressed his mouth closer, laving with his tongue, leaving her wet and wanting.

Kissing his way across her lower abdomen, he delved into her navel. Then he reached under the pillow for the condom and struggled to get it on. Smoothing her skin, he shaped her breasts together, then his mouth reached hers as he began his penetration. He caught her sharp breath with his own and drove himself slowly home.

"Merry Christmas," he gasped. "My God, Merry Christmas."

It was almost more than she could bear. She was overwhelmed with his insistent heavy presence, with his opening of her. Then he started to move and she moved with him in a timeless symphony.

Chloe didn't know how long they made love. It may have been a few minutes, it may have been much longer. She was in an altered state, focussed on Ross, his strong arms holding her firm and gentle, his big hands as they adored her body, his mouth taking her in, sucking her nipples. His penetration, his possession.

Then she reached that point, that pinnacle, teetered on the edge and finally tumbled over. He stroked her a few more times and followed her over the peak, grinding into her, his face muffling a groan in the pillow beside her head.

Chloe shifted on the damp sheet, pushing against his chest.

"Sorry." He moved to the side, taking her with him, their bodies glued together. He kissed her temple and cheek, tugged the sheet up over them, lay his heavy arm across her breasts and fell asleep.

Chloe cuddled in the warm afterglow of sex. Oh, it had been so long, too long, she just..... She dozed.

She woke to the feel of his arm shifting, rubbing her nipples against the dense curly hair. "Ross," she whispered. He lifted his head and kissed her.

"Hi, Chloe. How are you? Are you okay?" He smoothed his hand low on her stomach, then between her legs, gently rubbing. "Are you sore?"

She shook her head.

"That's good. Because I was hoping to do it again." He gave a breathless laugh and Chloe giggled into the hair on his chest.

"Again?" she said.

"Yeah. Don't say no, not yet anyway." His hands explored and his mouth followed.

"Just gently," she said.

"Oh, baby," he murmured against her breast, and pulled her nipple into his mouth. He fondled her breasts, lifting first one and then the other to the ministrations of his mouth. "You're so beautiful. Look at you."

Chloe huffed a breath and felt his skin with her fingers, running them lightly down his back and onto his buttocks. Suddenly she was on fire again, the embers flaming without warning. "Ross, don't make me wait." She panted against his chest.

"No, baby. I won't make you wait." He reached for his trousers and pulled a couple of condoms out, putting one on the night table. He slipped the other on and pulled her over him.

"Come on top of me, sweetheart." He rubbed his thumb back and forth low against her.

She pushed against his hand, then spread her legs across his hips and grasped him in her fist. She tried to lower herself onto his shaft.

He breathed heavily. "Chloe. Honey, take it easy. Oh my God." He grabbed her wrist and squeezed to release her grip. "I want to last a few minutes here." He took her hips in his big hands and guided her down. She folded over onto his chest and he wrapped his arms around her. They just lay there joined. He hugged and stroked, kissed her hair, her temple, her ear. Then she lifted her head and he leaned up to catch her mouth with his.

“Kiss me,” he said, so she did.

They slept, spoon fashion, she folded into the angle of his body, his arm across her waist and hand cupping her breast. She fell instantly asleep, comforted beyond measure by the heat and security of his physical presence.

~~~

Ross woke in the deep dark of the night, feeling the weight of her in his hand. Her nipple was distended, pressing into his palm. He breathed deeply, taking in the perfume of her body and of sex. His lungs expanded and moisture backed up behind his eyelids. His heart seemed too big for his chest.

He moved his thighs and felt the swell of her buttocks against his rising member. He grew hard. That was the way of it for him where Chloe was concerned. He wanted her, just by her teasing look and her laugh, sometimes sardonic, sometimes childish. Now he’d had her and he wanted her still. She was warm in his arms, lax in sleep. He heard the regular rhythm of her breath against the pillow.

What could he do? He hadn’t told her the truth. He’d lied by commission as well as omission. He didn’t know how to tell her now. Like the jerk that he was, he took her to bed before she found out he was a cop, not just any cop but one who was working the case of her missing husband. The truth was, he’d been afraid she wouldn’t let him into her bed if she knew.

So he made love to her anyway. He couldn’t say no. He had to have her. And he’d have her again if he could.

He held her until just before dawn. As she stirred he reached for his last condom. “Chloe,” he breathed. “I have to come between those beautiful thighs. Let me in, baby. Let me in.” He pressed his chest against her lush breasts and gripped her hips as he thrust inside. She pushed against him, moaning. Then he touched her between the legs and rubbed
~~~

until her breath came in convulsive gasps. When she contracted around him, he pinned her to the bed with his hands and drove himself in until he came in a rush. She was quiet in his arms for a long time.

"I should go, Chloe." He kissed her eyes, her swollen mouth. "We don't want Davey to find me here."

She shook her head, her eyes fastened on his in the dim light.

"Is that 'yes'?'

She sighed. "Yes, you should go."

She rested her head on his shoulder and he tugged her closer, holding her tight in his arms. "When can I come back?"

~~~

Boxing Day was wonderfully peaceful. The snow had melted. Chloe was in a giddy mood. She and Davey put on their helmets and rode their bikes up and down the drive. Davey determinedly peddled a little way up the wet trail until he was tired. He was improving rapidly with only the occasional spill. They had a nap after lunch, then made popcorn and watched one of the new movies Chloe had gotten him for Christmas.

Supper was in front of the fireplace with the tree lights on. They played cards then went early to bed.

Ross had said he was working tonight but would call her the following day to see if he could come by. She felt fabulous. Her body still tingled from his loving. She felt guilty, she was a married woman. She was anxious to see him again. She was nervous. She was scared.

Lying in bed, the sheets still scented from their lovemaking, she stretched luxuriously in the warm linens then shivered suddenly from memories of the night before. Ross was so focussed, it was mesmerizing. His hands, his large dark eyes, his mind. He'd loved her with his whole body, rubbing his chest against her, moving his legs to catch her to him, caressing her with his feet.
~~~

She flushed in the dark. She loved it, just the way Davey loved to talk to him, to play with him. Because he made her feel special, the centre of his attention.

~~~

"Ross Cullen? Sure, I know Ross Cullen."

Jayde looked animated today. She'd come over for an after Christmas lunch, and they were relaxing in the family room. She had news. Her son Will had brought his new girlfriend out for Christmas dinner with his mother and the boarder family. And they were engaged. He'd given the girl a ring for Christmas. Jayde was so excited, her face shone.

"A wedding, with no notice at all. Isn't that just like Will? Waits until I'm too old to look after the grandchildren." She laughed delightedly. "Probably babies pretty quick after that, he isn't getting any younger."

When she ran down on that topic, Davey started. He talked about 'Woss' this and 'Woss' that until Jayde finally laughingly asked, "Who's Ross?"

"He's the man who helped us on the trail when those men bothered us." Chloe slanted a look at her son. She didn't want to remind him of being scared. "You remember. He rescued us, along with Dog Two, of course."

Jayde smiled. "Yes, I remember. That was terrible. But that's all over now, isn't it Davey?"

Her son nodded. "But Woss gave me a helmet for Christmas, for my bike. And it gots a light on it, don't it Mum? It works, too."

"Let's see," said Jayde.

Davey ran off to find his helmet.

"So Ross is still coming around, is he?" She gave Chloe a meaningful look.

Chloe flushed. "Don't look at me like that. He comes every week or two to bike down the trail to the grocery store. He doesn't want us to risk going alone, that's all."

"That's all, is it?" Jayde raised her brows knowingly. "That's a right nice helmet, little Davey, and the light works real well. I like it."
~~~

Davey grinned and did a half summersault on the carpet so that his helmet fell off. He picked it up and took off after Plutie, who ran into the hallway. Jayde turned back to Chloe. “What’s Ross’s last name?”

“Cullen. It’s Ross Cullen.”

And that’s when Jayde said she knew him.

“You know Ross Cullen?” Chloe exclaimed. “How do you know him? He works security in town.”

Jayde snorted. “Security, huh? Well, I knew him when he was a kid, he was in the same crowd as Jannine. They all hung around together and got into trouble no doubt, the lot of them. He’s police, just like his father and older brother. They’re all police. They’re good people, the Cullens, even if Ross was a little wild in his younger days.”

Chloe’s mouth had dropped open and stayed there. Her face heated. “He’s police? What kind of police? He said security.....” Her voice trailed off as she stared at Jayde in horror.

“RCMP. His father before him, and then his older brother joined up as soon as he could. I think Ross went to university first then followed in the family footsteps.”

Chloe closed her mouth. “Ohmigod. He lied to me! He lied! He’s probably undercover, working on Jeff’s disappearance. They must think I did it, did something to him. Or that I’m a collaborator or something. My God!” She clapped her hand over her mouth. Her face went hot and she looked away. Her whole body shook.

Jayde put her hand on Chloe’s arm. “Chloe, I take it things have gone a little farther than bike rides down the trail for groceries.”

Chloe looked back at her and tears sprang into her eyes.

“Sweetheart, it’s okay. Everyone gets lonely. And it’s been a long time now. What, almost a year since Jeff disappeared?”

“Nine,” Chloe whispered. “Nine months.”

"Right. So you're not a saint. So what? Was Jeff? Probably not, all told. And Ross isn't either obviously. But he isn't a bad sort. I think he's grown into a good man, they're a good family."

"It was Christmas," she said forlornly. "Christmas night. I was just so lonely and he came over to see us and Davey was already in bed."

"You don't have to explain it to me. Christmas can be a damned lonely time. I was right glad to have that family living with me this year. Usually it's just me and the cat, when push comes to shove. Was it good?"

"Jayde!"

Her friend laughed. "Well, no use misbehaving if it isn't fun." Her eyes twinkled. "You needn't think I've been pure as the driven snow since the mister up and died. As I recall, Ross was a right handsome young man and had a nice body too. Jannine always fancied him but he didn't touch drugs and wouldn't have anything to do with all that."

"If you must know, it was fabulous." Her voice shook. "I thought I'd died and gone to heaven. The minute he left I missed him all over again." Chloe's face showed deep remorse at her enjoyment.

"That good, eh? Well, then." Jayde looked thoughtful. "You know there is probably a great deal Ross would do to further his detective work. Yes, he's detective now, his mother told me last time I saw her. So he'll do a lot of things to solve a case, I'm quite sure. But I'm equally sure he wouldn't sleep with you to do it. Think about it Chloe. What information did he get to further the search for Jeff that he didn't already have? He wasn't here for that. We can guess what he was here for but that's another matter." She chuckled.

Chloe batted her on the shoulder. "Stop it! I'm a married woman. I made vows and I've betrayed them. I can't pretend it's okay, I can't!" Tears threatened again.

Jayde looked at her sternly. "I don't know why not. I don't see any sign that Jeff's coming back. You could wait for years, Chloe. And what about Davey? He obviously likes Ross. You can see for yourself that he's taken with him. If Jeff comes back, well, that's a different situation. But it looks less and less like he will. Face it, the chances are slim. I'm not saying give up. But you've fought a long battle, swimming by yourself upstream and trying to keep your nose above water. And I'll bet you're tired as well as darned lonely."

She looked into Chloe's tear-glazed eyes and leaned forward to put her arms around her. "It's okay. Sometimes you have to look after yourself just to keep going."

CHAPTER THIRTEEN

Rainman lifted the last of the computers into the back of the truck and tucked in the straggling cords. He attached the cables that kept the cases from rattling around. Then he pulled down the camper door and locked it before going back in the house.

He had sixteen computers left. The others had been wiped clean, the hard drives removed and taken to be recycled. It was the day before New Year's Eve, and he was moving. He'd been packing for a week. The rental furniture had been taken away and he was sleeping on the floor on an air mattress. His clothes were in suitcases, he had books and kitchen items in a few boxes.

His next rental was in the suburb of View Royal. It was a fairly new house with plenty of electrical outlets, wireless internet service, a private drive and nice view. Not that he'd see much of that. He'd be busy in the back bedroom in the dark with the blinds pulled.

It was a lot of work closing down at the end of the year and getting ready to start up again in January. His briefcase was on the front seat of the truck with lists tucked inside. He'd closed down business two weeks ago, emptied and closed the bank accounts. He'd already opened a new postal box in his new name and would open new bank accounts in January.

His house rental was in that name as well. The car had been sold online for a pittance, but it meant he didn't have to abandon it somewhere or find a wrecker. Nothing wrong with the car, he was using this truck now in the name of Troy Smith.

He put the last bags into the cab of the truck, took his cleaning kit and started work. He went over the house with a fine tooth comb, picking up every bit of paper or scrap of cloth. He cleaned surfaces, the kitchen first. Inside and outside of the fridge, same with the stove and the microwave. Then he cleaned the cupboard door handles, the doorjambs and door knobs.

He was going up the west coast of the island with reservations at Point No Point cabins north of Sooke. He couldn't move into his new house until tomorrow and he'd decided to take a bit of a break, two or three nights at Point No Point with reservations in the name of Buster Ashmore. He liked the irony of that, Buster had just taken over the lease on the old house and was a little ticked off at him right now for having to shoulder that responsibility. But he'd get over it.

And then on the second of January Rain would arrive at his new home. He figured, with any luck, he'd be back in business in a few weeks and the money would begin to roll in again.

On the drive north he'd start to sort out the problem of Tom Dickson. He was in no hurry to deal with that issue, but it was beginning to haunt him. Dickson was out on bail. He'd demanded money but Rain wasn't worried about that. He'd decide if and when he paid.

Dickson had nothing to say to the police that wouldn't dig himself into a deeper hole than he was already. But at the same time, it would be better for everyone if Tom didn't go to jail. Anything could happen in there and maybe Dickson wasn't tough enough to handle it.

There was a huge divide between his rational side and his emotional side in the matter of Tom Dickson. Rationally, he could string him along and keep him onside, maybe even pay him a bit for his lawyers' fees. That just made good business sense. That was his mind talking.

Emotionally, he wanted to hang him out by his balls. Let him burn. The rage kept threatening to surge to the surface and drag him off track. Because rationality was Rain's lodestone. That was how he directed his whole life. The ultimate rational man. And this emotion kept rolling like lava, oozing through every chink in his logical armour and whipsawing him off course.

Maybe there was a way to rationally deal with his anger. He gave a fierce grin of black humour. The old 'two birds with one stone' trick, satisfying both sides of him at the same time.

A less pressing but more insistent problem was what to do now that Jeff wasn't here. Jeff was his conduit to legitimizing the income.

He needed a new plan. Because with Jeff gone, the building belonged to Jeff's wife. There were the shares, but he didn't know if they were of value anymore. She seemed to be doing okay, working her way through the pitfalls. It was an irritating situation and one that required some serious thought.

~~~

Ross called that evening, asking if he could come out. He'd just gotten off shift. Chloe stalled, he pressed. She didn't know if she'd welcome him when he got there or slap him silly. Likely the latter.

When the doorbell rang, she was in the bathroom while Davey cleaned his teeth. He jumped down from his stool and raced to the door just as she got there feeling slightly faint. "Hold on, Davey, we have to see who it is."

"It's Woss!"

Chloe looked through the peephole and sure enough, Ross stood on the step with a bouquet of flowers in his hand.
~~~

Davey was jumping up and down, his toothbrush splatting toothpaste on the front hall rug. Taking the brush from him with a trembling hand, she leaned past to open the door.

"Hello, Ross," she said, just as Davey leaped forward and tackled him around the legs.

"Woss, you came to visit," he said in a delighted voice.

The man stalled in the doorway. "Hey, Davey. What are you doing? You're in your pyjamas, you can't come outside dressed like that." He hoisted the little boy up in one arm, and held the flowers out to Chloe. "Hi, Chloe."

Chloe ignored the flowers and closed the door. "Hello," she said, her voice cool. She turned toward him and backed up a few steps, her arms folded across her chest. "What can I do for you?"

He gave her a suddenly guarded look. Moving forward with the flowers, he held them out again. "You could put those in water, if you wanted."

Chloe took the flowers but didn't move. "I understand you're RCMP," she said. "You work for the police."

He flushed guiltily.

Her voice rose. "You're police. You told me you were security!"

Ross held his hand up. "Chloe, I'm sorry. I came over tonight to tell you. I kind of got caught and didn't know how to...."

"You lied to me!" She hit him with the flowers, then hit him again until the petals were strewn around the hallway. Finally she threw them at him. "You lied to us!"

Davey looked startled.

Ross struggled to catch Chloe's hands as she batted at him, finally catching her wrist and holding on as she continued to hit at his chest with her other hand.

He finally let go and simply walked forward, wrapping one arm around her while the other held her son. She was trapped against him, beating weakly on his arm. Davey sniffled.

"Hold it, hold on now. Come on, Chloe. Don't upset him like this." Ross backed into the living room, tugging her along with him and sat on the sofa, pulling her down. She was half on his knee, fully against his chest as she gulped back her sobs. His hand stroked her back. Davey wrapped one little arm around Ross's neck and placed the other hand on her, patting her cheek.

Ross took a deep breath beside her. "Chloe, I'm sorry. I didn't mean to lie to you but once it started, I was caught. I didn't know how to get out of it. It's stupid, I know that. I came over tonight to put it right. And you would probably have been just as mad, anyway, after I told you."

He blew out a breath. "To be honest, I didn't want to risk what might happen when I told you, Chloe." He rocked her for a few minutes. "I'm sorry."

She nodded against his shirt then lifted her head to look at Davey. "Here, give him to me." She pulled her son onto her lap and cradled him.

"Atta boy. So much upset." Davey stirred and snuggled in closer. "There's a good boy." She held him, patting until he settled down again.

When she looked up, Ross was watching her guardedly, his jaw set in a grim line.

"Did you have me under surveillance? Did you get close so you could keep a watch on me?"

Colour suffused his face.

"You did!"

"No, no." He held up his hand. "I'll tell you everything, but I didn't get close to do some kind of undercover work, Chloe. I got close because I couldn't help it. I should have stayed away, but I couldn't seem to do it."

"Well? Were you working the case the whole time, while you rode up and down the trail with us? Did you think you'd learn something from that?" Her voice was low and tense.

"Chloe, no. Nothing like that." He kissed her to stop the flow of words. "Listen to me. I'm sorry. But I wasn't working, okay? I was so frightened for both of you after that attack on the trail that I came out to make sure you were safe going to the store. Honest. It was on my own time, because I needed to see you were safe."

He tugged her against him, kissed the top of her head. "That's not to say I wasn't working the first time, because I was." She tried to pull away as anger rose again but he wouldn't let her. "Chloe, you have to listen." She gave in, cradling a now sleeping Davey in her arms.

"I'll tell you but you have to listen to the end." His voice was pitched low to reach her without disturbing the child. "Should we put him to bed first? Or do you want to hear it all now?"

There was silence for a moment as she thought about it, then she roused. "I'll put him to bed."

"I'll help." He rose and lifted Davey out of her arms. She led the way down the hall, her son's toothbrush still in her hand.

"Were you cleaning your teeth?" he whispered.

She gave a strangled laugh. "Davey was cleaning his teeth when he heard you arrive." *And he raced for the door like his life depended on it.* She put her head down, trying to push that thought away.

Between them, Davey was tucked into bed and his nightlight turned on in the hall.

~~~

Ross stood in the kitchen doorway. He could see the hurt and anger on her face. Following into the living room, he took firm hold of her hand. "I need to tell you, Chloe. Will you listen?" He led her back to the sofa in front of the tree lights.

"I didn't meet you when you first reported your husband missing. I saw the interviews and I was in charge of the search. But we got nowhere and there wasn't anything to point in any given direction. On a balance of probabilities,
~~~

one spouse is usually involved when the other goes missing. So we were trying to keep an eye on you as well as follow any other leads that surfaced.

"I came out here a few times just to see what you did with your time. And I happened to be here when you took your bike and trailer and headed down the trail. Right away I thought, if Jeff was hiding, it would be a perfect way to contact him without using a method that could be traced electronically so I followed you. And you went to the grocery store."

He laughed softly as she tried to pull away, tugging her close again. "I know I shouldn't laugh. It's not funny. But usually when I'm following someone, we don't end up at a place like that. Anyway, I thank God that I was there that day, because of those men. The whole thing makes me shudder. It scares me every time I think about it." He fell silent, holding her too tight against his side. He leaned his head against hers and stared at the lights on the tree as she relaxed against him.

"That's a beautiful tree. It calms me down just to look at it.

"Yes, I like it too." She sighed, and pressed her face into his sweater, taking a deep breath. "Ross, we can't go back, can we? I'm a married woman. I can't pretend I'm not."

He stilled, an alarm sounding at the back of his brain.

"You know it's true. We can't, can we?" She gazed at him with apprehension.

"I don't know," he said. He put his fingers under her chin. "Look at me, Chloe." He laid his mouth over hers, and she kissed him back, gentle kisses that grew in power until his heart was thundering under his breastbone.

"Don't you see, Ross?" she said in despair. "I can't trust myself with you."

"But that's good, isn't it?" He kissed her again, placing his hand on her breast. "You're so lovely, Chloe. I can't seem to help myself."

She fell back against the cushions and his mouth followed her down as sensation swamped him. He opened her blouse to look at her.

"Oh, Ross. I just don't know." Grabbing his head, she held him against her. "I don't know. Jayde said…"

He switched to the other nipple. "I could play with you all day," he whispered. "You turn me on. I want to kiss you. Is that alright?"

She just looked back at him in indecision and he settled her on the couch and lowered himself over her. "You're wonderful, you fit me perfectly." He didn't speak again for a long time, his mouth exploring hers. She was open to him and giving.

Finally he pulled away and Chloe rested her head on his forearm. "Jayde said what? Is that how you found out?"

Chloe nodded. There were tears in her eyes. "She knew you when you were in high school. She said you were in the same crowd as her daughter Jannine."

Ross waited, but she had fallen silent. "Yeah, I knew Jannine. She was a bit wilder than I was, she used a lot of drugs and I didn't want to go there. It's a shame. She was a really nice girl who got going down the wrong road and couldn't find her way back."

"Do you still know her?"

"I've seen her a few times on the street. I know she lives rough. It must be really hard on her mom and Will. He was always pretty protective toward her, Will was, and there isn't anything he can do about how she lives. They just have to love her, because they can't fix her."

Chloe nodded. "Jayde cries sometimes, especially when she's been to town and can't find her. She's always worried that something bad has happened."

Ross shook his head. "Yeah, it's really tough on the families." He pushed her hair back from her forehead and smoothed it down her shoulder. "Your hair is so shiny, such a rich dark colour." He twisted a handful of it in his fingers and placed his mouth on it. "You smell so good, Chloe. And you taste like candy." His hand passed softly down her belly and lingered lower, his fingers searching. She groaned, looking at him helplessly.

"Kiss me again, Ross."

He finally raised his head, breathing hard. "I don't want to make love to you here. Davey might wake up and find us. Can I take you to bed?"

She nodded, raising her arms around his neck.

He fell onto the bed with her, ripping her skirt up. "Chloe, my God! I have to come inside you." He opened his pants and fumbled with her panties, tearing them down her legs as she pulled at his shirt. Then he was in her, thrusting, pushing in. He paused, panting against her temple.

"Ahhh…" He pulled out and lay back on the sheet, catching his breath. "Just a minute. I'm getting ahead of myself. I'm just a little excited." He groaned a laugh, and fumbled with his pants, pulling out a condom packet.

He moved over her, starting again with a deep kiss, pushing the blouse open and brushing his chest against her breasts, abrading her with his hair. Then he was pressing in again and she rose to meet him, thrust for thrust. He set a slow pace, but quickly accelerated. They reached their peak together.

Ross shifted and tugged her against his side. "Chloe, I can't let you go. The reason I didn't tell you I was police is I figured you'd toss me out and I needed to love you. I need you, damn it. And maybe you need me right now, too."

Chloe was silent. He thought she'd fallen asleep. "Jayde said," she started and he came awake from a doze. "She said that I've been strong for a long time, and that maybe I need to look after myself for a little while. Just to stay strong."

Ross tightened his arms around her and breathed in the perfume of her hair. *Thank God for Jayde.* He'd always admired her, and now he was her biggest fan.

~~~
~~~

"We've got a young woman, age twenty-six, Cindy Armstrong, picked up for dealing crystal meth. Turns out she was more the buyer than the seller, but she had an interesting story. Look at this." Parker shoved a paper across Ross's desk.

Ross was reading the daily lists, face to the screen but his mind was on Chloe. He needed to make sure he could see her, that she didn't block him out. What would he have to do?

"You need to see this, Sarge. She talks about Bob Humphreys, who used to work with her on a scam. She tried to trade this information for the cops letting her go on the drug charge."

Ross glanced at it. "Who's Bob Humphreys?"

"We don't know yet, but the scam is interesting."

"Okay." Ross sat back in his chair. "Fill me in."

"Well, she'd identify guys who ran a small business. Then she'd get friendly with them. If you saw her now, you'd wonder how effective she was but that crystal meth is pretty hard on a woman's looks. I imagine she was something to see before she started down that path. Humphreys would then funnel credit card receipts through the mark's business. Humphreys didn't have his own credit card account apparently, probably didn't want one, so had to use someone else's.

"Then the mark would get a visit from Cindy every week and she'd bring the account list with her. It would show how much had gone into his bank account, how much he owed Humphreys and how much he kept. The mark took about forty percent. That way he could pay the taxes and still come out ahead. And he had to pay Humphreys his portion in cash. Her job was to keep the guy happy. If he needed a little extra something, she'd provide it. Then Humphreys would give her a cut and keep the rest."

Ross stared into space for a moment. "Now on the surface, I have to say, free money to the small business guy, free money for Cindy. But where did it come from in the first place? What's it for? Money laundering obviously, but from where? Have you looked at where he lived, how he pays his mortgage, where else they put the money?"

"No, but I thought I'd check the banks, see if anyone has Bob Humphreys as a client. I can't find him in the databases. There are a couple, but both too old for this dude. She's given us quite a good description. Tall, dark hair, blue eyes, no more than thirty. Clean good looks, clean shaven, never drinks. She had an address for him, but the landlord says he's gone."

"Okay, follow it up, but don't spend too much time on it. We've got other things on the go."

CHAPTER FOURTEEN

Bill Hodson, John's lawyer, took a seat behind his desk. "Well, Ms Bowman," he said, "this is an unusual situation. There's an irregularity with the corporate shares. The records book shows fifty shares were issued, but when it was registered with the Company Records Office there were one hundred shares issued. One or the other is wrong. If it's the Company Records Office, it is one bitch of a job to correct, pardon my French. If the records book is wrong, then there are fifty shares out there held by an unknown person.

"Whoever holds them owns half the company. It means you can't deal with the company. You can't borrow money or bind the corporation because you have a silent partner. I've talked to our senior counsel and he thinks the best thing to do is to have a look at the original filing papers. Maybe there was an error, just because issuing one hundred shares is so common. That being said, the chances of error are slim to none.

"We'll contact Rowbotham, see what he remembers. We can advertise for the shareholder to come forward. The danger is if your mortgage company hears of it, they can get antsy."

Chloe felt physically sick and Hodson must have noticed her pallor.

"It's not hopeless," he added. "We'll do what we can."

Chloe headed to the hostel with a heavy heart. There was no clear road ahead, everything was obscured. Just like the way Jeff did business, murky, hidden in shifting shadows.

It may not be a bad thing to lose the building, as long as she was able to hang onto the house. She wouldn't like to lose both, but one or the other wouldn't be the end of the world. She had always thought they had too much, too soon.

She didn't know how many jobs Jeff had with his construction company but when she asked Fraser Hodges, he leered at her and asked how badly she wanted to know. She'd looked at him with intense dislike and replied, "Make up your mind, Fraser. You can tell me what you know, or you can answer in court. I have nothing to lose at this point."

Fraser grimaced. "Man, you don't have any sense of humour. No wonder Jeff took off. "

Chloe blanched but stiffened her spine. "We'll never know if it was me or you who made him take to his heels."

She pointed Fraser to the big lunch room table at the building, opened her folder and took out a pen. "Sit right here and start talking. Don't give me any trouble or by God, I'll call the police. With no records of payment for the work you did for Jeff, you're as guilty as anyone around here. Spill what you know."

Fraser glared at her, gingerly lowered himself into one of the chairs and reluctantly recited some jobs he'd worked on. When he was finished, Chloe said, "Good. That's a start, but only a start. Make sure you've given me everything. Because I have Mike LaTorre working here. I'll be picking his brains as well, and he seems a whole lot more cooperative."

Fraser's face flushed beet red as he squirmed in the chair. "Well, there might have been a few more." He talked for another half hour. Between them they drew up an approximate plan of the last calendar year. Fraser ended with a plea to leave certain jobs out of her report.

"They paid cash, Ms. Bowman, and no one would be the wiser if they weren't mentioned. Also, there's Mike, and Steve our labourer. We were all paid in cash. It's going to go hard on everybody if they get investigated and have to pay taxes after all this time."

Chloe didn't commit either way, but was especially interested in what work had been done on the building. She left the hostel feeling tense but with a lot more information in her folder. She'd even won a grudging compliment from him. "You're doing a good job, Ms. Bowman. I never figured you had it in you to pull things together. I doubt Jeff thought so either. He said he had to protect you from all the mess of the business. Guess he was wrong. I'm sorry he's gone."

Chloe gave him a hard look, but detected no sarcasm in his face. She simply nodded her head. "Thank you, Fraser."

~~~

Randy greeted her at the gym with enthusiasm. "Good timing. John's here doing his circuit today." Chloe waved to her brother and went in to change.

"Here's Mikki, she's going to work with you. She'll go easy, just to get you started."

Chloe grinned. Mikki was about twenty and weighed less than ninety pounds soaking wet. She began her warm-up. Several of the drills she showed her seemed designed for someone Miki's size.

"I can't lie on my stomach on the bench and lift my arms like that," she said. "My boobs are in the way. It just doesn't work." Mikki laughed and they found an alternate drill.

Fifty minutes later, John and Chloe looked at each other and burst out laughing. They were both dripping sweat, faces flushed. Mikki had gone slow with her but it had been a long time since she'd been there. They cooled down and stretched.
~~~

After a quick shower, Chloe talked John into going for lunch. She settled into the booth at Sato's Sushi restaurant, but not before checking with Sato. Sure enough, she had a credit there. Well, they'd start using it today.

Chloe arrived at the daycare in time to pick Davey up and get home to make dinner. Her son loved the squash soup in the fridge, and she'd make open faced sandwiches to go with it.

Dennis arrived home in one of his moods. He set the table, and after dinner he cleaned up the kitchen and bugged the others to pitch in. "Come on, guys. Chloe isn't a slave, she's just our landlady. We can help."

Amanda was willing, apologizing for not having helped for a few days. Beth was more reluctant but ready to do it because it was Dennis asking. She liked to look at him, blushed if he gave her any attention. Chloe told him it wasn't the boarders' job, but in fact she was grateful. The days were long and she fell into bed most nights beyond ready to sleep.

Don Murphy had no intention of helping. He grunted and headed for the stairs. But Dennis didn't want to let it go. "Hey, Don. You too good to help with a few dishes? Come on, man. You ate the food, now lift a finger here with the rest of us."

Don gave him a disgusted look and kept going.

"It's okay, Dennis," Chloe interrupted. She could see a fight brewing, his body language was getting tense. "He's not going to help, and none of you has to. It's my job to get this done."

She plunged the pots into sudsy water and turned to wipe the stove. "I've got it under control."

Dennis contemplated her for a moment. "So I see." He grabbed her round the waist and dragged her gently over to a chair by the kitchen table. "Sit here." He took the cloth from her hand and tossed it to Beth. "Here we go."

Amanda smiled at Chloe and stuck her hands in the sink. Dennis stacked the dishwasher and finished clearing the dining table. They chatted, and Chloe found herself joining in, telling them about interviewing Jeff's foreman. In a few minutes, everything was cleared away.

She sighed. "You guys are so good to me. I am tired, I have to admit. I stopped at the gym for the first time in months and it wore me out."

"Go to bed, Chloe, it's all done." Smiling, Dennis bounded up the stairs.

~~~

Ross stared at the calendar on the wall of his cubicle. He didn't just want Chloe now, he needed her. When could he see her again? He'd seen her two days ago, but it felt like thirty.

Her boarders were back and it was hard to get her alone. When he thought of how they had made love that night, how he'd pushed into her, placing his thumb down there between their bodies and rubbing her softly, how she panted.

She was looking at him but he knew she didn't really see him, she was looking inside herself, lost inside, and when he pushed deeper, nudging her in that secret place and she moaned, and he was flying, flying…

He shifted in his chair and tugged at the crotch of his pants. He was in trouble, all kinds of trouble. Not just so attached to her that he missed her bone deep. But in trouble because her husband was missing and he didn't know if the man was dead or alive. He was in trouble for his very job. What kind of cop slept with the wife of the missing man he was searching for? But he wouldn't give her up. The thought made him go cold. He shook his head vehemently, glaring at the wall.

"So what do you think, boss? You don't like it?"

Ross turned from the calendar toward the door, where Parker peered inquisitively round the wall of his cubicle.

"What?"

"The report I gave you, Bob Humphreys. What do you think?"
~~~

Ross waved him away. "I'll look at it in a minute." He stared blindly at the top of his desk. He was hooked for sure. He was sunk. He glared fiercely out the door at Parker's retreating back. They had to find this bastard, Sanderson. Fast. Before everything unravelled.

Parker returned. "You gotta hear this, Sarge. Bob Humphreys is connected to that flop house where Jeff Sanderson used to live. He was there while at university, then he moved out. I think he'd taken up with Chloe Bowman and the house didn't suit his new lifestyle."

"What house? I don't remember."

"There's this really run down house. Sanderson's friend Buddy Slots remembered the place. He lived there for a couple of months himself but found it too grungy. Anyway, Sanderson lived there until just a few months ago according to the landlord. That can't be right, but that's what he says.

"Well, Cindy Armstrong lives there, same house. She says Bob Humphreys used to pay the rent on the place. He'd let other people stay there and collect rent from them every month. So when I got back to the landlord, he says Bob Humphreys took over when Jeff Sanderson let the house go last year.

"According to the other people in the house, Humphreys has disappeared. But there's one more fellow to talk to, a guy called Buster. He's lived there longest and knew Humphreys. I'll call back there when I get the chance."

Ross nodded. "You do that. See if Buster's ever heard of Sanderson. Sounds like too much of a coincidence, the house and the money laundering, doesn't it? Gotta be connected."

Parker was back in less than an hour. "Sarge, this just came in from Edmonton. Tom Dickson was let out on bail but our guys have him under surveillance. He made a phone call to a cell phone, talked to someone named Rainman. Told him he'd saved his bacon while he was in the slammer and asked for a little help. Wanted some money for keeping information to himself, enough to pay his lawyer. Rainman was the name on the email to Sanderson to meet the morning he disappeared.

"The cell phone number is for a throw away phone, paid for in cash. But we have the bank account where the money for Dickson is supposed to be deposited. Rainman asked for a couple of days to get it together, they agreed on as close to twenty thousand as he could manage on short notice."

Ross frowned. "Okay, tell them we need to move on Dickson the minute the money comes in. That means the bank has to let us know the minute there's any activity in that account. We want to catch him accessing it. Then we've got him where we need him. We'll already have tied Sanderson to Rainman. And Rainman is probably the guy Buddy Slots is trying to remember, as Ran, or Ren. Ask him again."

Dan Parker shifted in the seat. "Yeah, I did. He thinks it might have been Rain. I can't find a Rain in the university records but I'm still looking. And still nothing on Rainman. I've been running databanks all week.

"I found a Rainier in the driver's license file, Rainier Murdoch. He got his license at age fifteen in Alberta. And he renewed at nineteen here in British Columbia. The picture's a bit fuzzy. That was almost ten years ago and it hasn't been renewed since, not in Alberta or BC. I've sent out a request to check the other provinces, just waiting for a response."

"Okay. Keep me posted."

"Will do. And I just talked to Buster at the flop house. Cindy was there and she faded into the woodwork the minute I showed up at the door. Buster didn't know Jeff Sanderson, he knew Bob Humphreys. But that isn't his real name, of course. He called himself something else before. Buster couldn't remember but said he'd think on it. I don't know if that means he'll contact Humphreys to get some pay for keeping quiet. He seemed pissed at Humphreys for abandoning the house. Maybe Buster will be pissed enough to remember his other name. That would be good."

After Parker left, Ross found a record in the police databank of an incident involving Cindy Armstrong. It was from months ago and unrelated to drugs. She'd been withdrawing a large amount of cash from an account on which it turned out she had legal signing authority. But the teller noticed the scabs on her face and arms and became nervous. Then she saw she was wearing a wig. She asked for ID and called her supervisor. Together they took the girl aside.

While Cindy waited for the cash to be put together, the supervisor called police. The police grilled her and checked the wig, but in the end the ID was okay. It was her, she'd just changed in appearance since it was issued, probably from drug use they surmised. They let her go.

Something didn't ring true. The ID was only two years old, according to the report. She couldn't have changed that much. Although he'd seen cases where he barely recognized the person. Look at Jannine Farrell, Jayde's daughter.

The last time he'd seen her she'd lost a couple of her teeth. Meth could have that effect on people. They called it meth mouth and it was a sad and irreversible side effect. But why would Cindy wear a wig? If she was using her ID, she'd want to look like herself, not try to look different. Better have another examination. Maybe Cindy Armstrong wasn't her name after all.

CHAPTER FIFTEEN

Ross and Dan visited the flop house together that evening. It was pouring rain. They shook the drops off their jackets as they stood in the narrow porch and rang the bell. Buster was very talkative. Maybe it was the effect of having a more senior officer in attendance, or maybe it was that he'd been in touch with Humphreys and hadn't been able to get any money out of him. At any rate, he was more forthcoming.

No, he didn't remember the name the guy used before he was known as Bob Humphreys. But he did remember an incident that had happened some months ago at the house. A fellow named Troy was there, a young man about Humphreys' age, and he'd rented Troy's ID from him. He was broke and needed the money. No, he didn't remember the guy's last name, and he didn't live at the house anymore, but he did drop by occasionally. If he came by, he'd call to let them know.

As they were stepping back out the door, Cindy Armstrong walked up the stairs. She stopped and tried to back down but Dan caught her arm. "Cindy, this is Detective Sergeant Cullen. We have a few questions for you."

Dan escorted her back through the dumping rain to the squad car and seated her in the back seat. They climbed in the front and turned around to address her. Cindy was trying the door handles but nothing worked. "It's okay, Cindy, we just want to talk."

Ross began. "We found a record of an incident in a bank a few months ago. It involved you trying to take some cash out of an account."

She stopped trying the handles and lifted her head in surprise. "I had the right," she blurted. "That account was in my name. They just got all twisted out of shape and called the cops for no reason." She looked belligerently back and forth between them. "It was legal."

"Well, for one thing the ID didn't look much like you."

"I can't help that, it's not my fault the pictures are bad on driver's licenses these days. That's their fault."

"Sure," said Ross. "So the other thing was, you were wearing a wig. Now, why would you wear a wig when you have such pretty hair? Why hide it?"

Cindy seemed at a loss for words. She ran her hand through her hair, staring at him cautiously.

Parker tried to hide his grin. "Smooth talker," he mouthed at him.

Ross hoped his red face was hidden in the dark of the car. He was getting more and more like Sanderson! "Come on, Cindy. This doesn't add up. Tell us what's going on. Cindy Armstrong isn't your real name, is it? Let's just run a check, Constable Parker. Type it in. We'll find out where Cindy Armstrong was born and who her parents are. Then you can tell us in your own words, Cindy, and we'll see if the answers match. This is a serious deal. Impersonation is a serious matter. We'd have to consider charges. More charges than you already face."

Cindy's face went white under the heavy makeup. She nervously fidgeted with her hair as she thought furiously. "Well, see," she said. "It's not me. The thing is, Bob used to get me different ID. I'd use it for a while, then he'd get me some more. That way, no one saw me for too long and got suspicious. You see what I mean? I'd get my photo taken and he'd take the photos away somewhere and have new ID made. Last time I was Candy, Candy Jones. Then I was Cindy. Bob thought I wouldn't have too much trouble remembering Cindy because it was so much like Candy."

Ross nodded thoughtfully. "Cough them up, all the aliases. What else were you called?"

"Nothing, honest. Nothing other than my real name, just Candy and now Cindy."

"What is your real name?"

"It's Trudy. Trudy Ashmore. You know, I'm Buster's sister."

Parker and Ross exchanged a startled look. This was like a spider's web, complicated and sticky.

"How many charges will we find on your rap sheet when we look you up?" asked Parker.

"None. I was a good girl, once," she said mournfully.

"And what name did Bob use, before he was Bob?"

Cindy looked scared. "I don't know, I don't remember. Let's see." She screwed up her face to try to look like she was thinking hard. "No, I can't remember."

"Not good enough, Cindy. Think it over for a minute, Parker and I are going to talk outside." The two police stepped out of the car and watched Cindy trying to open the back doors. Then she sat picking relentlessly at the scabs on her arms.

"It's raining too damn hard to stand out here for long," complained Parker. They headed over to the sparse shelter offered by a tree in the yard. A face peered out of the flop house window. "Probably brother Buster, seeing how Cindy's doing. So what do you think?"

Parker kicked at the leaves with his boot. "Sounds like quite a setup. Bob has a different name every once in a while, he gets a different name for his girlfriend. She wears wigs to go to the bank."

"Yeah." Ross breathed heavily through his nose. "It gets darker by the minute. Cindy had her own name, plus at least two aliases. So it's likely that Bob had the same. They'd probably change their names at the same time, leaving the old info behind and starting fresh so the old ID didn't lead anyone to the new identification. That gets rid of the trail. The scam starts over again, whatever it is."

"Ah, here we go…" Ross stared at the front door of the flop house where someone emerged wearing a rain slicker. The figure slogged across to where they stood.

"Uh, how's Cindy doing?" It was Buster. "She's a good kid, she wouldn't have anything to do with this, you know. Fucked up with meth, but otherwise a good kid."

Ross nodded and regarded him a moment. "You mean Trudy, don't you? Trudy Ashmore, your sister."

Buster halted in his tracks, then his shoulders seemed to hunch. "My sister, yeah. I ain't done nothin'," he said. "I work, I come home, I keep an eye on my sister. It's what any guy does if he can. She got hooked up with Bob and it looked pretty good for her, he spent money like it was going out of style. But she got in deep with the meth and I guess Bob didn't have no more use for her. So I stick around to keep an eye out, but that's all. Whatever was going down, I didn't have no part in it. And neither did Cindy, other than what Bob told her to do."

Ross said nothing. Parker stirred the leaves again with his toe.

"Well." Buster stood there indecisively. "Well, I remembered something else you might want to know. But you got to let Cindy go. She's got enough strikes against her without cops coming down on her."

Ross waved his hand. "Spit it out, Buster. What do you have of interest to us?"

"Bob's new name. It's Troy Smith. He was at the house a few months back. Bob borrowed his ID, an Alberta driver's license. Troy will remember, believe me. Bob gave him a good hiding with a two by four that he keeps behind the door in the hall. He won't have forgotten that in a hurry."

Ross nodded. "Okay, Buster. We'll finish up with your sister and then leave her here, won't be long, now."

Buster walked slowly back to the house.

He watched him go. "Must be a thankless task, keeping an eye on young Cindy here. With a crystal meth habit that won't quit. Now, Dan, we have Cindy's three names. And we have Bob's new name, all we need to get out of her is the name Bob was using before he was Bob. That's our goal."

They were in the car for another forty minutes. Cindy swore up and down she didn't know, then she said she might have known at one time but she couldn't remember because of the meth, it buggered her memory.

As the time ticked by, she cried despondently. Bob would hurt her if she told. He had always warned her, if she told he wouldn't forget it. He'd make her pay.

But ten minutes after that, they had it. He'd been going by the name Richard Meredith. Now they could look back as well as forward. Cindy climbed wearily out of the car and headed back to the flop house.

Ross got out. "Cindy," he called.

She paused, her head down against the rain that was still falling hard around them. "What?"

"Listen, crystal meth will kill you. I'm sure your brother, Buster, has told you that many times. He's worried about you. But you can't quit on your own and you have to want to quit. But if you don't, it'll kill you. Do you understand?"

She nodded, and turned away. "I know."

"Cindy. If you ever decide you want to quit, call me. Here's my card, put it in your purse and don't lose it. I'll find you a place where you can kick it, you hear? Because if you don't, there isn't any future for you. And a young woman like you deserves a future."

She took the card, looked at it as the raindrops speckled its surface. Then she looked up at him. "Thanks," she mouthed. Her tears mingled with the rain on her face.

Back at the office, Ross pointed Dan Parker to a chair at the work table in the case room. "I'll start. Here's what we have. Richard Meredith/ Bob Humphreys/ Troy Smith is working some kind of scam. He lifted real ID and had his picture put on it, so he was never caught out. The name, date of birth, place of birth, social insurance number always jibed with the system. He was working with Trudy Ashmore/ Candy Jones/ Cindy Armstrong. Rainman is nearby, perhaps it's the same guy. Jeff Sanderson is nearby, and Tom Dickson. Buster and those people are just associated, I don't see them as integral to this whole picture. You?"

Parker nodded. "I think the best way to tackle this is in two directions. Keep an eye on Dickson while he waits for contact from Rainman. Obviously he's hoping for money, but it's our only real lead to Rainman at this point. And the other direction is the banks. My bet is we'll find a number of bank accounts in each of these names. If we can get descriptions or photos from the bank's security cameras, we'll be finally making headway. These guys are very careful. Given how Sanderson's laptop hard drive had been wiped clean the week before he disappeared tells you they were pros and they were careful. There has to be a reason."

Ross shifted impatiently. "Well, let's get a move on. It's been nine months since this guy went missing. We have to make some progress here."

His fist thumped the table in frustration. "It's good to get the background, Dan, but Troy Smith is Bob's latest alias and he's probably still using it. We should be able to catch him with it. We could go back to Trudy Ashmore, get the names of the small business guys, the marks who washed the credit card deposits and coughed up cash. Maybe see what we can find from that angle. But concentrate on Smith. Canvas the banks, find out where he has an account and focus on that. We need to see him, we need a picture, contact, something. We have to find this bastard."

~~~

Jayde was in heaven. Will and his girlfriend were planning their wedding for Easter time and kindly consulting her on every decision. Now and then she'd muse aloud, dreaming about Jannine being well enough to take part in it or even just attend.

Chloe had met Will and really liked him. He wasn't an outgoing man, more of an introvert, very clever. And when he talked, he was worth listening to. He had a keen observation, a dry sense of humour and understood his mother very well. It was obvious to Chloe that he didn't hold any hope for Jannine attending the wedding but he always agreed with his mother if she mentioned it.

"Jayde, what could we do to encourage Jannine to enter rehab, to get herself off drugs?" Chloe wondered out loud. "Is there anything we could offer?"

In Jayde's opinion, most people tried to get help when they ran out of cash. When their family stopped giving them money, they'd finally accept a rehab programme. The ones who ended up homeless were the ones that had lost a bigger hold on themselves. They'd rather live on the street than give up their habit. Jayde didn't know what could be done to help Jannine that hadn't already been offered. But she kept herself cheerful, looking forward to the wedding.

Chloe put a beef stew in the slow cooker, ready to add potatoes a couple of hours before dinner. Most of her boarders liked her cooking, they liked coming into the house when it was cold and wet out and smelling the home cooked dinner that was prepared for them.

All except Don Murphy. He was a man who took himself pretty seriously. Chloe knew that the ease of getting boarders, especially out where she lived, was mostly due to the earthquake. Housing was at an absolute premium. But it didn't mean Murphy had to like it. She was almost at the end of her patience with him, her tolerance at an all-time low.
~~~

It was probably due to the constant pressure she was under, especially her dealings with StreetSmart. Their financial accounts never materialised, but the complaints continued. Now they said they'd pay part of their rent this month because the premises weren't what had been promised and they couldn't afford it due to falling donations.

Did they know she was a new business owner, were they trying to take advantage of the disruption caused by the earthquake or were they really under the gun financially?

She didn't know, and she'd never know if they didn't provide their accounts.

She'd put in another call to the Executive Director early in the day and he was just getting back to her now. Martin Barrymore should have had a baritone voice to go with his name but Chloe found his high nasal tone rather querulous. It was his supercilious attitude, however, that really grated on her nerves.

Today he was at his superior best. "To what do I owe the honour of your phone call this morning, requesting I reply immediately?"

"Did I say immediately, Martin? I don't recall. At any rate, now that you've called, I want to discuss the message you sent regarding the rent."

"I don't know that I sent a message, Mrs. Bowman, so much as informed you that we'd be paying partial rent, starting with the next payment."

"Yes, that's the message I'm referring to. Martin, rent isn't optional. It's not negotiable, it's mandatory. Your organization signed a binding contract. Now I offered to consider some change if you provided financial statements. You haven't done that. I have no choice but to enforce the rent."

There was a pause. She heard Barrymore take a deep breath. "Mrs. Bowman," he said in his most condescending tone, "Street Smart is a non-profit. We are not like the commercial business community. We don't provide services for fee and turn a profit." He said 'profit' like it was an undesirable situation. "Therefore, when things get tight we can't just conjure money out of a hat."

"Very interesting, Martin. You probably think I can. Who's your lawyer?"

Martin choked. "I beg your pardon? We don't keep a lawyer on retainer. We've never had the need."

"Well, you might now. If you don't pay the rent in full, on time, I'll take whatever steps are necessary to collect it. If that means I sue, then that's what I'll do. There are other steps, like attaching your bank account and whatever measures my lawyer recommends. There won't be any way to avoid it becoming public. And it won't look good for StreetSmart to default on their obligations.

"Now if you really have a financial shortfall, I'll be happy to look at the books. This is my third and final offer. Forward the books to my accountant, along with the details on your funding by the end of this week. If it arrives by then, I promise to have a look. But only if you want to. It's your choice. Either way, you have to pay the rent."

Chloe paused but Barrymore was silent. "As you know, from reading the lease," she was privately confident he'd never done any such thing, "You have the right to sublease your space, with my written approval. You could always consider that option."

Chloe hung up and found she'd been pacing the floor as she lectured the poor man. Poor man, because no matter how condescending he was, he was still probably having a hard time running his programme. Davey had been walking behind her as she paced, with Plutie bringing up the rear.

"All right, you two. Are you following me?"

Davey laughed in glee and threw his arms around her legs. Chloe picked him up and gave him a hug.

"What a day. Look at the weather, Davey. It's dumping down."

He looked thoughtfully out the window at the rain. "Can we have popcorn?" He turned his sober little face to his mother. "Popcorn's really good."

Chloe looked into the bright blue eyes just like Jeff's and swallowed hard. "I wonder, could we?"

Davey grinned. "Yes, we can!"

She put him down and went over to the bookcase. "Do you want to watch a cartoon or movie while you eat it?"

She started pulling video cases off the shelf. "There are a few here."

"Donald Duck! Donald Duck!" Davey jumped up and down, chanting. She looked at him speculatively. She'd bought a bunch of things over the internet and one had been some very old Donald Duck cartoons. He loved them. They weren't even that good, the picture was black and white, grainy and jerky.

She shrugged. "Okay. Let's get the popcorn made first." Plutie and Davey followed her into the kitchen.

He was settled on the couch, Plutie at his feet, with a bowl of popcorn beside him. Donald Duck was doing things only Donald could, when the phone rang again. It was Ross. He wanted to see her, when would be a good time to come out? Would she like to go to dinner and a movie, or maybe just a drive, although the weather wasn't all that good.

Chloe laughed at the thought. Dinner and a movie was kind of out of the question, she had to have dinner ready for her boarders every night.

Ross pressed on, suggesting lunch with her and Davey. He'd make sure she got back home at whatever time she needed to. They could even go to an afternoon movie if there was something she wanted to see, that Davey could go to as well, of course.

Chloe wavered. "I don't know Ross, it's a little difficult."

"But not impossible," he interjected. "How about Chinese food? Davey might like that, because there are all kinds of different things to eat and he could graze on all the dishes. Then we could shop around the stores in Chinatown. Have you been there lately? I'm thinking about Thursday, I'm off then. How about it?"

"That would be lovely. Thank you, Ross. We'll see you Thursday." Two days away. Davey went to daycare tomorrow and she was in town on business.

It seemed like forever since she'd seen him. She missed him every day. But with the boarders back, it was awkward. She shook her head and went to see what she could wear Thursday. This was a date, the first date she'd had since Jeff left.

Her heart gave a sharp hitch. And she'd already had sex with the man. What did that say about her? She was afraid to think. It seemed backward, but her whole life was these days. All backward.

She put it out of her mind and sat down to write a letter to StreetSmart, detailing her three offers to look at their books, and explaining the deadline. There, it was clearly laid out so there could be no misunderstanding.

~~~

When Ross came to pick them up he was driving a car with a child seat in the back. "Ross, that works. Where did you get the car seat?"

"My brother. He's got a little boy a bit younger than Davey. But the seat should be okay. They're standard until five years or a certain height."

"Is that so?" She gave him a look. "Did you look that up?"

He flushed. "I might have. If I'm going to take you out, I have to know what I'm doing, don't I? Come on, Davey." Ross lifted him into his arms. "Wow, I think you've grown. You're heavier than last time I saw you."

"I am?" He looked pleased. "I've been eating lots," he said seriously.

Ross laughed, and plunked him down in the seat. "Does this fit? It looks like it does. So you've been eating a lot, have you?"

"Yep."

Ross buckled him in and closed the car door. "Chloe." He opened the door for her and helped her in, then
~~~

climbed in the driver's seat and adjusted the mirror so he could see the little boy. "We're going to have some Chinese food. Do you like that?"

"Yeah!" Davey clapped and kicked his feet against the back of Chloe's seat.

Ross looked at her. "Does he like Chinese?"

"I don't think he knows what it is." They laughed as he started the car.

"Well, he'll find out."

Davey was very serious and on his best behaviour during lunch. He'd insisted on wearing his favourite sweater when he found out they were going out with Ross. It was slightly big on him, and very warm. His cheeks were red as he sat in the restaurant's booster seat and ate bean sprouts, tofu, broccoli, shrimp and egg noodle. They chatted and laughed like a little family, she thought with a pang.

Ross was patient, talked to him, helped him with his meal and treated his questions seriously until he realized Davey had just asked his twentieth question, and then teased him about it.

The big man ate an amazing amount of food. He must have a high metabolism. Of her boarders, Dennis was the one who ate a lot and he was a pretty physical guy. He kept ordering more dishes he thought Chloe would like until she protested that she was too full to take one more bite. They had the rest of the food wrapped up and he put it in the car.

Then they walked through Chinatown. There were the usual shops with Chinese bowls and utensils, dried products like mushrooms and noodles. Davey liked the little decorated dishes, so Ross bought four of them. There were fresh vegetable stands that Chloe especially liked. She stocked up on ginger and garlic, lemon grass, tea and lots of greens.

They went into the curio shops. The shellacked wooden boxes with glazed designs on them were lovely. There was sandalwood soap which she loved, so Ross picked up a few bars. There were all kinds of baskets, every shape, size and variety. Davey was enthralled with them. Ross said he could choose one for his toys, so they spent a long while examining each basket before the final choice was made.

By the time they headed home, Davey drooped in his chair, dozing, his little fingers clutching the basket. Ross looked in the mirror, then took Chloe's hand and held it. He ran his thumb down the thin skin at the front of her wrist as he focussed on the road. Finally he glanced over at her profile. "Did you have fun today?"

She smiled warmly. "I loved it. It was so relaxed, it's not often I do something - we do something," she corrected, "just for fun. Davey did like the Chinese food. He wanted to try everything just because you were putting it on your plate. Did you notice that?"

He looked bemused. "No, I thought it was more that you were eating it, so he was going to. He watches everything you do."

Chloe laughed. "Maybe. A little of both perhaps." She hummed along with the music.

After a minute, "Chloe, I know things are busy with the boarders back. I don't want to put pressure on you but I'm missing you something fierce. This was really nice today but I miss the other, too. The time alone with you."

Her cheeks went pink. "I know." She looked at him but couldn't hold the gaze. She fiddled with her purse strap.

Ross covered her busy hands with his. "I miss you, baby."

She laid her cheek against his shoulder and he concentrated on the road, his jaw clenched.

"Is there some way we can be together? I thought of coming over at eleven at night and knocking on your bedroom door. I thought of finding out what days Davey has a nap, coming over those days so we can have a nap too." He gave a rusty laugh. "Or when Davey goes to daycare. Maybe I can come just after he goes, or in the afternoon before you pick him up. Anything. Anything at all."

"I know," she said.

~~~

Parker laid a list on Ross's desk. "There you go. Every bank account for Troy Smith in the Greater Victoria area, as far as Sidney, Sooke and Nanaimo. There are fourteen of them, with names, addresses and phone numbers. I figure concentrate on the multiple accounts. Look, the one with five accounts all list the same PO Box number for an address. Gotta be that one."

"Right. Go for it. Parker, get out there and get me a picture of Troy Smith. Get Cheryl to help you with it."

Cheryl came in later in the day with a couple of photos in her hand. "Sarge, here are a couple of Troy Smiths that we ran down. This one," she pointed to a photo of an intense looking young man, tall and well-built with blondish hair and dark blue eyes, "He seems to be the Troy Smith that Buster was talking about. He hails from Alberta and is twenty-seven years old. Maybe we need to have a talk with him."

Ross looked at the address and grabbed his coat. "Let's go."

Cheryl hesitated. "Uh. What time would we get back?"

Ross gave her a narrow eyed look. "Marking the clock, are we?"

"No." She flushed. "I just have a date later and I wondered…"

"Cheryl, are you in or out?" Ross shifted his feet impatiently.

"I'm in," she said quickly. "I'll get my purse."

"Right."

They pulled into the driveway of an older shake-clad home in the Fairfield area. It had obviously been broken up into suites and the emergency exit staircases meandered unattractively down the sides of the once lovely building.

"That would be number three." Ross climbed out and headed for the entrance, not waiting for Cheryl. He rapped
~~~

on the door. No answer. They waited while Cheryl lifted the lid of the mailbox with her pen. Nothing inside but flyers.

Ross turned at the sound of an engine behind them. A motorcycle had pulled into the parking lot at the side of the house and a young man stood pulling off his helmet with gauntleted hands.

He spotted them and froze. Ross was already starting toward him as he turned and walked along the cement sidewalk to the front of the house.

"Looking for me?" His gaze looked innocent enough.

"That depends." Ross pulled out his ID. "Detective Sergeant Cullen, RCMP. This is Constable LeClerc. We're looking for Troy Smith."

The man bowed his head. "That would be me. What can I do for you?"

"Can we go inside?"

He looked toward the door then squinted at Ross. "I don't see why. What's the problem?"

"Mr. Smith," Cheryl said, "We have information that you rented your identification out to a man named Bob Humphreys last summer. Does that ring a bell with you?"

His fair skin flushed, Smith looked at her for a minute, then shifted his gaze to Ross. "Are you arresting me?"

"No, no." Cheryl put on her sexiest smile and Troy gave her back a slow grin.

"Than what's this about?"

"We heard that a man named Bob Humphreys borrowed your ID. Is that true?"

"He took it alright. He'd just hit me a couple of times in the ribs with a two by four and I was a bit stunned, if you want to know the truth. I was new in town and I was broke. And I might have had a drink or two." He grinned, a full smile this time. Ross could see his charm, wondered if Cheryl was moved by it. He glanced at her.

She was smiling shyly up at him. "I bet that hurt!"

Troy nodded. "So then he got friendly and asked to see what kind of ID I carried. I wasn't interested in talking to him about it. I was bull mad at the beating and more than a little drunk. But Buster suggested it would be in my best interests, so I pulled out my wallet and showed him what I had."

Cheryl nodded sympathetically.

"That's about it."

"Did he offer you money for it?" Ross' voice was brusque, he was a little ticked at his constable for buttering up to the guy.

"Well," he pulled his gaze away from her. "He took it for a few days. Buster said he was good for it. So I told him it would cost him a couple of hundred, and he agreed. That's all."

"Did you ever wonder what he might be doing with it?"

Troy gave him a thoughtful nod. "I didn't have a clue what he wanted it for. I was broke and needed the money." His eyes and voice were equally cool as he tried to stare Ross down.

Cheryl patted his arm to distract him. "Thanks so much for your cooperation. If we bring a photo by, can you have a look at it for us? Maybe tell us if it's the man called Bob Humphreys?"

"Sure." Troy gave her a wink. "Any time."

As he backed the car out of the driveway, Ross shot LeClerc a look. "You got pretty friendly there with the man we were questioning."

"Huh," she gave a humourless laugh. "They all warm up like that. They'll tell me anything, if I just pretend they're big strong men."

Ross snorted.

CHAPTER SIXTEEN

Ross worked for another hour. Just as he was clearing up to leave, a phone call came in and he was the only one left in the office to handle it. A worried woman started telling him a long story about her neighbour. It took Ross forty minutes to get off the phone. He suspected alcohol had something to do with her strong concern tonight, and told her that he needed a report in writing. They'd take it very seriously. He doubted they'd see anything from her, but he's been wrong before. He shrugged into his damp jacket.

It was just past eleven as he stood outside Chloe's gate and stared into the dense night. Dog Two was on the other side of the gate, growling softly, more in recognition than alarm. Ross opened the gate and the dog trotted out to see him. He sniffed his knees and shoes, then allowed Ross to rub his fingers across his head.

"Good boy, good dog. How you been?" He stood for a few minutes petting the animal, then walked through and closed the gate behind him.

The house was dark on the main floor at the front. A couple of dim lights glowed in the second floor windows, and one at the back of the house in Chloe's bedroom. He walked quietly around the garden and onto the deck, leaving Two behind to do his rounds. He stepped more softly now, not wanting to make noise and finally stood under the small roof sheltering the door to Chloe's bedroom.

A light shone behind the curtain. He knocked softly against the glass. A minute later the curtain was pulled back and he saw the pale oval of her face peeking out at him. He bent down and put his face close to the pane, and she smiled and waved. The door opened.

Ross stepped inside, dripping on the rug at the door. "Sorry I'm so late," he whispered. "A call came in just as I was leaving." He pried his boots off and stood uncertainly.

Chloe looked beautiful. Her dark brown hair was down, lying in curls on her shoulders. He was almost certain he could see through the housecoat she had on, but wanted to get closer to make sure.

"Give me your coat," she said and pulled it off his shoulders. The gas fireplace was on, sending a stream of warm air into the room. Chloe pulled a straight backed chair closer to the side of the fire and hung his jacket on it to dry.

"Come and sit." She indicated an overstuffed armchair and he crossed to seat himself. She plopped down on the footstool in front of him. "How are you?" Her face beamed up at him.

He laughed softly. "I'm fine, better now that I'm here." He took her in, from the top of her shiny hair to the bare toes peeping out beneath the hem of her nightie. "How are you? You look mighty fine."

She smiled, then turned her head. He could hear a little voice calling from across the hallway. "I had better see to him." She rose and walked gracefully to the door, disappearing into the hall. He could hear her murmuring and Davey's small voice responding. Then more words and silence.

He looked around the bedroom. He'd only been in here twice and had never really seen it before. It had been dark each time.

There was a table at his elbow with a bowl of some sweet pungent smelling leaves in it, and he leaned over to sniff. Everything around Chloe smelled good.

Books filled a small bookcase and overflowed in a stack on the floor. The bed had pillows piled high. Oh yes, he remembered those. An old fashioned dresser with a long table top stood against one wall. There was a tray on it, with a couple of glasses and a carafe. A covered dish sat beside it.

The door swung inward and Chloe stepped through, quietly closing it behind her. She paused, then picked up the tray and brought it over.

"Are you hungry?" She set it on the small table and lifted a lid. There were cheese slices, pieces of candied salmon, and a pile of herb crackers. She offered it to him, then reached to pour the wine. "I didn't know if you would want something to drink." He watched her expression, fleeting from concentration to eagerness to uncertainty.

"Whatever you want, Chloe. I'll do whatever you want."

She slid him a sideways look and blushed. "Well, what I want is for you to eat if you're hungry. Have you had supper?"

He nodded and reached for the salmon. "About four hours ago. So this will be very welcome."

"I have squash soup, I can warm up a bowl of it for you. That's what I'll do," and she whisked off to the door again and out into the hallway before he could protest.

Ross laughed silently to himself. He'd rather she was just here so he could be with her, but he was hungry now that he thought of it. Okay, a bowl of soup. Who ate squash soup? He did, as it turned out. It was delicious, and he told her so as he scraped the bottom of the bowl clean. She flushed with pleasure.

"Come here." He put the bowl aside and pulled her up onto his lap. "That's better." He placed his mouth over hers and settled into a long slow kiss. Her eyes were liquid when he drew back. "That's better, that's what I've been missing."

He kissed her again. "Oh, Chloe. You just bewitch me." Her head slid to his shoulder and he put his hand over her breast, feeling her shape and squeezing gently.

"Is it okay that I'm here?"

She nodded against his neck. "I've missed you, too," she whispered.

He huffed out a breath, pulling her tighter into his arms. "No kidding. Holy, these are very longs days."

"Did Two give you any trouble?" She gazed earnestly into his eyes. The serious expression was all Davey, he could see where the little boy got that look.

"No." He kissed her nose. "He growled a bit, but I just waited and he let me in the gate. Let me pet his head. I left him on guard out there."

She nodded. "He's a very sweet dog. I can't imagine what happened to One. He just disappeared at the same time as Jeff. Maybe he was with him…" Her voice trailed off.

Ross stilled, then tightened his arms again.

She looked up at him. "You don't like it when I talk about Jeff, do you? I'm sorry."

He stroked her hair and lifted her chin with his finger. "It's okay, Chloe. Talk about Jeff all you want. I don't mind. I'm sorry he disappeared. I truly am. It's been so tough for you and Davey. No one deserves that. But I'm glad I'm here. I want to be here, no matter what."

"I did feel guilty, at first." A tear trickled down her cheek. Ross wiped it away with his thumb. "But Jayde helped. And I don't think Jeff is alive. I believed for a long time that he was. I was almost paranoid about it. In some part of my brain, I thought if I stopped believing he was alive then that would condemn him to be dead. But I know that was just grief and some kind of twisted thinking." She sighed. "You could make love to me, Ross. If you want."

Ross smothered a laugh. He held her gently against his chest and kissed her temple, her cheek, her eyelids and then settled again on her lush mouth. His fingers strayed from her breast to the swell of her hip and then inward. He ground the heel of his hand lightly over her mound and she moved restlessly against him.

"Chloe."

She opened her dark liquid eyes.

"I'm clean, Chloe. I had my doctor run every test known to man. Everything came back clean. So the condoms are just for preventing pregnancy. Are you on the pill?"

She stared at him for a minute, then shook her head. "No, but I have an IUD."

He looked uncertain.

"I can't get pregnant with an IUD in place."

"Oh. Okay. So, do we need the condoms?"

Her gaze dropped to the buttons on his shirt and she slowly shook her head.

"I'll use them if you want me to. Chloe, what is it? I can use them, it's not a problem."

"No, you don't have to. I just never anticipated this conversation, that's all. It's so intimate. It's kind of what a husband and wife would discuss, I guess."

He realized how young she must have been when she met Jeff. She hadn't been with anyone else for a long time, and maybe Sanderson was her first. He didn't want to think about that and shifted restlessly in the chair.

"The way I feel about you is pretty intimate, believe me." His chest was tight and his eyes stung. He loved this woman and it was the last thing he could tell her. He flattened his lips against his teeth, then rose and set her on her feet. "Come to bed, baby. Let me make you happy."

When he finally pushed himself into her, her face seemed to glow up at him. The firelight flickered over her pale arms as they rose round his neck. Her breasts flattened against his chest and his forearm slid under the small of her back to angle her for his entry. His throat thickened and his heart expanded until it seemed to fill his chest. He was right where he needed to be.

~~~

Ross pored over the records from the five bank accounts of Troy Smith. It was late, but he did some of his best work when everyone else had gone home. Plus he couldn't see Chloe tonight so he might as well be here. He had to find Sanderson, it was imperative for his mental health, not to mention his physical well-being.

As he looked at the records, he noticed the deposits all came in from the internet, a company called Secure Source. So this was internet business. That was Fact One.

The money was deposited into one account, then it stopped and appeared in a second account. Then it would stop there and begin into the third. It was like filling trucks with grain. Except these accounts weren't full. They were all at about the same level. He started adding up the deposits, they totalled just over ten thousand dollars. When that limit was reached, it would switch to the second account and so on. That was Fact Two.

He leaned back in his chair and ruffled the top of his short hair. Where was that other file? A few strides brought him to his door, but Parker wasn't at his desk. He moved across the room and pawed through Dan's folders, coming up with the Sanderson file.

Toward the back were the bank reports for Humphreys. As he pulled them out he saw Dan's notes on his interview with Sanderson's lawyer. He'd been closemouthed of course, as lawyers were. But Dan noted at the bottom that he thought Rowbotham was nervous. It could just be the first time he'd dealt with police, or it could be something else entirely.

Dan had informed him that when a person is declared dead, the lawyer client privilege is nullified and they'd be back with more questions. Rowbotham turned green. Dan's words.

Ross frowned. As far as he knew, the lawyer-client privilege survived death. He'd have to look it up. If that was the case, Parker as out of line with his suggestion. But it was still an interesting observation.
~~~

With the Humphreys bank records in front of him, he started again. Sure enough, the deposits were made in one account, went to just over ten thousand dollars and moved to the next. The money came in over the weekend and the first days of each week. And the withdrawals occurred similarly. Once a week, cash was withdrawn from each account, usually around ten thousand dollars. Thus the balances continued to grow.

The Humphreys accounts had stopped receiving deposits after the first week of December last year. The withdrawals continued throughout the month until the accounts were empty and then they were closed.

He sat back in his chair. Was this the tip of the iceberg? Were there more accounts, say in Vancouver or up island, places that someone could access in a day from Victoria? He leaned over and sent a quick email to Parker to check it out.

Then he looked at the records again. He might be able to predict what Troy Smith, aka Humphreys would do next week. He'd made withdrawals on the first couple of days of each week. So there'd be deposits made over the coming weekend that would show up Monday and Tuesday in the accounts, and Smith would visit each bank to make a withdrawal.

It didn't seem like enough money. Looking at the records, it amounted to somewhere between forty and fifty thousand dollars a week. It was a lot of work for that much money.

He pulled out his calculator. On the other hand, if he pulled in that much cash each week, he was looking at somewhere between two and a half and three million dollars for the year. He whistled. That wasn't chicken feed. It was cash, and it was tax free. It was just a matter then of where did he put it? He had a sinking feeling he knew where it was used and Chloe sat right in the middle.

He wrote Parker another email to be prepared for Monday, have the banks staked out with undercover people and notify the branches to let the police know when Smith tried to access his bank account. They wanted to have a talk with Mr. Smith.

~~~

Rainman was nervous. Dickson had been talking to the cops, was probably still talking. He said he hadn't mentioned Rain, but there was no proof of that and Dickson struck him as someone who'd look after himself. The only thing that might hold him back was the secret they shared. Neither of them would benefit if the police knew.

But he would be anxious to minimise his time in jail and one of the best ways of doing that was to trade information. Possibly Rain would be part of that information. He had to be ready.

Cindy had been questioned here in town. He didn't know what she'd said, but he could make an educated guess. Buster was mad at him for abandoning the house. It meant if he and his sister were to continue living there, he had to step up to the plate and deal with it, not something Buster liked to do. Rain thought his visit tonight might shed a little light on things.

As he stepped through the door, he smelled the damp coming up from the basement. Why didn't the fucking landlord bulldoze the damned thing? It was next to worthless and probably making everyone sick who lived here. Too bad it hadn't been demolished in the earthquake.

Buster was in the kitchen with his back to the door, talking to someone out of Rain's line of sight. He eased sideways to get a look. It was a cop, he'd seen him talking to Cindy one night just outside in the yard. He pulled back and reached for the door handle behind him as the cop moved to rise. Whipping the door open, he ran.

He was out of sight in seconds, the rundown neighbourhood affording plenty of overgrown shrubs and bushes into which he could blend. The police officer stood on the doorstep looking carefully around. Rain knew he was
~~~

invisible, pressed behind the hedge of the house across the street. He waited.

The cop finally walked to his beat up truck and drove away. Buster stood in the doorway for a moment then stepped back inside and the porch light went out. He waited some more.

Finally the older man was back out on the step, his hat on and shrugging into a rainproof jacket. Rain moved up behind him and grabbed his shoulder. He was tall, not as tall as Jeff but he still had an edge over old Buster.

"Don't move." He grabbed his arm and shoved his cell phone into his back. "It's Bob Humphreys. And I'm not happy to see you talking to the cops."

The man froze. "Bob," he panted. "Listen man, I didn't tell him nothing. They got Cindy in their sights and I was trying to soften him up a bit. She don't deserve it. She's got enough strikes against her already. She don't need the fuzz all over her!"

Rain could smell heat from the sweat rising off his body right through the jacket. "Buster, you must think I'm a dimwit. What did you tell him? I need to know."

"Nothing, man." Buster made to turn and Rain jammed harder with his cell phone. He stood stock still. "Listen. I know they been asking about you, but we didn't tell them nothing. They been asking about a guy named Jeff Sanderson, but none of us know that guy. We got nothing to tell them. Honest, Bob. Word of honour." He stood still, breathing hard.

"You listen, Buster. Go back in the house and stay there. Don't even think about looking out the window. Understand? And next time the cops come round, if you tell them anything about me, anything at all, I'll know. This is no threat, Buster. This is a promise. I'll come for you."

Rain walked back to his truck parked on the next block. Things were heating up. He should have seen it coming. After the crazy way Jeff disappeared, he should have known then. But his pride stood in the way, his almighty ego.

He knew best. Oh, right. Rain was the man! He ran the show, he controlled the elements, he made it happen. So he'd decide when the show was over. Except now he didn't have that luxury, because it looked like it was over and there wasn't a fucking thing he could do about it. He'd make another visit to Jimmy off East Sooke Road. He needed some more supplies.

~~~

"What do you mean he's gone?" Ross roared from behind his desk. He stood in a rush, his chair rocketed out behind him and crashed into the wall. "What the hell!" He pushed both hands through his hair and glared at Parker, standing dripping before him.

He knew he was on edge. He hadn't been able to see Chloe, to be alone with her in five days and it was driving him up the wall. He was right on the border of losing control. But this was the last straw.

"Tell me." His hand slashed the air with impatience. "What?"

"He did his rounds last week." Parker flicked water off the papers in his hand. "All the accounts are empty. He took some in cash and some in cashier's cheques. But it's all gone. He must have been tipped off. Something. Because he cleaned them all out.

"The post office box is the only address we have. We have a description and registration of a pickup truck in Troy Smith's name, although the address is phoney. But we can put out a watch on the truck. We've got a few good photos from the bank cameras. We can send them out with the vehicle watch. But he must be gone. Why else take all the cash? Didn't bother to close the accounts, because there isn't any need to, is there?" Parker hung his head.

"Fuck! Fuck fuck fuck! We were all ready for him. Every branch was covered, from the moment they opened their doors this morning."

Ross stood with his hands on his hips, glaring out at the room. He shook his head in frustration, blew out through
~~~

his lips and kicked the leg of his desk hard enough to spill the coffee in his cup. "Parker, I swear. If we can't catch this guy to talk to him, to peel some information out of him, there's something seriously wrong. He's the key to Sanderson. We have to find him, so help me God. We've been trailing this sonofabitch for six damn months!"

"I know. I know." Dan threw his hands in the air, wet paper flapping. "We'll find him. But we're going to have to move fast now. Nothing from the tap on Dickson? You'd think he'd be getting antsy about his money."

Ross just glared.

"Okay," Parker shrugged out of his raincoat. "Back to the drawing board."

"Just get that watch out on the vehicle, don't wait for the photos. We can send them out as follow-up. If he took all the money last week, he could already be gone. Do it now. Mention Duncan, Nanaimo, Vancouver, Calgary, Edmonton. He's got ties in all those places."

Ross threw himself back into his chair. Nothing was breaking! It was tied so fucking tight, he never got a lead. If Rainman and Sanderson were tied together, Rainman may have had a hand in whatever happened to Sanderson last spring. And if Dickson and the rest were connected, maybe Dickson knew what happened as well. They had to have been so incredibly careful that no one else knew anything. Whatever they were up to, they'd taken extraordinary steps to conceal it.

Parker had found a couple of guys who funnelled cash from Secure Source and knew Cindy Armstrong. These were guys who were used as part of Rainman's scam. One was a serious young man who'd just started a used car lot. Cindy came in to look at a car and talked him into doing a bit of work for her on the side. She told him her uncle needed the help.

From the guy's discomfort level it looked like maybe Cindy slept with him as part of the deal. But his car lot went broke even with the extra cash, so the relationship came to an end.

It didn't tell them what the scam was, but it gave them another way to follow the trail. This was another method the Rainman used to wash his money. Is that why he was called Rainman? Maybe it had nothing to do with his real name, and everything to do with laundering cash.

Ross kicked his desk again. *Fuck*! He was all out of patience. The case was going to literally drive him crazy. He was in limbo with Chloe. He couldn't take her out, couldn't call on her at home. He was *persona non grata*. He snorted in disgust. He should have taken Latin in school, he didn't feel too clever right now.

He whirled in frustration, grabbed his jacket, stalked through the office. He was going to make a mistake if he didn't calm down. "Parker, get on it. I'll be back in a few."

~~~

By the time he'd reached the Westshore, he was feeling more in control of himself. He steered down the long narrow road across the rickety bridge to the Esquimalt Lagoon and pulled out onto the heavy sand, parking his truck against one of the huge logs that washed up at high tide. Getting out, he walked.

The gravel and rock beach was heavy going but he trudged along. Rain pelted down, rolling under his collar and drenching the front of his shirt. He kept going, movement being the best solution. His mother always used to say that he couldn't sit still when he was sorting something out and it was best if he kept busy. By heaven, he needed to be busy now.

His life was falling apart, not that it had been under his control in the first place. But this thing with Chloe ate at him. He wanted her. He wanted to take her out, bring her to meet his family. He couldn't do that. His brother and father would be in an uproar over his dating a woman whose husband was missing, presumed dead of unnatural causes and believed to be involved with a money laundering scheme.
~~~

They wouldn't be quiet about their disapproval either, both being highly opinionated and vocal men and both aware that Ross was involved in the investigation of the aforementioned events. His mother would be aghast. He couldn't do that to her. He walked faster through the heavy gravel.

Damn it, he wanted to be free to see Chloe in public, take her to a show. Take her and Davey around town. He was proud of her, he was in love with her. And he knew in his heart, if not his head, that Chloe was not involved, had never been involved with anything illegal. He knew her family from their investigation, and more importantly he knew her.

How he knew her! It made him catch his breath. But he also had to listen to his brain. That was his job, to make sure he did everything required to find out the truth. He put back his head in anguish, his teeth grinding together. The rain pelted his face. His hair dripped, runoff pouring down his neck.

Where to go with this, what to do? He stood in the rain and cried tears of angry frustration.

CHAPTER SEVENTEEN

Three hours later Ross was back at his desk. Only dogged, thorough police work was going to solve this case and he was determined to get it solved. Parker was surprised to see him in at quitting time, but said he didn't have any plans so would stay and help.

They spent the evening on it, going back over all the notes, all the interviews. They highlighted who needed to be spoken to again, who might have more information, what kind of information they were now looking for as the investigation shifted direction. They'd put pressure on Secure Source, as they hadn't received anything useful from their first query. They were an American company, but most of these internet secure service providers were very cooperative with police. Their business depended on being incorruptible.

Ross kept going back to Sanderson and wanted to see another interview with his parents, maybe get permission at the same time for DNA samples. That might get their attention, and they'd likely need that information anyway when the time came.

His other target was the landlord of the flop house. He'd been the subject of a cursory interview early on, but it was worth another effort. And what about Rain Murdoch?

Why wasn't there a current driver's licence for him in Alberta or BC? Had he gone to another province, or state? Or had he disappeared too? Was he dead? Better track down his family, see what they could find.

Had they ever asked Sanderson's university friends about the Rain Murdoch name? Parker leafed through the notes but couldn't find any reference, so added it to the list.

Ross made a mental note to ask Chloe again if she knew Rain or Rainman. If Davey knew the name, why not Chloe? He felt disloyal, but forcefully crushed the emotion. He had to get to the bottom of this, no matter what the picture looked like when he got there. The turmoil was driving him crazy. And it was better to face it than put his head in the sand.

Another loose end was the woman in the apartment block. There'd been one suite that Dickson and Sanderson had been able to show a prospective investor because the tenant was a friend. A friend of who? How were they involved in the swindle? Parker put it on the list. By ten they were both wiped. Ross was shrugging on his coat when his email beeped.

"Aw, just leave it."

But Parker leaned across and waved at the keyboard. "Come on. You never know what it might be."

Ross chuckled tiredly. "Too true. Let's see." He clicked on the icon. Up popped the report of another phone call from Tom Dickson to Rainman. The conversation was transcribed in the text.

They leaned forward excitedly. "Listen to this, sir. It's a new phone number, sent to Dickson's phone by text message. He called Murdoch back at about four o'clock today Alberta time."

They both scanned the wording. The two men discussed how much money Dickson needed and when it might be deposited. Dickson made some threatening noises about information he had that would put Rainman in deep trouble with the police. Rainman replied that Dickson was more culpable than anyone else.

They postured with each other, then Dickson said, "If what happened at the potholes ever got out, you'd be finished. There'd be no future for you."

"You were there too," Rainman replied. "Don't be stupid, man. You're putting nails in your own coffin."

Dickson replied, "Well, share the loot then, and we'll both be okay. Don't be greedy, Rainman. I need money for the lawyer and you have the money, so cough it up. Get it into the account, end of the week at the latest. I need to give my lawyer a deposit or he's going to dump me. And if I get dumped I'll be a dangerous friend. Very dangerous."

Rainman made a commitment to do his best. They hadn't been able to tell where Rainman was, just the general area in the mountains somewhere near Banff. That at least was a start.

Then there was a second phone call about twenty-five minutes later. Dickson sounded like he'd been drinking. "I've been thinking, Rainman. You're just as liable. Accessory, and it carries the same sentence. Don't think you can get out of it. You're in just as deep as I am. I can hear you trying to weasel out. Trying to say it was all me. You were there too, you're in deep shit."

There was quite a pause. Then Rainman replied, "He was my friend, Dickson. And I would never have done what you did. So suck it up. Don't you threaten me, you shitfaced bastard. I don't care what you think you can tell the cops. You'll pay big time. So keep your head and quit talking on the phone. You're going to blow everything." And he hung up. The position of Rainman's phone was still imprecise but approximately the same as the first position.

There had been a third call an hour later, where Rainman answered, listened to Dickson for not more than half a minute. Dickson sounded drunk, slurring his words, and the call was ended. No position was located.

They stared at each other. "So where's Rainman now? Banff area in the mountains. These phone calls are about five hours old. Let's get that out, he's must be travelling east. Hop on it, it could be the break we're waiting for. That truck may be the link we need to pick him up."

Ross thumped the table with his fist. "Tomorrow we'll look at the potholes reference. Might mean the Sooke Potholes, they were both operating out of Victoria. And we'll pull Dickson back in for questioning. Maybe both of us go and see what we can get out of him. He's one mouthy bastard. Thank God."

~~~

They took a quick trip to the Sooke Potholes the next day. "We could have it dragged," Dan suggested doubtfully, looking into one of the deep wells in the river as the water boiled through. "It would be quite an ordeal."

Ross looked back at the heavy forest growing up both sides of the water course. "It would be one hell of a job, alright." He blew out through his nostrils. "We don't have any evidence that would justify dragging it, just gut instinct. At the end of the day, that might be what we have to go on. But first let's get some of this other information in, try to complete at least a part of the picture."

He looked back up the river. "We need to know who was here and where they were located. If they climbed up higher, we'd have to start up there and work our way down. Mind you, if there's anyone in this river, there are a lot of hiding places, all the pools. And maybe they're not in the river, maybe they were out in the woods above here. Easy to hide a body."

They walked back to the car. There'd been a complaint about a guy who lived on his own along East Sooke Road and fired his rifle at passersby. The neighbour was scared of him. "He drives a big expensive truck and has no visible income," he'd added. "What's that about?"

Ross thought it might be sour grapes on the neighbour's part, but it was worth looking into. There were a
~~~

lot of marijuana growers out here and on first inspection, the junior officer who went out to take a look thought that was what he was going to find. But what he found instead was a small but well-built house, a satellite dish on the roof, and the owner a grizzled older guy who lived alone, sporting a long grey and black beard to the middle of his chest. He'd been gruff but cooperative, and denied owning a rifle. Said the neighbour was just nosy and he hadn't welcomed the guy's questions. He owned his own land, was a logger by trade. Other than that, he declined to answer questions.

Ross pulled his truck into the yard just after sunset. There were a few lights on in the house, but the porch and front room were dark. He approached the door, Dan staying by the truck as he scanned the yard. He knocked loudly and waited, then knocked again. There was no answer, no sound from the interior. He knocked a third time and came down a couple of steps to walk around the side of the house.

"Hold it right there, buster," a gravel voice grated out behind him. He heard the snick of a rifle hammer pulled back.

Ross put his hands in the air. "Hey, no problem." He turned slowly to find Dan holding his gun on the man and watched as the rifle was carefully lowered.

He pulled out his ID and held it up, although it was too dark to read. "Police," he said. "RCMP. Are you James Dolan?"

Dolan lowered his head in frustration. "Who wants to know?" he growled. "What is this, police harassment?"

Parker snorted and took possession of the rifle.

"We'd like to ask you a few questions, Mr. Dolan. I guess we could start with a look at the license for your rifle. Can we go inside?"

Dolan shook his head. "Nope. No one goes inside my place."

Ross pondered him for a second. "Well, we can just arrest you for possession of a firearm without a permit and for pointing it at a police officer. Then we get a search warrant. Does that sound better?"

Dolan kicked the dirt. "I got a license for that rifle and I can show it to you. But no one comes onto my land without an invitation. I wasn't threatening you. I didn't know you were police. I was just protecting my property."

"Parker, put the handcuffs on him and we can phone in for the permit."

"You don't have to do that! I can get the permit, it's right there in the front room. Alright, come in." And he started for the door.

Ross held up his hand. "Just a minute. Hold it there. Parker, put on the handcuffs."

"What the fuck! I'm cooperating, you asshole! Let me get the permit."

Parker had one hand cuffed and was reaching for the other. It turned into a tussle with Ross and Parker both on the ground, Dolan between them with his hands finally cuffed. Ross rose and brushed the dirt off his jeans. "Shall we add 'resisting arrest' to the charges?"

"Fuck!" Dolan wheezed on the ground. "Why didn't you just let me get the permit? I'm allowed to protect my property, dammit. Let me up and I'll go get it."

Parker reached down and grabbed his arm, hoisting him to his feet as Ross ushered them toward the house. "It's unlocked," Dolan growled. "The light switch is right inside the door."

They stepped into the kitchen. It was very neat, a few dishes in the sink but otherwise tidy. Dolan led them over to the end of the counter where a large folder lay.

"Just inside there, under firearms. Have a look."

Ross poked into the files and found it, pulling the document out. James Arthur Dolan had licensed the rifle four years ago. "Looks in order," Ross said. He put it back in the binder and stepped into the living room to look around.

Again everything neat and tidy. There was a big screen television and a desk in the corner with a couple of desk top computers and a laptop, two printers and a file cabinet. On the floor beside the cabinet stood a large piece of equipment that Ross didn't recognize. "Looks like you have a few gadgets here." He looked back at Dolan. "Do you have internet?"

"I use the satellite. The reception's good. Met a real pretty lady through the internet. Might get married again." His grin showed surprisingly even white teeth.

Ross nodded. "Well, Dolan. I guess I'm going to let you off the hook this time. I don't like how you handled yourself tonight, but I can see you're a man of privacy. However, I'm taking the rifle with me. You got any more firearms around here?"

"Naw, you got it."

"Okay. Keep your cool, because you don't want to be on the receiving end of what we can hand out. You understand?"

"Yessir." Dolan jingled the handcuffs. "I guess you're going to take these off before you go."

Parker looked at Ross, and took out the key at his nod. He put the cuffs back on his belt.

Out in the truck, Ross pulled away from the house. About a half mile down the road, he stopped on the verge. "Okay, Dan, call it in. Find out any priors and get the confirmation on that rifle license."

A few minutes later, they sat in the dark cab in silence.

"So the gun license was a phony. Probably counterfeit. I've seen enough of them to know it looked exactly like it was supposed to look. What has he got going there? A counterfeit service? Look at all the computer and printing equipment and the satellite dish. It's a natural. He doesn't need to grow pot, because this is a steady income and there isn't any season to it. Phone it in, we're going back to arrest him. We can get the lab guys out in the morning. We'll move now before he starts destroying evidence."

Dolan's arrest was a bigger tussle than Ross had anticipated and both men were breathing heavily by the time they got him cuffed and handed over to the two officers in the squad car that had just pulled in. Ross rubbed his eye where he'd taken a heavy blow.

"This had better not turn black or there'll be no end of ribbing."

Parker laughed and dabbed at his split lip. "Maybe we need a bit more practice," he suggested.

Ross snorted and headed for his truck.

The next day the lab guys had a lot to say. The big machine on the floor was a laminator. It also did plasticising which is what was required for the new drivers licenses. The licenses were printed plastic and this machine could match care cards, social insurance cards, driver's licenses, credit cards, even laminate for passports. They thought it was worth upwards of a quarter of a million dollars. The computers were full of prototypes of different kinds of identification. Ross was anxious to get a list of the all the names in the database but that was going to take some time.

Meanwhile they questioned Dolan. At first he had nothing to say, other than his name and address. Finally he acknowledged he needed a lawyer so they called legal aid. When Dolan finished his interview with the young lawyer who came, he said he was waiting for a new lawyer and he'd answer questions in the morning. He didn't mind staying in jail another night.

They got him to sign a *consent to stay* and locked him up. At about three the next afternoon Ross got a call that the new lawyer had shown up and Dolan was ready to talk.

~~~

Chloe parked her truck in the side lot and entered the low rise commercial building. She climbed the stairs and seated herself in the reception area. She had an appointment with the accountant. He'd said it was important, so she rearranged her schedule and Davey's daycare.
~~~

Cliff Greening came out with a smile and a warm handshake and escorted her into his office. The last time she was here they were finalizing the year end accounts for Sanderson Holdings. It had been a tough task but Chloe's sleuthing had paid off. As far as Jeff's construction business went, she'd tracked down most of the jobs Fraser Hodges and Mike LeTorre told her about. It was a pretty complete picture. The accountant said he'd do his best with it.

Now he had a different document before him on the desk. "We've heard from Revenue Canada. They're not happy with the return we filed and they want to do a modified audit."

Chloe's heart stuttered for a moment. In spite of trying to hide from reality, she couldn't deny what she knew deep in her gut. Going through the bank statements and the files she'd put together, the money didn't add up. She had huge questions about the source of the capital. She sometimes thought she knew less and less about her husband as time went by. He was like a stranger, someone she might have never really known at all.

She straightened her shoulders. "What do we have to do?"

Cliff stared at the paper before him. "Well," he lifted his gaze. "I'm not sure. I've never been in this situation before, with no records. Let's see. They want the source of the money for the down payment on the building. I know we don't have documentation and there are many other companies in the same situation after the quake. So we can plead that. But we need a viable source. Is there anywhere he might have borrowed it? From family, from friends? Would he have sold something? The problem, of course," he added, "is that it came in small and consistent sums for deposit. And it was all in cash."

Cliff squinted, not looking so much at her as at the picture in his head. "Could he have, say, sold some assets, borrowed it, or both and then put in some cash from the construction business to come up with the total down payment? What are we looking at here?" He flipped through the statements. "Something like six hundred thousand dollars. That's a lot of cash. Given the lack of records, we probably don't need the entire amount. And then of course they're going to want to audit the construction business."

Chloe sighed. "Well, that won't be so difficult. I think I found most of the jobs and contacted all the customers I could find.

"But where are the payroll numbers, the expense receipts?" Cliff looked at her with a piercing gaze. "You have to admit it's thin."

Chloe looked away. "He paid his carpenters in cash, Cliff. That's what they told me. So there is that." She looked glumly back at him.

"Yeah, this is like a snowball rolling downhill. There're going to be all kinds of arms and legs sticking out of it before it hits bottom." Cliff tapped the paper thoughtfully. "Well, put on your thinking cap and see what you can come up with. Maybe contact his family and friends, see if anyone knows anything. He probably talked about it to someone." He flushed self-consciously, realizing how that sounded.

Chloe nodded to herself. *Right, if he talked about it, he should have talked to me*. She left in a hurry.

She stopped in to see John, but he wasn't in his office. Brent was between clients so she visited with him for a few minutes. He suggested she call Jeff's parents again in Florida. "I know they haven't been that supportive, but you never know. He's their only child. They might have helped him out, even if they didn't see him often."

When she finished at the gym, Vivienne was just arriving. "Chloe! You should tell me when you're coming into town and we could work out together then grab lunch." She looked fabulous, and Chloe told her so.

She glowed at the compliment. "Well," she leaned in confidentially, "I think I have a new beau."

"Mum! Really? That's nice. Where did you meet him?"

Vivienne put her finger to her lips. "It's kind of on the hush-hush right now."

Her eyes narrowed. "Is he married?"

Her mother drew back. "No! He is not! But it's just that his wife has only been dead a year, and she was sick for a long time before she died. His kids are pretty protective, so we're being careful. But he's nice, you'll like him honey. He's a very good man and I'm feeling positive about this."

She gave her a hug. "I'm glad, Mum. I really am. It's no fun being lonely, is it?"

Vivienne looked at her daughter sadly. "No, sweetie. It isn't. And I know you loved Jeff very much. But little Davey is probably lonely too, and life is short. Don't wait too long."

She hugged her again and headed home. She had other things on her mind, like a Revenue Canada audit and the fear of losing her house. And she had Ross.

What to do about Ross? What would everyone think if they found out? It was more likely *when* they found out. It was shocking even to her, when she thought about it. She flushed with embarrassment and fear. Her husband was missing, not even proved dead, and she was having an affair with a police detective.

What kind of woman was she? Loose? Immoral? Even her mother, who'd been a widow for more than six years, retreated hastily from the very suggestion of going with a married partner.

She had to break it off with him, she just had to. Her heart stuttered at the thought but she couldn't see any other choice. And yet every time she thought that, then she'd think of how it felt to be with him. Her whole body vibrated at the memory of his love making. His physical presence was powerful and she was vastly moved by him.

And Davey loved him. He sat on his knee, held his hand, leaned on his leg. He wanted to touch him and so did Chloe. She gave a choked laugh and changed gears as she took off down the highway on-ramp. It was like a Catch 22. There was no good answer. She lost either way.

That night she had a message on her home phone from Jeff's father in Florida. Jeffrey Sr had called not long before she got home, but she didn't pick up the messages right away and it was too late to call back now with the three hour time difference.

Plus, he sounded drunk. Chloe couldn't understand everything he said, he may have been crying. But the police had apparently come to see him again with more questions and they'd asked for DNA samples from him and his wife. They'd use that to identify a body.

Chloe was in shock. Did this mean they'd found a body? Why didn't she know about it? The beeping of the phone in her hand recalled her to reality and she hung up.

Then she hastily picked it up again and dialled Ross's number. He answered on the second ring. "Cullen."

"This is Chloe."

He barely skipped a bit. "I see. I'm in a meeting right now, but can call you back in a few minutes."

"Okay," she whispered.

"Sounds good." The phone went dead.

Three minutes later the phone rang. "Chloe? What's going on? What's wrong?"

"Did the police find Jeff's body?"

"What?"

"Did they find Jeff? Did you guys find him? I just had a message from Jeff's father and he seems to think they've found a body."

"No. That is, not that I'm aware of. Just a minute."

She heard the tapping of keys, then Ross called to someone. She waited.

His voice came back low into the phone. "Nothing like that, Chloe. Someone would come out to see you if they did. We certainly wouldn't tell other people first. We don't work that way."

"Okay." Chloe took a deep breath. "Okay. Jeff's father left a message. And he said the police asked him and his wife for DNA samples to identify a body. He sounded really upset."

"I see." His voice was tight. "Well, that was clumsy."

She heard him inhale.

"By the way, Chloe. Do you know the name Rain or Rainman in connection with Jeff's business, or Jeff?"

"No. They asked me that before, but I don't recognize that name. Other than the email, that was from Rainman, for Jeff to meet him. But I'd never heard it before. Anyway, sorry to bother you at work, Ross. I'll let you go."

"You don't bother me, Chloe. Not with your phone calls anyway." He gave a husky laugh. "You just bother me in other ways. Can I come out to see you tonight? I should be able to be there by ten. Would that be okay? I miss you. This arrangement isn't working too well, is it?"

"No," she said, "it isn't. I think we should stop seeing each other. It seems so risky. And it makes me nervous. I don't know why, but I kind of do. I mean, I'm married and I'm in a difficult position right now. I just don't know…"

"Well, let me come out and we can talk about it."

"But if you came out, you know what would happen!"

"I'm counting on it." His voice was intimate. "And I think you are too."

She was silent for a moment. "Okay," she whispered. "Come out."

CHAPTER EIGHTEEN

Before Ross left the office, the interview with Rainier Murdoch's parents came in. They were an elderly couple who farmed outside Moose Jaw, Saskatchewan. Rainier was their only son, they had a daughter living in Airdrie with her husband and baby.

Yes, they heard from their son frequently. He lived in BC, moved around a lot so they didn't have a phone number for him but he kept in touch. He called them every other week.

What did he do for a living? He was a travelling salesman. Not sure what he sells.

Yes he grew up on the farm. He went to high school in Moose Jaw, had some nice friends from that time. Sure, they knew Jeff Sanderson. Jeff had been in Moose Jaw for a year during high school, grade eleven. They remembered him coming out to the farm on weekends. He and Rain had been close friends. Then Jeff's folks moved on, and he left.

The two boys met up again at University in Victoria. Jeff even came out and spent Christmas with them one year, that was a while ago now, must be six or seven years. They hadn't seen him since.

Did they know the name Rainman? The father had laughed. "That was Rain's nickname after that movie came out. You know, the one with Tom Cruise and that other fellow, Dustin Hoffman, that's it. Yeah, when that movie came out Rain's nickname became Rainman because he was so clever with computers. I haven't heard that in years. Why all the questions? Is Rain in trouble? Has he been hurt?"

"No sir, nothing like that. Just following up on a few issues. Just routine."

Could they let the police know when they next heard from Rain? They had a few questions for him. The parents looked dubiously at each other. Sure.

~~~

Chloe left her bedroom door unlocked and returned to find Ross lounging in the comfortable chair in front of the fireplace. His boots and jacket lay on the rug by the door. She'd just tucked Davey into bed and settled Plutie down beside him. The dishwasher was on and the boarders were diligently working away upstairs.

All but Don Murphy, who'd stayed out for a work-related function. It made things much more relaxed when he wasn't there.

She closed the door behind her and switched off the overhead light.

His eyes crinkled in a smile. "Hi."

"Hi, yourself." She couldn't help smiling in return.

"Come here." He held out his hand. She walked across the carpet and put her hand on his big palm. His fingers closed slowly over hers and he tugged her closer, onto his lap. "That's better. Hi."

He examined her face with concentration. "You look a little tired. Have you been working too hard?"

"More worried than overworked," she said.

"Yeah. I'm sorry, baby."

"Davey misses you."

Ross paused and searched her face. "He does?"
~~~

"Yeah, he's just a little guy, and he's attached to you. He misses you."

"Oh. I didn't know. Well, maybe we better go back to having some daytime visits." He thought a minute. "When is he in daycare this week?"

"He was in today and goes again on Thursday."

"Well, I could come out Wednesday. We could bike down to the cafe and have lunch if you want. You don't still need to get groceries that way, right? The shops are all open now and gas is easier to get. If it's dumping rain we can stay home and I'll bring lunch."

"I don't mind going, even if it's raining. And Davey's protected in the trailer, so we can go rain or shine."

"Okay. Two days in one week. Wow." He placed his mouth over hers and she sank into the comfort he offered. A few moments later, he came up for air, feathering kisses across her overwarm cheeks. "How are you? What are you working on?"

"I'm going to be audited by Revenue Canada."

"Huh." Ross stared at her a minute. "Because why?"

"Because I can't find all the records for the construction company and the purchase of the building."

"Aw, baby." He cuddled her against his chest and stared into the fire. "Did you see it coming?"

She nodded dejectedly against his shirt. "Kind of. I mean, whatever records there were went with Jeff. I don't have anything but the bank statements. And I don't even have the cheques for most of the year. So it doesn't look good."

"Have you got an accountant working on it for you? What does he say?"

"Yes, and he seems pretty good. He says we'll do our best."

Ross nodded. His hand moved slowly down the front of her blouse, undoing buttons one by one. "Oh my." He spread the lapels. "What do we have here?" His mouth sank onto her skin in a slow burn. "Enough to give a dying man hope," he breathed.

"Are you a dying man, Ross?" she teased, feeling her temperature soar.

"I thought I was until you said I could come out to see you. Now I have hope."

Chloe giggled. The ridge of his erection was hard under her hip and she wriggled lightly, rubbing on him.

"Chloe! Take it easy. Lord above." He placed his hand gently over her breast and watched his fingers flex around her flesh and rub across the swollen nipple. "I can't give you up, Chloe. I can't." Her heart eased as he lifted her to the bed to lay her down. "Make love to me. Sweetheart, let's make love together."

She smiled up into his eyes and raised her arms to welcome him. She couldn't give him up either. The thought made her chest go tight and moisture flood her eyes. Give him up? Then what would she do, where would she get comfort then? She raised her hips to welcome him.

~~~

Ross left at four and Chloe went back to sleep. Her body was tired but when she woke to the sound of Davey and Plutie across the hall, her mind was busy. She worried about having to lose Ross. She didn't have the intestinal fortitude to refuse him. She felt so good after they made love and spent time together.

She liked the bigness of him, the thick arms and muscular legs. His hands were broad and heavy, capable. He was covered in hair down his chest, on his arms and legs. She liked to rub it, and the hair on his head was so thick and short it was like a pelt. It felt crisp and capable, no nonsense and trustworthy. She grinned to herself, all that from his hair.

She wanted to be able to phone him if she had a problem and get his view on it, simply have him in her life. Davey missed him. He hadn't been out during the day for a couple of weeks and Davey had asked where he was. Was he sick? Was Woss not going to come anymore?
~~~

She'd tell him this morning that Ross was coming out on Wednesday and they were going for a bike ride together. She gave a slow, luxurious stretch in the bed. Her body still hummed from his attentions, she wasn't giving that up without a fight.

She called Jeffrey Sanderson that morning, it was close to noon in Florida. And Mr. Sanderson was sober. She resolved from that discovery to always phone early.

"How are you?" she asked. "Are you alright? You sounded shaken up yesterday."

"Yeah. I was. Those stupid cops really did a number on me. Have they found his body?" His voice was unsteady.

"No. I phoned and checked. They haven't found him. They told me I'd be the first to know, they'd come and tell me in person before anyone else and they'd tell you as well."

"I know." She heard him take a deep breath. "It's just wearing. Well, you know better than anyone." There was a pause. "How are you doing with your little boy?" Chloe noticed he never said, *how is my grandson*. As if Davey wasn't related to him.

"We're managing. Things are more difficult at the moment because the government is going to do an audit on Jeff's construction company and the purchase of a commercial building that happened just before he disappeared. So that's going to be a trial, I guess, in more ways than one."

He snorted out what passed for a laugh. "A trial, alright. It'll be that. What's the main issue?"

"Well, Jeff wasn't big on keeping records. They want to know where the down payment came from for the building. It's about six hundred thousand dollars, and I don't have anything to show for it. Jeff ran a construction company and I assume the down payment came from there, but that's a lot of cash to come up with."

"Well. That is a problem. What does your accountant say?"

"He says we'll do our best. He seems knowledgeable, so that's good. He suggested I find out if any of his friends loaned him money, but I don't know who his friends were. So I don't have anyone to ask other than the few people around here, and none of them know anything about it."

"Well, you know Jeff. He had angles, always had angles."

"How is Alice?" Chloe asked.

Jeffrey choked up. "She's in bed right now, won't get up. She hasn't been herself since we heard about Jeff, and I don't know how she's going to be. It's been pretty tough."

"I'm really sorry, Mr. Sanderson. It must be terrible for both of you. I'll try to keep you informed of anything I hear at this end."

"Okay. Good girl, Chloe. Thanks for the call." He hung up.

Chloe had a short list of people to talk to. None of them were positive. Even Fraser Hodges was sympathetic but unhelpful. "I don't know, Mrs. Bowman," he said. "Jeff kept things pretty close to the chest. But I always got the impression he had someone who supported him in the finances. He was never short of cash. It had to come from somewhere. I hope you find out. Cause it would be a shame to lose the house or something. That's a real nice house." Chloe was pretty wobbly after that conversation.

She went back to the accounts. The down payment came out of the company account by way of a cheque for five hundred and eighty-six thousand dollars. There had been regular deposits from the construction company account into Sanderson Holdings of about eighty thousand dollars each over the previous months. That second account showed the money coming in from smaller amounts deposited once or twice a week, and totaled something like fifteen or twenty thousand every week. But there were other deposits coming and going as well, so it was hard to tell. She printed out the statements and rubbed her forehead wearily. She couldn't figure this out and didn't know how to explain it to Revenue Canada.

The money was there, where did it come from? This is probably what the police were wondering as well. Was Ross working on that? Was he listening to her complaints but back at work instructing people to comb through the bank accounts looking for illegalities?

She might go crazy thinking like that. She had dinner at her mother's that night so she hustled around to get a meal ready for her boarders then got Davey changed and into the truck.

It was a fun evening. Low key, but everyone was there. Rosemary's pregnancy was definitely showing now. She lay on the floor for a while to ease a backache and didn't complain once. She wasn't even making nasty comments.

Chloe looked at John, but his attention was focussed on his wife. She made a face at Diana sitting beside her.

Diana laughed. "I know, it's a brand new world. How are things with you?"

"Well, my cranky boarder has taken to staying out for dinner a couple of times a week, for which we are all grateful. And I'm being audited by the feds. Other than that, things are quiet."

John looked over at her. "Being audited, huh? That's no fun. They audited after Dad died, made a hell of a mess. Luckily Dad was such a straight shooter there was nothing to find. But it can be tense. Are they auditing you personally or the holding company?"

"It's Holdings. And probably the construction account as well. So Jeff. But Cliff Greening seems optimistic."

"Yeah, he's good. What are they looking for?"

"The down payment for the building. I can't even answer that." She saw John exchange a glance with Brent and sighed. "I know. You asked about it a long time ago. I just don't know." She shrugged. "I've combed through everything looking for information."

John frowned. "You could have asked him." His tone was abrupt.

"I did ask!" Chloe lowered her voice when Davey's head whipped around at her tone. He was sitting on Uncle Brent's knee and they were playing with a couple of Lego figures he'd brought with him.

"I didn't get any answers. I don't know if there were answers that he could give. Ones that would be acceptable. If I lose the building, then so be it. I can't manufacture information."

Vivienne rose to get more coffee. "John, this isn't Chloe's fault, or her doing. It's her responsibility now and she's trying to pick up the pieces, but it wasn't hers when the deed was done."

John's face was dark but he didn't reply. Rosemary reached a hand to stroke his cheek. "It's okay, John. Chloe's doing the best she can, and that's all she can do."

Chloe sat with her mouth open. Had Rosemary just defended her? She looked at Brent who winked. She closed her mouth. After a moment she said, "Thank you, Rosemary. I am doing the best I can. Because Jeff isn't here, because there are no records, because of the earthquake, I don't honestly know what they'll do. It's almost funny."

The conversation had gone on to other things, when Davey said to Brent, "Woss is coming tomorrow. We're having a bike ride and a lunch. It's fun."

"Woss is coming tomorrow, is he? Who's Woss?"

"He's Mummy's friend. He plays with me."

Brent looked over at Chloe who was staring at her son in horror. "Hey, Chloe." Everyone paused in their conversation. "Who's Woss?"

"What do you mean?" Chloe yelped.

"Davey just told me Woss is coming tomorrow. Who's Woss?" Brent grinned, knowing he had everyone's attention.

"Uh," Chloe stalled, looking at all the interested faces. "Ross is the guy who saved us on the Wilkinson Trail last fall, you remember. He came out sometimes to ride the trail with us on his bike, just to make sure we were safe. Didn't he, Davey?"

"Yep. And he likes to play. He brought me a helmet for riding my bike and it gots a light on it too. And he gave us lunch at that place, Mum, what was it?" Davey screwed his face up in confusion.

"At the Wilkinson Cafe." Her cheeks burned.

"Aha!" Brent was grinning again.

"Oh, stop it!" she said crossly. "Don't you start, I'm warning you."

"No, no, but this Ross guy saves you on the trail." Davey nodded and Brent patted him on the head. "Good man, you keep track of what's going on." He looked back at Chloe, "Then he comes out and rides with you to get groceries all the time."

"I didn't say all the time!" Chloe sputtered.

But Davey was nodding, "It's so we're safe. That's why Woss comes. And he likes us." He smiled beatifically up at his uncle. "He likes me and Mummy, too."

"I'll bet he does," Brent nodded. "Sure he does." He grinned at his wife. "And here we were feeling sorry for Chloe, out there by herself...."

"Oh, Brent," Diana laughed. "Stop it. You're the biggest tease. Chloe, you know better than to listen to anything he has to say."

Chloe looked furiously around the room and happened to catch a speculative look in Rosemary's eye. "Don't you even think it!"

She was outwardly outraged, and privately couldn't have been more humiliated. Tears formed in her eyes. "I mean it," she choked. "You stop."

"Hey, hey." Brent moved over onto the sofa beside her, Davey still on his lap. "Come on, Chloe. We have to be able to laugh, just a little bit. Come on, now. I didn't mean anything by it, I was just teasing."

Chloe leaned on his shoulder.

Brent gazed around at the others with a confused look on his face and Davey reached over to pat her head. "Now you've done it," she heard John mutter. When the tears subsided, Vivienne passed her the tissue.

"There you go," her mother said. "Nothing clears the air like a good cry."

The men pulled in their chins. "Sure makes me feel better," Brent muttered.

On the way home, Chloe did feel more cheerful. Maybe her mother was right.

~~~

Ross got there at ten the next morning with creases still pressed into his cheek. He grinned and admitted he'd been short on sleep so had taken the opportunity on his day off to try to catch up. Chloe made him toast and coffee, and Davey sat beside him and chatted about dinner the night before at Nana's house, and about his Uncle Brent and Uncle John.

"He has aunts too," said Chloe.

Davey nodded. "I gots aunts too."

She set out some things to thaw for dinner and cut up vegetables for the evening meal. Davey wanted to ride with him, so the two of them went outside and rode up and down near the house, with Davey's helmet listing to the left at a rakish angle. After a while they came back in. "He's a pretty good rider," he remarked. "But not ready to ride the trail yet, I'm afraid."

"No," Chloe agreed. "He'll be in the bike trailer for a while yet."

They had a good bike ride to the cafe. The little boy got over excited and laughed hysterically as the sandwiches appeared. Chloe took him outside to run completely around the cafe, then back in to go to the washroom. By the time they returned to the table, he was calm enough to eat the rest of his lunch.

Ross thought that was hilarious. "So that's how it's done. You run him ragged for a few minutes, then let him
~~~

take a leak." He snickered. "Does it just work on the little guys?"

Chloe blushed and glanced at her son. "Hard to tell," she said. "If you get out of hand we'll find out."

Ross gave her a grin. "We'll see, will we?"

She laughed at him and Davey joined in.

By the time they were back home, Davey had wound down. Chloe sat him with Plutie and a bowl of popcorn in front of the television and put on Donald Duck.

She turned to Ross. "Would you like coffee? Or do you have to go now?"

He gave her a steady look. "I'd like you," he said. She flushed and he shook his head in embarrassment. "Sorry, Chloe. No, I don't need coffee. Just come here and sit with me for a minute. I need a kiss." He pulled her toward the living room, away from the television noise.

She took his hand and kept going, tugging him along the hallway. When they got to the door to her bedroom, he saw it was dim inside, the blinds still drawn. He went willingly, closing the door softly behind him.

He thought after that it was like a dream, just walking into that dim room and suddenly his hand was on her naked breast and she was pulling him down on top of her, between her legs.

He was inside her and looking into her wide dark eyes as he came. The sweat stuck his shirt to his back, and his breath laboured mightily. They were too slow, he could hear the television in the other room and knew Davey was right there. They were too fast, it was over already.

CHAPTER NINETEEN

The next day the auditors arrived at Chloe's house at eight seventeen in the morning. She opened the door to a little posse on the step. They introduced themselves and she invited them into the living room, offering chairs.

"Now, what's the procedure?" she inquired.

Zeke seemed to be the lead and he leaned forward in his chair, resting his forearms on his bulky briefcase. "We begin with a close look at all documents, then if there appear to be discrepancies we go for a court order. That gives us the right to seize everything and conduct a complete audit. We always hope it won't go that far." He gave a tight smile and Chloe gave one back.

"And why are you here? Wouldn't it make more sense to work with my accountant? I don't want to pay him to come out here whenever you have a question."

Zeke shook his head. "We need to be where the documents are."

"That makes sense," she said. "The documents are at the accountant's office."

Zeke frowned and the other two looked at him. "I understood your office is in your home."

Chloe waved vaguely in the direction of the hall. "It's right there. But none of this business occurred from my office. We've reconstructed whatever we've been able to. Are you aware of the circumstances?"

They looked confused.

"You knew my husband ran this company?"

They nodded in unison.

"Do you know that my husband disappeared at the end of April last year?"

Zeke nodded more slowly, the other two froze.

"He disappeared along with his car and whatever papers he had with him. The car was found burned out in Washington State. He hasn't been found. You'd have to ask the police what evidence they have, they don't share that with me. I wasn't involved in the business until after he left. There were no records, no documents. They disappeared along with my husband. So, what we have are documents I've found after the fact, and they're all at the accountant's. Does that make sense? So perhaps that's where you should be."

Zeke looked longingly down the hall to her office. "What do you have in the office then?"

"Nothing whatever to do with the company. Everything, absolutely everything is at the accountant's office." She felt like a parrot. Just keep saying it over again. On the other hand, Cliff had warned her, as had John. *You cooperate, you bend over backwards.*

"Why don't you come down and have a look?" she suggested. The three leaped to their feet.

She led the way down the hall and opened her office door. Davey was playing Lego in the corner and looked up. "Hi, Mum." He watched the crew behind her. "Who's here?"

"Just some people to see the office." Chloe waved toward the desk.

"That's my laptop. The company laptop is in the hands of the police. So you could go there to see what financial information there might be on it. Any documents you see are for this calendar year, everything else has been given to the accountant to reconstruct the books."

Zeke regretfully backed out the door. "Okay, people. Let's head downtown."

They left as abruptly as they'd arrived. Chloe ran to the phone and called Cliff Greening to warn of their arrival, but he was already prepared.

That night there was another phone call from Jeffrey Sanderson. He was slightly inebriated, but also talkative. Chloe tried to tell him about Davey, what he looked like, what his personality was like. He listened patiently.

What he kept going back to was the money Jeff had used for the down payment on the building. How much was it, how was it paid, in what amounts? Chloe wondered if he was going to claim that it was his, and if she was going to finish this conversation with a debt owed to Jeff's father that she couldn't afford to pay.

But she found copies of the bank documents on her desk and laboured through the details with him. At least he was showing interest in something about Jeff.

Before, she often wondered if he and his son had parted company on such bad terms that the father couldn't get past it to care about his son or the fact that he'd gone missing.

Chloe mentioned that the auditors had arrived and begun work with her accountant. She didn't know how useful it would be, because all they had to work with was an incomplete pile of documents that she'd dug up after the fact. Finally she rang off.

Well, two phone calls from Florida in one week. This was a record.

~~~

Ross and Dan arrived in Edmonton in a blizzard. They suffered ribbing from the other officers about coming from an island in the Pacific, and how tough it must be. They had both spent time at the Edmonton detachment and already knew some of the officers. They were taken into the
~~~

lab and listened to the original recordings of the Dickson - Rainman conversations. When they'd run through the conversations several times, Ross turned to Parker. "What do you make of that? What does it sound like to you?"

"It sounds like Dickson is trying to bully Rain and Rain is keeping his cool."

"Yeah, but what else? I'm thinking it sounds like whatever happened out at the potholes," and here Ross used his fingers to make quotations around the word, "happened because of Dickson, to someone who was a friend of Rain, and Dickson is hoping that Rain's presence during the incident makes him culpable. That way he can pull Rain in tight, and keep a hold on him. What do you say?"

Dan looked doubtful. "If Dickson killed someone and Rain helped him bury the body for instance, or helped him get away. Then Rain gets to share the criminal liability. Something like that?"

"Yeah. So maybe Dickson would like to talk about it. He might think he can shift all the blame onto Rain and save his own skin. Let's go see."

They interrogated Dickson that afternoon. They were back in the same room where Ross first talked to him, the same dented table and chairs, scratched doors and dingy walls.

"Feels like home," were Tom Dickson's opening words.

Ross sat down across from him and motioned Parker to the chair beside his. "Mr. Dickson," he said. "This is Constable Dan Parker, I'm Detective Sergeant Ross Cullen for the record. We're from the Victoria, British Columbia RCMP Detachment and you and I spoke before, some weeks ago."

Dickson leaned back comfortably in his metal chair. "I remember," he smirked. "But I don't appreciate being hauled in here to answer more questions. We had a deal and we signed it. Then I got released on bail. And until I go for trial or get convicted I'm a free man. So what's this about?

The cops come back out and pick me up for no reason? I'm not happy."

"I'm not happy either, Mr. Dickson." Ross leaned forward, all business. "Last time we talked we made a deal."

Dickson frowned. "That's right. It's all signed and sealed. My lawyer saw to that."

"Yes, he did. But there seems to be a problem."

Dickson sat up straight. "Ain't no problem. You agreed to it and you signed. You're stuck with it."

"The deal was that you'd tell us everything you know about a scam concerning selling a fictitious interest in an apartment building. And that included telling us what you know about the other participants. Do you recall that?"

"And I kept my part of the bargain! Now you keep yours, and leave me the fuck alone!" Dickson stood, as if ready to leave.

"Sit down, Mr. Dickson. I don't want to have you restrained."

"Restrained? What the hell!" Dickson sank back in his chair. "What is this? You guys don't have to abide by your own word anymore? I'm calling my lawyer. I got rights."

"You probably should call your lawyer. We have a real problem here. You didn't tell us everything you know."

"I told you everything."

"No, you didn't tell us who Rainman was, or what happened at the Potholes. You held back essential information. So there is no deal."

Dickson blanched. He looked down for a moment and put his hand up to shield his eyes. "Let's see, I told you about Jeff Sanderson and his part in the scam and that I knew about Rainman. I just never met him. He was Jeff's sidekick, not mine. Jeff dealt with him. Yeah, that's about it." He looked sideways at Parker. "That's about it."

"No. That's not it. You spoke to Rainman by phone just a few days ago. You wanted to know how much money he was going to give you to help pay your legal defence. That tells me you know him and you know how to get hold of him."

Dickson's gaze locked with Ross as he sat motionless in his chair. His eyes flicked over to Parker and back again. He licked his lips, then clamped them shut.

"Then you talked to him about what happened at the Potholes. You were quite drunk on the third phone call so you weren't as careful. You talked about whose fault it was that Rainman's friend got hurt."

Ross could see the wheels turning.

Dickson leaped from his chair. "This is a setup. I want to see my lawyer. Right now!"

"Sit down, Dickson."

Dickson paused and sank slowly back into the chair. "I want my lawyer. I'm not talking any more without my lawyer."

"We're holding you for questioning so let's get that call over with."

The lawyer came by the holding cell at three thirty in the afternoon. By five they were back in the interview room. Ross introduced everyone for the recording and settled back in his chair, Parker at his side. Parker went over the former agreement and why it was now void. The lawyer made token protests but had to agree. Then they got down to what Dickson knew about Rainman.

Dickson said he wanted to make a clean breast of it. Rainman had called a meeting.

Ross interrupted. "How do you know Rainman?"

Dickson looked surprised. "He and Jeff worked together. If you were going to do business with Jeff, you had Rainman as part of the deal. His specialty was processing the money. That's what he did, and Jeff didn't. They thought it was safer that way, a division of labour. Kind of communistic, if you will." Dickson smirked, obviously comfortable again.

"What was Rainman's real name?"

"Huh? Uh, well, I just know Rainman. That's all he's ever called."

Parker leaned forward. "Is this Rainman?" And he fanned out a half dozen photos on the table between them, the best of what they'd garnered from bank surveillance. It showed Bob Humphreys - Troy Smith in various poses, sometimes with dark hair, sometimes with bleached blond hair.

Dickson leaned forward and examined them. "Well, I dunno." He pawed through them. "This one is him. I don't know about the rest. Although," and he pointed to another one, "That could be him, but what's with the tooth? Anyway, this one is definitely him."

The photo showed a good full frontal of Bob Humphreys with dark hair cut short and brushed back off his face. Parker shuffled the photos together, that one on top.

Ross started again. "What kind of business did Sanderson do?"

"He had a construction business, which seemed to be on the up and up. And he was interested in this scam idea."

"Whose idea was the scam?"

"That was mine. I tried it on my own and knew I needed a sidekick, someone to close the deal. That was Jeff."

"How did you meet Jeff?"

"In a bar. He was always hanging around, throwing out ideas. I pulled him aside one day and bounced a few things off him. He was intrigued and the rest is history, as they say." Dickson grinned, looking very relaxed.

"So, back to the meeting at the Potholes."

"Right. So Rainman called the meeting. He was doing some business out near there anyway and he needed to talk to Jeff and me. Rainman didn't meet in town or coffee shops and bars or whatever. He kept a very low profile. So he suggested the Potholes."

"Are we talking about the Sooke Potholes, northwest of Victoria?"

"Yeah, that's it."

"Okay. When was this?"

"Uh, like, do you mean the day of the week?"

"No, the date. When was it?"

"Well." Dickson gazed at the wall for a minute. "I don't know, must have been the first of May, something like that. I don't really remember."

"How did you get there?"

"Jeff and I travelled out together in his car. Rainman met us there."

Ross looked at Parker, so Dan stepped it to continue. "Did you meet in the parking lot?"

"No. Rainman didn't like to be seen with us in case someone remembered. He was very careful. So he told us to hike up the trail and meet him at the top of the falls. I didn't know where that was but Jeff did, so I followed him."

"What happened?"

For the first time Dickson looked uncertain. "We walked up the trail and met Rainman."

"Describe where you met."

Dickson hitched his chair forward and leaned an elbow on the table. "If you go up the trail it kind of peters out. You follow a faint path that goes back into the woods but circles around to the top of the falls. Rainman was sitting on a stump waiting for us. He saw us first because he was just sitting still and it was raining pretty hard."

"What time of day?"

"Just after lunch, about two thirty."

"Okay. Go on."

"Rainman hailed us and we walked over to talk to him. He was absolutely drenched, we all were. It was raining buckets. I complained about being wet and Rainman called me a pussy which really ticked me off. I'm no pussy, I just like to stay dry. So we walked back under the shelter of the trees near the river at the top of the falls and talked."

"What were you talking about? What was the meeting about?"

"It was about laundering money. How were we going to cash the cheque and get the money without it being traced back to us? Rainman was mad. He said he didn't do stuff like this, it was stupid to get involved in it. He said it was too hard to stay in the shadows and on like that. But he had lots of ideas, he was the idea man for that part of the scam."

Dickson paused and glanced around cautiously at the faces before him, then seemed to come to some decision. He took a deep breath. "We were just talking and then suddenly Jeff slipped. He kind of stumbled and his boot slipped on the rocks and he fell into the river. Just went head first down the falls. We both yelled and I ran and tried to grab his jacket but I couldn't reach him and he disappeared."

There was silence for a moment. Then Parker took over. "When did you next see him?"

"I didn't! I never saw him again! He was gone. Down the falls and gone. Those Potholes are a mess. You can't find nothin' once it hits the water. There are so many pools and so much swirling water, you never see anything again." Dickson pursed his mouth and drummed his fingers on the table. "That was it. Never saw him again."

Parker waited but he volunteered nothing more.

Ross got up and walked to the door, tapped on it lightly. "We'll take a ten minute break."

Standing by the coffee urn, he stirred his cup thoughtfully. "What do you think, Dan?"

One of the things Parker liked most about working with Ross was it wasn't all orders. Ross liked to pick his brains and he appreciated it. It gave him a chance to air his own theories.

"Well, it could have happened that way. But it doesn't gibe with what Rainman said in the cell phone conversation, or what Dickson said for that matter. There was real blame to be spread during that phone call. And here Dickson is claiming an accident. So what happened then? Why the dead dog, the burned car, a record of Sanderson travelling back into Canada a few days after he's dead? Too much doesn't add up."

Ross grinned. "Exactly," was all he said. "Let's phone in, see if the officers have been out to the Murdoch farm again with the photographs. See what's cooking there."

Parker got on the phone while Ross went for a chat with the commanding officer at the detachment. He came back in a good mood. "They're going to keep Dickson in for questioning. Maybe we can get some cooperation in having him contact Rainman, try to pull him in for a meeting with Dickson. Any news?"

"Revenue Canada is conducting an audit of Sanderson Holdings and Sanderson's construction company. Just started today apparently." Ross simply nodded, and hoped to hell his neck wasn't as red as it felt. This was not news to him.

"And the officers are back from the Murdoch farm. The folks were pretty hesitant, tried to pretend they didn't recognize him at first but then the father confirmed. The photos are all of his son, although he said the blond hair and crooked tooth would have thrown him off if he wasn't looking closely."

Ross took the photos and leafed through them again. "Yeah, you know, that tooth was a stroke of genius. This is one smart man. And never meets in public, not even coffee shops. He means business but not in a tough guy way, in a smart guy way. Must be lonely, though."

Dan gave him a strange look but made no reply

Back in the interview room, Ross put it to Dickson. They wanted him to phone Rainman and arrange a face to face meeting. It looked like Rainman was heading east from Vancouver, but they didn't know how far he'd gotten by now. Ross was of the opinion he would be taking the time to get rid of his truck and provide himself a different vehicle. That should slow him down a bit.

Mc Lean hemmed and hawed. He wanted his deal back if he was going to cooperate that way.

Ross appeared to ponder that. "The question is, have you told us everything you know?"

Mc Lean thought a moment. "Only that we walked down the river looking for Sanderson. We thought it was possible he'd crawled out on the bank farther down but we didn't see him. At one point I jumped into the water because I thought I saw his jacket but it wasn't him. Had a heck of a time getting back out."

"What happened to his car?"

Mc Lean looked blank for a minute. Then his colour darkened. "Let's see. I drove it back to town but didn't want to have it in my driveway, didn't know exactly where to leave it. So I took the ferry to the mainland." He looked Ross right in the eye. "I went across the border to the States at Blaine and got rid of it down there."

Ross stared back. "How did you get rid of it?"

Dickson flushed. "I drove it to an isolated spot and torched it."

Ross waited.

He fidgeted.

"Go on," said Ross.

"Go on, nothing. That's it. I burned it."

"Now, why would you do that?"

Dickson was breathing heavily. "I didn't want the car around my place, like I told you. So I took it away and burned it."

"Hmm. What do you think, Constable Parker? He goes to all that trouble, crosses the American Border and burns the car. What does that say to you?"

Dan pulled at his lower lip. "It's odd. That's all I can say, damned odd."

"Odd?" Mc Lean sounded aggressive and his lawyer laid a restraining hand on his arm.

"Calm down, Tom, or you're going to blow this." The expression on the lawyers' face said it all, he'd already blown it.

Dickson sat back in his chair and huffed for a minute. "I burned it because I didn't want my finger prints to be found on the car. I didn't want to be connected to it in any way."

"Sounds like a big reaction. I mean, Jeff's death was an accident. He fell. Simple as that. And here you drive his car to the ferry, carry on to Blaine, enter the States as Jeff Sanderson. Where did you get the ID?"

"Jeff left it in the car. He always did that." He grated his thumb nail along a groove in the table top. "I just panicked. We were doing something that was illegal and then someone died. I panicked." He looked up, triumphant.

"So you burn the car. How did you manage that?"

"Siphoned some gas out of the tank onto the upholstery. Lit it on fire. Tossed in the keys and the siphon. Walked out to the road and on down to the nearest little town."

"Must have taken some time."

"Yeah, it took time. It was about a five hour walk. But I managed okay."

They talked round and round the timing. Mc Lean started to sweat. He wiped his forehead and caught the trickle running down in front of his ear.

Finally Parker commented, "Doesn't sound like panic to me. Too planned, you know?" He looked at Ross. "Panic is more confusion and adrenaline and spur of the moment. Not much confusion here. This sounds methodical and orderly. As if you had a real plan, a purpose."

"I did have a purpose!" He was breathing heavily. His lawyer leaned forward and suggested a break.

Ross stood up. "Good idea." They stepped outside.

The lawyer followed a few minutes later. "It's time to wrap it up for the day. I have to go, so we won't be able to question him further tonight. However my client is willing to try to contact Rainman by cell phone. He says he can probably get him to agree to a meeting. Is that useful?"

Ross nodded.

The lawyer held up his hand. "What does he get in exchange for his cooperation? I don't like to see him getting deeper in trouble for your benefit alone. That's not how the system works, officers."

"No, you're right. And if he leveled with us, we'd have a deal, but he doesn't."

"I think he is."

"Not from what other information we have. Not by a long shot." Ross gave him a hard stare. "Maybe you should tell your client that."

~~~

Mc Lean tried to reach Rainman by phone but there was no answer. They waited twenty minutes and then tried. Again no answer. They agreed to come back later that night and try once more. He was taken to a holding cell.

Ross and Dan went for a bite to eat with one of Parker's buddies and spent some time deciding what Dickson should say when he got Rainman on the phone. They were back at the cells at nine thirty, gathered in the interview room and tried again. No answer.

In his hotel room, Ross tried Chloe's cell but she didn't pick up. He left a message and lay on the bed staring at the television screen. They were close, so close. As soon as they got back, they'd interview James Dolan again about the equipment at his house and organize a drag of the Sooke River from the waterfalls down, through the Potholes if necessary, and out to the ocean. He hoped they found something. It was too much to carry on with this ghost hanging over everyone.

People did, of course. He knew of a couple of cases just in the Victoria area where the answers were never found. The families limped along trying to put it behind them but having it resurface all the time, hovering like a dark bird of prey looking for any show of weakness. They never knew if their loved one was dead or still alive. They didn't know if they should be praying for a soul released from its body, for someone who'd been kidnapped and was still held hostage or even someone who had left of their own accord out of estrangement or mental illness. It was a desperate way to live.
~~~

He watched part of a hockey game, then muted the sound and tried Chloe's phone again. Still no answer.

He wondered idly what Rainman did with his money now that Jeff was gone, because almost certainly Jeff had been the one who put the money to work. That had to be how the down payment for the building was arranged. Without Jeff, Rainman had money but nowhere to spend it other than on himself. And he didn't live that kind of lifestyle.

He didn't drink in bars and go out to nightclubs, living the high life with expensive women and fast cars. He was the clever one. He needed Jeff. Jeff ran the construction end and the money got put to use. That must be how it had worked. Rainman must have a truck full of cash.

Next morning early they were back in the interview room. Rainman answered on the fourth ring. Dickson was sweating before they even started to talk.

"Hello."

"Hey, Rainman."

"Dickson."

"How you doing buddy?"

"Not bad."

"Listen, I didn't hear from you so got kind of worried." Dickson had instructions to keep him talking as long as possible so the position locator could be used effectively.

"You don't have to worry, man. Where are you?"

"I'm sitting at home. Just wondered where you are and when you might be able to get that money to me."

"Pretty soon. It's not a problem." A pause. "Where did you say you were?"

"I'm just here on my couch, waiting to hear from you."

Ross had a stunned moment of insight. Rainman was sitting outside Dickson's house, he'd bet his future on it. He tore out of the interview room and motioned the guard over. "Get me a phone, direct to the detachment. Now."

He sent a plain clothes team to Dickson's house but was sure it'd be too late. Rain Murdoch was so smart, he'd be gone in a flash. When he returned to the interview room, Dickson was sitting with his head down, the phone in his hand.

He looked over at Parker.

"He's gone. Said he had an emergency and would get back to him. He hung up. No location, no meeting."

When the plain clothes team reported back, no vehicle was sitting outside and no one had seen a vehicle. Was there a back alley? Yes, there was.

Ross and Dan met and decided to try one more time. They couldn't hold the man for questioning much longer. They didn't have murder and they didn't even have manslaughter unless they got Rain Murdoch to tell his side of the story.

And they had to get to Murdoch before they could get his story. That might take a while. He was proving alarmingly elusive. Ross was convinced they didn't know what he was driving or what name he might be using. He could have red hair by now and a goatee with fake overbite teeth, a pair of rimless glasses and a Viking's ring in his ear.

And he didn't suffer from a lack of money. It was going to be very difficult.

But at the end of the day, they couldn't shake Dickson's version of the story of how Sanderson died. They headed back to Victoria with empty hands.

CHAPTER TWENTY

Rainier drove down an Airdrie, Alberta, side street and pulled his muddy brown 1995 Datsun four-door into the curb. He waited with the motor running. He hadn't called his sister beforehand because he didn't know which phones might be tapped. It was best not to take chances.

He could tell someone was home. The lights were on and he saw shadows moving about the kitchen. He'd wait. Meantime he scanned the street and side street for surveillance cars, but saw nothing that raised an alarm. He turned off the engine.

Finally his sister came out of the house, tugging her coat on. Susan worked nights, four on, three off. It was tough on the family but they were paying down some big student loans and saving for a house. They thought it was worth it.

Rain climbed out of his car and walked along the sidewalk to intercept her at the curb. "Hey, sis."

She gasped and whirled around. "Rain!" She ran to give him a hug, banging his arm with her huge carry bag. "What are you doing here? Why didn't you call to let us know you were coming?" She stepped back to get a good look at him. "You look different. Your hair, it's way lighter."

"I know." He ran his hand over his close cropped head. "Just a phase I'm going through," he grinned. "How are you?"

"Okay. It's so good to see you. But I have to run or I'll be late for work. Why don't you go in for a visit with Darrell? I'll be home about four and we can catch up tomorrow morning."

"I can't, sis. I've got a schedule to keep. Listen, it's good to see you. I wanted to leave something with you. It's in my car."

"Alright," she said doubtfully. "You really can't stay the night and have a visit? It's been so long. Mum and Dad are worried about you."

His head turned swiftly. "How do you mean?"

"They phoned to ask if I'd heard from you. You usually call them and you haven't called. Plus the police have been around asking a lot of questions. Last time they came they brought pictures and asked them to identify you. It scared them. What's going on, Rain? Are you in trouble?"

"Maybe, sis," he said. "I'm not sure. Here, this is what I want to give you." He pulled a duffel bag out of the trunk and took it over to her car. "This is for the folks. You're not to give it to them until summer. You understand? It's a surprise. There's a letter in there for them, they'll understand. But not till summer. Can you do that for me?"

"Sure. You know I can. What's going on? You're scaring me, Rain. What kind of trouble are you in?"

"Nothing that can't be fixed. I love you, you've always been the best big sister. Now, you take care of your little family and I'll see you soon. Okay? Don't worry, just take good care. And this is for you. Don't use it for about a month, then have Darrell's folks deposit it in their bank account and give you a cheque, so it won't be a problem." He leaned down and kissed her cheek. "Take good care, sis. See you soon."

He turned and walked rapidly away so he didn't have to see her tears.

~~~

Ross arrived back in Victoria with a massive headache and severely sleep deprived. He thought he was either a little cranky or simply ready to rip the head off the next person to cross him.

He dropped Parker at home and rode the cab to his townhouse. Dragging his suitcase through the door, he threw it into the hallway. It gouged a hole in the hardwood. He roared with rage and kicked it across the floor.

A head popped out of the living room. "Welcome home, little bro."

He gaped in astonishment, then put a hand to his throbbing head. "What the hell are you doing here?"

"They told me you were due back this morning so I took a chance that you'd be calling in at home before getting to work." Bob looked pointedly at the suitcase lying on its side. "Offended you, did it?"

Turning around, he headed for the bathroom. "I've got one bitch of a headache. Give me a minute." He rummaged in the medicine cabinet until he found a bottle of painkillers, then popped four and took a long drink of water. He stared at himself in the mirror as he refilled the glass. He looked like hell, big shadows under red-rimmed eyes. What the fuck was Bob doing here?

Back out in the hallway, his brother was still standing at the door waiting for him.

Ross huffed with exasperation. "Well? Obviously something brought you out here." He stomped into the kitchen. "I know I gave you a key," he tossed back over his shoulder, "But that was to check on the place when I'm away, not drop in uninvited."

He turned in the noon light from the kitchen window to face him. "What's up?"

"Pretty edgy," Bob frowned at him. "How'd it go in Edmonton?"
~~~

He blew a breath through flared nostrils. "All kinds of ways, every direction imaginable. This is one clever character and we only have half the story from the other guy."

Bob pulled out one of the kitchen chairs and plunked himself down. "Tell me about it."

They talked for more than an hour. Ross always welcomed his brother's insights, infused with his greater experience. When they wound up, he realized his headache was on the mend. Rising, he went to the fridge. "Would you like a drink?"

"Yeah, you got a soda?"

He pulled two off the shelf and handed one to his brother. "So what's new with you? You working today?"

Bob nodded. "Actually I'm on shortly, just taking a break. Sit down. I have a few more questions for you."

He raised his brows. "You got a case that borders on this one?"

"Kind of."

He seated himself and popped the top on the can, taking a long swallow. "Okay, shoot."

"How long have you been seeing Ms Bowman?"

Ross choked on his soda and spewed fluid across the table. "What? What kind of question is that?" He leaped to his feet, fists clenched. "By God, Bob, you've gone too far now. Get out. Go on, get out of my house." He was furious, trembling with emotion. He turned away, trying to control himself. "Get out," he breathed. "Get out before I hit you. I swear, this is too much."

Bob said nothing, waited.

He turned around and ground his teeth. "Bob, get out!"

"I'm not going anywhere. Sit down and talk to me. Someone saw you. You were with her and her little boy down in Chinatown. It was one of our guys and he came straight to me. I told him it was part of the investigation but totally confidential. He wasn't to tell another soul. He said he hadn't because it looked too bad. He told me because we were friends and he thought I should know. For your sake, Ross."

He stared at his brother, heat climbing his neck.

Bob continued. "The officer said you looked totally besotted. You were chatting with the little boy and holding his hand, and you had your hand at her back helping her through the door. If you weren't looking at her face, you were looking at her chest. He did confirm that it was a chest worthy of a second look. She laughed at something you said and you looked, well, I don't know what the word is. Infatuated."

He averted his gaze. His face was florid, his jaw inflexible, his clenched fists braced aggressively on his thighs.

Bob gave him an appraising glance. "What's going on?"

He looked back at him helplessly.

"Come on, Ross. This isn't like you. You're single minded, you're a hard worker, you're a clever guy. This isn't clever. I want to know what's going on. Have you lost your mind?"

He looked at his fists as if he had never seen them before, then slowly unclenched them, flexing his fingers one by one. Helplessly he gazed at his brother. "I'm in love with her."

Bob sighed. After a minute he ground out, "I was afraid of that. I couldn't think what would make you do something so stupid."

Ross let that go.

"It is stupid, you know."

He nodded. "I'm well aware of that fact." He turned his face away, staring sightlessly out the window.

Bob examined his palms for a minute, turned his ring on his finger a few times. "What are you going to do?"

"Well, for starters I've been trying to find out what happened to her husband. I mean, it sounds crass but if he's dead, well..." Ross shrugged. "If he's dead, then there's a chance for me. Maybe not today, but sometime. And for another, I've been trying to put this case to rest because as long as it's open, we can't see each other. Theoretically." He slid a glance at his brother.

Bob snorted inelegantly. "Theoretically speaking, are you screwing her?"

The colour rose again in his face.

Bob grunted." Of course you are. Did she play the helpless female –my husband's gone, I can't manage, and please don't suspect me in all this? Or did you jump in as the rescuing hero? You know that some of the firemen from the 9/11 disaster in New York ended up leaving their wives and marrying the widows. They were still rescuing." Bob shook his head in disbelief.

"I've thought about that."

Bob turned his head slowly toward his brother.

"I mean, I heard that story too, and I thought about that. But it's not like that. I spent my time at Victim Services just like you did. And I could see the pain and loss and sometimes the hopelessness of those people, mostly women. And it was hard to see. But this is different."

He opened his mouth and closed it again. "It's just... different. I love her." His arms tensed against the table top as he sank back into his chair. "I mean, I miss her so much when I can't see her. And my chest is tight when I think about her. And Davey. He's the cutest little guy, and clever. He sees and remembers everything."

His eyes lit up. "He even remembered a comment his father made about Rainman, the partner we've been trying to track down. He's very observant."

Bob smiled slightly, then gave a short laugh. "Well, you're hooked for sure. I can see that. So what to do about it?" He pinched the bridge of his nose.

"Have you told Dad?"

Bob slanted him a look. "Are you kidding? He'd be sitting outside your door roaring for blood with a loaded shotgun in his hands. I haven't told a soul. Believe me, Ross, no one can know." He thought a minute. "Well, what are the ground rules? You can't go anywhere with her. Nowhere. I can see from your face you've been going places with her. You can't!"

"Yeah, I know. I know."

"Okay, so you can't go anywhere with her. You can't phone her from work or on your cell phone. Do you hear me? Only from home, or better still a throwaway phone. The best scenario is not to see her. Could you do that? Tell her the investigation and the rest of your work load is so intense right now you can't take the time to see her."

Ross looked belligerent.

"I know," his brother said. "Pretty tough."

They both looked out the window for a bit. "You know she'll probably break it off when you find Sanderson, alive or dead. She'll have to process it and it won't happen with you on the scene, plus it makes her look bad. And she'll have a problem with that."

Ross's jaw bulged. "I'm aware of that. It's one reason I haven't cut it off because I know she'll want to do it herself soon. It's pretty hard to face, frankly. It's helping to drive me crazy."

They exchanged a sympathetic look. "Yeah. I remember with my wife."

Ross choked out a laugh. "She gave you an easy time, you lucky bastard."

Bob grinned. "Well, it wasn't that easy. But yeah, we both knew right off what we wanted to do."

"No pun intended," Ross chipped in.

Bob laughed at that and flashed him a look. "No pun intended." He whistled tunelessly through his teeth for a second. "Okay. Well, let's get this case put to bed. Go over the main points again, then we'll focus on what can be done immediately."

~~~

Dragging the Sooke River was a perilous job that involved police divers and draggers for miles up and down from the Potholes. They started at the falls and moved from
~~~

there through the heavy mist on down the body of water. Most of the bottom was too uneven to be dragged and the divers had to go down with headlamps and do a visual search.

The Potholes themselves posed a different problem. The sides of the holes were fiercely steep, allowing no purchase for the divers and the water moved so fast and furiously through the gorges they needed a different solution.

They ran long lines anchored on the bank and the divers methodically moved from hole to hole, searching every crevice. On the second day, there was a hail from the watchers on the bank. They'd found something in the fast moving waters. When it came up it was a child's jacket, caught in a crack of rock at the bottom.

False alarm. The search continued. Ross was stretched to his limit. He hadn't seen Chloe and Davey since before his trip to Edmonton. His brother's visit had given him pause, and he was thankful for Bob's way of handling it. He hadn't liked it but he'd needed it. Someone had to yank his chain and who better than the brother he trusted and respected. He could talk about the case with him now, knowing that he understood how much it meant to put it to bed. So to speak.

He bought a throw away phone and gave the number to Chloe. He called her a couple of times but it was so painful to talk to her knowing he couldn't see her, it was almost easier to just keep working. On the fourth day, word came back that something had been found - a body, or at least body parts.

They found a leather jacket caught in the branches of a submerged tree in the river bed close to the mouth of the river. It was in a back eddy, without much vigour to the wash of the water. Most of the bones were intact. They were hauling it in and Ross could see it first thing in the morning. He cleared his desk and headed out of the detachment office.

They had the final transcripts of the interviews with Dickson and Ross couldn't find it in his heart to go over it again. He handed it off to Parker, along with the information from Jimmy Dolan's computer programmes. There was a list of pieces of identification that he'd produced that he needed Dan to go through, primarily by date. What had been produced from the time they caught on to Rainman as Troy Smith, until the time they arrested Jim Dolan? It might give them insight into what alias Rainman was currently using.

He went straight to the gym, put on a pair of headphones with Collective Soul pounding out the beat and did a punishing workout that took most of the early evening. Then he stopped for a quick bite to eat at the neighbourhood Vietnamese place and went to the theatre, buying a ticket for the next movie to start.

He entered and sat near the back. He thought he might doze but actually got caught up in a surprisingly good plot and felt refreshed when he walked back out. He had achieved some distance for a moment. He wasn't so tightly tied up in the case. He might even sleep tonight.

~~~

Chloe called Florida after the boarders left for the day and she delivered Davey to daycare. She'd received a third call from Jeff's dad, a message left on her voice mail while she was out. Again, he hadn't sounded too sober.

She grimaced. What would it be like to live with someone who was drunk every night? Must be pretty tough for Mrs Sanderson. The phone rang a few times and Alice answered.

"Hello, Alice? This is Chloe Bowman calling from Victoria, Canada. How are you doing?"

"Fine." The women's voice sounded guarded.

"I'm glad to hear that. Last time I talked to Jeffrey, he mentioned that you were having a hard time since Jeff disappeared. I'm so sorry."

"Yes, it's been tough. You have no idea."

Well, actually I do. She let the silence drag, she was so aggravated with that comment. Finally she said, "Is Jeffrey there? He called last night and I wasn't home. So I'm returning his call."
~~~

"He did?" Alice seemed to think about that. "He's just gone down to the store. I'll tell him when he gets back. Thanks for calling." She hung up rather abruptly.

Chloe spent the next hour gathering her own bank documents the auditors had asked for. Cliff Greening had said she didn't need to produce these personal items as the audit was of the company.

But when she agreed to bring them in, he said, "Good girl. The more we cooperate, the less likely they'll come back for a full audit. They'll know there isn't anything else to find. You have no idea how unhappy that can be. They come into your house and simply scoop everything and take it away. They don't care if you need it right then or not. Very nasty. I've seen them empty file cabinets into garbage bags, and you get it back in the same horrible condition. Because there's no actual source of documents in this case, they're going to have to make decisions based on what they can lay their hands on."

Chloe thought he was being optimistic. She snapped an elastic around another batch of cheques, then started on her credit card accounts. The phone rang. It was Jeffrey Sanderson returning her call.

"Hello, Chloe. Thanks for calling back." His voice lowered. "Alice didn't know I'd called you, so it shook her up a bit. Sorry about that."

"Oh, that's no problem, Jeffrey. How are you doing?"

"Well, thanks for asking. I'm doing a bit better. It makes me feel good to talk to you. Maybe it's because you saw Jeff in the last few years and we didn't. But it eases my heart. How is your little boy doing today?"

Still that non-relationship status for her son. She reined in her patience and tried to sound warm and friendly. This was Davey's grandfather, the only one he had. "He's doing pretty well. He's at daycare today. He goes three days a week and loves it. He's very social, just like Jeff. And now that he's five, it's probably time to give him more play time with other children."

Jeffrey listened, and Chloe rambled on a bit. "That's nice," he said when she stopped. "That's real nice. He sounds like a good little guy. Maybe we'll get to see him sometime."

This was the first offer Chloe had heard and she dove right in. "Yes, I'd love it if you could meet him. Maybe some time when you're travelling in this direction. I won't be doing any travel for a while, I guess."

"Yes, it sounds like you won't be able to afford it, what with auditors and such. That's really why I called. You gave me good information last time I talked to you and I've been thinking about it. I gave Jeff a ton of money in the last year or two before he disappeared and I think that's what he used for the down payment on your building. You said about six hundred thousand dollars. Canadian, of course. Well, I can surely come up with a record of that much."

Chloe's mouth opened and then closed but no sound came out.

"Hello," he said, "are you there? I might have lost you."

"No," she squeaked. "I'm here." She cleared her throat. "That's a lot of money, Jeffrey. The auditors would want proof that you gave that to Jeff. They're combing through everything here, and there's no record of a sum like that coming through any of the accounts. I'm not sure how…" She trailed off.

"I don't think it'll be a problem," he said. "I told Jeff to use an American bank, and he said he had one in Washington State. Maybe near Seattle, I don't remember. He could bring it up in cash if he wanted, I guess. No record of that. I don't know what he did. I just know he took the money. I can write up a letter to give details. What's your address, so I can get it to you?"

Chloe reeled off her mailing address and hung up in a daze. What had just happened? As far as she knew, Jeff was barely in touch with his folks. She'd suggest they call or send a picture of Davey, and he'd brush her off.

Would the auditors be satisfied with this? She put her hand to her forehead and tried to think. Better call Cliff Greening.

Cliff was disbelieving at first.

"That's how I felt," said Chloe. "These people barely know I'm alive and they have no interest in Davey whatsoever. But he says he gave Jeff that much money and likely that's what supplied the down payment. If he sends the documents, and that's a big 'if', do you think the auditors will accept that? Will that satisfy them?"

Greening was silent for a moment. "I honestly don't have a clue. I've never had a case like this. Let me knock it around with my colleagues, see if anyone has any suggestions. If it comes, call me right away and I'll let you know if we come up with anything from this end."

~~~

Today was a day at home with no one to look after, just her. That hardly ever happened and Chloe wasn't used to the extreme quiet in the house. Usually there was noise, Davey chattering, Plutie playing with him. She'd called Ross to let him know she was home alone for the day but he'd been almost too busy to talk. She let him go, and made plans for a day by herself.

She put some music on and pulled out her list. There was some baking and prep work for dinners for the rest of the week. She had a few busy days coming up. The hostel needed some of her time and she was meeting with the maintenance people for the building. There was a list of things that needed attention, drainage basins to be pumped, the roof checked. The windows hadn't been washed in the year they'd owned the building, the parking lines on the older part of the parking lot were entirely worn away.

Her mind left the list and wandered back to Ross. Would he like to meet for lunch? She could take him to the sushi place. It was quiet there and they could eat in a booth for privacy. She called him again but there was no answer and no message service. He'd changed his phone number.
~~~

She missed him, especially when she went to bed at night. She had to be really tired or she didn't sleep. She'd hear noises in the night, even with the boarders in the house. Or she'd imagine a tap on her bedroom door but there was never anyone there. She hadn't seen him since he took them down the trail for lunch at the cafe and then came into her bedroom while Davey watched cartoons.

They shouldn't have done that. But she'd wanted him so much, it was so intense to be with him. And she still wanted him with a bone deep ache. But he was busy and a little distant right now. Maybe things had changed. Maybe he'd moved on and she was hanging onto something that didn't exist anymore.

A tear leaked from the corner of her eye and she bent over her list. She wouldn't jump to conclusions, she was the one who'd thought they should stop seeing each other. It was dangerous for both of them.

She paid a visit to Jayde, who was deep into the manufacture of table centrepieces for Will's wedding. She had small plastic containers spread all over her table with squares of dense florists foam crammed into each one. Sprigs of lavender, baby's breath and other dried flowers were scattered about.

"See this," she said. "Eucalyptus is fabulous for this kind of thing and Will's girlfriend really likes it."

"What's her name again, Jayde? I don't think you told me."

"It's Jasmine. Imagine that. Someone calling their child Jasmine. Mind you, she's pretty cute, kind of suits her. People name their kids anything at all, it seems. I remember once I took Jannine to see a children's programme at the Royal Theatre when she was little. The guy running the show had a list of names of kids who were having a birthday that week and he called them up to get a balloon. Anyway, one of the little girls was called Blueberry Sunshine. Can you imagine? What if you had to go through your life with a name like that?"

Jayde pressed her lips together in disapproval and Chloe couldn't help but laugh. She loved coming here. "Did I tell you I'm being audited by Revenue Canada?"

Jayde paused. "Well, you did say they'd written to give you notice but I didn't know they'd arrived."

"They came this week, Monday morning. Wanted to see everything I've ever done in my life."

Jayde laughed. "Yes, I imagine that's what they'll want. What do you think will happen? What with the earthquake and all, and Jeff disappearing, it's not surprising you can't come up with the paperwork. Do they understand that?"

Chloe shrugged. "I just keep giving them everything they ask for if I have it, and go from there. My accountant is working with them to try to answer questions, so I'm relying on him. I don't know anything."

Jayde gave her a piercing look. "Chloe, don't worry. It'll probably work out fine. We both know Jeff didn't share information. You've told me that before. So what will be, will be, I guess. There isn't much you can do to change it, is there? So worrying would be a waste of time. And you don't have time to waste.

"Here, help me with this. What do you think? Shall we have all dried flowers, or use the dried ones as backdrop and add some fresh ones into the mix? It's going to be almost spring. I imagine the daffodils will be out. But daffs aren't a good choice for this. Probably carnations or something."

When Chloe got home she was in a good mood. The best since they spent the day with Ross. She pushed that thought away and started dinner. She'd finish gathering her credit card accounts after dinner and take them in when she and Davey went to town tomorrow. They were spending the afternoon with Vivienne and having dinner at Uncle Brent and Aunt Diana's. Davey was pumped.

CHAPTER TWENTY ONE

John got back into his office late. It had been another heavy day, construction was going slower than planned. There was a chronic shortage of decent grades of plywood and oriented strand board. The common replacement products used in the industry didn't have the strength and resistance to water that plywood had and it was stretching their creativity to find ways to get the construction done.

His carpenters were good, the labourers not so much. Most of the labour had come from out of town because of the offer of big wages, and they were fed up with the living conditions. The hostel served its purpose but only for a limited time. Then he sent the guys back home. There was no future in keeping them here longer.

They started fights, got belligerent on the job, things simply fell apart. The weeks were sixty to seventy hours long. The guys were damned tired when they went home and that was a bonus because it kept the number of fights down.

Mike LaTorre had turned out to be a good straw boss. He kept order with a genial face and an iron fist. The first guy he bounced had set the tone for the rest of them and things had settled down to a dull roar. But he had to send that message again every so often to keep everyone in line. He thought Maria must be tired of it, yet she had a calming influence especially on the younger men.

He sifted through the messages on his desk, putting aside those he'd get back to before he went home. Then one caught his eye, a call from Detective Sergeant Ross Cullen, RCMP.

John felt an immediate frisson of alarm. Was this the Ross that Davey had been talking about the other night? That made him perk up. He quickly dialled the number. Cullen answered on the second ring.

"This is John Bowman, returning your call."

"Thank you for calling, Mr. Bowman. We have a situation here that I wanted to talk to you about."

"Go ahead. Is it about my sister Chloe, or something else?"

"Yes, it's about Ms. Bowman. We've found a body and made a positive identification for Jeff Sanderson. We're ready to inform Ms. Bowman but we wanted to make sure there was a family member with her. Since you came in for her police interviews, we thought you might be the person to be there when she receives the news."

John took a deep breath, and his voice shook slightly. "You've found Jeff Sanderson?"

"Yes, we have. We have identification from his dental records, and although we'll be doing DNA tests as well, I don't see the need to wait. The dental record match is a hundred percent. And Ms. Bowman has been waiting long enough to get the news."

"So, he's dead."

"Yes, sir. He is."

John didn't know what to say. He rubbed his jaw, feeling the bristles scratching his palm. "I'm kind of lost for words."

"Yes, I can imagine. We thought someone should be there with Ms. Bowman when the police arrive. Would that person be you, or is there someone else we should call?"

"No, that would be me."

"Well, perhaps you need some time to gather yourself before we set this in motion."

"Are you talking about right now?" John looked down at his work clothes, dusty from the day, his dinged up steel-toed boots. Well, Chloe had seen him like that many times before.

"If you can't manage it now, we can arrange for a later time. But I find it's best to get the word out as soon as we know. That way there's no hint that we're holding back information. Family members have usually been waiting longer than they ever thought they'd be able to, so we like to let them know as soon as decently possible." Cullen's' voice was very formal.

"That's for sure. Okay. Well, I'll just call my wife and get myself out there. Can you give me an hour?"

"An hour is fine, Mr. Bowman. No rush."

"Will you be there yourself, Detective Cullen?"

"No, Constable Dan Parker and Constable Cheryl LeClerc will be the ones coming out. We try not to make a circus of it, and Ms. Bowman has dealt with both of these officers before. I think she'll be comfortable with them, if comfort is possible under these circumstances. But with you there, at least she'll have some family. You can ride out with them if you prefer."

"No. No, I'll go in my own car. I'll probably be staying longer. How did he die?"

"We aren't releasing that information just yet. However, I can say he's probably been dead from the time he disappeared. This is not a recent death."

"Was he murdered?"

"I can't say at this time. All we can really do is let her know that we've found her husband's body. There're still a lot of questions to be answered."

"Right. Okay, I'm glad you called me and didn't just go out there and tell her without… well, without some support."

"I'll tell my officers to arrive at her home at approximately seven thirty. Does that give you enough time?"

"Yes, yes that's fine."

~~~

When the doorbell rang, Davey was forking the last bite of dinner into his mouth. "Yay," he yelled, "Someone's here."

Chloe was relieved he didn't say, "Woss", because that was his usual reaction. Amanda leaned over to lift him to the floor and he ran to the door.

"Wait for me, Davey. We have to see who it is. We don't just rip the door open. Oh, hi, John," she said in delight. "Haven't seen you for a little bit. Come on in."

"Uncle John!" Davey threw himself into John's legs and swung around.

"Wow! This is pretty exuberant. Is this what it's going to be like when our child is four?"

Davey frowned up at him. "I'm five."

"Come in. Let Uncle John in, Davey."

John grabbed the youngster under the arms and swung the door closed behind him. "How are things?"

"We're okay. Davey's healthy, I'm healthy. What more can we ask? It'd be nice to see the end of this audit, but that's another issue. Have you had dinner? There's lots, it's roast chicken tonight with mashed potatoes and gravy, cranberry sauce. I do this once in a while."

"No, thanks. I just ate." He looked at his watch. "I could use a soda or something."

"Well, I've got sparkling water…"

"That's perfect. A squeeze of lemon?"

"Yes, I can do that."

John walked into the kitchen and sat Davey down on the counter. "Hi, Amanda. How are classes going?"

Amanda blushed. "Fine, thanks."
~~~

"Are you into mid-terms already? Probably not till just before Easter right?"

"Next week," she said. "I have two on Monday and one every day till Friday. It'll keep me busy."

John grinned. "Thanks," he said to Chloe, taking the glass from her hand. "Looks good. Amanda, could you take Davey upstairs and keep him busy for a bit? I just need to talk to Chloe for a few minutes."

"Sure, no problem. Come on, Davey. You know I have that game on my iPod that you like to play." Davey skipped happily after her as she left the room.

Chloe looked alarmed. "What's going on, John?" She turned her head when she heard the doorbell. John opened his mouth, then closed it at the sound. He saw recognition in her eyes, a fatalistic look.

Following her to the door, he waited while two police officers filed in and introduced themselves. He led them into the living room, seated everyone, then sat beside Chloe and took her hand. The police said their piece.

Chloe looked stunned, like she wasn't taking it in. She didn't speak but nodded a few times. John tried to ask questions, whatever she would have wanted to ask had she been able. The officers gave them the same answers he'd gotten from Detective Cullen. This was an ongoing investigation, there were a lot of unanswered questions, they would keep her informed as soon as things developed. No, there was no doubt that this was Jeff Sanderson. They had a positive identification based on dental records.

Chloe just sat there. When they finished talking they looked at her. She seemed to struggle with what was expected. "Um." She looked at John. "What…"

"Nothing, Chloe. You don't have to do anything. Is there something you want to ask them while they're here?"

"I don't…" She looked at the officers, then at John again. The hurt and loss was so naked on her face that he could barely look at her. He patted her hand and she leaned her face against his arm. John motioned to the officers and they rose to leave.

"Our sincere condolences, Ms. Bowman," the woman officer said. She crouched in front of Chloe. "Here's my card. If you want to talk about it, or if you have any questions, I'll be happy to do my best to answer them."

Chloe nodded into her lap.

After they left, John came back and sat down beside her. She didn't move. He put his arm around her shoulders and she leaned into his chest. "Oh, John. I knew, but I never really believed that he was dead."

She started to shake and near-silent sobs escaped her throat into the flannel of his work shirt. After a while she calmed and he rubbed her head. "Aw, Chloe. He was too young to die. And you're too young to be a widow. A widow? It seems ludicrous, doesn't it?" They sat together in silence.

~~~

Chloe turned down John's offer to stay the night, to call a family council and have everyone come out. She was worn out and needed to be alone. He offered to tell the rest of the family for her and she gratefully accepted.

"But don't let them come out tonight. Tomorrow will be soon enough."

Vivienne called an hour later. "Aw, sweetie, I'm so sorry. Really, I am. I know how much you loved him and what a loss this is for you. And for Davey. I think he's lonely for a man and he feels the loss, too."

Chloe cried on the phone.

"John made me promise not to come out to see you tonight. Are you sure? I can be there in twenty minutes."

"No, Mum." She wiped her eyes with the back of her hand. "Really. I'm so tired. And I have things to do. Everyone can come tomorrow, that's soon enough. Come in the morning, I'll be ready for you then."

She trundled Davey into bed and read him his story. Plutie turned around three times and settled on the mat beside his bed. Then he whined because Chloe had forgotten
~~~

to let him outside before starting the bedtime ritual. She climbed the stairs wearily and knocked on Amanda's door.

"Yes."

"Amanda, it's Chloe. Can I talk to you for a minute?"

"Sure," Amanda opened the door. "What's wrong? You look all upset."

"I just need to talk to you. The police came to tell me they found my husband. His body, I mean." She stuttered in confusion for a moment. "I kind of knew but I didn't believe it, you know?" She sat down wearily on the chair and Amanda settled on her bed.

"That's so sad. I'm really sorry, Chloe."

"Thanks. Would you tell the others when they come in? It just saves me having to say it over for each one. And there will be people coming and going, I guess, over the next few days."

She gazed into space as she wondered what this would mean. A funeral, of course. Someone had to arrange it. And other consequences that she simply couldn't think about right now.

"Anyway, if you'd do that, I'd be grateful. Thanks, Amanda. Don't let it upset you or disturb your studying. Jeff has been gone a long time and…" Her voice caught in her throat and she couldn't finish the sentence. She waved and headed for the door. "Thanks."

Chloe drifted into her bedroom. She started to undress but couldn't seem to focus. Finally she stripped, dumping her clothes on the floor, and crawled under the covers. She lay there, numb. Kind of how she felt when Jeff first disappeared. All her emotions had leaked out, bit by bit, until she was an empty shell. She could feel things rattling round inside.

She dozed and was wakened by the sound of crying. Her pillow was wet and her throat sore from sobbing. Calmer, she rose to check that she hadn't disturbed Davey. He was sleeping the sleep of the innocent, his face driven straight into the pillow. She eased him to his side, adjusted his blankets and wandered back to bed.

She lay staring at the ceiling, then at her radio. It was only twenty minutes after eleven, and she was rigid, her whole body tense. *Was it too late to call Ross*? She picked up the phone and held it against her chest, clasped in both hands. *Should she call him?* She wanted to hear his voice. Just know the comfort of his presence, even remotely.

She gripped the phone, her hands hurting from the sharp contact, then put it down on the night table. She couldn't lean on him for this. It wasn't right and she knew it. He must know it too, because she hadn't heard from him and the one time she'd caught him on the phone, he'd been too busy to talk. She was simply alone, as she'd been since Jeff disappeared. Alone, with Davey.

She slept not at all after that. She rolled around, tangling the sheets and trying not to think about how Jeff might have died. Not knowing what had happened was beyond bearing. Jeff must have been into something that she knew nothing about. There was too much evidence pointing in that direction. All this money that came into the accounts. She didn't believe that Jeffrey Sanderson had given his son six hundred thousand dollars. They didn't even speak.

She rolled again and tried not to think of what might have happened. There were all kinds of possibilities and none of them good. If he'd been into drugs, he might very well have been the one to sell drugs to Jayde's daughter, Jannine. The very idea made her gag, the thought of the pain in that family because of her addiction.

Finally she couldn't bear it any longer and got up to watch television. There was nothing on but old reruns and she fell asleep on the couch, with the sound on low. She awoke preoccupied with Jeff, how he'd been in the last year or two of their marriage. Absolutely driven. And he wouldn't share with her, share his vision or whatever was driving him. He'd been closed down.

She'd tried to be patient. When she was small her parents had gone through a rocky patch, where her father was putting in long hours building the business. Her mother had been very hurt, stuck at home with three young children and a very busy schedule of baseball practices, ballet lessons, hockey games, conducting this family orchestra on her own.

Things had finally smoothed out for them and Chloe didn't know whether it was because the business moved into a new, more manageable phase or her father understood Vivienne's concerns and pulled back to engage again.

With her own family as guide, she'd tried to get Jeff to understand that she didn't want to be a single parent, that she had experience to offer his business and she wanted him to let her in. But he couldn't seem to hear her.

If she were honest, it hadn't started in the last year. Jeff had always been that way. At first she found it charming, he'd simply look after everything. But then she found it annoying. But by then she was pregnant with Davey. After the baby was born, it was as if Jeff thought she had company now so he was free to spend all his time on business.

She heard the boarders stirring upstairs, so clicked off the television and dragged herself off the sofa. Davey would be awake soon.

~~~

Her family arrived just after eight o'clock. John and Rosemary came first. Rosemary took one look at her and went to make tea. John engulfed her in a hug and walked her in his arms out to the kitchen. Davey sat at the table eating his breakfast and grinned in delight at the sight of Uncle John. Before they could sit down, Vivienne rang the bell and let herself in, followed closely by Brent. Diana couldn't get the day off work. She'd be out later.

"Does that mean this is a sit in?" Chloe asked wearily.

"A sit in? Good idea," said Vivienne. "Yes, we need to be together and there are things to talk about, decisions to make."
~~~

At first Chloe was convinced she was too tired to handle all of them. But as the hours went by, she relaxed. The talk bounced leisurely back and forth between memories of Jeff to stories of their father and forward to arrangements that needed to be made.

John had directed Jeff's body be taken to the funeral home that had handled their father's funeral but they were waiting on the Coroner. Apparently they were safe to set a funeral date.

Chloe was surprised that she could face the discussion that followed between her brothers and her mother whether burial of the body or cremation, church or funeral home service, the question of a life insurance policy.

She was baffled by that question. She'd never heard of a policy, they hadn't even considered life insurance. Although she did remember it being an issue when Jeff bought the building. She'd check with the mortgage company.

"Anyway," she said, "I have money in the company. I can manage the funeral."

Everyone protested but Chloe stood her ground. "I'll manage what I can. I promise to let you know if I can't."

Her brothers continued to bristle and it made her smile at her mother in amusement. Even Rosemary was supportive. Chloe couldn't believe the change in her sister-in-law. She was more than six months pregnant, showing proudly. She was loving with John, less self-focussed and more compassionate than she'd ever seen her.

At some point in the day, Chloe remembered Jeff's parents. She was suddenly swamped with fatigue and John offered to call them.

Diana came at five with Chinese food and the boarders arrived home shortly after. Dennis came in first, kicking his shoes off at the door. "Chloe," he called, "Are you there? Hi, Davey, where's your Mum? Oh, there you are." He looked at her pale face. "Hey, listen. I'm really sorry. Amanda told me last night but you'd already gone to bed. What can I do? There must be something." He turned as John appeared in the living room doorway.

"Dennis, this is my brother John." She carried on with the introductions when the rest of her family appeared. "As you can see, I have lots of help."

"Okay." He looked down at Davey. "Want to me amuse the little guy for a while? Maybe you have things to talk about."

Chloe shook her head. "You're a great guy, Dennis. Thanks for the offer. I may need to take you up on it later, but we're fine for now. Dinner will be on the table at six thirty. Who else is home tonight, do you know?"

"I don't know about Don. But Beth and Amanda were staying late for something or other and said they'd be home later but would like supper."

She smiled wanly. "Sounds good."

Dennis nodded to the others and vaulted up the stairs.

"Well." Chloe turned back to her family. "What do you want to do?"

"I think we should call the Pastor of our church and let him know what's happened. Maybe he can meet with us tomorrow for a prayer service and that would put everyone's heart at rest." Vivienne nodded knowledgeably. "Then we can get on with our day and Chloe, you can let us know what arrangements you have with the funeral home."

Diana set the table with Davey telling her where everyone sat. "Well, some of them won't be here for dinner, will they?" Chloe heard her say. "So we can move the chairs around a little bit, because the rest of us are here. Where do you sit?"

She sat with Vivienne as her mother made the call to the Pastor, nodding at the suggested times until it was arranged. Vivienne hung up and took her daughter's hand. "You know, Chloe, there's no good age to be a widow. It's something we can't control, something that happens. It's never easy, whether you've had your husband a short time or a very long one."

They both cried. Chloe pressed her mother's palm with her fingers. "I know, Mum. We weren't very sympathetic with you when Dad died. We thought you should pull it together and get on with life, didn't we?"

"You were young and hurting. Your father was a big part of your lives, each of you. And in one way you were right. You have to pull it together and get on with it. It's just not easy, that's all. It's damned hard, but it's necessary. You have Davey to consider.

"No one here is looking for you to act the bereaved widow. You've been in mourning for a long time. This is simply the end of the long illness, you could say, that finally and permanently takes Jeff away. It's getting toward the end of the mourning hopefully, not the beginning, sweetheart."

Diana poked her head in. "Dinner's on the table."

Ross called her that evening just as the family was making its way out the door. Chloe said she'd call him back but once everyone had their coats and were gone, Amanda and Beth arrived. She directed them to the Chinese food for reheating and listened to the account of the speech they'd heard about eco-something.

In the middle of it, Amanda remembered what had happened. "Oh, my God. I'm sorry, Chloe. Here we are going on and on about us, when you have all this to deal with."

Beth's eyes grew big. "Amanda told me." Her gaze fell to Davey who was trying to brush out Plutie's ears. "I'm so sorry. It must be terrible." She looked at her in embarrassment.

Chloe smiled. "It's okay. I'll be okay. I know it's hard to think of the right words to say. But it means a lot to me to hear your concern." She gave the girls a hug.

As they climbed the stairs, Chloe looked around the kitchen and realized it had been days since she'd done any cleaning.

Despair rose in her chest and a tremendous weariness came over her. Suddenly her limbs were incredibly heavy, and she couldn't summon the energy to do the simplest thing. She tumbled Davey into bed, teeth unbrushed and prayers unsaid. She fell into bed the same way, falling instantly asleep. She didn't hear her phone ringing in the office.

~~~

Chloe couldn't pull herself out of her lassitude. Vivienne showed up that afternoon with a cleaning service and had them go through the entire house, including upstairs in the boarders rooms and bathrooms. Meanwhile she went through Chloe's closet and found clothes for the funeral service, laying them out for her on the bed.

"Come on, Davey," she said. "Let's see what you have." Not much, as it turned out. "Don't worry," she told him. "I'll find you something really nice. Maybe dress pants and a jacket."

She found her daughter in the kitchen. "These cleaners will be finished in half an hour. What do you have planned for dinner?" She looked in the fridge. "Looks like leftovers."

Chloe nodded. "Hot chicken sandwiches with a salad. There are cupcakes for dessert."

Vivienne looked doubtfully at her. "You don't eat that, do you? Bread and gravy? That's not like you."

She looked at her mother in despair. "Mum, does this really matter right now?"

Vivienne dropped into the chair across from her. "Of course not, what was I thinking? Would you like me to bring Davey home? He needs something to wear to the funeral and I want to take him shopping tomorrow. He said he wants to come, don't you Davey?"

Chloe looked blearily at her son. "That would be fine, Mum. I don't have the energy to deal with him anyway. It would be good for him to get out of the house."

Vivienne watched her face carefully. "Okay. I'll take Davey and finish with the cleaners. Then you have dinner and
~~~

go to bed. Maybe you could stay in bed tomorrow, is that possible? There can't be anything you absolutely have to do. And the funeral is the next day. Why don't I keep Davey two nights? Brent is going to come out to get you for the funeral and we can meet at the Church. Come on, Davey, let's pack your pyjamas and toothbrush."

Ross called again that night. He said he knew Jeff's body had been found. He was calling to give her his condolences. He sounded so formal on the phone. "Thank you, Ross. That's very kind."

"How are you doing?"

"I'm holding my own. My family has rallied round and is giving me a lot of support. They've helped with the arrangements. The funeral's on Saturday."

"So I heard. It was in the paper."

"Yes, of course." There was a lull.

"Is there anything I can do?" His voice sounded odd, as if he had a cold or some throat restriction.

"No, that's okay. I'm fine."

"Nothing? Do you need a driver or someone to pick anything up?"

"No, my brothers are doing that for me. Thanks, Ross."

"Right. Well, okay. Call me if you need anything."

"Thanks, Ross, and thanks for calling. Bye."

Stonily, she put down the phone. She felt a compounded loss because it appeared that Ross was no longer her friend, her helper, her lover. Even though she didn't want to see him right now, there was a huge hole in her heart.

Her chest hurt and her eyes ached from unshed tears. Finally she collapsed into her pillow in misery and cried her eyes out. Now she felt worse, with stuffed sinuses, sore throat and that continued hollowed out place in her breast. She pressed her hands against the tender area and that's how she fell asleep.

CHAPTER TWENTY TWO

Rain continued driving in the snow. He had chains on the half worn tires of his dark green pickup truck. There was little weight in the back to keep his traction steady, all the computers had been cleaned and recycled. He had nothing left but a laptop to keep tabs on his accounts and to get email and other necessary information. He'd arrive in Saskatoon this afternoon with the clothes on his back and a single knapsack and he was looking forward to it.

He'd find a little cabin on the edge of town for the rest of the winter, a place to hole up and recuperate. That's what he needed right now. His license plates were from Saskatchewan so wouldn't raise any questions. The city was big enough but not too big, he could mingle and live unnoticed. He had new ID, his name was Victor Landon, Vic. He could get used to that.

He was worried about his family. They seemed upset and he didn't want them to fuss. He was okay, he could ride this out. While riding it out, he needed to find another way to live. This life was finished.

He kept himself current with the BC news and Victoria in particular. He'd heard that Jeff's body had finally been found. It was about time. Man, that had taken an eternity. Surely they'd be able to tell how he'd died. If everything he read about police resources and methods was true, they must be able to figure out that one basic fact. Then would they be coming after him or Tom Dickson?

Rain didn't know, but he meant to be prepared. He wasn't going down for this alone. If he got caught, he was taking someone with him.

~~~

Ross walked the sidewalk, heading for his meeting with the coroner. He was a few minutes late, but Dan Parker had caught him as he left with an update on the baseball coach. It looked like they could ditch that one. Some parent overreacting, apparently.

He stopped to let an older fellow pass in front of him and found himself face to face with Chloe. She had Davey by the hand and her other hand was holding onto the arm of the fellow who walked beside her. His gaze flew to her face and then ricocheted off to the tall, lean man who was escorting her.

"Woss!" He looked down to see Davey let go of his mother's hand and torpedo toward him. He grabbed him around the legs and laughed. "Woss. Were you waiting for us?"

"Davey!" Chloe called nervously, her hand outstretched.

He put his hand on Davey's head and rubbed his hair, keeping his eyes on the woman. "Hi, Chloe. How are you?"

Her face was pale and her eyes looked like bruises in her face. He wanted to touch her, embrace her. But the man she was with was giving him a hard look and moved his arm protectively around her back.

Okay, he thought. *Is that the way it is?* Maybe he shouldn't jump to conclusions, yet his heart was beating a rapid tattoo in his chest and he was having trouble breathing. He looked down and tapped Davey on the back. "How's it going, little guy? Are you being good for your Mum?"
~~~

"Yep. When do you come to see us? You never come no more." His lower lip trembled. "How come? Don't you want to play?"

"Davey!" Chloe's voice was insistent. "Ross is a busy man, he doesn't have time right now to come see us."

He gave her a reproachful look and she had the grace to glance away, gesturing to the man beside her. "Ross, this is my brother, Brent Bowman. Brent, this is Detective Ross Cullen."

Brent put out his hand and Ross shook it. He didn't mind the once over he was subjected to, now that it was clarified this was her brother. "Pleased to meet you, Brent." He glanced down at Davey, then squatted so he could talk to him.

"Mummy's right, I'm pretty busy, so I haven't had time to come out. But when things slow down, I'll come and see you. Okay?"

"Promise?"

"Yes. That's a promise, Davey. I'll see you."

The little boy nodded solemnly. "Okay."

Ross watched them walk away and turned toward the government office. But his mind wasn't on the case anymore, it was on Chloe. It was like a blow to the chest to run into her like that and he needed a minute to catch his breath.

The coroner had an interesting situation before him. They'd found most of Sanderson's bones, certainly the head and torso were all there, anchored in place by the leather jacket wrapped around it. Bones from the lower parts of the body had been scattered where they drifted with the water, the backwash minimal at the mouth of the river. The divers had stayed with it until they'd extracted everything possible.

When the body was assembled they were only short a few small bones. The dental records matched. The height of the body was right, the gender was male. The broken left femur matched an old injury his parents informed them about.

The main issue was cause of death. Because there was no tissue to work with, they didn't have a lot to go on.

Ross wasn't surprised that there was no firm opinion. The Coroner couldn't determine if Sanderson died by drowning or if he died before he entered the water. But he did have two items to point out. The head had suffered serious damage, with a crack in the bone in the front of the forehead and a caving in of the bone on the back. Neither of those was inconsistent with what Tom Dickson had told them, that he fell head first down the falls. So if he'd been injured prior to falling into the water, they couldn't prove it by the evidence on the skeleton.

The other item was a fracture in the collar bone. Was that possible as an accidental injury when the body fell into a rushing river? The coroner couldn't say. He did feel that it was broken from a frontal blow rather than from the shoulder being damaged while tumbling in the water. Just something to add to the list of things they may never be able to explain.

~~~

Chloe arrived with Brent at the Church a few minutes early for the funeral service and found the rest of her family waiting. They gathered in a side chapel as the mourners collected. She was surprised how many people attended. She didn't take in much of the service and was glad to be preoccupied with Davey who was wiggling against her legs and itching at the neck of his new dress shirt. Brent pulled him off her lap and settled him down for the prayers.

In the reception afterward, she was touched to realize a lot of the people there were connections of hers from school and from her father's and brothers' lives. Two men approached her together, friends of Jeff's from university. They introduced themselves. Uhjal gave her his card and said if she wanted to talk, he'd be happy to meet for coffee sometime.

"Talk?" she fumbled.
~~~

"Well, just about Jeff. I think a lot of his friends were not your friends and you might be curious about his life before you two met."

Chloe smiled for the first time that day. "Thank you, Uhjal. That's so kind." He flushed and moved off with Buddy in his wake.

Then across the hall she saw Ross standing with a small group, a few of them in police uniform. He looked tense, his hands clasped together. He caught her eye and held it. Chloe nodded and he detached himself and made his way over to her.

"Hi, Chloe." He took her hand. "How are you holding up?" His eyes seemed to pierce her.

"What are you doing here?" She was suddenly having trouble breathing.

He went red. "Well, as usual I'm working. But I'm also here for you. I care about you, Chloe. And I haven't been able to tell you because of this investigation, it's always been between us." He ran a finger around his collar as if it was too tight. He looked smart in grey flannel dress pants and a navy jacket. His hair was as brutally short as ever, his large eyes intense.

"You're staring, Chloe. Do I look funny or have you forgotten what I look like?" His mouth took a sardonic twist downward.

She ripped her gaze away and glanced across the room. Immediately she saw John studying her and the man she was talking to. Damn him. He was like an eagle, with his eyes everywhere, documenting everything. She whirled back to Ross. "My brother is looking at us, so I don't want to talk now. I might call you later."

Ross gave a small bow and walked away. She followed him with her gaze. Where did they stand, the two of them? She couldn't tell. At the same time she almost didn't want to know. This was too muddled. The timing was bad. She couldn't take up with someone the next week after her husband's funeral. It was crazy. She was crazy.

They went back to John's place, a few friends and business acquaintances following. Eventually Chloe asked Brent to drive them home. She was so tired she felt incapable of anything.

Saying goodbye took forever. Everyone wanted to express their condolences and the hugs went on and on.

Davey got cranky and cried most of the way home. "Never mind, Davey," she tried to soothe him. "We won't do anything tomorrow. Or for a few days. Maybe a half day of daycare just to have some fun." She was talking to herself, mumbling under her breath.

Brent took her hand and squeezed it. "It's okay, Chloe. It's okay."

There was another message from Jeffrey Sanderson. She couldn't possibly call him tonight, it was too late. And she wondered where she'd get the intestinal fortitude to call him tomorrow. She sighed and slowly fell into bed.

~~~

The phone woke her. She looked blearily at the clock and realized with a shot of panic that it was nine thirty. She leaped from bed. Davey! She hadn't heard him get up. Was he wandering around the house by himself? Or had he gone outside? She raced across the hallway, pushing open the door. The little boy was sleeping peacefully, although Plutie was looking a bit anxious. The phone had stopped ringing, but started up again right away.

She pulled the dog out of the room by his collar and grabbed the phone on the way to putting him outside. "Hello?"

"Hello, Chloe." It was someone crying into the phone, a man's voice.

"Who is this?"

"It's Jeffrey, Jeffrey Sanderson. Oh, my God. He's dead, my boy is dead."

"Jeffrey?" She was momentarily lost for words as she watched Plutie race across the patio and squat to do her
~~~

business in the middle of the lawn. "Did the police come to tell you?"

"Yes, they came. Alice answered the door and there they were."

She heard him sobbing.

"I'm so sorry, Jeffrey. I'm so sorry. What can I say?" She was almost out of words, especially for this couple who didn't seem to care one way or the other for their son and grandson. "When did you find out?"

"Yesterday I guess. No, the day before. We had a dinner party last night, so it was the night before."

She couldn't believe it. A dinner party? What kind of people were they?

"Well." She didn't know what to say. "I guess it will take a while to get used to the idea. I don't think that happens quickly. I mean, he's been gone for ten months, Jeffrey, and I don't feel much better. How about you?"

"Not much, no." He rambled on, seeming to find some relief in talking to her.

Finally, she was too tired to carry on. "I'm sorry. I have to go, there's so much to do without Jeff here."

"Yes, of course. Thank you for talking to me, Chloe. It comforts me. Thank you."

"You're welcome," she whispered.

After she hung up she felt absolutely drained. Poor man. Maybe he had no one else he could talk to about his son. Maybe it was Alice who didn't care, not Jeffrey. She couldn't figure them out and couldn't be bothered to try. She and Davey grazed their way through the day, with cereal and other snacks. They watched Donald Duck for a while and she saw what charmed Davey about the silly old cartoons.

The rain stopped around noon, so she got jackets and helmets down and the two of them rode their bikes up and down the drive and a little way along the trail. She couldn't even garner the energy to call in on Jayde.

She didn't phone Ross. What was there to say? She wanted to see him but couldn't. Why start it up again? And

Davey loved the man, mourned when he didn't come round. If she encouraged him to call, Davey would get his hopes up that Ross was going to be a regular part of his life. He had suffered enough loss without being set up for another one.

The next day she dragged herself out to pick up the mail and found a manila envelope from Jeff's dad. Turning it over in her hands, she put it in her bag. There was a pile of other things, one from Revenue Canada. That could wait as well.

She dropped Davey at daycare for a half day and did grocery shopping. When she got home, she barely got the perishables into the fridge before she fell onto her bed for a nap.

It was after dinner when she remembered the mail. Davey was playing quietly, Lego spread all around him on the family room floor. She flopped into the arm chair and put her feet up, laying the envelopes on her lap.

The first piece she opened was from Mr. Sanderson. She pulled out a sheaf of papers and placed them on her propped up legs. There were three cancelled cheques made out from Jeffrey Sanderson to Jeffrey Sanderson, totalling just under five hundred and fifty thousand dollars. They were all dated last year, several months apart. It was confusing, it would be hard to show whether it was the father or the son who received the money without some closer scrutiny.

The other papers in the envelope consisted of a letter covering several pages, attesting that Jeffrey Sanderson of Florida, USA had given his son, Jeffrey Sanderson of Victoria, Canada, a total of five hundred and forty-two thousand dollars in American funds between January and December two years ago. The money was a gift to his son and not expected or demanded to be repaid. He didn't know how his son spent the money.

The bank stamps on the cheques showed they'd been deposited in an American account. The letter had a seal affixed to it, and a separate document from a notary who had received Sanderson's sworn statement.

Chloe sighed and laid it aside. She'd read it again in the morning. Her mind didn't work that well right now, too foggy and weary. She put her head back on the chair and was only roused when Davey's hand landed on her thigh. "Mummy, are you tired again?"

She laughed and looked down into his sparkling eyes. "Yes, Mummy's tired again. Are you?"

"Nope." He went back to the castle that he was building.

"Well, it's almost bedtime, so ten more minutes and then it's off to clean your teeth."

He made a face. She made one back at him and reached for the rest of the mail. A few bills, a flyer for a new restaurant and the letter from Revenue Canada. She ripped it open with a fatalistic shrug.

The audit was finished, and given that the records were incomplete, they'd been unable to come to a definite conclusion. They couldn't determine a source of some income but had found an amount that wasn't reported on any of Mr. Sanderson's tax returns. Therefore income tax was due. They were referring it to their superiors for a final decision on the amount owing. Zeke, the team leader had signed the letter, a copy to Cliff Greening.

She didn't have a clue where that left her. It might mean they seized the building for taxes. She'd heard of that. Or would they seize the house? She supposed she and Davey could live at the building. She could carve out a spot there for the two of them.

She snorted. Not likely. Her brothers would have something to say about that. Well, she wasn't going to move in with Vivienne.

She put the letter with the other mail and heaved herself from the chair. She almost didn't care what happened. She was numb, just like right after she lost Jeff.

And she didn't have to play around with the words this time. She wasn't wondering if he left, vaporized, took off, was mentally ill, or any of those crazy thoughts she'd had. He hadn't been abducted by aliens, he didn't just drive away and forget to come home. He'd died in the Sooke River. Drowned in the Potholes. No one would tell her how or why. He was just dead. It was almost as bad as knowing nothing at all.

"Let's go, Davey. Bedtime." With what seemed like superhuman effort she negotiated her protesting son down the hall.

~~~

Inspector Marsh motioned Ross to the chair in front of his desk. He finished reading a paper that lay before him, then pushed it aside and pulled a list forward.

"So, where are we, Ross?" He ran down the list, getting an update on each case. Ross provided details as they rolled through the files.

"So the coach is clean?"

"Yes, sir. We didn't find anything. A number of the little guys said he touched them. When they described it, he was lacing boots, pulling gear over their heads. We think a parent overreacted. The guy's doing a good job. Too bad about the report because he's volunteering his time, but at least now he's been thoroughly screened."

Marsh pursed his lips. "Too bad is right. Waste of our time." He looked at the next item. "What about Sanderson? He's no longer a missing person. He's been found. What do we have on cause of death?"

"Inconclusive. Nothing that would determine whether death was by drowning. The injuries to bone could be consistent with falling down the falls and being tossed onto the rocks by the rushing water." Ross explained the damage to the head, the broken collar bone and various minor injuries.

"The coroner found an old fracture, a broken leg that the father told us about. So there's plenty of support for the ID of the body."

"Good. Where do you go from here?"
~~~

"We need to find Rainier Murdoch. We don't have any leads, so it's more or less on the back burner. Murdoch has a knack for moving under the radar and he hasn't contacted his family or other known associates. Not that there are many. We don't know what he looks like now or what name he's using. We don't know what he's driving. He changes vehicles every couple of months, along with ID. He pays cash for a car and sells it for cash. The next vehicle he buys is in a different name. And he's not short of cash. So at the moment, we don't have anything.

"Tom Dickson is our other contact and he's told us everything he knows. But until we have more information, we can't prove that. Sort of stymied."

"Okay." Marsh pulled at his sideburns as he stared out the window. "Let me think on it. Why not make a public appeal? Talk about how the family can't put their son to rest, a murderer may be getting away with his crime. People can't resist something like that," he said.

"It's a failing of humanity. They want to be the person who leads you to the culprit. If there's a reward, then that brings them out of the woods. People like solving riddles and this is a great riddle, a man who can change his looks so much that no one recognizes him.

"Meanwhile keep at the Russell case, that's our new priority right now. Pull Parker off Sanderson and let's move as fast as we can. Russell is high profile and it's serious."

"Yes sir."

Ross put together a file with the photos from Murdoch's old driver's licence, the bank and Troy Smith and Bob Humphreys ID from the counterfeiter Jimmy Dolan's computer. He gathered the four best pictures and sent it down to the promotions department for publication release. They had a good cross section. Murdoch would be hard pressed to come up with some new look that wasn't similar to at least one of these.

He was excited. It'd take a while for results to come in and a great deal of work to weed out the candidates. He hoped it would be worth it.

But meanwhile he was stuck in limbo again. Pulling Parker off the case meant Sanderson was on hold. It would be an ongoing investigation, eventually a cold case that hung over their heads. They were already ten months in. He wouldn't be expected to solve it but he was cut off from Chloe Bowman. He was in a black mood when he got back to his townhouse that evening.

He called Chloe and left her a message as she didn't pick up. She didn't have to call back, he told her, he was just checking to see how she was. But if she needed anything, she should contact him right away. He hung up feeling more depressed than he'd ever felt in his life.

CHAPTER TWENTY THREE

Cliff Greening didn't know what to make of the letter from Jeff's father. He read it twice, then examined the cancelled cheques back and front.

"Well," he said eventually. "It's not for me to decide. I'll take copies of these for our file and forward them to Zeke and company. We aren't even outside the grace period. Good timing, is all I can say."

Chloe giggled, feeling somewhat lightheaded. "It's odd, though, isn't it? I mean, how would I be able to explain how that money left the Washington State bank and got into Jeff's accounts here in town? I can't. But I guess I don't have to. I didn't do it and it's not up to me to explain it."

She rubbed her forehead tiredly. "I can't see them taking it seriously but it's worth a try." The other thing that rang false about this whole thing was the relationship between father and son. But she was the only one who would be aware of that so she didn't comment.

Taking her copy of the documents, she spent the rest of the afternoon at the building. John didn't usually bother her with the details of running the hostel but there'd been some damage to the place. She expected the worst and wasn't disappointed. When she stepped inside, she smelled smoke and wrinkled her nose. Mike LaTorre came to meet her at the door.

"Hi, Mike. I thought the guys weren't allowed to smoke." As she looked around, her eyes widened. Air ducts hung from the ceiling at odd angles. Cubicles at one end of the space were torn apart. The smoke smell came from a pile of clothes in the middle of the entrance that Mike had been shovelling into garbage cans. "Okay. I see."

Mike grinned. "I hope not. It was quite a picture but it's all over now."

"That's not good. You and Maria have to live here, it's not right to be in fear for your lives. What happened?"

He chuckled. "Not exactly in fear of our lives but it was lively. A couple of the guys got into it, one of them had had a bit to drink before he came home. He was mouthy and the other guy had enough so a fight started. Then a few more thought it looked like fun and dove into it with them. It became a bit of a free for all.

"I recruited some of the older fellows to help me and we waded in. It didn't take long to calm them down. But the clothes burning thing was too much. We tossed that guy out and warned everyone else. It's under control, don't worry."

"Hmm." She looked into the lunchroom and walked down a few of the aisles. "Not entirely under control. It's going to be months before we can get anyone to come and look at that ductwork, let alone repair it."

"Don't worry, Ms. Bowman, it's all taken care of. One of the guys staying here is a licensed sheet metal worker and he's going to look after it. The carpenters will repair the cubicles and it'll all be back to order in no time. No harm done."

Chloe looked at him in astonishment. "I'll take your word for it," she murmured. She wasn't going to borrow trouble. If it really was under control, she had too much to worry about to question it. John assured her he was docking wages to cover the cost of putting the space back into shape, so none of them were going to be out of pocket.

However, food had become an issue. Maybe the restaurant was tired of the contract, because she heard so many complaints it gave her a headache. After a consultation with the chef and the restaurant owner that hurriedly grew heated, she was left without food. No supper that day, in fact.

Maria was worried. "I can't do it," she said. "It's too many men and not enough facilities. I could throw together something out of tins, or make sandwiches for a day or two if I had to. But I can't cook here."

"I don't expect you to, Maria. This restaurant shows serious bad faith in cutting us off with no notice, just because I questioned the quality of the food. But I've got someone else in mind. I'll go and see what they can do for us tonight. Perhaps they want to take on the contract. I'll call you as soon as I know."

She walked back to the truck and checked her watch. Better call Jayde. There was no going home until she'd sorted out the food. Forty men and no dinner was a dangerous combination.

Jayde said she had no problem getting Davey tonight. She'd look forward to it, in fact. She'd high tail it up there in about an hour and bring him back to her place, keep him there until Chloe called.

Hanging up, she blessed her willing and cheerful neighbour. Who was she to feel so down when Jayde lived day to day with the defeat of her daughter's situation? She started the truck and drove a couple of blocks over to Tony's Place. Tony was a friend of her brother Brent, and Chloe had met him a few times when the boys were in high school together. Now he had his own restaurant and seemed to be doing rather well. The food was certainly good and the establishment well respected.

Tony wasn't in. Chloe explained to the shift manager what she needed for the night and the next day, dinner for forty men and breakfast and lunch delivered the next morning by seven thirty. Was that possible?

When she mentioned that she knew Tony, the manager asked her to wait a few minutes. He brought her coffee and a cookie while she sat at the counter. Ten minutes later he returned with the phone. "Tony wants to talk to you," he smiled.

Tony was effusive over the phone. He absolutely remembered her, Brent's little sister. What had become of her? Was she in business, too? Well, the whole family seemed to be in commerce. He was pleased to make contact again. Then he got down to business himself.

He'd get dinner over there by seven that night, his manager assured him they could do it. The menu was flexible was it? Good, because they couldn't do forty dishes on the spur of the moment that were all the same. They'd probably have three different choices tonight. And he'd provide food for the following day as well.

Could he work on some figures, talk to his manager and get back to her? He didn't want to jump into it without some thought and prep time to ensure a good product. "Don't worry," he added, "If we don't come to an agreement, I can still provide the food on a short term basis until you line someone else up. But I'm pretty sure we can do it, it'll just take some organizing."

Chloe was so relieved to have this settled, even temporarily, that she thought she might not have the energy to drive home. It was like the air had been let out of her balloon. She got in the truck and called Maria, reassuring her that meals had been arranged. They were coming from Tony's Place.

Maria was thrilled. "Chloe," she gushed. "You're a miracle worker! Can you imagine what it would be like here with no dinner? Chaos. Thank you so much. Actually," her voice became thoughtful, "Tony's Place has good food. The men should be really happy. What are they bringing for dinner?"

Chloe explained the possibility of three choices, reassured her again and hung up. One more thing off her mental list. She didn't even have the energy to smile over that. She took the time to go back into Tony's Place and order take out dinner for six, then started up the truck and headed for the highway.

~~~

There was another phone call from Ross that evening. She didn't answer the phone, but he left a message similar to the ones before. If she needed anything or just wanted to talk, she could call him. She thought about it but didn't call.

His message prompted a memory, though, and she dug out her dress purse from the funeral. There it was. She fingered the business card that Jeff's friend Uhjal Singh had given her. On impulse she called the number and left him a message. She'd like to meet him for coffee.

Singh met her in a coffee shop near his office in an industrial park north of town. There was no one there she knew, but he waved to several people already ensconced at tables and led her toward the back and a more private spot in a small booth.

"This is good, Mrs. Bowman. What would you like?"

Chloe smiled. "Whatever you're having, Uhjal. And call me Chloe, everyone does."

He went to the bar to get their coffee. When he brought it back, a clerk followed with some cinnamon buns on a tray.

"I don't know about you, but sometimes I just need a bit to eat mid-morning." He settled in and doctored his coffee. Chloe thought him a handsome man. He moved with confidence, wore a wedding ring on his finger.

"How long have you been married?"

He looked up, obviously surprised at the question. "Uh," he laughed. "You caught me off guard there. Almost three years. We met at university."

She smiled. "So tell me, how did you know Jeff?"

"We were in the same classes first year, taking business. Jeff didn't study too hard but he seemed to do okay with his grades. I don't remember him being in any of my
~~~

study groups and I'd be surprised if he was in anyone else's either." He laughed. "He was in a hurry and went as fast as he could, through as many courses as he could. He was one bright man."

"What classes did you take together?"

"Well, let's see. First year English, Mathematics, business systems. That's probably all, because I was also taking Japanese and French."

"Really? Were you in business or languages?"

He laughed again. "That's what my father kept asking. I dropped the languages after first year. They were fun but I knew my future was in this." He gestured in the general direction of the industrial park.

She nodded. "Funny how what our family does impacts us so much, isn't it?" She sipped her coffee. "What did you know about Jeff and his family?"

Uhjal gave her a direct look. "Not much. I've thought about that quite a bit since he disappeared and the police came around now and then to ask me questions."

"Really? How did they even find you in the first place?"

"They'd been asking for anyone who knew Jeff or had any information about him to contact them. I thought it was a long shot, my information was pretty old but I called the detachment, told them I knew him at university. They found that interesting and interviewed me a couple of times. You never know what might prove helpful in something like this. I was shocked to hear he was dead. It must have been terrible for you. I'm really sorry, Chloe."

He saw she was overcome with emotion and busied himself with a cinnamon bun, gently pushing the other one across the table toward her. "So, about his family," he continued. "Jeff was nineteen in first year, same as me. He was living on his own in an old house with about five other guys. It was grungy and damp. But he didn't care. He had a plan. He seldom spoke about his family. But once I remember him saying that his mother was difficult to deal with. He'd had a bit too much to drink and he said she was stiff and cold. He couldn't get along with her. His father drank his life away because he was tied to his mother."

Uhjal sipped his coffee. "He hardly spoke to his folks. They'd agreed to support him through university if he remained in Canada. It wasn't clear if they didn't want him near them or it was cheaper here because he was a Canadian citizen. But he was to stay in Canada, didn't even see them over the holidays or summer break. They didn't come here and he didn't go there."

He munched his cinnamon bun for a few minutes and washed it down with more coffee. Chloe picked at hers, ending up eating half of it.

"I talked with Buddy after the funeral. You saw him, he was there with me. We hadn't seen each other in years. We started comparing notes about Jeff because I had offered to talk to you." He dimpled. "Buddy thought I was very brave to make that offer, by the way."

Chloe laughed.

"Here's what we agreed on. Buddy lived in the same house as Jeff for the first couple of months of first year. He moved out because it was too disorganized for him. But Jeff thrived on it. He rented the house and collected rent from everyone else. Buddy's pretty sure he lived off what he made on that. He didn't go to classes because he thought he knew more than the Prof. Now it might have been true some of the time because he was smart. But mostly it was that he had a different plan, he wanted something else. I'm not sure what it was but he spent more time bandying ideas for business then in getting any kind of education.

"He wanted to get his education in the real world. You know, the school of hard knocks. And I also think he was trying to prove something to his father. Buddy agreed with me."

"Prove what? Because Jeff's father calls me now and then, surprisingly."

"Why would that be a surprise? You were married to his son."

"For the first four years I never heard from them. Jeff never phoned them and they never phoned us. Nothing at Christmas. I'd send cards and pictures of the baby but we never got anything in return. They don't acknowledge our son, Davey. It's very strange."

Uhjal looked uncomfortable. "That's pretty sad. From what I gathered, Jeff's dad was a really accomplished guy, well educated, went to work for a big oil company early out of university and travelled his whole career. They were in Norway, Japan, Beirut, Texas, you name it. And he was the boss. I think Jeff wanted to measure up, know what I mean? I think that's why he was in such a hurry."

He saw the stricken look in her eyes. "Ah, don't listen to me. Buddy told me not to go there. I'm sorry Chloe." He patted her hand.

"You know what? It makes sense. From what I've learned about Jeff since he disappeared, it kind of makes sense." Her eyes shining with tears, Chloe shook Uhjal's hand. "Thank you for talking to me. It's helped a lot."

~~~

George Atwell was astounded to receive a visit from the police regarding his banking practices. He looked chagrined. As he'd told his wife earlier, he wasn't entirely comfortable depositing those cashier cheques.

"There's no problem, sir." The police officer squirmed in his chair. "We're just following up on some information. Can you tell me where you got them, what it was for and who paid it to you? It's a perfectly legal way to pay money but we have an interest in those particular ones."

Atwell relaxed. "Oh, well then. That's no problem. My daughter-in-law had them. Apparently their bank wouldn't take them but ours would. So we deposited them and gave them the cash, my son and her, that is."

The officer nodded. "Where can I find your daughter-in-law?"
~~~

Susan and Darrell Atwell received a visit that evening. Susan was flustered at the questions from the police and when they didn't stop she started to cry. She retreated into the bedroom and her husband finally went after her when she didn't reappear.

"You can't just stay in here," he whispered. "They aren't going away. What's the problem?"

"You know what the problem is! Rain gave me those to help us out with the loans, and now I think they must be bogus or something."

Darrell thought a moment. "They weren't bogus. Dad would have let us know soon enough. The bank would have reversed the deposit and called him. Come on, Susie. You have to talk to them. If Rain hasn't done anything wrong, there's nothing to worry about."

"I know." But her fear was Rain *had* done something wrong. She went back to the living room where the police officer was patiently waiting. "Sorry," she murmured. "What do you want to know?"

The officer smiled. "I just have some questions about the cashier cheques. George Atwell deposited them into his bank account. He said you gave them to him."

Susan nodded.

"Are you Susan Murdoch?"

"Susan Atwell now, but yes, I was Susan Murdoch."

"Is Rainier Murdoch related to you?"

Tears filled her eyes again but she nodded. "He's my brother."

"Okay," he made a note in his small book. "And where did you get the cashier cheques?"

"My brother gave them to me. We have a pretty heavy debt load and he said he wanted to help."

"I see. When did he give them to you?"

She looked at Darrell. "About a month ago," they both replied.

"Yes, about a month," Susan repeated.

"And where did you see him?"

"Uh, he came here to the house."

"How long did he stay?"

"Oh, he didn't stay. Darrell didn't even see him. He stopped me on the sidewalk as I was leaving for work and talked to me for a few minutes, gave me an envelope with the cheques in it and said he had to go. He had a schedule to keep, he said."

"What was he wearing that day?"

Susan looked unsure. "I don't remember."

The officer gave her an odd look.

"It was dark out and he was only there a few moments. I didn't notice what he was wearing."

"I thought he stopped you on your way to work?"

"Yes, I work night shift at the hospital. It was just before eight o'clock and at that time it's totally dark now. He just came up behind me and said my name. I recognized his voice, and gave him a hug. And he gave me the envelope and left."

"Do you know what he was driving?"

"Uh, I'm not very good with cars."

Darrell snorted a laugh at that. She looked over at her husband. "Well, I'm not!"

He grinned, "That's for sure."

Susan looked back at the officer. "It was an older car, a dark colour. That's all I really noticed. I drove away before he did because I was going to be late for work. I didn't get a good look at it."

After a few more questions, the officer left. Darrell turned to his wife. "Susan, that brother of yours is going to get us into trouble one day if we aren't careful. I wondered at him giving us that much money."

Susan glowered at him. "It's not the first time he's given us money and we were glad of it last time, too."

"I know. He's been generous. It's just, we don't know where he gets it."

Susan looked miserable and he tugged her into his arms. "Don't worry. I'm sure he's safe."

~~~

Jayde knocked at Chloe's door the next morning. "Well, miss, it's a glorious day and it's time to come out and pick daffodils."

"Daffodils?" Chloe looked uncertainly at the dark cloud cover, her eyelids heavy. "A beautiful day?" She frowned at Jayde blearily. "What are you talking about?"

Jayde laughed and grabbed Davey under the arms. "Aren't you ready to come outside, youngster?"

"Okay." He ran for his coat.

"Come on, Chloe. It's time to get out and smile a little."

They wandered down the Trail and into Jayde's field. "See the daffs? There are tons of them."

They got absolutely soaked. The grass was deep and sodden and their shoes were flooded. But they returned with an armload of flowers and Chloe put them in great vases around the family room and kitchen, one in the entryway. Refreshed and energized after Jayde left, she whipped around cleaning all the bathrooms before they had lunch and walked down to the daycare to visit the children.

The phone rang that night and Davey answered. He was listening intently as Chloe entered the family room. "Who are you talking to, Davey?" she asked curiously.

He ignored her. "Okay," he said into the phone. He listened some more, then said, "Not right now." He looked at his Mum but focused on the phone. Finally he took the phone away from his ear and handed it to her.

"Hello?"

"Hi, Chloe. It's Ross. How are you doing?"

Her pulse speeded up at the sound of his voice. "We're doing okay." She pictured his intense gaze and turned away as if he could see her through the phone.

"Good. I wondered if I can could out tomorrow to see you."

At her pause, he added, "Davey wants to see me."

Chloe couldn't help a small groan. "Well…"
~~~

"Come on, middle of the day, what could it hurt?" His voice was teasing.

Chloe went hot. Ross knew better than anyone what could happen in the middle of the day. There was an awkward pause. "What do you say?" he prodded. "Can I come out?"

She had trouble catching her breath. This was why she didn't answer the phone, she didn't trust herself with him. He was dangerous, he could talk her into anything. She loved the sound of his voice.

"What do you say, Chloe?" he almost purred through the phone.

"Okay," she said. "Okay. Come out."

As soon as she hung up, the phone rang again. "Ross, did you forget something?"

"No," said Brent, "This is your brother and I didn't forget anything."

Chloe slapped her hand over her mouth to hold in the gasp of dismay.

"So, is this the Ross that Davey likes?"

"None of your business."

"But is it the same guy?" Brent's tone was no longer joking.

"Yes, it is."

"Okay, keep your shirt on. I was just calling to pin down Easter dinner. Mum says she'll bring the apple pies. That's a plus, she makes the best pies."

Chloe's laugh was rusty. It was a family legend, primarily sponsored by their father. "What do you want me to bring? I have squash soup, sounds awful, tastes absolutely delicious, and I can do appetizers. Plus I have homemade spicy apple butter for the ham. Jayde and I made it from our crab-apples."

"Wow, you're turning into a farmer. Well, I'll let Diana decide. Just make sure you come at five thirty and bring Davey."

"Sounds good."

"Oh, and Chloe. About Ross."

She met that with stony silence.

"If it is the Detective Ross Cullen we met on the sidewalk, and I trust it is…" He paused, and she gave a noncommittal grunt. "I just want to make sure you know that he's in love with you."

"Brent, you step over the line!" Her cry was from the heart.

"You're stubborn sometimes. I got a good look at him that day. And once he understood that I was your brother and not his competition, he never took his eyes off you. And the second time I watched him watching you was at the funeral. Again, he never stopped looking. Just keep that in mind." He dropped his voice. "Be kind, Chloe. Don't trample on his heart."

Chloe hung up in absolute turmoil. She paced the floor and walked round the entranceway, through the hall to the kitchen, back to the dining room and out to the hall again. Plutie trotted after her until she put him outside.

Don Murphy came in late in the midst of her turmoil and wanted his dinner. She told him dinner was over, so he could get it out of the fridge and warm it up. He raised his brows and got it. That was the way to deal with touchy boarders, tell them to fetch.

Her sudden spate of energy lasted until Davey was in bed and she'd vacuumed the main floor of the house. Then she fell into the bathtub and lay there like a limp noodle.

What was she doing? She was in an impossible position. Everything was confused in her mind. She didn't know what was safe, and she worried about getting entangled with someone else when she was just beginning to deal with her loss. Or at least to understand her loss.

She'd promised herself she'd stay away from Ross. He was too persuasive, she had no willpower where he was concerned. He looked at her and she melted, forgot she had responsibilities, forgot everything but wanting him. He was a dangerous man.

CHAPTER TWENTY FOUR

Ross arrived on his bicycle at eleven the next morning. Davey ran around the entrance hall yelling, "Woss is here! Woss is here." He bent down and scooped the little boy up.

"Hey, good to see you." He hugged him. "Are you allowed to come out for a ride?"

"Yes, I am!"

Ross laughed. "Okay. Sounds good. Hi, Chloe." Chloe smiled and grabbed Davey's jacket. Ross bundled his little arms into the sleeves and stood him back down. "You can't go without a helmet." Davey tore down the hall and Chloe turned to get her coat.

"Chloe, how are you doing?" He took her jacket to help her into it. "Everything okay? Or at least, as okay as can be expected?"

"I'm pretty good," she said.

"Are you mad at me?"

She looked over her shoulder at him.

"Well," he shrugged, "You didn't take any of my phone calls, so I figured…"

"No, I'm not mad." She looked past him to the door.

"If not mad, then what?" He crowded her with his body, backing her up at the foot of the staircase. "What?"

She kept her gaze on the buttons of his shirt. He looked down. "Have I got food on my shirt?"

She swatted him and put her hand against his chest to move him backward, then just left it there. "You're teasing."

He laughed a little, "Yeah, I guess I am." He bent his head, raised her face at the same time and planted his mouth over hers. The kiss took her breath. After a minute he lifted his head. "You're teasing, too," he said in a strained voice.

Davey barrelled back into the entrance, his helmet on his head with buckles flying, his jacket trailing. "I'm ready," he yelled.

"We better get him outside before we go deaf." Ross opened the door and followed the boy onto the steps. They rode with Davey till he'd worked off some energy, then put him in the trailer and went for lunch at the Wilkinson Cafe. By the time they got there, Davey had calmed down. On the way back they picked up Davey's bike and the three of them cycled as far as Jayde's house where they stopped for tea.

"Ross Cullen, as I live and breathe." Jayde came out on the step to give him a hug. "You big galloot. You don't even look that much different but what happened to the hair?"

She waved them into her kitchen and turned to Chloe. "His hair used to be down on his shoulders, all wavy and brushed back. The girls sure liked that."

Chloe laughed, Ross was red in the face.

"Jayde," he warned. "Don't tell too many tales out of school. I have a few I could tell about Will, so keep a lid on it."

Jayde laughed delightedly and motioned them to sit. "I don't have much to offer you," she said. "I haven't done any baking for a few days."

"Don't worry about it, Jayde," Chloe said. "We just had lunch."

Ross pulled Davey up on his knee. "How's Will? I hear he's getting married. When's the big day?"

Jayde looked ecstatic. "It's Easter Saturday. We've been working away on the preparations. It's not a big wedding, you know. About fifty people, mostly family and a few close friends. But you have to go through all the same process for fifty, I guess, as you would for a hundred and fifty. So it's been keeping me busy. Will, not so much."

Ross laughed. "Yeah, I can't see him being too involved in planning a wedding. Not that he couldn't, just that he won't."

"Well." She set a pot of tea on the table, and checked on Davey who had moved off to play with the kitten. "This is a nice surprise, imagine seeing you two together." She had a little smile on her face. "Looks good though, from this view."

"Jayde," Chloe blushed. "We just went for a bike ride up the trail."

"Sure, sure you did." Jayde poured the tea and refused to look at her. "Did I tell you I got my dress? Let me show you, I want to get your opinion. I think you'll like it."

Ross left as soon as they got back to the house, but with a promise from Chloe that she'd go out to dinner with him Easter Friday. "I'm working most of the holiday so I won't be free other than that. Can you get a sitter, or should I try to find someone?'

Chloe watched him ride away and closed the door. Now what? She raced to her bedroom to haul out all the dresses in her closet. Maybe she had to go shopping because everything in here was at least a year old and a lot of it much older than that. She went into a tailspin. He hadn't kissed her before he left.

~~~

Tips from the public started flowing in. Given so many different pictures to choose from, most were wildly inaccurate. But Ross knew that amongst them could be the one that led them to Murdoch. His screening crew was soon overwhelmed. He had to wait again, and waiting was tough.
~~~

He was seeing Chloe now, out in the open, and he needed this case closed. Granted, Sanderson had been found and buried. But there was more to this case than Sanderson.

He had plans and they didn't involve putting his relationship with Chloe on hold for the next year or two. That one kiss in the hallway at her front door had nearly set him on his heels. The smell of her, the feel of her soft hair against his wrist as he raised her face to meet his. The firm pressure of her lips had shot a wave of heat through him that was staggering. That shut the door on waiting, that one kiss.

He thought of his brother. Bob had been monitoring him and brought up mention of Chloe again. Ross was very clear, he was going to see her openly. The body had been found, she wasn't implicated. He wasn't waiting for the case to be closed and if he had to ask to be taken off the investigation, then he would.

Bob was furious. It was unprofessional, he declared, it was downright dangerous for his career. He couldn't believe Ross was so stupid.

He'd finally cut through the flow of words. "Bob," he shouted. "This is my decision. This is my life and by God, I'll live it the way I think I should."

"Well, you better tell the old man then, because he'll hear about it from someone." Their father had plenty of contacts in the force, and weekly conversations with some of his old cronies who were still working. He heard everything that went on, especially when it had anything to do with his sons.

Ross went straight to Inspector Marsh and slid into a ten minute slot the older man had in his schedule. He bared his soul. Marsh looked at him long and hard. "That's a difficult position to put yourself in, Detective Cullen."

He realized Marsh was getting very formal, definitely a warning sign. "I understand that, Inspector. I've tried to hold off, it's more than ten months since the missing persons report was filed. The husband's been found, the funeral's over. The wife hasn't been implicated in any part of it. I know it doesn't look good. But I've waited and it's time to take some personal steps that I thought I should inform you about. Ms. Bowman is willing to date me."

He knew his face was red. He was overheating and shifted uncomfortably, sliding a finger inside the collar of his shirt. "I'm in love with her, sir," he choked, but doggedly continued. "And normally I wouldn't bother to tell you something personal like this, but the investigation is still open with regard to Sanderson's partner. Ms Bowman was cleared of any suspicion." Ross realized he was rambling and shut his mouth.

Marsh sat there, looking at him. Finally he moved in his chair and fingered his moustache. "Well," he gazed down at the paper on his desk, his hand over his mouth. "I think you should carry on until something turns up, then come see me about how we're going to handle it."

He held up his hand. "I won't be hanging over your shoulder. If I didn't trust you to do the job I'd give it to someone else. But we have to make this look good, as well as have it work on an ethical level. So keep me posted. If I have a change of mind on this, I'll let you know." Marsh waved him off, watching thoughtfully as he walked out the office door. Ross had the wild idea that he'd been trying to hide a smile behind his hand.

~~~

Dinner with Ross on Friday was charming. He arrived dressed in grey flannel dress pants, a button down shirt and silk jacket. His hair was freshly cut, his shave so close his jaw gleamed. Davey was being looked after by a neighbourhood girl who'd had him in the bathtub when Ross arrived. He went in to chat with the little boy for a few minutes, watched him playing with the toys in the bathwater, then left him in Katie's care.

As he waited at the door for Chloe to get her shoes, he gazed appreciatively at her outfit. "Wow, you look great." He glanced quickly at the low neckline of her top and then away. "Do you have your coat? It's chilly out there."
~~~

He'd made reservations at a trendy little Asian bistro that served a wide variety of eastern foods and had lovely atmosphere. "Not too loud," he said, looking around the entry as he took her coat and handed it to the maître'd. "But the music's nice." There was a pianist in the corner playing a meandering melody.

Ross seated himself across from her and asked what she'd like to drink. She pursed her lips ruefully. It was true, they knew each other intimately, but didn't even know the other's taste in drinks. They had never been on a date, unless she called lunch in Chinatown with Davey a date. Somehow, it didn't quite fit the description.

"I'll have a cranberry juice and soda for now." Ross ordered a beer from a local brewpub and sat back to look around the cosy room. Chloe studied him for a minute. He was different, more edgy. She sensed a real tension in him.

When he glanced at her, she had a sudden need to rearrange her napkin while their drinks were served. Ross asked about growing up with a businessman father and two older brothers.

Chloe grinned. "It was fun. That's all I can say. The boys claimed Dad spoiled me, and maybe he did. But they teased a lot and he'd make them stop, so they'd whine. But Dad was easy. He was smart and had a great sense of humour. He listened, really listened to us."

Sudden tears sparkled in her eyes. "I still miss him. He died too young. No one knew he had a heart problem, he just collapsed one evening, sitting in his easy chair after supper."

Ross took her hand in his big one and stroked her fingers. "How did your Mum take it?"

"Oh, she went right off the deep end. She lived for him, we all did. It was very hard on everyone. John was still in his twenties and he was suddenly taking over the whole construction company with jobs on the go, some half completed and quotes out, none of which he got because he was seen as too young and untried.

"It was a struggle. He'd finished university and been doing his carpentry apprenticeship with Dad. Right away he had trouble with some of the guys who wouldn't accept him as boss, that's one of the reasons he's so hard. He had to bull his way through to pull those jobs to completion with the banks hounding him and his workers questioning every step he took.

"We all worked then, Brent, John and I, to add what we could. Brent worked out on the crews because then John would hear what was being said and done out there. I worked in the office to make sure his interests were looked after there. And of course Ralph, what a loyal guy. He worked for Dad for years as foreman and stuck right by John, advising and supporting. Anyway, how did I get on this? Good heavens." She ran a finger under her eyelash to catch the moisture and turned her face to watch the musician.

Ross tugged on her fingers. "Is that when you met Jeff?"

She turned back to stare at him for a minute. "I met him four months later. He came into the office for a quote on a job." She smiled and tugged her hand back to allow the waiter to place her dinner in front of her. "Oh, that looks wonderful, and smells so good."

"What about you?" she said, when the waiter left. "I know you have one brother in the police."

Ross nodded, and poked at his spring rolls. "One older brother in the RCMP. His name is Bob, Robert named after our father. And one younger sister."

"Oh," said Chloe. "Just like my family. Two boys and then a girl. How strange."

"Not quite," he said. "There were three boys. Another brother, younger than me, his name was Sandy. Alexander. He died when we were young. He was walking on the train tracks with his friend and when the train came Greg got off but Sandy was still running and didn't make it." Ross drummed his fingers on the table.

Chloe watched them for a minute, then placed her hand gently over his restless fingers. He paused, watching her face then flipped his hand over and grasped hers. He gave her a wonderful little smile that made her heart turn over in her chest.

"How old was he?"

"He was eight, I was ten and Bob was thirteen. Our sister, Allie was just four. She doesn't really remember him."

"That's so sad." She watched him take a bite of his rice noodles. "Is it good?"

"You won't know if you don't try it," he laughed.

Chloe thoroughly enjoyed herself. When Ross brought her home, she turned to invite him in. But his expression was so determined, almost grim, that the words caught in her throat.

"I'll drive the sitter home," he said.

"Oh. Okay."

He took the key from her hand and unlocked the front door. The sitter went to get her coat and shoes on and Ross took the opportunity to tug Chloe into the kitchen.

"Thank you for coming to dinner, Chloe. I really enjoyed it. Can I call you? Will you answer the phone if I call?"

Chloe nodded, wordless.

"Good." His arms slid around her waist under her coat and he leaned his head down to hers, his mouth claiming a fierce kiss. It soon softened, his lips moving over hers in surrender as much as possession. He pulled back and lifted his head, taking a deep breath.

"Well," he said as he stepped back. "I'll call," and he turned and walked out the door with Katie hobbling behind, one shoe still untied.

Chloe listened to his truck start up outside, then the lights swept round and were gone. She collapsed on the stairs, her feet resting on the bottom step. It was so difficult, she didn't know where she stood. He'd asked her out yet he barely kissed her goodnight before he darted out the door.

"Chloe?"

She looked up to see Amanda peering down at her over the railing from the landing up above.

"Are you okay? You could have asked me to babysit Davey, you know. I like to."

"Oh, Amanda, thank you. But you have mid-terms and papers due. I don't mind getting a sitter." Her chin landed on her hand.

Amanda crept down the stairs. "Are you okay? How did the date go? Katie said he was a real big guy and handsome." She giggled.

"Yes, he's handsome." Chloe choked back a sob. "It went okay."

"Just okay? That's too bad. Didn't you like him?"

Chloe rolled her head sideways to look at her boarder. "Is it wrong to be dating someone so soon after they found Jeff? I'm muddled in my head. I can't seem to think it through. I don't know anything for sure, anymore."

Amanda put her hand on her shoulder. "Oh, Chloe. You've waited so long. Ever since I met you, you've been alone. That's the word that always came to mind. Alone." She slid her arm along Chloe's shoulders as she saw the tears begin to fall. "Sorry, Chloe. I didn't mean to make you feel bad."

Chloe shook her head, wiping her nose with her wrist. "You didn't. I can do that all by myself."

~~~

"Boss, we just got a call from Saskatoon reporting a Rain Murdoch lookalike." Parker still had one arm in his jacket as he leaned around the wall of the cubicle. "A young woman says he's staying in a rental cabin at a place where she works on the edge of town, been there a few weeks. He doesn't let her into his cabin to clean and he doesn't have a job. But she got a photo of him with her cell phone, clever girl, and the lab says it's a match with the Bob Humphreys and Troy Smith shots from the bank cameras!"
~~~

Ross froze in the process of rising from his chair. "Good, good. Let's move. Send word to bring him in. Do we know what he's driving?"

Parker nodded and came into the small room, his jacket dragging on the floor. "He's got a ten year old black Ford pickup. He cooks in his room, goes to the local grocery, sometimes eats at a small diner nearby. A couple times a week he goes to the local bar and has a few. Not much else. Spends a lot of time in his cabin, she says."

Ross hunched his shoulders. "So an early morning raid. Get them to scope it out first and make sure they know where he is, which cabin, the entrances to the property, the cabin doors. Traffic patterns, you name it. Don't screw this up, Dan. This guy is like an eel, we can't lose him. If we put someone to follow him, he'll be gone in a flash.

"Call the Saskatoon detachment, find out who's going to be handling this. Have them call me. We need to coordinate this with a knitting needle, it's got to be done just right." Ross sat back in his chair, the papers in front of him forgotten.

This was their chance, maybe the only one for months to come. If they blew it, there was no knowing where Murdoch would hide. Ross couldn't believe he was still in western Canada. Why not go east or to the States, even Mexico? He had enough money. It was hard to take a ton of cash across the border, but not impossible. And Murdoch was the kind of guy who seemed to thrive on strategic planning.

He wanted to see this photo. He leaped from his chair and headed for the door.

~~~

Chloe hosted the family dinner Easter Sunday. They'd been at church together in the morning, then came out in the afternoon to the house. Davey raced around the kitchen with Plutie at his heels. He steamed up to the door and screeched to a halt each time the doorbell went.
~~~

There were no boarders today. Dennis had gone home Friday with a younger brother who came down island to drive him back. Amanda caught the bus Thursday night for home. Beth had gone with her. Don was staying at a friend's house. So for a few nights, Chloe and Davey had the house to themselves.

There was a ham slow cooking in the oven, smothered in brown sugar and hot mustard. The others were bringing vegetables and Vivienne was bringing pie. Chloe made hot-cross buns. It was only her second attempt, but they turned out well. Davey liked the cross cut into the top of each bun and had laboriously made his own with some of the dough she gave him to work with. His slightly grey looking rolls were cooked in a separate pan and cooling on the counter when the family arrived.

Diana phoned at the last minute and asked to bring a teacher from school who was new to town and didn't have family to spend the weekend with. Chloe set an extra place at the table. And Vivienne was bringing her new beau, Edward.

There were nine of them. Edward turned out to be a nice man who'd been in business, had two restaurants that were taken over by his kids when he retired. He and John had a lot to talk about, especially the issue of handing over the reins to the next generation. Diana's friend was an attractive man teaching grade seven in the elementary school where she worked.

"This is Chris," she said when they arrived at the door. Chloe liked him instantly. He was one of those people who made her feel at ease. She raised her brows at Diana who smiled delightedly from behind his back as they came into the house.

Chris had come into the school district as vice principal, and handled a lot of the physical education classes. Chloe didn't mind him there, Easter was a time to spend with family and friends. There were loads of leftovers, and she parcelled it out as they left.

As she hugged Vivienne goodbye, she whispered in her ear, "He's really nice, Mum. I'm glad for you."

Vivienne beamed and took Edward's arm as they went down the front steps. Chris hung back to say goodnight, his eyes roving round the entry hall. Finally, as the last family member left, she put out her hand. "Goodnight, Chris. Thanks for joining us. It was nice to meet you."

He took her hand in a warm grip. "Thank you, Chloe. I really enjoyed myself."

"Not at all," she said, tugging a little. He finally released her.

"May I call you?" he asked. "Maybe we could go for coffee or lunch sometime." His grin was engaging.

Chloe laughed. "In a bit, perhaps. Not right now, no."

He nodded understandingly. "I know something of your situation. Diana mentioned it on the way out, but of course it's been in the papers."

Her smile became strained. "Yes, well, not yet. Thank you, anyway." She turned up the wattage on her smile and moved to close the door.

He edged backward.

"Chris," Diana called from the car.

He turned his head at the call. "Be right there." Then he looked back. "In a few weeks, then. Chloe, I'll call and see how you are."

She maintained her smile until the door was shut.

"What does he want to call for?" Davey demanded, frowning up at her.

"Good question," she muttered.

Ross had phoned to wish them happy Easter, but didn't say when he'd see them. She was upset by the uncertainty. She compensated by keeping as busy as she could. Davey asked about him again, when would he come over so they could play? Or when would they go on a bike ride with Woss?

Her chest hurt. Maybe she was getting some kind of infection, like pneumonia, although she didn't have a cough. She was hot and chilled by turns, totally discombobulated.

Monday night he called to invite them to dinner at his folks place. "It's Dad's birthday," he said, "the family will be there. I'd like you and Davey to meet them. There'll be a couple of other children around his age, my brother's boys. I'll pick you up."

Chloe hung up in turmoil. *Meet his family?* That sounded so different from what she'd imagined. It put an entirely unique spin on it. She turned it over in her mind endlessly, until she thought she might go crazy.

CHAPTER TWENTY FIVE

Rain was arrested just before four on a cold morning in Saskatoon. He heard a tremendous banging on the front door of his cabin that woke him from a light sleep. He'd been thinking it might be time to leave. He'd seen the pictures of his face as Troy Smith and Bob Humphreys, they were posted in the paper and shown several times on the news on television. The police were getting close. It had been nagging at him, and even though he'd decided to spend the winter here, he had a sudden urge to move on. He'd had a restless night.

When the banging started, he grabbed his pants, a heavy shirt and a handful of keys on the nightstand before moving silently toward the back door. He shifted the curtain aside to see the face of a uniformed police officer waiting in the light skiff of snow on the back step.

Pulling his pants on, he walked to the front entrance. When he opened it, three officers bulled in and forced him backward onto the couch. He'd known it was just a matter of time. He almost welcomed it. No more running, hiding, shifting in the night. It was over.

He offered his Victor Landon ID and watched silently as they searched the place, tossing it methodically and collecting everything in garbage bags. They turned all the furniture upside down, tossed the bed and examined the mattress.

They pounded on the wall in the back of the closet, lifted the area rug to check the floor for loose boards. He reached for his shirt and was immediately restrained. Then one officer was assigned to watch him while he found his socks and pulled them on, then a tee shirt and heavy over shirt. He got his boots and coat, knowing he wasn't coming back here.

They dumped the sofa onto the floor, having removed all the cushions and tore the lining down, unscrewed the legs. They took his truck keys and tossed the truck, cab and bed while they waited for the tow to take it away to police storage for searching. Then they cuffed him and hustled him out to the squad car that was waiting in the light drifting snow.

As they drove away, he looked back through the early morning light at the small faux log cabin fading from view. This is what it came down to. This was all there was left, a little rented cabin sitting in the snow at the edge of a city in the middle of the prairies. He had been reduced to the clothes he stood up in.

He had his one phone call when they finished processing and booked him at the Saskatoon detachment headquarters. He called Susan, caught her just before she left for night shift at the hospital. "Susan," he said. "It's Rain. I'm at the police station in Saskatoon and they've arrested me. Now I want you to listen."

Already he heard her protests and weepy panic seeping through the phone lines.

"I need your help, Susie. You have to listen." He looked around the cubicle where he'd been given access to a phone. Was he being monitored? He had no choice any more in how he handled things.

"Listen, Susie. Listen. Remember, I mailed you a set of keys about two months ago. They were in a manila envelope and I told you to keep them in a safe place. Do you still have them?"

She sobbed into the phone.

"Susie, do you still have them?"

"Yes," she gulped, then got a grip on herself. "Yes, I still have them."

"Okay, they're keys to a storage locker here in Saskatoon. I need you to come out here in the next few weeks, bring the keys and go to the storage locker. The address is written on the card inside the envelope. Do you still have it? Good. It's locker number twenty-two. Remember that. Locker number twenty-two. Inside is a trunk, an old travelling trunk. The first key is for the door to the locker, the second key is for the trunk. And there are bags in the trunk. You have to get the bags. Now, Susie."

He stopped as the crying started up again. "Susie, come on."

"Okay," she said wetly. "Go ahead."

"There are bags in the trunk, you have to get them back to your place. It's not dirty money, Susie. It isn't drug money. There's tax owing on it, but other than that it's clean. You should drive out here, because it'll be hard to fly with that much cash in your luggage. Best call Dad and get him to help. You could use his truck. Can you do that?"

"Okay. Yes, I can. Darrell and I, one of us will do it."

"Good, because I'll need money to pay my lawyer, and that's where it's going to come from. "

He heard her take a deep breath. "Okay, Rain. We can do that. Who's your lawyer? We can get some money to him right away out of our own account."

"Don't worry about it, Susie. I won't be here that long. I'm wanted for questioning in BC and that's where I'll end up, so I'll let you know who to send it to and when."

~~~
~~~

Ross arrived at the house a few minutes early to pick them up. Davey swung on his leg, then dragged him off to his bedroom to see the dress shirt he was going to wear. Chloe appeared in the doorway minutes later to hustle him into it.

"He's not wearing it now, because we wanted it to stay clean as long as possible," she explained as she stuck his arms into the sleeves of the dress shirt. She buttoned him up and tucked the tails in, then adjusted his belt. It was black with a silver horseshoe buckle. Davey stuck out his stomach to show it off. "From Uncle Brent," he said and shone it lovingly with his hand.

"Very nice," said Ross. "Very nice, indeed." But he was looking at Chloe.

She straightened and smiled shyly. Her skirt was knee length, swirling gracefully around her legs and her sweater was cut on the bias and moulded to her figure like a second skin. He couldn't take his eyes off her, suddenly wondering how his brother was going to behave. He stiffened at the thought.

Rain Murdoch had arrived in Victoria that afternoon. Ross hadn't seen him yet but knew there was no way to get near him, he was lawyering up as quickly as possible. He hoped with all his heart that this was the end of the case. If he could just get the real story from Murdoch about the Potholes, then he was determined to put the whole series of events to rest. There were always a few details left, the questions didn't all get answered, but hopefully this would fill in the big picture.

The charges Murdoch faced would likely include money laundering, tax evasion, extortion plus murder or manslaughter, depending on how the story went about Sanderson's death. Dickson would have more to say on that score because it was possible that the two of them worked together to kill Sanderson and share the profits. That would suggest a charge of 'conspiracy to commit' as well. Any way he cut it, Murdoch was facing some heavy penalties and would likely want to make a deal. He'd have to spill his info, and Ross couldn't wait to hear what that was going to be.

As he brought Chloe and Davey out to his truck, he pondered how to broach the subject with her and decided there was no way to do it.

The evening went well. There was the moment he observed Bob eyeing Chloe's sweater and had to stare him down. Then Greg seemed to be caught by the same sight and he'd reached across him for the potatoes and nudged him heavily with his foot.

Finally, dinner over, Dad took the men downstairs to show them the renovation he was doing, taking out a wall to make the recreation room bigger.

Robert Cullen was no fool and he made a pointed if gentle nudge at his eldest son and Greg, Sandy's old friend and honorary family member, to keep their eyes on their own women. Bob protested, claiming it was actually a police matter to ascertain whether the reports of the chest were to be believed. Ross nearly clocked him for that comment, but then Greg stepped in to contribute that although he hadn't heard said reports, he had to believe they were true.

He hung his head in frustration, having caught the humorous glint in his father's eye. "Okay, guys. You can stop now. I think I've got the point." He looked up ruefully to the guffaws of the others.

His father finally wiped his eyes and gave him a one-armed hug. "Never mind, Ross. Their tongues are hanging out and that's all you need to know." He broke into chuckles again, but finally pulled himself together. "Aw, she's a fine looking woman, Ross. And I think she's a true one, too. And her little boy is charming. He's playing with Bob's two like there's no end in sight. It's cute to see.

"He's a good little guy," Bob chipped in. "You'd think it would've been very difficult to keep him balanced, with what's gone on over the past year. Yet he seems okay. And she does too. A bit tentative, maybe. Probably not sure how we'd receive her, knowing the background as we do."

Greg looked curious, so Bob quickly filled him in. "The husband's body was finally found," he finished.

"And we just arrested his partner in Saskatchewan," said Ross. "He arrived in town today to face charges."

His father and brother both turned to him soberly. "Whoa. That's good." Bob thought a minute. "Does she know?"

"I haven't told her. I'm caught, just like we discussed. I won't talk about it until there's an official message for her and that'll come from Marsh."

Greg was perfectly at home in this conversation, he'd attended many of them over the years, both as a child when Sandy was alive, and later when the family had simply accepted that he was still part of the clan. When Bob and then Ross joined the force, it was a given that the conversation tended to drift in that direction.

"Well," Bob stroked his jaw thoughtfully. "If you can keep your hands off her until the job's done, that'll be a miracle. And if tonight's any indication, I don't hold out much hope."

Ross reached over to give him a hefty shove and they laughed, but he caught the sober look in his father's eyes.

When he escorted Chloe into her house, carrying a sleeping Davey in his arms, he tensed. Keeping his hands off her was getting harder and harder. She didn't help, looking up at him cautiously from those dark eyes, sweeping her hair back over her shoulder with her hand.

That's what he wanted to do, put his hands in her hair, feel its silky texture. It was just one of the many ways he wanted to touch her. It didn't really matter what she did or how she moved, it tempted him. He turned away and looked toward Davey's bedroom. "Shall I carry him straight down to bed?"

She nodded and preceded him, turning on lights as she went. Between them they shuffled the little limbs into pyjamas and tucked him under the covers. Chloe showed Plutie to the door, then checked the counter in the kitchen.

"Okay, Dennis isn't home yet. We have to leave the lights on for him."

Picking up her coat from the floor where she'd dropped it, she hung it in the closet. "Would you like a coffee or something?"

He looked down at her, the whole package of woman. *What I want doesn't come in a mug.* He shook his head. "No, thanks. Come here, Chloe."

She came to him willingly, moving into his arms and laying her head on his chest. He hugged her tight, his chin resting at her temple. He could smell her perfume and her own scent like a light musk beneath. It was powerful, tugging at him relentlessly. Even sitting at dinner, he caught her scent. He'd kept turning to brush his hand across the back of her chair and touch her hair with his fingers or rub his fingers lightly down her thigh as she sat so primly beside him. It had been irresistible, like an aphrodisiac. He knew exactly what Bob had been teasing him about.

She wound her arms around his back under his coat, her palms flattened against him. He shuddered. This was a formidable force and he didn't know if he'd survive it unscathed. He lowered his head to kiss her and she opened up to him like a flower responding to the warming sun.

He sank like a stone, his lips opening over hers and his tongue sinking into her mouth. Within seconds he was breathing heavily and had an erection he couldn't hide.

He heard the door open behind him and jerked back, pushing Chloe to the side as he turned to face the intruder. A younger man stood there, his dark head turned to stare at him.

"Hi, Dennis," he heard Chloe say behind him.

As he drove his truck back into the city, he reflected morosely on how fate seemed to have a hand in everything. Or maybe it wasn't fate at all, but God's plan for him. If he took a certain path he'd end up at a certain place, no matter how long it might take him to get there. No matter how fast or slow he travelled, he'd still end up there. He'd been about to get in deep with Chloe tonight, too deep to pull himself back.

But no, Dennis the boarder had arrived and put the kibosh on that. But he'd end up there anyway, he was determined, life plan or no life plan. He smirked ironically to himself. Ross, the philosopher. Definitely not.

~~~

Chloe had had a meeting with Bill Hodson about the shares and that night she turned the issues over in her mind. If the shares were owned by someone else, then she'd only have half ownership of the building. On the other hand, would that mean that the other shareholder was also liable for the tax debt? There was nothing she could do, it was out of her hands. It was almost more frustration than she could bear.

As she readied for bed, her thoughts went to the dinner at Ross's parents. It had been nice to be included in what was obviously a close family. She liked his mother right away, she was warm and welcoming. His father was a bit more reserved and she'd been prepared for that, knowing his background and expecting him to be suspicious about her character. But when they left he'd given her a real hug and said he hoped to see her again soon. That had made her feel good.

Davey enjoyed himself. With two other boys to play with, one older, one younger, he was entertained all evening running back and forth and up and down the stairs to the basement.

Ross's sister Allie was there with her husband Jesse, a plumber. He and Greg had talked back and forth when the conversation got too full of police work, although they joshed good-naturedly about how they had to stay on the straight and narrow in order to keep a place in the family. Chloe had been uncomfortable at that comment, and glanced around but didn't see anyone looking at her sideways.

What she'd been anticipating was Ross bringing her home. The way he kept touching her during dinner had
~~~

distracted her terribly. She could feel his leg pressed against hers under the table, or his arm barely touching her shoulder as he leaned on the back of her chair while he talked down the table. At one point he turned and planted one foot on the rung of her chair and his knee gently rubbed her thigh, back and forth. It drove her mad.

And when they got home, just when he kissed her, Dennis arrived. What timing. Ross shot out the door like a bullet, couldn't get out of there fast enough. Was he embarrassed? Surely he was too mature to be thrown off his stride by a twenty-two year old university student who greeted them and bounded up the stairs?

No, it was something else. It was as if he'd decided to keep their relationship on a strictly friendly basis. And yet he kept taking her out. She couldn't figure it out, and it was so damn frustrating she felt like wringing his big neck for him.

She collapsed on her bed in absolute agony, her headache escalating to painful peaks. Levering herself up, she took a handful of pain pills and fell back into bed.

~~~

"Can you believe this?" Chloe asked.

"No, I can't say that I do."

She had dropped by John's office with coffee. Davey played in the corner with the action figures he kept there.

"So let me get this straight. The lawyer says there were fifty shares issued but he filed a report with the Company Records Office saying that one hundred were issued. No one knows where those extra shares are. Revenue Canada says they can accept some of the money Jeff's dad gave him but not all the money. And the mortgage company is holding a life insurance policy on Jeff for a million dollars." He laughed and sipped his coffee.

Chloe's head jerked around. "It's not funny, John."

He snorted. "It is, kind of. Come on, Chloe. This is stranger and stranger, you have to admit. Was Jeff some kind of alchemist, turning salt into gold? Do you really believe his
~~~

father gave him six hundred thousand dollars and he brought it into the country in cash?"

She just stared at him. "I don't know. It's so odd I almost believe it. I can't prove it one way or the other, but the documents looked genuine. Where would he get them if he didn't do what he claimed?"

John shrugged and leaned down to hoist Davey onto his lap where he settled in to play with the toys on his desk. Chloe watched them for a minute.

"How's Rosemary feeling these days? That baby isn't too far away."

John flushed. "She's pretty good. Tired of being pregnant, says her belly gets in the way of doing things but she feels okay."

"Are you excited?"

His colour deepened." Yeah." His gaze slid to the side.

"It's okay to be excited," she said. "I think it's wonderful, you'll be a good dad. A lot like our father, and he was the best."

John smiled in spite of himself. "You would think that, he always took your side."

Chloe laughed. "You keep telling yourself that, John."

CHAPTER TWENTY SIX

The first session with Rainier Murdoch was one of the toughest Ross had ever been involved with. He was a very private individual. Each question was weighed and measured before it was answered, usually in as few words as possible. They spent most of the day at it and got next to nowhere. Finally Ross called another halt and motioned Murdoch's lawyer out into the corridor.

"I'm not sure where we're getting on this," he said.

The lawyer nodded. "He is cautious."

Ross snorted, and the lawyer gave a reluctant grin. "Admit it, you've never had a client this careful in your whole career."

The lawyer nodded. "Maybe once or twice," he said and waited.

"Well, I'm not inclined to quit now. We can go all night. We need his cooperation and it's only been, what?" He looked at his watch. "Ten hours, I vote we go another six, then break for four and start up again with a second team. What do you think?"

The lawyer eyed him carefully. "What's the full range of charges he's facing?"

Ross reeled them off. "Plus anything else we can dig up. So with murder and perhaps conspiracy to commit in the mix, you'd think he might like to cooperate."

"What's your evidence?"

Ross gave him a hard look. "Suffice it to say, we've got everything pretty well pinned down. We need information on his accomplice, Tom Dickson."

"Let me talk to him, then we'll break for dinner. That will give him time to think about it, and we can reconvene at eight. How does that sound? If we have to go all night, so be it."

Ross nodded and sent his crew off to eat while they waited. At eight o'clock, the lawyer was just emerging from consulting with Murdoch. "We need more information," he said. "My advice to my client has been to get that information before making a decision. What do you have in the way of evidence against him with regard to Sanderson's death, Tom Dickson's involvement and the money laundering charge? If we can see that, we can make a decision."

They arranged to meet first thing in the morning. Ross went back to his desk, going over the file, finding the loopholes and seeing how persuasively he could present the evidence. Parker popped his head in. "How's it going, boss? I heard the Murdoch interview is short circuited."

Ross nodded. "Only for now, we meet again in the morning. They want to know what the evidence is before they decide on a plea bargain. How did things go with you?"

"It went well. Trudy Ashmore and her brother are both ready to come in tomorrow and identify him as Bob Humphreys and Trudy can ID him as Troy Smith. That's as good as it gets for impersonation. Uhjal Singh is coming as well, he knows Rainier Murdoch, so can ID him. I haven't got Buddy Slots yet, but if I do, then we'll have impersonation nailed down."

"Thanks, Dan."

He looked at his phone, then his watch. Could he call Chloe this late? He needed to talk to her, if just to wish her good night. He hesitated but finally dialled the number. It rang and he waited. When it went to voice mail he left a short message. Now, that could mean she was either out or sleeping and didn't hear the phone.

He was in a cold sweat. What if she was out with some other guy? He hadn't exactly laid claim to her, he'd been back on his heels, trying to keep his feelings under control. At least, not out of control, which is what it was like when he went to bed with her. He lost perspective. He lost good judgement. He lost his head.

He paced. Should he drive out there and see if her truck was in the garage? That was too degrading for words. He either went out to see her or he went home. He grabbed his jacket and went home.

~~~

The second interview with Rainier Murdoch didn't go well. Ross presented his case persuasively, but with Tom Dickson insisting Sanderson's death was an accident, he didn't have enough to tip the scales. He consulted Marsh and they came up with manslaughter. Even that charge was tenuous and would likely have to be dropped if it went to trial.

Without further evidence, he wasn't going to get anyone pinned for the death of Jeff Sanderson. And maybe he had to accept that death through inadvertence was all that had happened.

That left money laundering, impersonation and tax evasion. He didn't want to see Murdoch get off so lightly but the will to continue this case from those in charge was waning. They wanted it wrapped up. With Dickson on the hook for extortion and fraud in the apartment scam, they wanted to put it to bed.

Ross thought he'd never worked on a case for so long with so little to show. After consultation with his lawyer, Murdoch said he'd think about what he was willing to do. Ross left in total frustration.
~~~

James Dolan, however had gotten tired of sitting in a cell and decided to talk. He met with Parker and arranged a plea bargain that involved doing time in the community, given that he had only committed 'a victimless crime.'

Parker reminded him someone had died in the middle of this business but Dolan wouldn't budge. No one died because of what he did. He might have helped people commit fraud, but no one died from it.

Dolan identified Murdoch as his client and when given access to his equipment, he pulled up all the information in his file under the name Richard Meredith, the name he was using when Dolan first met him. When they went through that file, Ross found Murdoch had used seven aliases with Dolan's help, and had half a dozen others in reserve. There were another four aliases for Trudy Ashmore.

He went back at Murdoch, adding fraud to the list of charges. Murdoch was still thinking, so Ross offered to move ahead on the charges immediately and let the chips fall where they may.

Then a call came in from Edmonton. Dickson had been questioned again and the interrogating officer had let him know Rainman was arrested and talking. Tom seemed petrified by the new. He began to spew information, ranting about how Sanderson died.

They met Murdoch at the head of the Sooke Falls, he said. Murdoch was waiting for them. He was angry they were trying to pass a cheque, it was a stupid move after all the care they'd taken to stay under the radar. But Sanderson wouldn't back down and told Murdoch this was a part of the deal, either get on board or their partnership was finished.

Murdoch had a savage temper, Dickson had seen it before. He flew into a rage, picked up a heavy branch from the ground, whirled around and nailed Sanderson in the chest, using the piece of wood as if it was a baseball bat. He teetered on the edge of the bank and Murdoch hit him again across the forehead. He fell head first into the falls.

Ross was on fire. He had his evidence and he was going to nail Murdoch to the wall. This story tied very well with the one of Murdoch hitting Troy Smith in the ribs with a two by four. The man was going down for murder. He felt the familiar adrenaline rush as the end loomed near, that great feeling he always got when the evidence fell into place, when the proof finally landed in their hands. Rainier Murdoch was their man.

Soon, he could be with Chloe. Chloe and Davey were a part of him and he hurt badly from the gap in his life, from the wanting that gnawed at him. But he was close now, so close.

He called Chloe that night, but found he couldn't just chat. It made the separation that much more painful. He talked with Davey for a few minutes, then told her he'd call soon and hung up. His neck was so stiff he could hardly turn his head. He hit the gym at midnight.

~~~

Chloe's meeting with tax lawyer Ian Moreau was Chloe's first stop of the morning. He laid out the final proposal from Revenue Canada. They had come up with reasons for their determination, and Moreau found them quite encouraging. None of the deposits into the corporate account or the construction account were traceable, with the exception of transfers from the tenants of the building for rent. That meant it was all cash and therefore suspect. They were willing to accept the construction jobs as legitimate income.

"In other words," said Moreau, "they've also accepted the five hundred and fifty thousand building down payment, given the proof that the money was given by the father to the son by way of gift. Everything else is taxable income. Zeke told me they didn't bother deciding whether it was illegal, there's no one to charge."

Chloe's face froze. Moreau paused and scrutinized her. "Ms Bowman, I don't know what your husband did or
~~~

didn't do, I'm not passing judgement. I'm simply trying to give you the best outcome that I can."

She nodded and tried to smile. "Good. I appreciate that."

"Okay." He flipped a page. "To skip to the bottom line, they gave in on the money from the father and stuck to their guns on everything else. That leaves," he swung the sheaf of papers around to show her the figures, "This much owing in taxes. All the accounts at Revenue Canada will be closed, yours, your husband's, the construction company, the corporate account. They'll put it all to rest. They can't come back at you if any further information comes to light.

"I realize that's a lot of money, but they've bent on the time frame. I've negotiated a three year period to pay. That's the best I could do. And I have no way of knowing if this schedule is feasible, but it's a generous decision, they're seldom that lenient. I think the earthquake is having its effect, many people are in similar circumstances."

Chloe left the office with a copy of the file in her briefcase and a strange weightless feeling of relief. It was a lot of money and the company was in a risky position. Maybe she could manage, maybe she couldn't, but at least she knew where she stood. And the whole issue was dealt with, off her plate.

There were other issues standing right behind that one waiting for her to tackle, like the life insurance. The mortgage company was 'holding' it pending some decision on their part. *What decision?* To see if they could legally grab it? If they took it, that was one million dollars less she owed on the mortgage. If they couldn't take it, then they had to give it to the company. Just another little battle to fight, one that she was afraid to take on until the shares were sorted out.

The only thought keeping her going was that at this point, it looked like she'd keep her house. They wouldn't lose their home, and if all else failed, she'd take boarders and get a job and they'd manage.

She met Vivienne at the gym and they did a workout together. Her mother was seeing a lot of Edward and he'd finally gotten his nerve up to introduce her to the family. They'd been thrilled to meet her and Vivienne glowed with happiness.

~~~

Chloe arrived home to a household of hungry boarders. Don Murphy was the most vocal, wondering aloud why dinner couldn't be a regular thing in a household where people paid room and board. She stiffened in affront but continued cutting vegetables as the chicken cooked in the oven. She moved the rice off the burner.

As she arranged a vegetable plate, Murphy sat at the kitchen table, his legs stretched out. Chloe had to move around him as she carried dishes into the dining room. On her way back she tripped over his feet. "Don, would you please move? You're in the way."

He moved an inch and gave her a flat stare.

"Move your feet, Don."

He shifted slightly.

Chloe met him stare for stony stare. Finally she braced a hand on her hip. "What is your problem, Mr. Murphy? You're rude and belligerent. Go and take your petty moods out on someone else. I'm not interested."

He glared. "Dinner was supposed to be ready half an hour ago."

Chloe threw up her hands. "That's the last straw. Pack up your stuff and leave. This is your final night here. I don't care where you go. I'm going to refund your payment for this month. Just get out and leave me alone."

She crossed to the stove, pulled the chicken out of the oven and shoveled the pieces onto a platter. There was silence behind her.

"But I don't have anywhere else to go."

"I don't care. It has nothing to do with me." Chloe kept working, digging the rice out of the pot and dumping it into a serving bowl.
~~~

"Dinner!" she called and carried the food to the table.

"But I can't!"

She finally had his attention.

"This is the last month of school, I only need this month. What's your problem?"

"You," she said as she walked by with the basket of rolls and a dish of butter. "Just pack up. I've had enough and I'm not going to put up with you anymore." The others thundered down the stairs and Chloe got Davey into his booster seat at the table.

Later that night, with Davey in bed, Chloe was catching up on her email when a quiet knock sounded at her open office door. "Come in," she called, and looked up to watch Don Murphy sidle into the room. His face was flushed and he stood uncertainly before her.

"Can I talk to you for a minute?"

"Sure." She pushed her chair around, but didn't ask him to sit.

"Well, about you asking me to leave…" He hesitated.

"I didn't ask you." she said. "I told you. I'm finished with your rude manners. I don't want you here anymore."

"Yeah, that's what I meant. I just wanted to talk about that."

"What about it?"

"I was hoping I could stay." His gaze fell away and landed on a spot on the floor near her feet.

"Why would you want to stay? You don't like it here, you've made that plain."

"Well, I don't mind it here. That is, I like it well enough." He risked a glance at her, but obviously decided he wasn't doing that well. "It's just, that is… this is the last month of school and then I'll be going home. It's going to be hard to find another place for such a short period of time."

Chloe said nothing.

His face went a darker shade of red. "I apologize for my behaviour. I don't know why I do that, but sometimes I forget to use my manners. I'm sorry, Ms. Bowman. I won't do it again. I wonder if there is any way you could manage to let me stay."

Chloe was silent so long he finally had to look at her. "You see, Don," she said. "The fact that you apologized has left me speechless. That is so out of character from what I know about you. Are you that rude at work?"

He shook his head.

"No, I don't imagine so. They would've hustled you out of there the first week. I don't know why I've put up with you this long."

"So, does that mean I can stay?" He slanted a look at her.

"I don't know. I'll have to think about it. Tell you what. You pay me an extra month's rent for the aggravation of putting up with it this long. Then if you can manage to control your tongue and your attitude, you can stay."

He went beet red. He looked at the floor for a long time, then nodded. "Okay, I can do that."

"Good. That's the only way you can stay." She had his cheque in her hand before she turned out the light.

Lying in bed, she smiled at the irony of making Don Murphy pay two months' rent to stay till the term ended. She never thought she'd be that tough, but sometimes her good humour just dissipated and another Chloe appeared, one who wouldn't put up with the Don Murphys of this world.

She glanced at the window, where a sliver of moon showed above the trees. It had been a tough day. There were still some huge hurdles to cross before she could get her life under some semblance of control.

Ross seemed to have given up calling. She didn't often answer her phone and when he left messages, she hesitated to call back. She'd answered last night but he didn't talk long, just chatted with Davey and then promised to call again soon. She was despondent. She was lonely and heartsick.

She sank into despair, feeling giddy and weepy by turns. She was desperately lonesome, surrounded by her boarders. She sighed weakly into her pillow.

CHAPTER TWENTY SEVEN

Ross planned to see Rain Murdoch with a list of demands and a fist full of evidence. Before he could get in to begin an interrogation, Rain's lawyer contacted him. He was meeting his client that morning, and they'd like to see Ross at eleven to talk over options. He promised to have further information for him. Ross held his fire. He was getting more information by the minute. What else could there be?

He took Parker with him to the meeting. Parker was the only one who knew as much as he did about this case and a second opinion would be helpful. The lawyer had just wound up his talk with Murdoch, and came out with a pad of paper in his hand. They went into a side room.

The lawyer settled down at the flimsy metal table and shot his cuffs. "Well, gentlemen," he said. "We have a proposal. My client is willing to provide information on the death of Jeff Sanderson and on an apartment building scam in which Tom Dickson took part. In exchange, he'd like to deal on his sentence for impersonation and tax evasion. He says there's no basis for fraud charges."

The conversation went back and forth, and finally Ross left to contact Marsh. He was sceptical about Murdoch's ability to prove what had happened at the Sooke Potholes, so he didn't think any deal they came up with would hold water. But he badly wanted to hear his story. It was afternoon before the arrangement was in place, signed off by the Attorney General's office.

Ross had had five hours sleep and felt more than a little testy. He marched into the interview room with an attitude.

"Okay, folks, let's get this show on the road. By the way, Murdoch, this is your last chance to cough up what you know. My patience is completely gone."

The lawyer raised his hand. "No need to threaten my client, Detective Cullen. We have a deal and my client's quite aware of his responsibilities." He nodded to Murdoch.

Murdoch sat as still as a statue in his chair. In spite of the orange jumpsuit, he looked cool and totally in control. He gave Ross a measured look. "Where would you like me to start?"

"With the death of Jeff Sanderson," he shot back.

Murdoch nodded his head and rested his clasped hands on the table as the handcuffs clanked against the metal top. He fixed his eyes on Ross and began to talk.

He'd met with Sanderson the week before he disappeared and Jeff had floated the idea of the apartment scam. Murdoch said 'no'. They were in a relatively legal business and he didn't want to muddy the waters.

Ross's eyebrows climbed at this outrageous claim but Murdoch's expression didn't change. He continued calmly.

He thought Sanderson had accepted his position. Then he got an email setting up a meeting at the 'third position'. That meant the Sooke Potholes.

"What were the first and second positions?" Parker interrupted.

"We had other meeting places, six different ones in all, set up but not recorded. That way we could get together without articulating that information by either phone or email."

Ross filed away 'articulating' for future reference.

Rainier arrived before Sanderson and was waiting on a stump back under the trees out of the rain when the others arrived. He was considerably surprised to see Tom Dickson. He'd assumed Sanderson was coming alone.

"Had you met Dickson before?"

"Yes. Once. I wasn't impressed."

Ross smirked. Compared to the superficially affable and slightly ineffective conman, Rainier Murdoch was both more restrained and had a more subtly dangerous aura about him. He motioned for the prisoner to continue.

The two men arrived at the top of the trail and looked around for Murdoch. When he stood to gain their attention, they approached. He greeted Sanderson and asked what the meeting was about. Because Dickson was there, he suspected it was about the apartment scam that Sanderson had floated at their previous meeting and he was right. The man was there to try to talk him into it.

Again he said 'no'. Dickson talked harder, Murdoch said 'no' a third time. Dickson got angry and started shouting. Sanderson told him to calm down and asked Murdoch to explain his reasons for refusing the deal.

He replied that washing a cheque was a totally different animal from washing cash. He didn't think it was possible. It didn't fit into any risk category he was willing to entertain.

Dickson was spitting mad. He shouted disparaging remarks at him, made veiled and not so veiled threats. Reaching down, he picked up a stout branch and hammered it on the ground as he made his point. Murdoch remained silent.

Sanderson tried to reason with him, and Dickson turned on him. He accused him of backing out of an iron clad agreement, called him derogatory names. Sanderson grinned at him, laughed a little. He opened his mouth to say something else and Dickson nailed him in the upper chest or throat with the branch, swinging it like a baseball bat.

Jeff stood for a second, weaving on his feet. Murdoch lunged to grab his arm but Dickson hit him again in the middle of the forehead before he could reach him. Sanderson toppled like a bowling pin headfirst into the Falls.

Murdoch fell silent at that point. There was no sound in the room. Ross stared at him as he returned the stare, his gaze calm. This was exactly the tale Dickson had told in his jail cell, except for the laughter and the second blow. Who was telling the truth?

"I thought Sanderson was your friend," Ross said roughly. "Did you just stand there and watch him drown?"

Rain looked down at the table and seemed to gather himself. "Dickson ran. He dropped the branch and went back down the trail beside the Falls. I was right on his heels," he said.

"I thought I might be able to see Jeff in the water and haul him out. I ran along the river, going in and out of the bush. At one point, I thought I saw his jacket. I shrugged out of my coat and dove in, but it was just an old shirt caught in some branches. I couldn't get back out on the bank, it was so steep and slippery. I pulled myself downstream until I got to a place where I could get some purchase and climb out.

"I panicked. I felt if I took too long getting out of the water, I'd lose my chance to see if he went past in the river. I ran further, past the Potholes and stopped at the bridge. I was cold by this time and dripping wet. I climbed under the bridge. In the Potholes the water moves so fast, he could whip through there and end up near the bridge before I could get there. But I couldn't see anything. There was no one around, it was getting dark. I walked back up toward the Potholes still looking for him. Then I realized Jeff's car was gone from the parking lot. I thought perhaps he'd pulled himself out and, not seeing me, had gone home in his car."

He took a deep breath. "I walked back up the path toward the falls. I had to get my jacket where I'd dropped it when I dove into the water, and my cell phone and car keys were in the pocket. Once I got my phone, I tried calling him but there was no answer. I called several times. Then I got my car and drove into town."

Ross interrupted. "You're very concise on detail. It sounds like you've memorised this story."

Murdoch stopped talking for a minute, considering him across the table. He glanced at his lawyer, who motioned for him to continue.

"I drove out to Jeff's house. I'd only been there once while he was building it. I'd never been inside but I knew the layout. Jeff kept his car in the garage at the back. So I parked on the road and walked through the trees behind the garage. I looked in the windows, but his car wasn't there. I called his cell phone again."

He paused. "Then I went home."

"What time was this?"

He thought for a minute. "Close to eleven thirty."

"Who saw you come home?"

"No one."

"Who can corroborate your story?"

"Tom Dickson, for part of it. I doubt if he knows what happened after I dove into the water. I got the impression that he took off. I didn't see where he went after that."

Ross took a deep breath. "Tom Dickson told the same story, Mr. Murdoch. But he said that Sanderson slipped and fell into the water and that he, Dickson, dove in trying to save him, but only found an old shirt in the water."

Murdoch stared at him for a second, then a slow cold smile lit his face. "Did he? So he hung around longer than I thought. Well, well."

"What do you say to that?"

"I say he's lying. A lying sack of shit."

"Well, why should I take your story over his?"

Murdoch gave him a stare. "Because I can prove my story, he can just make his up as he goes along."

Ross banged the table with his fist. "Ten minutes to regroup," he said and headed for the door.

"What do you think, Parker?" They stood at the vending machine. Ross pulled on a bottle of water as Dan stirred a murky looking cup of coffee.

"Well, he's cool. Not much emotion showing there. But when you asked if Sanderson was his friend, I thought he was going to crack."

"Yeah, so did I. It surprised me. His hands were shaking and his knuckles went white. But which one of them is telling the truth? At this point it's a case of he said, he said."

"Yeah, but he says he has proof. This is one smart mother. Let's see what he has."

"Okay, back to work." They crowded into the drab airless room.

Murdoch looked like he hadn't moved, his stillness was commanding in the small space, almost ominous.

"Let's see what we have," Ross interjected. "We have both you and Dickson saying how this went down and the stories don't match. And there are no other witnesses. Why should I believe your version?"

"I have proof," Murdoch repeated. "When Jeff and Tom Dickson approached me at the top of the trail I took their picture. The date and time is on that picture and I'm quite sure you can identify the site by the background in the photo. Then I recorded the conversation. The date and time are embedded in the recording." He fell silent.

Ross was dumbfounded and hoped his mouth wasn't hanging open. He looked at Parker, who shrugged. "Where are the recording and photo?"

"They're on the laptop that was with me when I was arrested in Saskatoon."

~~~

Later that day Ross listened to the recording with Parker, running through it two or three times as they pieced together the events. It definitely supported Murdoch's version, although it sounded violent and chaotic, so much more out of control than in his calm retelling of events. At
~~~

the point where Dickson must have hit Sanderson, he heard Murdoch let out such a bellow of rage it startled him even now, listening to it in his office.

Finally he went straight to Marsh. If this was true, they were looking at an entirely different scenario. What about Dickson's story? He must have known that once Rain was found, his chances were narrowing dramatically, although it was doubtful that he knew about the recording.

Ross sat down with a senior member of the Attorney General's department and revamped the charges. Once he got full disclosure, it looked like tax evasion and impersonation were all Rainier Murdoch faced. Although he'd lived a life undercover for a number of years, he hadn't done anything else illegal.

"But where did the money come from?" asked Marsh.

"They ran an Internet gambling site, although he didn't have a license. They didn't want to pay taxes, so they laundered it into cash and funnelled it through Sanderson's construction company. In order to stay out of sight, Murdoch had to keep changing his identity and opening new bank accounts. That way he avoided notice. He lived on part of the cash and supplied the rest to Sanderson.

"They had plans to go straight as soon as they made their nest egg. But the horizon of enough money, how big that nest egg needed to be, kept retreating. Sanderson always argued for more. Murdoch was stuck in the shadows while Sanderson had a life. Murdoch was tired of it.

"At the same time, he wasn't going to take shortcuts. He wasn't going to get caught doing stupid stuff like laundering cheques after all the care he'd taken to keep himself invisible. That's why he refused Dickson's deal. And when Sanderson agreed with his partner, Dickson lost it. He attacked Sanderson and sent him down the falls to his death. We'll never know if he was dead when he hit the water or drowned in the river."

"No, but it doesn't matter. The penalty's the same."

"True." Ross thought Sanderson's family might think it mattered.

"Well, wrap it up, Ross. This one has taken far too long. Let's put it to bed. Murdoch gets a slap on the wrist, I suppose?"

"We've come up with an agreement on charges that will result in two years' time served in the community and testimony against Dickson. And he'll have to settle with the Government for taxes. We've turned over his records to Revenue Canada."

"Won't that lead them straight to Ms. Bowman?" Marsh had a keen look in his eye.

Ross looked right back. "They've been dealing with her for some months, sir. I believe she has just made a settlement with them."

"I see." Marsh eyed him thoughtfully. "How's that going, by the way?"

"Sir?"

Marsh's moustache twitched. "Are you still seeing Ms. Bowman?"

"I haven't seen her often, sir. This case has taken a lot of time, I haven't had a day off in two weeks. And to be blunt I haven't felt comfortable seeing her while I was questioning her husband's business partner. But now that it's finished, I'll be going out to see her again." He pressed his lips tight.

Marsh nodded. "Good, good."

But Ross knew that time was not yet. Chloe needed to be informed how her husband died and what he'd been involved in. The reports would inevitably appear in the newspaper and it wasn't right that she learn of it that way. He still had to wait.

~~~

Chloe had lunch with Tony after she'd sealed the deal with him for meals at the hostel and Brent joined them. She enjoyed the teasing and good-natured bickering between the two friends. When they were finished, Tony drove her home.
~~~

She'd just received a call that morning from her lawyer regarding her company's missing shares.

"I've been contacted,' he said. "A lawyer in town has a client who claims to hold them. Apparently they can produce the actual shares."

She'd been astounded.

"If this person has the physical shares," he said, "Then they own half the company. It means you have a partner. I'm sorry I can't be more help, Ms. Bowman, but you'll have to work with what exists. Art Rowbotham's role in this is still a question. I've already contacted the Law Society and they'll be investigating. It won't impact you, just an interesting sidelight."

She was left with a half-finished story. A company that she didn't own? Her hands shook throughout lunch when she thought about it.

Tony coasted to a stop in her drive and turned the engine off. "Let me get the door, Chloe." He gave her a hand out and glanced up at her house. "This is a real nice place. I know your fellow's gone but you've got something to work with here. Thanks for letting me have a chance at the meals for your hostel. I appreciate the business. Almost like keeping it in the family, right?"

He laughed and leaned in to give her a hug. "Take care."

Chloe let out her breath in a nervous whoosh as he drove away. She'd spotted Ross's bike leaning against the fence as they came into the yard. Sure enough, he stood like a statue just inside the door.

He gave her a steady look. "I stopped in and had a visit with Davey and Amanda. It's probably time to go." He was immobile, almost daring her to say something.

"Ross. You could have phoned."

"I have, several times. I don't seem to catch you in."

"It's been days since your last call."

"Yeah, and it's been days since I've had an hour off work." He stepped closer. "So, you're seeing someone else, now."

She felt faint, the blood left her head. "No."

"Could have fooled me." He looked flushed and frustrated, as if he knew he should shut up before he bullied her into saying something that he didn't want to hear but couldn't reign himself in. The adrenaline was pumping, she could see a vein pulsing in his neck. He crowded her with his body.

"If you're not seeing someone else…" He paused to let her speak but she pressed her lips tightly together. "Then who was that guy that just dropped you off and gave you a friendly hug?"

She stared up at him, reading the confusion and anger in his face, then laid her palm in the centre of his chest. "Ross," she said. Nothing else, just his name. Then she leaned forward and kissed him.

His reaction was instantaneous, moving against her and wrapping his arms tightly to align her body with his. He deepened the kiss until she was bent over his arm and had to grip his shoulders to keep her balance. His breath came fast and heavy. Her own heart was pumping frantically. She'd unleashed a storm.

They both heard the sound of running feet. "Woss. I thought you was gone," Davey said happily. "You're still here! Hi, Mummy. He came to visit."

Chloe stepped back, holding the man at arm's length. "Hi Davey. Yes, I see Ross is here." Her voice was not quite steady. "Did you have a good time with Amanda?"

Ross moved away and turned his body to gaze out the window. She saw his chest expand in a deep breath.

"Yep." Davey whirled around. "Woss said we could ride bikes, but then he forgot."

She took Davey's hand. "Maybe Ross would ride bikes with us now." They both looked at him as he turned to meet their matched dark gaze. He seemed to search Chloe's eyes.

"Please, Ross," she said.

He nodded stiffly. "Okay, I could do that."

"Good. Let me get changed and I'll be right back. Hey, Amanda. Thanks for babysitting."

Davey rode round and round the yard, Plutie following, while Ross led Chloe onto the deck out of hearing. "Chloe, this is driving me crazy. I have to know if you've started going out with someone else, or if we're still… uh."

"There, see? You don't know what to call it, because there's no word for what we have. An on-again, off-again relationship? Does that describe it?" Her voice was sharp with irritation and Davey glanced over.

Ross put his hand on her arm. "Listen. I've been caught in a trap, partly of my own making. We've arrested Jeff's partner."

Chloe's breath caught in her throat. "What do you mean, partner? He worked on his own. He didn't have a partner."

"See, that's the thing. Here I am investigating your husband's disappearance and there are all kinds of issues coming up, which I know about but you don't. And I'm dating you. Do you think that works?"

She shook her head in despair. "No, I guess not." Her eyes filled with tears. "Then why are you here? If you can't see me?"

"Because I miss you." His whisper was fierce. "I can't sleep at night for missing you. It's like someone cut off my right arm." The colour went high on his cheekbones. "I want to talk to you, I want to date you, I want to sleep with you, damn it!"

He tried to pull her resistant body into his arms. "Sex with you was like nothing I've ever had. It wasn't just sex, that's why. It was something else entirely. Something that doesn't have a name. I want more, I want it all the time. I want it now!"

He finally succeeded in pulling her against him, and his erection was hard against her stomach. She subsided against his chest, swamped with confusion.

"I've missed you, too." Her cheek rested against the rise and fall of his shirt. "I didn't know what was going on. You took me out and suddenly you didn't call."

"I've been working. We needed to put this case to rest. And I was caught in the middle."

"What does that mean, put the case to rest? Have you solved how Jeff died? Or is it about the money, do you know where it came from?"

He heaved a sigh into her windblown hair. "See, that's exactly what I'm talking about. It's complicated."

She gazed sightlessly out at the yard. "I know it is. You don't have to tell me. I've been dealing with it for nearly a year. But besides being complicated, it's dark and shadowy, and that's even harder to bear. Like living in a murky world. If there's light, I want to see it." She turned in his arms and gazed into his hard face. "I need to know what you've found out."

He looked into her eyes. "Kiss me, Chloe."

He laid his mouth over hers and she sank into the comfort of his kiss. His hand skimmed her throat and down the front of her sweater, coming to rest on her breast. He groaned, pressing his face into her hair and inhaling as he flexed his fingers around her.

"Well," he said, breathing deeply. He paused as if to gather himself. "We've made progress."

She turned her face up to him. "Tell me."

"It's best if I don't."

Her mouth turned down.

"Chloe, it's best if we follow procedure. That way you get all the information, not some of it or the bits that I focus on. That way there's a record that you've been informed. And it won't come between us." His eyes pleaded with her. "That's the main thing. I don't want you to blame me for finding this stuff out."

She looked away and watched Davey drop his bike and chase Plutie toward them, thundering onto the porch. "The next step," he said, "is to have you come into the station and meet with officers to fill you in on what we know. The same officers as before, Dan and Cheryl. There'll be charges laid against a number of people and it'll be in the news. You need to know before that happens. Maybe you want your brother to come with you again."

Chloe took Davey's slightly dirty little hand and swung it thoughtfully. Then she admonished him, "Go play, Davey. We're talking. Way you go." He raced back to the yard.

She glanced up at Ross. "Is it bad news?"

He looked sober, moved his head stiffly sideways. "I'd say so."

She stared out at the trees and sighed. "Well, the sooner the better than. I'll call John, you find out when they could meet with us."

"I already have that information." He pulled a card out of his pocket. "Here are the times, they'll meet you at the detachment offices. It's better there. More formal, more procedure."

She took the card and folded her fingers around it.

"Chloe, will you go out with me?"

She looked at him but didn't answer.

"See what I mean?" he spat in frustration. "It's damned complicated. Shit." He stared stonily across the drive.

"I didn't say I wouldn't go out with you," she said, her voice low.

"You didn't have to," he bit out. "The look said it all."

"I doubt it."

He turned back to her.

"You see, I've missed you so much and you didn't come around so I decided I couldn't have you, that I'd just put you out of my mind. And here you are again, asking me out. I don't know what to do." A tear leaked from her eye, and she brushed it impatiently away.

"Do you want to see me?" He breathed a huge sigh of relief at her small nod. "I sure want to see you. I've put my career at risk by being in contact with you. I had to talk to my supervisor and give him a warning that we'd been dating because rumours were starting to go round the force. Can we do something soon?"

She hesitated.

"We can take Davey. Maybe just a bite to eat and a movie. Would that would be okay?"

She nodded. "Okay."

"Alright." He looked determined. "Are you seeing someone else? Who was that guy who drove you home?"

"Just a friend of my brother."

"Yeah, Uncle Brent's friend. He owns a restaurant."

Chloe gave a small smile at his out-of-sorts expression. "Davey was talking, was he?"

"Yes. Davey's my buddy. He tells me stuff. So, are you seeing him?"

"I went out to lunch with him and Brent. He just took on the contract to supply meals for the worker's hostel that John's running in the building."

"So you took pity on him." He huffed his irritation. "Are you taking pity on me too?" he demanded. "Is that what this is?

"Maybe," She gave him a meaningful look.

His neck turned red and colour washed the lean planes of his face. "Don't tease, Chloe. By God, I'm damned near to just taking what I need." His jaw tightened and he turned his head away. She rubbed his chest with her palm and he dragged her in so her breasts flattened against him, his arms like steel bands around her.

CHAPTER TWENTY EIGHT

Chloe thought she'd almost recovered from losing Jeff, but the session at the RCMP headquarters came close to breaking her. John came with her to meet Constables Parker and LeClerc. She wasn't that surprised to learn that Jeff was involved in a money laundering scheme. She hadn't been able to think of many other explanations for the amount of money that flowed into his accounts.

But the volume left her speechless. To think that he was passing between two and three million dollars a year in cash was staggering.

She was astounded to find he had a partner. Never had there been the smallest hint that he was working with someone else. It had been Jeff making decisions, running the construction crew and buying properties. In all the time they were married she'd never heard of Rainman, save for that one final email on his laptop. The information reinforced what she already knew. She'd been living a lie, her relationship with her husband had been a sham. It was demeaning, it was humiliating.

She tried not to let the shock and dismay show, but John must have read it on her face. He called a halt mid-point and asked if they could take a break. Constable LeClerc showed Chloe down the hall to the women's restrooms, then brought coffee and water into the meeting room. It was twenty minutes before everyone was back in their chairs and ready to continue.

Then they covered the activities of selling a sham interest in an apartment building with a third partner. They told of the meeting at Sooke Potholes and Jeff's death down the falls. Chloe only heard half of what was said after that. She left it to John to ask questions. When they dealt with how Jeff died, she was rendered speechless, her head reeling and her heart beaten to a pulp. John clarified everything he could think of, looking at Chloe for guidance but getting none.

Constable Parker thanked her for coming in and left the room. LeClerc offered to meet with her again when she was ready. "It's a lot to take in, and when it is about someone you loved, it interferes with your ability to hear what's been said," she commented. "You'll probably have more questions. I'll be happy to answer them if I can."

Chloe noticed the past tense for 'loved.' She thought it was suddenly very appropriate for how she felt about Jeff.

John stood with her on the sidewalk outside police headquarters. "What do you think?" He examined her expression.

"I don't know what to think. I didn't see any of that. None of it. It must mean I'm pretty stupid, stupid and unobservant."

John took her arm and walked her down the block. "Don't think that Chloe. You're not stupid. You're a clever girl. What you have to admit is Jeff Sanderson was a very smart man. The fact that he was able to hide this from you is phenomenal. You were in love and you believed what he told you. That's all.

"And he didn't do it alone. Their system was already set up long before he met you. His partner was even more clever. This Rainman, whoever he is, must be a genius. The police should hire him. It sounds like he's the one who set the standards, judging from the argument at Sooke Falls."

Chloe gasped for air. "I can't go there right now, John. Let's not go there."

"I'm sorry, little one." He put his arm around her shoulders. "Sorry for being insensitive, but also sorry that you had to hear all that about your husband."

~~~

Ross called that night. He'd been looking out his window when Chloe and John left after the meeting. Her body language had shown how stricken she was at what she'd learned. He couldn't go to see her, and secretly didn't think she'd want him there, anyway.

"When do your boarders leave?" he asked. "You'll be all alone when they do."

"I know, and I can't wait. One's already gone and another leaves tomorrow, the rest by the end of the week. Four months with the house all to myself. It seems like a dream."

There was a frown in her voice as she continued, "Of course, there are people out there who are still struggling to find a place to live. Maybe I should look into that, because I'll have extra room....'

Ross shushed her. "Give it time, Chloe. Maybe nothing on the agenda for a while. Can I come out to see you tomorrow night? I'll be off then, I have some free time."

"Oh." There was a long pause. "I'm very tired, Ross."

"I know, baby. I won't take any entertaining. I just want to see you for a little while. I won't even stay late."

"Not yet," she whispered. "Not yet."

~~~

When Chloe heard from her lawyer that Rainier Murdoch had come forward with the missing shares, she was stunned. "Who," she said blankly into the phone, "is Rainier Murdoch?"

Then it clicked into place. This was her husband's business partner. She felt sick. How could she be in business with a criminal, someone who'd been involved in Jeff's death? It was impossible. It was preposterous. She'd kill him!

She gasped at the thought, that she felt murderous toward this man. She didn't want to meet him, didn't want to feel dirtied by association. The thought was abhorrent.

Her lawyer arranged a meeting later that morning at his office, with Chloe and the legal counsel representing Murdoch. She almost didn't go. But after a lot of self-talk and dithering, she got herself there to hear what was presented.

As she listened, she put together a picture in her head of this man. When the lawyer was finished, she asked for a drink of water and they took a short break. Then she sat down, and asked him to repeat it all again.

"Okay, of course," he said. "This is a lot to take in. I understand. Here's the situation. Mr. Murdoch was Mr. Sanderson's business partner, albeit a silent one."

He looked questioningly at her lawyer, noted his nod and continued. "When the company was formed, Mr. Murdoch took fifty shares in actual, rather than having them stay in the corporate registry. He owned half the business, but didn't want his name on the paperwork."

He paused delicately. "I don't need to speculate as to why."

Everyone in the room nodded. No one here is in the dark, she thought. They all know why Murdoch's name wasn't to show on the books.

Chloe left the meeting feeling numb. She must not have any feelings left. They'd been battered out of her. She lay on the couch when she got home and fell asleep, barely waking in time to fetch Davey from the daycare.

The next day passed in a fog. In the afternoon Jayde brought some seedlings to add to her vegetable garden and stayed for a cup of tea once the plants were in the ground. She was full of news, bursting with excitement. Will and his wife were expecting. She was to have a grandchild at last. She couldn't contain her enthusiasm.

"Just think, Chloe! This time next year, the little rascal will be four months old and trying to crawl. It might be a girl, but then a boy would be nice too. Boys are fun, aren't they, Davey?" Davey grinned at her and some of his hot chocolate leaked out between his teeth and down his chin.

Jayde laughed and Chloe spoke sharply, "Davey! Cut that out."

"Chloe, it's just a dribble. You look a little tired, haven't you been sleeping?"

She looked surprised. "I feel like I do. But I am tired."

Jayde nodded knowingly. "What's going on, Chloe? You can tell me. Sit down here, let's talk."

Chloe hesitated, then sat. "I haven't told anyone, Jayde. Something has happened with the building."

Jayde listened without interrupting as Chloe talked about the proposal from Murdoch. When she was finished, Jayde sat back and thought about it for a minute, then gave her a searching look. "That sounds generous. He's going to pay the taxes. He wants the insurance money to go against the building mortgage. And he'll let you take the income for managing the building. What could be wrong with that? How do you feel about it?"

"I don't know." Chloe's face was morose. "At first I didn't want anything to do with it. Now I'm not sure."

"Well," Jayde took her hand. "Is this an evil man, then?"

"I have no idea. I've never met him. I didn't know Jeff had a partner!"

Jayde nodded. "From what I've read in the paper, he was there when Jeff died."

"Yes, but he didn't kill him, if that's what you mean."

"Okay, but didn't he try to get him to cheat a woman out of her money with a phoney investment in an apartment?"

"No," she shook her head. "That was a different guy, and they tried to get Murdoch to work with them on it but he refused."

"Why would he refuse? He was going to make money off it."

"Apparently he thought what they did was pretty honest, just evading taxes. He didn't want to be a part of the other."

Jayde looked thoughtful. "There was something else I read in the paper, let me see. Oh, yes. They said he got caught giving money to his sister to help pay her student loans."

Chloe nodded.

"So," said Jayde, he's a pretty mean character, helping his sister out and refusing to take part in ripping off women. He just doesn't pay his taxes."

Chloe stared at her for a minute, then pulled a face. "I get your point. He has more in the way of morals than Jeff did. Maybe that's part of my problem. You don't know how hard it was to listen to them telling me that Jeff tried to pull Murdoch into this apartment scam, and he said 'no'."

She thought of what the lawyer had said. *Mr. Murdoch understands about the cost of running the building, he understands about the taxation issues that you've settled with Revenue Canada. He knows there's an insurance policy that's been paid to the mortgage corporation. He has a proposal to make.*

Chloe had been beside herself. No wonder she had to get the lawyer to say everything twice. Having to deal with a silent partner was one thing, having to deal with a partner who was a criminal was something else. She had no reference point from which to make a judgement. And she kept thinking about John, his disapproval of Jeff and his business ethics. And Ross, what would his reaction be? He'd be livid.

She turned to Jayde. "He's actually been generous. I didn't want to see it that way. I wonder what he's like."

"You won't know unless you meet him, I guess." Jayde gave her a searching look, nodded and stood. "Well. I'd better get along. I'm knitting a baby blanket, did I tell you? I guess it'll be yellow and green, that way it will work no matter what, won't it?"

As Jayde walked back down the trail, Chloe thought with longing of the wedding and baby in her friend's life and the cool blank spaces in her own. She loved Davey with all her soul but there was still that empty place that longed to be filled.

CHAPTER TWENTY NINE

Ross called in the afternoon. "Can I come out to see you tonight?"

"Okay. Do you want to come for dinner?"

He laughed. "No, don't do dinner. I'll just come for a few minutes. I'm working, so around eight-thirty. Then it won't be too late for you."

She gave a choked little laugh. "That's fine, I'll see you then."

Davey was just going to bed when he arrived. The little boy quickly finished his prayers and demanded a story. So Ross lay down beside him on his bed and read the recipe for chilli from his children's cookbook.

When he was finished, he kissed him on the forehead and heaved himself up. "Do you always read him recipes?" he asked as he pulled the bedroom door closed.

Chloe laughed. "No, only once a week."

"Really?" He was incredulous. "It was pretty boring."

"I know. He loves that book for some reason. It drives me crazy, so I only let him choose it every now and then. You lucked out on chilli. Pancakes are pretty good too. The rest of those recipes will make you insane."

Ross chuckled and tugged at her wrist. "Chloe, come sit down just for a minute. I promised I wouldn't stay long and I know you're tired, but I need to talk to you."

He urged her along and seated her on the sofa, lowering himself beside her. He took her hand in his own big one and flattened it on his thigh. "Listen. I know this has been a tough week, and there's been a lot to absorb from what Dan and Cheryl told you. And most of it would have come as a surprise."

"You have no idea." Her head fell back against the sofa. "I felt..." She shuddered and covered her mouth.

Ross hesitated, then drew her into his arms. "Sweetheart, I never thought you were involved. I'm not surprised you were blindsided."

He rocked her gently as she relaxed against him. "I just don't want us to be put on hold, to have to start at the beginning again. We've done that a few times, every time something new comes to light. And I'm afraid we won't be able to get back to where we were." He wasn't making much sense and fell silent for a few moments. She smoothed his shirt with her fingers and it was almost more than he could bear.

"Chloe," he started again as sweat gathered on his chest. "I want to see you and spend time with you. And I want to do it out in the open. Can we do that?" His heart was thudding fast as she stiffened in his arms.

"I know you've been through a lot," he continued doggedly. "And it's been weeks and months of tension, waiting for things to happen, waiting for news." He smoothed her hair back from her face.

"I know all that. I'm not trying to make it any harder. I can wait, as long as it takes. But I want to be part of your life. I don't want to hesitate and wonder if you want to see me, or whether it's awkward with your family." She didn't reply, so he plunged on desperately.

"You know yourself it's hard on Davey not to see me. I'd like to be here for him, too." He lifted her chin with his fingers. Her face was still and pale, her eyes searching his.

"What? What do you want to hear from me? I love you." It might be too soon, but he'd been thinking it for such a long difficult time.

She buried her head against his chest. He heard her mutter against his shirt. "What did you say?"

"I said, it took you long enough."

"Took me long enough?" He put his head back and burst out laughing, then was suddenly cold sober as he focussed fiercely on her pale face. "I was afraid, afraid I was rushing you. Afraid you couldn't see me because of the new stuff you kept finding out about Jeff. There was never a good time."

He studied the shadows beneath her eyes. Gently he put his thumb there, then to the side of her mouth. "I love you, Chloe. I want to take you to bed. I want to marry you."

He tenderly pressed his mouth against hers, waiting for her reaction.

Her mouth was soft and lush. He knew he'd lose control the moment he kissed her. His heart was beating hard in his chest, the blood rushing in his head. "Chloe, let me take you to bed. It's been too long, I can't wait anymore."

His hand slid to her breast and squeezed. "Oh, God. I've missed you so. You can't imagine." He stroked her slender waist and the swell of her hip. He pressed inward. "Come to bed. I need you, baby."

The bedclothes went sailing onto the floor. He laid Chloe back against the cool sheets, and she pulled him down for a deep kiss. He lost track of time, of place. Her clothes came off and he heard something rip. He reared back to tear at his shirt, struggled with his belt buckle. Her hands were there too, and between them it was undone. He unzipped his pants and shucked them off.

He took a steadying breath and moved onto the bed, his hands on her legs, caressing slowly up her flesh, his mouth following in an open kiss. She caught her breath as he pressed his mouth there and sealed his lips over her. He kissed her, licking and gently suckling her tender places until she moaned and called his name, her hands tangled in his hair. She tasted sweet, like honey, like flower nectar.

Then he was on top of her, kneeing her legs apart, laying his weight onto her, into her. She caught her breath in the back of her throat. He tried to slow down. But he was already there, deep inside, pressed inside. Her inner muscles contracted, adjusted, and he pinned her hips desperately to the bed. "Don't move, don't move baby. I'm not… I can't…"

Sweat poured off him as she clawed at his shoulders, dragging him down. He pressed against her, flattening her breasts under his weight. Then he plunged and she reared up to meet him, and again. He went suddenly deaf from the roar of blood in his ears. He couldn't slow now, could only keep moving, driving toward that goal, so close, almost within reach. He clamped his mouth over hers to muffle her cry and relinquished his fierce efforts at holding back to follow her over the edge.

When he became aware, he was lying on his side with Chloe's head on his arm, her body gathered snugly against him. Her eyelashes brushed his skin and he knew she was awake. His palm smoothed upward, shaped her breast and he lifted his head to lave her nipple with his tongue. She quivered under his hand and his heart quaked.

He gathered her close again, and rocked her against him, laying her head on his shoulder.

"I love you, sweetheart. I want to marry you, you and Davey. Marry me, Chloe."

CHAPTER THIRTY

Chloe gazed with satisfaction across her big yard. The dahlias were in full bloom, showing salad-plate sized blossoms down the side of the lawn. The air buzzed with dragon flies, bees and the conversation of more than two dozen guests. Croquet wickets were set up at the end of the long garden and a game was in progress with what looked like much abbreviated rules and highly competitive players.

Rainier Murdoch and his family were here, his parents and his sister Susan and husband Darrell with their three year old daughter, Chantelle. The little girl had been hesitant at first to leave her mother's side, given the number of small boys tearing about the place.

But Davey had taken to her and led her around by the hand, showing her where to get a drink of the juice punch Chloe set out for the children on the picnic table. Then he introduced his dog, Plutie. She immediately took a shine to the little animal. She petted him and took him by the lead to show her mother.

Chloe glanced over to where Vivienne had seated herself beside Rain's parents, carrying her newest grandchild. John and Rosemary had a little girl, Gemma, who'd been born in early July and held the reins of their entire household in her tiny hands. She had the Bowman colouring, jet black hair with pale skin and sky blue eyes and John's own eyes never left her, as if she'd come to harm if he wasn't right there. Rosemary trailed behind Vivienne, anxious that the child be safe.

Chloe sighed. There had never been born a child as wonderful as Gemma. Then she couldn't help smiling to herself, because she could remember feeling the same way when Davey was new.

She glanced around to see where he was, and found him helping Chantelle tug Plutie over to meet the group of small boys who were playing marbles on the patio.

Rain approached her. "Is there anything I can do?"

Chloe grinned at him. "Got beaten out of the croquet game, did you?"

He grimaced. "I'm not sure about the rules."

Chloe gave a ladylike snort. "I imagine not. Those rules change hourly, if I don't miss my guess. You have to watch John like a hawk, and Brent is even worse."

Rain threw back his head and laughed. "Is that right?" He gazed speculatively back at the group of men just finishing up their game. "I'll have to remember that for my next turn. Can I start barbecuing for you?"

"That would be great." Chloe turned and led the way into the house. "I have chicken breasts and halibut steaks, so everyone has a choice. I know sometimes people from the prairies aren't always as fond of fish…" She glanced over at him with a question in her voice.

"Good guess. I love it, myself, but my folks not so much. Now if there was a good piece of cow…"

Chloe snickered and handed him a metal tray. "I'll remember that for next time. Here, I'll bring the sauce and basting brushes. The tongs and flippers are already out there."

Rain gave her a level look. "Thank you, Chloe. For everything, but especially on behalf of my family." He turned without giving her time to answer and headed outside.

Rainier Murdoch had been surprisingly easy to deal with over the building. Once Chloe managed to assimilate all the information, she'd decided to go ahead with the dual ownership. She looked at it as a trial run, she'd give it a year and see how it shook out.

But so far, it had been fine. He didn't try to interfere with how she ran the business. He just asked to be kept informed and left it in her hands. She'd been more worried about how Ross would take it, that she was in business with a criminal.

She looked around for Ross. He was holding a croquet mallet, leaning on it as he chatted with John and waited for his friend Greg to take his shot. Between Greg and Brent, the game was nearly sewed up. Davey swung on his leg, creasing his linen trousers, his own mallet abandoned on the ground beside them.

Davey seldom left Ross's side for long. Since the wedding, he'd been so thrilled to have him there, telling him all his secrets and having physical contact, on his knee, leaning on his arm, swinging on him, being held. Chloe had tried to get him to back off a little, saying he was too big to be carried all the time. But Ross had said, no, this was fine. Let him get used to having him there.

"When the new baby arrives," he added, "There'll be a lot to adjust to, so let him have the time." He'd run his hand over the slight swell of Chloe's belly as a thrill ran through her.

They'd managed to put together a life in the midst of chaos. Ross was what she'd dreamed of. He was what they needed, she and Davey. They had become a family.

Jayde's Squash Soup

Cut open a 2 lb butternut squash and remove the seeds.
Cut into uniform sized pieces:

2 lbs squash	1 white onion
2 large carrots	2 stalks celery
2 apples, core removed	6 garlic cloves (whole)

Toss together with 2 Tbsp olive oil, 2 Tbsp curry paste.
Spread on a baking sheet and roast in 375 F oven for 40 minutes.

Remove squash from skin, put all ingredients in a large pot and bring to simmer with 1 quart vegetable stock and 1 cinnamon stick. Cook over low heat 40 minutes. Remove cinnamon stick and puree mix till smooth consistency.

Season to taste with salt and pepper.

also by Sylvie Grayson

LEGAL OBSTRUCTION

When Emily Drury takes a job as legal counsel for an import-export company, she doesn't make the decision lightly. She needs to get away to someplace safe.

Joe Tanner counts himself lucky. He's charmed a successful big city lawyer into heading up the legal department of his rapidly expanding business. But why would a beautiful woman who could easily make partner in the high profile legal firm where she works, give it all up to come to a place like Bonnie?

A mystery surrounds her arrival that wraps them both in ever tightening tentacles. As Joe realizes she has become essential to his happiness, his first reaction is to protect her. But he doesn't know the whole story.

Can Emily trust him enough to divulge her secret? Will he learn what he needs to know in time to stop the avalanche that's gaining speed as it races down the hill toward her?

see website for Sylvie Grayson
www.sylviegrayson.com or contact her at
sylviegraysonauthor@gmail.com

also by Sylvie Grayson

SUSPENDED ANIMATION

...romantic suspense at its best -

Be careful who you trust...

Katy Dalton worked hard to save her money. And working with her friend Bruno to invest it seems like a safe bet. But her job disappears and she needs her money back, everything Bruno has already loaned to Rome Trucking. When Katy insists he return it, Bruno stops answering his phone and bad things start to happen.

Brett Rome is frustrated. The last thing he wants to do is leave a promising career in hockey to come home and run his ailing father's trucking company. What he discovers is not the successful business that he remembers, but one that is teetering on the very edge of bankruptcy and a young woman demanding the return of the money she invested.

With the company in chaos, Brett hires her. But danger lurks in the form of Bruno's dubious associates. What secret are they hiding and why are they willing to kill Katy? Can Brett put this broken picture back together, and is Katy part of the solution or the problem?

A thrilling roller coaster of a story...

Sylvie Grayson has found her niche, you'll love this book...

Sylvie Grayson's next book from Great Western Publishing to be released in 2015 - romantic suspense in a fantasy world...

The Last War: Book One

Emperor Aqatain has been defeated and his holdings torn apart. New territories have arisen from the old Empire, new ways of governing, and the citizens swear they will never need to fight again after the long and costly war. The country of Khandarken lies along the Catastrophic Ocean with Adar Silva to the south as its most valuable ally. Jiran is a western tribal land that has ties to no one.

Bethlehem Farmer is working with her brother Abram to hold things together in south Khandarken, looking after the dispossessed on their land, keeping the farm productive and the talc mine working in the hills behind their fields. But when Abram comes under attack, and then takes a trip with Uncle Jade into the Northern Territory and disappears without a trace, she's left on her own, undefended, and suddenly things are not what they seem and no one can be trusted.

Major Dante Regiment is sent by his father, the General, to discover what has happened to Bethlehem Farmer in the Southern Territory. What he finds shakes him to the core and fuels his grim determination to protect Bethlehem at all cost, even with his life.

"... a spellbinding fantasy of love and betrayal, old anger and a brand new world..."

April 2015 2015

ABOUT THE AUTHOR

Sylvie Grayson has lived most of her life in British Columbia, Canada, in spots ranging from Vancouver Island on the west coast to the North Peace River country and the Kootenays in the beautiful interior. She spent a one year sojourn in Tokyo Japan.

She has been an English language instructor, a nightclub manager, an auto shop bookkeeper and many other professions. She found her niche at university and completed a bachelor's degree in Sociology and doctorate in Law. Now she works part time as the owner of a small company, and writes when she can.

She still loves to travel, having recently completed a trip to Singapore, Thailand, Viet Nam and Hong Kong. She lives on the coast of the Pacific Ocean with her husband on a small patch of land near the sea that they call home.

Other books by Ms Grayson include *Suspended Animation* and *Legal Obstruction.*

If you enjoyed this book, please consider leaving a review on Amazon. You can learn more at - **www.sylviegrayson.com** or contact the author at **sylviegraysonauthor@gmail.com**

Made in the USA
Charleston, SC
25 February 2015